I Don't Love You

Vanessa Tello

ISBN 13: 978-1-7355125-0-1

To all those who have loved and lost
and still believe in finding love again

Prologue

*D*owntown Los Angeles: It was the middle of an afternoon in the beginning of May. Hordes of business executives crossed the streets, talking on their cell phones, hurrying back to work from a power lunch. In the midst of it all was Cassandra, standing on Wilshire Blvd. cell phone in one hand, wondering what had happened to her and what was still to come.

Cassandra Greyson was an overachiever, one who always got her way no matter what. She constantly tried to control everything, but this situation was completely out of her control. She strived for the best, but sometimes came up short. In the past, she had never come up short; she had won each time. What had happened to her luck and strength? Had she lost it? She had nowhere to turn and did not know what her next step would be. The one person who came to mind would probably not help her—heck he probably wouldn't even answer the phone if she called him. She stood there helplessly. This time, there was no turning back. Cassandra had always made mistakes, but they were fixable. This mistake couldn't be fixed even if she tried. At this point, the only option would be to return to Manhattan, but she did not want that. Not yet. She was not ready to go back, but most of all she didn't *want* to go back.

What should I do? she wondered, still standing on Wilshire Blvd. The only thing to do was to pick up where she had left off. She lifted her head, stood up straight, and told herself that she had accomplished a lot of things and would continue to do so. Then and there, she decided that nothing was going to stop her—not after all she had been through. She headed toward her office located in the Aon Building.

Cassandra walked past Julie Chow on the same street, without even as much as a glance toward her. Julie was what most people would call ordinary. There was nothing really special about her or her looks. She, like most women in LA, was looking for true love. Julie had just left the Aon Building—she worked there—and wondered when her day would come for true love. She thought to herself: *I have a good job, make decent money and, above all, I can treat a man the right way. Why haven't I been able to find one?* It had been two years since her last serious relationship and now she was ready for a new one. With these thoughts, Julie headed toward her car for lunch.

On the other side of town, Ryan Scott looked at his watch and realized he was late for his appointment. *Another day of work*, he thought. He didn't entirely loathe his job as a merchant sales representative for Wells Fargo, but it had its days. He got into his car and was grateful that his appointment was only a few blocks away. After, he would have to fight his way through traffic to get home. He was content living in South Bay where he was close to the beach and bars. Like most men Ryan's age, he was happy to be single, living life without major responsibilities. On the way to his appointment, he thought, *one more deal to close and I am top sales rep for the third straight month!* That put a big smile on his face.

Eric enjoyed working from home when he could. It was another typical day for Eric: work, workout at the gym, and then sleep. He didn't change much in his routine for fear of losing control. He had not been in a monogamous relationship in a while and didn't really care much for it. Working out was his passion—besides his kids. Looking at himself in the mirror, he thought, *I have an awesome body.*

In Newport Beach, Eugene Conrad sat behind his massive desk staring at his blank computer screen. It was just a little after 8:00 a.m. *Do I really need to be here?* he asked himself. *I should be sitting on the beach or playing golf!* Eugene couldn't sit there all day when the sun was shining through his floor-to-ceiling windows. He got up from his chair and left the office.

Cassandra continued walking toward the Aon Building, prepared for what the day had to offer and what was yet to come. *Stay strong*, she told herself.

Chapter 1

It was a typical day in May. The weather in LA was above eighty degrees and you could feel summer around the corner—if it wasn't already there yet. Julie Chow was walking to Starbucks during her fifteen-minute break from the bank where she worked. She thought to herself: *Another day at work . . . I have to meet my sales quota before I take off to Hawaii at the end of the month.* Julie was a sales representative at one of the largest banks on the West Coast. She had been in this job for about two years and every day was the same—open more accounts than yesterday.

Julie walked into Starbucks, packed with its typical weekday morning crowd—men and women in suits ready to take over the world—and stood in line to get her usual Vente. Julie looked around for any good-looking men. Since she worked in the financial district of downtown LA, there had to be some men she could meet. She spotted a rather good-looking man wearing an expensive suit, watch, shoes, and nicely combed hair, waiting for his order. *Probably an attorney*, she thought. She looked at him and smiled. With just one glance at Julie, he took his coffee and walked out. *What is wrong with me!* Julie thought to herself.

Julie was a mixture of Chinese and Russian ethnicities, which made her have pale skin, slightly Asian brown eyes, and dark brown hair. She was five feet seven inches tall with a slender figure. She was average looking—nothing exceptional, but pretty in a nonconventional way. Julie got her coffee and walked back to the office, hoping true love was waiting around the corner.

Cassandra was sitting at her desk, typing a letter for one of the partners she worked for. At this point in her life, she had ruled out law school. It was not for her and she was ready to move on to something else. What that was, she

1

wasn't sure yet. Cassandra had been working for two partners in a law firm in downtown LA since last October, after she had finished yet another degree at The Fashion Institute of Design and Merchandising. It was another degree for Cassandra to add to her pile—which now totaled to three. Cassandra basically did anything and everything for the partners who could not stand each other. Sometimes she had to act like a referee between them. *Partnerships are like marriages*, she thought, *everything is nice and sweet at the beginning; then you wake up one day and you can no longer trust or stand to be with each other.* As she was finishing the letter, Cassandra's coworker Christian approached her.

"Hey hon, what are you up to?"

"Nothing much, just thinking about what I should do next," Cassandra responded.

"Honey, you just need to get out of this firm and do something else!"

"I know, but I am not sure what that is yet," she replied.

"Are you going to happy hour tonight?" Christian asked.

Christian Romero was a good-looking man with dark features that made him look Middle Eastern. Like Cassandra, he liked men, which made it easy for her to talk about her man problems.

"I do have to make an appearance," Cassandra replied. "But first I must go to the bank and straighten out the firm's business account, which is screwed up yet again."

Cassandra got into the elevator and went down fifty-three floors in seconds. What a ride! Every time she came out of the elevator, she could hear her ears pop. She walked through the lobby and then to another set of elevators to get to the bank. Heads turned as Cassandra walked into the bank.

Cassandra Zea was gorgeous; she came from a mixture of Peruvian and Greek descent. Along with her long black hair and dark brown eyes, Cassandra stood tall at five feet eight inches with long legs, amazing olive skin, and a smile that no one could refuse. She noticed men looking at her, but chose to ignore them because each one was no different than the next. Always being told "You are really beautiful" or "You have nice eyes and a great smile" got mundane for Cassandra. She wished a man would approach differently. Maybe compliment her ears?

Cassandra was looking for the bank representative that the partners always talked about. She could never meet her when she came to the bank. This time, Cassandra decided to ask one of the tellers if they knew where to find her firm's bank representative. One of the tellers pointed toward the direction of a young woman. Cassandra walked toward her desk and introduced herself.

"Hi, I am Cassandra, it's nice to finally meet you," said Cassandra, holding her hand out for a handshake.

Julie Chow got up from her chair. "Hello, I am Julie Chow." She shook Cassandra's hand. Cassandra sat down and immediately received bad energy from Julie.

"I work for Matthew and Mark upstairs in their law firm."

"I know Matthew and Mark very well. How can I help you today?" Julie asked.

"Well, there seems to be yet another problem with the firm's business account and I am wondering if you can help me fix it," Cassandra replied.

"Sure," Julie said. "Let me just take a look at the accounts."

As Julie looked at her screen, Cassandra started examining Julie. She looked like she was in her early thirties, but was not sure. Cassandra could tell Julie was a mixture of different races, but couldn't pinpoint. Regardless, she could sense bad energy from Julie. Cassandra was blessed in that way. On meeting someone for the first time, she could instantly sense if the person had good or bad intentions, and from what she was feeling, she knew it was bad.

"I see the problem here," Julie said, drawing Cassandra out of her thoughts.

"What is the problem?"

"There were some charges on the checking account and checks happened to come in at the same time, causing the account to become negative. I can refund some of the overdraft fees, but the account is going to still be negative. The partners need to transfer money into the account," Julie concluded.

"I will let them know as soon as I get upstairs." Julie was looking at Cassandra with a kind of envy that most plain girls have for pretty girls. Julie was thinking to herself, *Cassandra probably does nothing upstairs and just sits there looking pretty.*

"Have you been working here long?" Cassandra asked.

"For about two years."

"How long have you been working for Matthew and Mark?" Julie inquired.

"Since last October," Cassandra said.

"Do you ever go out around downtown?" Cassandra asked curiously. She needed someone for happy hour because all her other friends were busy that night.

"Not too much, I usually just go to the Library Bar or the Standard."

"What about you?" Julie asked.

"I live downtown and frequent most of the bars around here."

"Are you going to happy hour today?" Cassandra asked.

"I am not sure," Julie responded.

"Well, I am going over to the Library Bar after to work; you are welcome to join me if you want," Cassandra offered.

"Sounds like fun," said Julie. "Great, here is my number; call me if you can't find me," Cassandra said.

"Okay, see you there!"

Cassandra got up from the chair, waved goodbye, and headed for the door. As she waited for the elevators, Cassandra thought, *I hope Julie is somewhat fun because she looks like a bit of a drag.*

Julie, sitting at her desk, thought to herself, *finally here's someone I can hang out with. I wonder if she is any fun.*

Cassandra returned to her office and talked to Christian.

"I invited the bank representative to come out for drinks."

"Why?" Christian asked.

"She looks like fun and it's always nice to befriend people."

"Well, honey, I hope she is fun and knows how to drink," Christian retorted.

"You are coming to happy hour, right?" Cassandra checked.

"Only for one drink!"

"Whatever you say, Christian. One drink turns into three or four."

"I know, honey, I can't help myself," said Christian with a laugh.

Chapter 2

*R*yan Scott had your typical all-American boy looks, with spiky light brown hair, light brown eyes, perfect features, and a killer smile. He was able to charm his way through any situation. Women were definitely not a problem for him. Ryan had grown up in Chicago, Illinois, and, soon after completing his degree at Ohio State, realized he had a knack for selling. He started working at a small marketing company, followed by a medical supply company. Somewhere in between his jobs, he moved to LA with his girlfriend, but that was two years ago, and the girlfriend was the only thing that hadn't stuck around.

Now he was working at Wells Fargo as a merchant sales representative. He enjoyed the perks of a high-paying commission job and making his own schedule. Ryan had only been working at the bank for four months and had already outshined his mentor, ranking in the top three in sales for the state of California. He didn't think much about it; it was what he was good at.

Ryan entered yet another client's office, ready to close a deal that would make him the top salesperson for yet another month.

"Hey boss, how are you doing today?" Ryan asked, flashing his killer smile.

"Hanging in there," the client responded.

"Well, let's close this deal and it will make us both very happy," Ryan said. Handing him the pen, he showed the client where to sign.

Easy as cake, Ryan thought. *In a couple of minutes, I will be out of here to enjoy the rest of my day.*

A few towns away, Eric Dubas sat in his home office trying to close another deal. He had been working at Wells Fargo for two years and his job as a merchant sales representative had become more and more stressful.

"Close this deal, close that deal," he remembered his boss saying to him at a recent meeting. Eric cringed remembering his boss's voice.

"I need to find a new job," Eric said to himself.

Eric was a native of LA. His parents had migrated to LA from Mexico decades ago. He was a first-generation Mexican American, but that didn't stop him from wanting to achieve better things in life. At thirty-five, he had one failed marriage behind him, which had produced a son and a daughter—both were the loves of his life. Eric was a great father, but he was unable to make his marriage work. He was determined to give his kids the best stable life he possibly could. Being in a relationship was the furthest thing from Eric's mind. Ever since his divorce nine years ago, he hadn't found anyone he wanted to get involved with. He'd dated occasionally and had one serious relationship that didn't last, partly due to him. He was not big on the idea of change and hated anything that came between him and his routine. Eric had everything down to a science. Work during the day, work out at night for two hours, and sleep. He had mastered this schedule with an occasional outing here and there, but nothing that required him to break from his schedule.

Eric looked at his monthly sales numbers. *How am I going to get enough deals to meet my quota? I guess I am going to have to come up with some brilliant plan.* He noticed Ryan Scott's monthly numbers and thought, *how does he do it?*

Ryan was recommended by Eric for the merchant sales representative position. It was the only way one could get hired for this particular position. Eric and Ryan were not the best of friends; neither did they care much for each other. Deep inside, Eric hated Ryan because Ryan was younger and had broken the sales record without even trying. Eric thought, *I have to beat him one way or another.*

Every morning during the beginning, middle, and end of summer, Eugene Conrad always contemplated getting up and going to work. It was always a struggle between going to the office or the golf course. Eugene loved the game of golf and had mastered it by the time he had reached high school.

Eugene, born and raised in Orange County, had it all since the day of his conception. Besides being born with beautiful sparkling blue eyes, brown hair, and a perfect height of six feet, his master plan had been laid out for him the moment his parents knew they were expecting. Being born third-generation American, he was given a simple plan: get through middle school and high school, attend the University of Southern California, then join the family business of real estate development in Orange County, eventually running the entire company—plain and simple, without a change in plan. With little argument, Eugene knew that he had to follow this plan and he always did what everyone expected him to.

This particular morning, Eugene looked out of his bedroom window thinking about the last three years of his life and what had happened to him. He agreed that he no longer was going to do anything for anyone, except make himself happy, if he only knew where to start. With that in mind, he looked in his closet, picked out one of his many tailored suits, took a shower, got ready, and headed to another long day at the office.

Cassandra was looking forward to happy hour today. *Yet another friend to add to my list,* she thought. Cassandra had made her mark in downtown LA in the last year and a half, having frequented all the bars and restaurants every night. She had established a reputation as a party girl with very important contacts. She looked at herself in the mirror making sure her makeup was perfect. She didn't like using makeup and thought she looked better without it, but makeup was a prerequisite for nightlife. Cassandra looked at her watch: 6:00 p.m.—longer then she had anticipated staying at work, but Christian didn't get out of work till then and most people didn't either. There was no point going to the bars early because they didn't get crowded until later.

Cassandra walked back to the office.

"Are you ready to meet the man of your dreams?" she asked Christian jokingly.

"Oh honey, yes, let's go!"

They headed over to the Library Bar, which was across the street from their office building on Hope Street. Every time Cassandra walked into a bar, she could feel men staring at her. Cassandra and Christian headed straight to the bar and ordered two Stella Artois, the happy hour beer.

"Cheers," Cassandra said to Christian.

"Cheers, honey."

They started drinking their beers, found two empty stools, and sat down eyeing the room.

"Do you see any hot men?" Cassandra asked.

"Only the bartender, honey. Give me a piece of that and I will be happy all night," Christian retorted.

"Oh, Christian, there's more to life than one-night stands!" She was not too sure she believed her own statement. Soon after, she spotted Julie walking in and waved to her.

"Hi Julie, I want you to meet Christian, my coworker."

"Hello Christian. It's nice to meet you," Julie said, holding her hand out.

Christian shook her hand, "Nice to meet you too."

"Would you like a Stella?" Cassandra asked.

"I only drink Jack and Coke or Belvedere and Spirit," Julie responded. Cassandra and Christian looked at each other and made a funny face. Julie flagged down the bartender and placed her order of Jack and Coke.

As the night progressed, Cassandra and Christian grew tired of Julie. She had a way of being condescending to people and thought she was better than everyone around her. She held on tight to her Louis Vuitton bag, making sure it was always on display as if she were the only one to own that brand.

"I am out of here," Christian remarked.

"Why? Where are you going?" Cassandra interjected.

"Home. I have to take the metro and I cannot pass out on the train. Someone might take advantage of me," Christian said with a smile.

"Oh, please, you would enjoy it more than anyone," Cassandra smiled back.

"Fine, leave me with her; I will manage."

"Okay honey, don't drink too much. I will see you at work tomorrow."

"Muah," Christian said as he left.

"Love you tons," Cassandra said, watching him leave.

"Why is Christian leaving so early?" Julie inquired.

"He has to take the metro home to Long Beach," Cassandra replied.

"Oh, I see," Julie said.

Cassandra started looking around the bar trying to find someone she could speak to. Unfortunately, tonight was one of those nights where the crowd was dull, and everyone was engaged in their own conversations.

Cassandra looked at her cell phone and realized it was close to 8:00 p.m. She was tired from the day's events. She drank the last of her beer and stood up. "I am going to go home. I am tired."

"Okay, I should go as well," said Julie. She gulped her drink down and they both headed out the door.

"I live a block over and I am headed this way," Cassandra said pointing down Sixth Street.

"I am in the parking garage. Do you want a ride home?" asked Julie.

"No, I live only a block away. I can manage walking."

"Okay, have a good night."

"Good night," Cassandra said as she turned and walked toward her loft located in the Milano Loft building. Julie walked toward the garage to her car. Cassandra's two-minute walk home brought a lot of memories rushing into her head. What was she going to do now? Drinking only made matters worse. Cassandra could feel herself get more and more dizzy as she reached her apartment door. She turned the knob on her door and entered her quiet apartment. *Home at last and no one is waiting for me.* She turned on the light and looked at her semi-furnished apartment. It made her sad to be in the loft by herself. She was too exhausted to keep thinking. She went straight to bed, threw herself on it, and closed her eyes.

Julie got in her car and headed home. At twenty-eight, she still lived at home with her parents, but she wasn't embarrassed. She was planning on moving out someday. She drove home with random thoughts in her head. *Does Cassandra like me? Does she think I fit in? Will I ever meet anyone?* Apparently, the five Jack and Cokes didn't help her thoughts! She kept driving hoping tomorrow would be a better day.

Chapter 3

*I*t had been two days since Cassandra had hung out with Julie, and she really did not care to relive those moments. Cassandra was staring out of the law firm's conference room windows on the fifty-third floor of the Aon Building. On a clear day, mountains could be seen at a distance, but Cassandra wasn't sure where they were located. It was on days like this that she hated feeling lonely and depressed. The alcohol didn't help much either; it only made her feel worse. She continued staring out of the windows and Eugene Conrad popped into her head. *I wonder what he is up to.* Cassandra had neither seen nor spoken to Eugene in over a month, but that was typical in their relationship. They would talk on the phone one month, and then wouldn't speak for two months and so on. Most of their communication was through text messaging. Cassandra hated that Eugene was always so inconsistent with her. She was not sure what he wanted and mostly she could not read him at all.

It had been over a year since she had first met Eugene Conrad at the Standard Hotel. Cassandra had been in the hotel lobby speaking with one of the security guards when Eugene and his cousin Sam had approached the guard, asking to be granted entry to the hotel's lavish rooftop—known to be one of the LA's best outdoor bars. To this day, Cassandra still remembered what Eugene was wearing: a blue Dodgers baseball cap with a dark blue T-shirt and black pants. When Eugene and his cousin had tried going up the escalator, the guard had stopped them because they had drinks in their hands. They had to finish their drinks downstairs before going to the rooftop. As Eugene and Sam were finishing their drinks, Cassandra had started a conversation with them. "Do you guys come here often?" she had asked.

"Sometimes. We just left a Dodgers game and decided to stop by. I love the steak sandwich from the hotel's restaurant," Eugene had replied.

"I see, and where do you live?" Cassandra had inquired.

"Orange County."

"How general," Cassandra had said with a bit of an attitude.

"What does that mean?" Eugene had asked.

"Well, Orange County is rather large . . . and you just saying 'Orange County' means that you don't want me to know where you live."

"Interesting," he had replied.

"Well, just for the record, I live in Laguna Canyon."

"That's nice. And you, where do you live?" Cassandra had asked Sam.

"Laguna Niguel, a couple of minutes from my cousin."

"Well, I live across the street in the Pegasus," Cassandra had informed.

"Really, right across the street?" Eugene had asked.

"Yes, I come here often," Cassandra had replied. She thought, *an Orange County guy—not my cup of tea, but he seems nice enough to know.*

"By the way, my name is Cassandra."

"I'm Eugene, and this is my cousin Sam."

"Nice to meet you both."

"Are you guys ready to go upstairs and drink?"

"For sure!" Eugene had replied. With one look from Cassandra, the security guards had let them upstairs. Since that night, Cassandra had not been able to stop thinking about Eugene and she did not exactly know why. Eugene was your typical Orange County guy, tall, brown hair with beautiful blue eyes, smart, successful, and fun to be with. It wasn't like Cassandra didn't encounter these types of men on an everyday basis, but there was something different about Eugene. She couldn't pinpoint yet, but there was a reason why she kept calling him all the time even though he was not a true friend to Cassandra. She decided to stop thinking about him because she would only torture herself.

She went back to her desk and her phone rang. "Cassandra speaking."

"Hi Cassandra, its Julie from Wells Fargo. How are you?"

"Good, thank you. And yourself?"

"Glad that it's Friday!"

"Me too," Cassandra said. *Why she is calling me?*

"I was wondering if you have any plans for tonight. If not, maybe you would like to go to happy hour?" Julie asked. Cassandra tried thinking of a good excuse, but couldn't get one. She really did not want to go home and sit in her apartment all night.

"Where were you thinking?"

"Maybe the Library Bar or Standard Rooftop?" Julie said.

"How about the Library Bar?" Cassandra asked.

"Great. I will meet you there around 6:00 p.m.," Julie said with an upbeat tone.

"Okay, see you then," Cassandra said and hung up. *It was either this or hanging out alone at home.*

Ryan Scott walked to Julie's branch "First Tower," which was one of the many branches he covered as a merchant sales representative. It was Friday afternoon and he was geared to get this day over with and start his weekend. He went to the empty desk that was located near Julie Chow's desk.

"Hey Julie."

"Hi Ryan, how are you?"

"Good. Ready to start the weekend."

"Me too."

"Any plans for this weekend?" Ryan inquired.

"Not much, just laying low."

"How about yourself?"

"Hanging out by the beach and having a couple of drinks," Ryan stated.

"Nice. Hope you enjoy yourself," Julie said with a smile and turned her attention back to her computer screen. This was a typical conversation that took place between Julie and Ryan. She had no interest in him other than being his coworker, and Ryan thought Julie was somewhat cute, but wasn't his type. Their paths rarely crossed and when it did, it was a simple "Hello" and "Goodbye." Ryan went back to his desk and started crunching numbers. *The sooner the better*, he thought.

Cassandra decided that she had had enough of work today and left early to take a nap before happy hour. She would need her strength to hang out with Julie. It wasn't that Julie was a bad person; Julie didn't know how to socialize with other people. As she walked home, she started dialing away, inviting people to come to the Library Bar at 6:00 p.m. *The more the merrier,* she thought. Reaching her apartment, she turned on the TV. Maybe she could catch an episode of *Law and Order,* one of her favorite TV shows. While watching TV, Cassandra started dozing off, but was awakened by text messages. Some friends said they would meet her at the bar; others said they had previous engagements and would catch up with her later.

About an hour later, Cassandra woke up from her nap and got ready to leave. She loved living alone some days, but on other days it drove her crazy. Then, a quick memory of Eugene popped into her head. She needed a drink.

Cassandra headed over to the Library Bar. Some of her friends were already at the bar, with tequila shots. "Hey beautiful," they called out to Cassandra. She smiled, a smile inherited from her mother and maternal grandmother; although Cassandra had never met her maternal grandmother, she knew she resembled her in some way.

"Hi guys! Are you drinking straight tequila again?" Cassandra exclaimed.

"Come on, Cassandra, you know us better than that by now!" said Oscar.

"You guys are too much!" Cassandra waved down her favorite bartender, Carlos. She had met Carlos when the Library Bar had first opened up last summer. Back then it was only a couple of patrons and Cassandra. She became familiar with him and Cassandra was his favorite customer.

"What can I get you, love?" Carlos asked.

"Grey Goose and tonic with a lime," Cassandra said with a smile.

"Anything for you, love."

"I know," Cassandra responded with a wink.

As she got her drink from the bar, she spotted Julie approaching her. "Hi Julie, how are you? How was work?" Not like Cassandra really wanted to know, but she was being polite.

"It was okay, long . . . and drama at the last minute with certain coworkers!"

"Wow, sounds rough," Cassandra said as she looked around for her friends.

"Are you getting a drink?" she asked Julie.

"Yes, definitely." Julie went to the bar to order and Cassandra spotted her friends. She sat down at the table with them and everyone started chatting about their day. Julie got her drink and joined the table.

"Everyone, this is Julie," Cassandra told the table.

"Hi Julie," everyone replied. Julie sat down in between Cassandra and Oscar. Oscar put his arm around Julie and said, "You are too cute."

"Thanks," Julie replied with a sour voice, trying to shrug her shoulders so Oscar could get the hint. Oscar looked over at his sister, Lila, and made a face. Cassandra wanted to agree with the face Oscar made, but decided not to.

"And where is Mr. Eugene Conrad tonight?" Lila questioned with a giggle.

"How should I know?" Cassandra shrugged.

"I haven't spoken to him in over a month. Plus, I am over it. I have moved on. He is yesterday's news," Cassandra said proudly.

"Right, in about ten minutes, after you have another vodka tonic, you will start talking about him again."

"Nope, not this time. It's done. I can't spend my time waiting for him. He doesn't like me and that's it,' Cassandra said loudly.

"We'll see," Lila said with a smile.

As the night progressed, Julie started pulling herself apart from the group's conversation. "What's her problem?" Oscar asked.

"I'm not sure, she seems a little weird. She acts as if she is better than everyone else. She lacks people skills," Cassandra interjected.

"Maybe. Or she just needs to get laid," Oscar said.

"Right, let's see if that happens."

They both looked at each other and laughed. Soon everyone was at the bar doing tequila shots. Two shots later, Cassandra could not believe she was doing this again. *If I end up kissing someone, he better be cute*, she laughed to herself.

Oscar and Cassandra scoped out the place for potential hookups and noticed some candidates.

"Look at him, Cassandra. He has been staring at you all night."

"I don't think so."

"He has blue eyes and blond hair, and we all know how you're a sucker for that," Oscar said laughing loudly.

Cassandra smiled and said, "Yes, I am." She walked over to him and introduced herself.

"Hi, I'm Cassandra. Can I guess what you do for a living?" The man looked surprised and said, "Sure, why not?"

"Okay, so you're not a banker or a lawyer. Let me see. I've got it, you work in commercial real estate development."

"Something of that nature," the mystery man said.

"And what's your profession?" the man asked Cassandra, his blue eyes intense and piercing.

"I make dreams happen," Cassandra said with her sexy smile and walked away. Barely two seconds later the man came up to Cassandra to introduce himself. "Hi, I am Matt."

"Hi Matt," Cassandra said. Cassandra introduced Matt to Oscar who sitting at the bar making faces behind Matt's back.

"Matt, this is my friend Oscar. Oscar, this is Matt."

"Hello Oscar," Matt said as he extended his hand out for Oscar to shake. Oscar had a great big smile on his face as he shook Matt's hand.

"So, what are we drinking? Tequila shots?" Matt asked.

"No way, no more tequila for me," Cassandra said.

"I'll take one," Oscar said.

"Of course, you will, because that is all you drink," Cassandra said with a laugh. As both men took their shots, Cassandra noticed Julie staring at them and waved for her to join them. "Matt, this is Julie."

"Hi Julie," Matt said. "Would you like a drink?"

"No, thank you. I'm fine," Julie responded. She seemed to be sending out signals that she was jealous. Cassandra started getting closer to Matt, who of course didn't mind.

"So, Matt, what's your story?" Cassandra questioned.

"What do you mean?"

"You know, how many kids, how many wives, and so on."

"Oh, I have four kids and two different wives, one on each coast," Matt laughed.

"Nice, I have a husband, boyfriend, and lover. And we all live together," Cassandra said nonchalantly.

"Hope you have a big place," Matt said with a smile.

"Actually, I am not in a relationship, never have been married, and no kids," Matt stated.

"Ah. You must be gay then."

"Never and not likely. I just haven't found the one."

"Well, tonight is your lucky night, Matt."

"Oh, really. What is that?"

"You met me tonight; that should be lucky enough," Cassandra laughed. They continued their conversation. Matt was in awe of Cassandra's eyes. Julie continued staring in envy because the attention was on Cassandra. Matt was a cookie-cutter guy, the type of men Cassandra had always met since her move to LA over a year and a half ago. He was a successful real estate developer with offices in LA and Orange County, in his mid-thirties, and with houses in Hollywood Hills and Laguna Beach. *Wonder if he knows Eugene*, Cassandra thought during the conversation. Later that night, Cassandra started drinking a lot more as Matt kept buying her and her friends drinks. *I need to stop drinking*, Cassandra thought to herself, *before I black out*, but she kept drinking anyway.

Before she realized it, Cassandra was on her eighth vodka tonic and making out with Matt at the bar. Oscar looked on, wishing he was the one kissing the gorgeous man. Julie ignored them and paid attention to something else. As it was nearing closing time, Cassandra and Matt left the bar together against Julie's wishes. Julie said, "Cassandra I can take you home."

"No, I can take myself home, thank you," Cassandra responded.

"Fine, whatever you want," Julie said angrily.

"Matt, would you like to take me home?" Cassandra asked Matt seductively.

"Of course, don't you live down the block?" Matt asked.

"Yes, I do. Want to come over?" Cassandra asked as she kissed him again.

"Definitely," Matt said. Cassandra and Matt kissed some more before heading toward Cassandra's apartment. Julie left, simply saying "goodbye." Oscar and everyone else left too.

"Bye baby," Oscar said as he kissed Cassandra on her cheek. "Don't do anything I wouldn't do."

"Right," Cassandra said as she slightly lost her balance walking down the stairs of the bar. "Ready?" Matt asked looking into Cassandra's eyes.

"Yes!" They started walking toward Cassandra's apartment.

Chapter 4

*S*aturday morning sunlight was hitting Eugene Conrad in the face. After some minutes of trying to ignore the sunshine, he finally gave in and opened his eyes. He stared at the ceiling trying to recap the events from the previous night.

He and his buddies had started out with dinner at the Cheesecake Factory in Fashion Island in Newport Beach and then had headed next door to the Yard House for drinks. Somewhere after arriving at the Yard House, his memory had started fading. Finally, he remembered getting home and passing out on his bed, naked of course. Eugene Conrad was not one for sleeping with clothes on.

Flashing moments from the previous night started popping into his head. He was speaking to several girls, asking them for their numbers, then drinking some more. As he waited for another memory to pop in his head, he heard his cell phone ring. It was his sister calling him. He hit the ignore button. *I can't right now*, he said to his phone.

He wondered what time it was. It was only 9:00 a.m. As he got up from bed, his head was pounding. *No more drinking*. This, of course, was a usual comment for Eugene. He threw on a pair of shorts and his red USC T-shirt. He headed downstairs for some water and aspirin.

Taking a bottle of Fiji water and aspirin from the kitchen, he headed to the couch and turned on the TV. Another memory popped into his head. *Did I kiss someone last night?* He remembered trying to kiss a girl after his seventh glass of chardonnay, which also included three vodka tonics during dinner. He shook his head as if erasing the memory. He sat on the couch, leaning his head on a pillow.

As he was watching TV, a commercial came on that reminded him of Cassandra. He was not sure what the connection was between the commercial and Cassandra, but she was in his head now. *I should call her*, he thought. He always wished he could be a better friend to Cassandra, as she was to him, but he usually failed. Eugene was not the type of guy to flake on people and not return calls. This was the problem. He had always done what everyone expected him to do and now he was taking a break from it. It just happened that Cassandra had walked into his life while this was happening. He wasn't ready to get involved with anyone yet. The last two years of his life had been a roller coaster, and the ride was finally coming to a complete stop—or so he thought. He would learn in a couple of months that his drinking would spiral out of control resulting in a second DUI.

The noise coming from upstairs disturbed his thoughts. His phone was ringing again. With a sigh, Eugene said, "I guess I have to start my day." He got up from the couch and headed upstairs to see if it was his sister calling again. She had a tendency to call and call until he picked up the phone.

Startled, Cassandra opened her eyes, and froze. *Where am I?* It took her a couple of seconds to realize that she was lying in her own bed. Relieved, she buried her head into the pillow. *I can't believe I did this again. I had told myself I would not drink like this anymore.*

As she turned around to lie on her back, she suddenly felt nauseous. She tried to ignore the feeling, but it worsened. She ran to the bathroom and started vomiting. All that came out was the bile from her stomach lining. Cassandra had not eaten anything the night before when she had started drinking. When the vomiting stopped, she lay back in bed. Eyes closed, she started praying that the feeling would go away.

Since recently, whenever Cassandra drank she would immediately vomit the next day. This had never happened to her before. It was as if her body was having a bad reaction to alcohol. She grabbed her iPhone from the nightstand. Several missed calls and five text messages waiting to be read. She started reading them. One was from a guy named Mark: "Great meeting you last night, hope we can together soon." *Who's Mark?* She wondered. She continued reading the rest of the messages. There was one message from Oscar, "Hope you had fun all night with the delicious guy; call me later for details."

Why did he always relate men to how food tastes? Cassandra went through her missed calls which were the usual—Mom, best friend from back home, a couple of extremely drunk friends at 4:00 a.m.—and Julie. *What did Julie want?* Cassandra looked at the time: 10:00 a.m. Her head continued to pound, but she knew she couldn't stomach aspirin.

She got up, hoping she wouldn't feel nausea, and walked over to her water cooler. She drank some water, turned on the TV, and lay down on the couch. Flipping through the channels, she started watching an episode of *The Hills*. She knew life wasn't always as perfect as they made it to be.

Julie Chow was having breakfast at home with her parents. This was typical on a Saturday morning since she still lived in her parent's house. At twenty-eight, Julie still had not moved out and started her own life.

Unbeknownst to most people, Julie had a fear of leaving her parent's house. More accurately, a fear of failure. She couldn't stomach the idea of not being perfect in front of people even though she was far from what the definition of perfection was.

What she didn't know was that her pretending to be perfect and well-mannered in front of others was a façade, which could be seen right through. If anything, it made her very disliked by most people she encountered.

"How was last night, dear?" her mother asked.

"It was okay. A friend that works in the same building and I went out for happy hour, which of course turned into an all-night affair," Julie replied.

"Tell me about this new friend," her mother asked.

"She works for the law firm that has an account with Wells Fargo. Her name is Cassandra and she's rather a nice person," Julie replied.

"How nice," her mother responded.

As she was eating breakfast, Julie started going over the details from last night. She had fun hanging out with Cassandra and her friends, but she did not meet any new men. Neither did any man approach her nor did anyone offer to buy her a drink, like they did for Cassandra. She wondered why. Julie knew she was pretty—her parents told her all the time. So why didn't any men try to talk to her? Maybe it just wasn't her night. *I need to be more sociable*, she told herself.

As Cassandra lay on her couch, she remembered the text message she had received from Mark. She remembered the guy she had met at the bar and the drinks she had kept pounding as if it were a contest to see who could get drunk the fastest.

What a mistake.

She barely remembered leaving the bar with him.

Somewhere after her fifth vodka tonic and tequila shot, Cassandra had blanked out. She remembered kissing him a lot. He must have been a nice guy since he didn't stay over, and Cassandra had invited him several times. *I wish I could remember what we spoke about,* she thought. She tried to go through as many details as possible to make sure she hadn't embarrassed herself last night. Cassandra had a tendency of getting really drunk and then doing something funny, which resulted in embarrassing situations.

Even though most people found it hard to tell when Cassandra was drunk, half the time she could not remember details from the night before. She laughed, remembering the embarrassing stories that her friends had told her about herself.

Cassandra hated the days after the drinking: they were the most depressing. She wondered about this guy Mark—another man she would add to her damaged goods list. Cassandra had created her "damaged goods" category right before she had left Manhattan to move to LA. Since then, every man she had encountered fit her damaged good criteria: successful, rich, good-looking, not married/divorced, and thirty-five or older—these were the requirements to be part of the "damaged goods list." Every man Cassandra had met was an eligible candidate.

Mark was no exception. *I am sure he's a nice guy, but most men are not looking for relationships. Who can blame them? They're successful, rich, and lived in LA, which is equivalent to living in Fantasy Land, where nothing is real*! Suddenly, Cassandra remembered Eugene. She knew out of all men she had met, Eugene was an exception. She felt like calling him, but decided against it. He probably wouldn't answer the phone anyway. Her phone started ringing and she carefully got up to answer it. It was Julie. "Hello," Cassandra said softly.

"Hi, what are you doing?" Julie asked.

"Trying not to throw up my liver."

"Are you okay? What happened?"

"I had too much to drink last night and, of course, I didn't eat before my drinking marathon."

"Ouch. I totally feel you. I didn't feel that good either this morning, but I had some breakfast and felt better," Julie said.

"Lucky you," replied Cassandra.

"What are your plans for today?" Julie inquired.

"Hopefully not to throw up anymore," Cassandra remarked.

"Are you interested in getting a manicure and pedicure today?" Julie asked. Cassandra thought about it and looked at her feet. She *did* need a pedicure but was wondering what would be more painful: hanging out with Julie or not getting a pedicure? She finally agreed.

"Okay, what time do you want to go?" Cassandra asked.

"How about noon?" Apparently, Julie wasn't as hungover as Cassandra.

"How about 1:00 p.m.? I need more time to rest," Cassandra said.

"Okay. I will come pick you up," offered Julie.

"Okay, see you then. Bye!" Cassandra hung up. She lay back on the couch and continued flipping through the channels until she saw something she liked. She was not looking forward to the afternoon ahead.

It was 11:00 a.m. on Saturday morning, and Ryan Scott was just driving home from playing cards all night at The Hollywood Park Casino in Inglewood. His hair disheveled and eyes red, Ryan looked extremely exhausted, but he'd had a great time playing poker all night. If he could become a professional poker player, he would, but his mother would have never approved.

Even at twenty-nine, Ryan still valued his mother's opinions. He had grown up on the outskirts of Chicago. His parents had divorced when he was little, but the most cherished moments were with his father when they both went to the Cubs baseball games. His father had season tickets back then and Ryan had never missed a game.

After Ryan's father left, it was just his mom, him, and his maternal grandparents. His maternal grandfather became a father to Ryan and his father just became a distant memory.

He thought about how much money he had lost and won while playing poker. He was up $500 and that was good enough for him. No matter what he tried his hand at, Ryan always excelled, and this time was no different. He was a thinker, and his head was always filled with thoughts about his next step in life.

He had moved to LA after finishing at Ohio State with his girlfriend. Ryan had decided to stick it out in LA, but his girlfriend hadn't, and it had broken his heart when she had gotten on a plane to move back East, but he was better now. It had been over a year and his heart was healing. Not completely healed, but in the process of it. He wondered if he was ever going to meet someone truly special or did he let *the one* slip away. Ryan always thought he wasn't meant to be married, perhaps be a playboy forever. He was still young and was in no rush to get married. He pulled into a parking space in front of his apartment, happy to be home. Going upstairs to his room, he threw himself on the bed not bothering to take off his clothes.

Around 1:00 p.m., Julie came to pick up Cassandra at her apartment in downtown LA. She sent Cassandra a text message when she was a couple of blocks away. Cassandra was still lying on the couch. When she got Julie's text, she got up to get ready immediately. She really didn't care what she looked like today, given how she felt from last night's drinking session.

She threw on some clothes and put her hair up; even without makeup, Cassandra was still beautiful. She walked to the elevator bank, waited patiently, and then finally emerged in the lobby. Her building, like most buildings in downtown LA, was new, having recently been built during the many renovations that were taking place in downtown LA. It was a well-equipped building with a gym and rooftop deck that could host parties. Cassandra waved at the security guard and exited the building. It was a beautiful Saturday afternoon. She got into Julie's car.

"Hey Julie, how are you?" Cassandra asked.

"Good, and you?" Julie inquired.

"Feeling better," Cassandra said with a smile. "Where are we going to get our nails done?"

"Down in Irvine," Julie responded.

"Irvine, like Irvine in Orange County?" Cassandra asked surprised.

"Yes, it's by the Irvine campus, next to Newport Beach."

Great, Cassandra thought. Going down to Newport Beach and Irvine only reminded her of Eugene. She could never seem to get away from him.

"Is there a problem?" asked Julie.

"No, not at all. Look forward to the drive!" Cassandra said with a smile.

Chapter 5

*I*t was the middle of the week and Cassandra was tired from getting up early every morning. She woke up at 9:00 a.m. and had to be at work by 9:00 a.m.——which translated into 10:00 a.m. for her. She didn't understand why she needed to be at work so early. Nothing really started at the firm until after 10:00 a.m. This particular morning, Cassandra was researching the money line for the Lakers Game later that night. Cassandra loved to gamble, and recently sports gambling had become one of her addictions. She had won big during Super Bowl 42 when the New York Giants had won. Since then, she started learning the difference between the money line, plus or minus, and total points. She had got the hang of it and loved the adrenaline of betting on games and then watching to see if you win.

It was the beginning of the NBA playoffs and Cassandra needed to get in on the action. There was a game tonight and she needed to bet on it. She found out the odds and placed her money on a straight line for the Lakers to win. An easy choice with a minimum payout of $110 for every $100 she bet, but it was better than nothing.

"What are you doing tonight, hon?" Christian asked.

"Watching the Lakers game at the Library Bar. Wanna come?" Cassandra asked still looking at the computer hoping she had made the right choice.

"No, honey, I can't. I have dinner with my two roommates who are going to leave me at the end of the month."

"How sad. Where are you going to move to?" Cassandra inquired.

"Honey, I don't know yet, somewhere in downtown Long Beach."

"Well, you know what I say, you should move to downtown LA," replied Cassandra.

"But it's expensive. I need drinking money," Christian explained.

"Christian, you always say that when you're broke; maybe you should stop drinking," Elizabeth said.

Elizabeth Dowell was the new girl the firm had recently hired and Cassandra had taken a quick liking to her. She was petite and pretty. She was only twenty-two and had been married for over a year. Elizabeth reminded Cassandra of herself when she was that age.

"That's true, Christian, you are always broke or something in that respect," said Cassandra. They all laughed.

"Are you betting on the game?" Elizabeth asked Cassandra.

"Yes, I have to call some gambling company located in San Jose, Costa Rica. I place my bet with them over the phone and then wire them the money," Cassandra explained. "I know it sounds a bit shady, but that's how it's done."

"How much are you betting?" queried Elizabeth.

"Not much, enough where it won't be too bad if I lose," Cassandra responded.

"Wish I had that kind of money to waste . . ." Christian stated.

"Me too!" Elizabeth concurred.

Cassandra did not have that much money to bet or lose. Ever since she had moved to LA, she had not divulged any information about her family to anyone here. Her parents, fed up with her constant moving around and indecisiveness, had cut her off completely, leaving her to fend for herself in LA. Cassandra didn't care if some days were hard; she had complete freedom in her life and she was willing to pay the price by having no money. Cassandra's family in New York was extremely wealthy. Cassandra had always experienced a very comfortable life, but those were just material things to her. In reality, Cassandra couldn't have the one thing she always craved for: a family that was always together and there for her. From an early age, Cassandra had learned that money could not buy everything; it was just something that people used to shelter themselves from seeing the truth. The temptation of what her parents were offering her always stuck in the back of her head. Were she to return to NY, all of Cassandra's problems would disappear, but then she would be bounded by their rules and guidelines. Cassandra knew nothing in life was free and for now, she didn't care to return to that life.

"What time is the game?" Elizabeth asked.

"Starts at 6:00 p.m. I am going to the Library Bar to watch the game with Hank, and I think Julie is coming as well," Cassandra said.

"Is Julie your new BFF?" Christian said with a smirk.

"Oh, no, not at all. She is someone good to keep around. I think I may need her for something, but I don't know what it is yet," Cassandra laughed.

Cassandra indeed was a good person. She may have done hurtful things to others, but sometimes she couldn't help herself. This was the result of being brought up spoiled without any restrictions.

"Well, good luck with her. You could not pay me to hang out with her!" Christian stated.

Glad that the workday was over, Cassandra was looking forward to happy hour. It was 5:45 p.m. She asked Hank, "Ready to go?"

"Yes," Hank said. Hank was a temporary employee that was hired by one of the firm's business associates. He secretly had a crush on Cassandra, but would never admit to anyone because he knew Cassandra was out of his league. They walked toward the elevator together. "I can't wait to see the game; hopefully the Lakers win," Cassandra said.

"The Lakers will win. They have to, they are the best!" They got into the elevator and Hank remembered how just last month Cassandra had tried to kiss him one night when they were hanging out. Cassandra had drunk too much champagne and was intoxicated. Not knowing what was happening, she had tried putting the moves on Hank. Hank, a gentleman, did not take advantage of the situation. Although sometimes he would have liked to know what it would be like to kiss her.

The elevator doors opened. Exiting the elevator, they took the escalators down to the street.

The Library Bar was right across the street of the Aon Building that housed over a hundred companies in downtown LA.

"I hope there are seats available at the bar," Cassandra said.

"There should be; it's still early." As they walked up the four steps to the bar, they could hear the loud sounds of the TV coming from inside. The bar was pretty packed for a Wednesday night. Cassandra walked in first. She always caused a stir whenever she walked into a place, heads turning her way.

"There are seats toward the end," Cassandra shouted. Hank followed her to the end of the bar. They sat next to each other on the bar stools.

"Hey, what can I getcha?" the bartender asked.

"A Stella, please," Cassandra replied. Stella Artois was the drink of choice during happy hour for Cassandra. The bartender looked at Hank. "Water for me," he said.

"Why are you not drinking?" Cassandra asked.

"I am taking it easy for a while. Until Memorial Day weekend," Hank said. Cassandra glanced at him with a weird look, but got distracted when her Stella was served.

"What time is Julie coming?" Hank asked.

"She should be here by 6:00 p.m." Cassandra and Hank continued to talk and watch the previews before the game started. Shortly after 6:00 p.m. Julie entered the bar and spotted Cassandra and Hank. Cassandra waved at her. They all greeted each other.

"The table up front is empty; do you want to move over there?"

"Sure, let's go," Cassandra said. They sat down at the table and Julie went to order her usual Jack and Coke. When she got back, she announced, "I invited a coworker to come over and watch the game."

"Which coworker is this?" Cassandra asked. "One of the merchant sales representatives. He was in the office today and I mentioned I was going to watch the game and invited him."

"Fun! Is he cute?" Cassandra asked

"He is cute, but I am not interested. Not my type," Julie said. *Who is your type?* Cassandra thought in her mind. Several minutes passed and Julie kept looking out of the window for her coworker. Finally, he walked in and spotted Julie.

"Hi Julie," he said.

"Hi Ryan, I want you to meet Cassandra and Hank. Cassandra and Hank, this is Ryan," Julie said. Ryan shook hands with them and sat down next to Julie, across from Cassandra and Hank. Ryan Scott was an attractive young man, with boy-next-door looks. He had average height with dark brown/blond spiky hair, piercing brown eyes, and a smile that could get him out of anything. He was wearing a black suit with a white shirt and red tie that was tailored to the smell of future success!

Cassandra took one look at him and knew that she had to have him. Ryan looked at Cassandra and thought how pretty she was and how long it would take him to sleep with her. Whether it was work or women, he was always on top of his game.

Ryan got up from the table to order a drink. He returned with his second favorite beer, Hefeweizen. Miller Light was his first.

"I'm sorry, I didn't catch your name in the beginning," Cassandra said.

"It's Ryan, Ryan Scott," Ryan said with a smile. Cassandra smiled back at him. *This was just too easy,* she thought.

"Well, Ryan Scott, it's very nice to meet you." They all continued talking, waiting for the game to start.

"Does everyone want to order some pizza from Wolfgang's?" Julie asked.

"Yes, let's order the BBQ chicken pizza; it's to die for," Cassandra said.

"That sounds good," Ryan said. Julie put the order in for the pizza to be delivered at their table in the bar.

"Ryan, Cassandra bets on sports as well," Julie said.

"You do?" Ryan asked.

"Yes, I love betting on sports, I have a bet on this game and the Lakers better win," Cassandra said. Cassandra kept noticing Ryan looking at her all night. Even when he spoke to her, he would touch her hand from across the table. The pizza was delivered from Wolfgang Puck and was finished in a matter of minutes. After, Ryan asked Cassandra if she would like another beer.

"Yes, please," she said. Being the gentleman he was, he asked Julie as well.

The night continued with Ryan paying attention to Cassandra and exchanging information with her on where they grew up and where they lived now. When Julie left the table to go to the restroom and Hank left to go home, Ryan gave Cassandra his business card.

"This is my information; my cell phone number is on it," Ryan said.

"Does this mean I can call you any time I like?"

"Yes, whenever you like." There was something Cassandra liked about Ryan. He wasn't like the cookie-cutter guys that Cassandra dated. He was sweet and smart. Cassandra, of course, enjoyed the attention. The Lakers won the game and Ryan got up and said, "I have to head back to South Bay."

"Leaving already?" Julie asked.

"Yes, I have had too many beers and have a bit of a ride home," Ryan said.

"It was nice to have met you," Cassandra said.

"Same here," Ryan said.

"Bye Julie."

"Bye Ryan." Ryan left and Julie said, "What do you think?"

"He's adorable. You don't like him?" Cassandra checked.

"No, he is just a coworker," Julie said.

"Are you ready to go?" Cassandra asked with a yawn.

"Yes, I am," Julie, said. Both women left the bar. Cassandra never once told her that Ryan had given her his business card.

The next day, Cassandra arrived at work.

"How did last night go?" Elizabeth asked.

"As good as it could, given the fact that I was hanging out with Julie and Hank, but Julie brought a coworker named Ryan, and he was cute. He gave me his business card and told me to give him a call."

"Wow, does Julie like him?" Elizabeth asked.

"I asked her, but she said no."

Later that day, Cassandra sent a text message to Ryan about betting on Friday's game. It wasn't until Friday afternoon that Ryan replied to Cassandra's text message: "I consider you a lucky charm since you were with me last time the Lakers won. You should come down and watch the game with me."

Cassandra messaged back, "Where are you watching the game?"

"At Tony P's in Marina Del Rey."

"Sounds like fun, count me in." Now Cassandra needed to convince Julie to go because she would be Cassandra's ride down there. Ever since Cassandra had moved to LA, she didn't have a car. She did not need one. *LA would be like Manhattan*, she had thought. What a shock Cassandra had received on her first day in LA when she realized that there were no taxis like Manhattan.

"Hey Julie, it's Cassandra. What are you doing?"

"Working hard on a Friday, which I hate," she replied.

"Oh, where were you planning on watching the game tonight?" Cassandra asked.

"I am going to my aunt's house because they are having a porch party. You can come, if you like?" Julie asked. Cassandra thought, *who in their right mind goes to porch parties and hangs out with their aunt?*

"I have a better idea. Ryan just texted me and invited us down to Tony P's in the Marina. Would you like to go?"

"Really, he texted you? How did he get your number?"

"We exchanged numbers at the Library Bar on Wednesday," Cassandra explained not telling her the truth. Julie didn't know that Cassandra had reached out to Ryan.

"Sure, I want to go!" Julie exclaimed. "I will go home, change, and pick you up and we'll head down there."

"Okay, sounds like a plan," Cassandra said. She hung up the phone and turned to Elizabeth who had been standing next to Cassandra during the conversation.

"*Us? He invited us?* I believe he only invited you," Elizabeth said.

"I know, but I had to make the story believable to where he invited *us* and I do need a ride down there," Cassandra stated matter-of-factly.

"You are too much," Elizabeth said with a laugh.

"I am helping the girl out by getting her some friends. If it weren't for me, she would be at a porch party at her aunt's house. Who does that?" Cassandra said sarcastically.

They both laughed and went back to work.

While Cassandra and Julie were driving down the Marina, they started to discuss the evening that lay ahead of them.

"Do you think Ryan has a lot of friends?" Julie asked.

"I am sure he does," Cassandra replied.

"Are you sure he invited both of us and not only you?" Julie asked.

"Yes Julie, he invited both of us."

"Tonight's going to be fun," Julie said excitedly. *I hope so*, Cassandra thought. They arrived at Tony P's and the parking lot was completely full. Julie gave her car to the valet and they walked into the bar.

"There's a $10 cover charge," the bartender announced.

"A cover charge for what?" Cassandra asked curiously.

"For tonight's game. It's the best place in town to watch," the bartender stated.

"The game already started. Why should I pay the whole $10?" Cassandra inquired with a sexy smile.

"Okay, just because you have a nice smile, you can pay $5."

"Thank you," Cassandra said as she handed him a $5 bill. They walked in and started looking for Ryan. From the back of the restaurant, Ryan spotted Cassandra and Julie and raised his hand to indicate where they were sitting. Cassandra saw Ryan and started walking over.

"Hi Ryan," Cassandra said. Ryan got up and gave Cassandra a big hug and said hello to Julie. "Everyone, this is Cassandra and Julie. This is Alex, Shawn, and his girlfriend Stacey," Ryan introduced everyone. Cassandra sat down next to Ryan and Julie sat across the table next to Alex.

"You work at Wells Fargo too?" Alex asked Julie.

"Yes, I am a personal banker," Julie replied.

"Shawn and I both work as merchant sales representative for Wells," Alex informed. "Cassandra, do you work at Wells too?"

"No, I work for a law firm located in the same building as Wells in downtown LA." The waitress came around to take their order for drinks.

"I'll have a Miller Light," Cassandra stated.

"Jack and Coke," Julie said. Ryan started talking to Cassandra, touching her arm every now and then. Cassandra loved the attention Ryan was showering on her. Every time Ryan looked at her, she could tell that he liked her. The bar started getting louder because the Lakers kept making three pointers. The Lakers game came to an end and the group decided to head over to the Circle Bar in Santa Monica.

"What kind of a bar is it?" Cassandra inquired.

"It's a laidback bar. They play good music," Alex responded. "You will like it."

The group headed out the door. It had been raining when they were inside, but it had just stopped, leaving the beautiful smell of rain in the air.

"This is the second time it has rained in LA since I have lived here," Cassandra stated. Julie and Cassandra waited for the valet to bring the car. Since they were the last ones to leave the parking lot, they were a bit behind and finally caught up to someone else's car in the group.

"This is fun," Julie said. Cassandra thought, *has she never hung out before? Every time we do something, it seems foreign to Julie.* She made a mental note to ask Julie if she had ever hung out with people. After driving for fifteen minutes, they all pulled into a parking lot and met outside their cars. Upon entering the bar, the security asked for their IDs. Cassandra entered first and noticed the bar was a bit of a dive bar, small with an oval bar in the middle and some booths to the side and in the back. The lighting was very dim.

She made her way to the back of the bar and everyone else followed. It was still early, and the crowd was light.

"What are we all drinking?" Cassandra asked.

"Jack and Coke for me," Julie said.

"Me too," Ryan said. Cassandra ordered the drinks and they all started chatting at the bar. Ryan stood very close to Cassandra and told her how many times he came here and how he liked it. Julie and Alex were talking to one side, and Shawn and his girlfriend Stacey were gazing into each other's eyes. The bar started to get full. Ryan enjoyed talking to Cassandra. She had a pretty smile and great hair. He wondered what it would be like to kiss her. Everyone kept drinking more and more and Ryan grabbed Cassandra's hand, "Come with me," he said.

He pulled Cassandra and she followed him toward the front of the bar where there was a booth and they sat down with their drinks.

"Can I tell you something?" Ryan said. "Sure," Cassandra responded.

"You have really sexy hair," Ryan said. Cassandra smiled and Ryan leaned in to kiss her. Cassandra pulled away and sipped her drink.

"Why did you pull away?" Ryan asked, his face still very close to hers.

"I am not sure if this would work out," Cassandra said.

"I don't think so either," Ryan said and leaned in to kiss her again, and without a second thought, Cassandra kissed him back. The kiss lasted for about five minutes straight and they finally came up for air. They both smiled and sipped their drinks. Cassandra thought, *wow, he can really kiss*. Ryan didn't say much after the kiss; he just smiled and looked at Cassandra.

"I need to get some cigarettes," Ryan said. They got up and walked to the door of the bar. It began raining so Cassandra said, "I am going back to the bar."

"Okay," Ryan said. She turned around and walked back to the bar and just like that it was over.

Back at the bar, Julie was looking for Cassandra.

"Hey Stacey, do you know where Cassandra and Ryan went?'

"No, I don't," Stacey said. *That's weird*, Julie thought to herself. A couple of minutes later, she spotted Cassandra walking toward the bar.

"Where did you go?"

"Ryan and I went to get cigarettes, but it started raining again and he decided to go by himself," Cassandra said.

"Oh, you guys have been gone for a while," Julie said.

"Really? It didn't seem that long," Cassandra said motioning to the bartender for another drink, which she needed desperately.

Ryan crossed the street to get a pack of Parliaments, as thoughts raced through his mind. He really liked Cassandra and kissing her was insanely great. He wanted to continue kissing her, but he knew the relationship would not work out in the long run. Cassandra was one of those girls that you would madly fall in love with and then she would break your heart on purpose, and Ryan didn't need any more heartache. He knew that leaving it as a friendship would be good enough.

"Hey Cassandra. I want you to meet my friend, Eric. He also works for Wells Fargo," Alex said.

"Hi Cassandra." Eric took one look at Cassandra and knew he wanted to spend the rest of life with her. Later on, he would find out that Cassandra had set up her master plan that he, Julie, and Ryan would become victims of.

"Hi Eric," Cassandra said still thinking about Ryan's kiss. She looked away and stared at the dance floor. Eric came up from behind her. "Do you come here often?"

"This is actually my first time," Cassandra said.

"Do you want to dance?" he asked.

"No, not right now, thank you." Cassandra went back to the bar and noticed that Ryan had returned and was speaking to Julie. She could automatically tell that Ryan was putting the moves on Julie. He had her hand on her back as he spoke to her. Cassandra was a bit confused; not that she wanted to pursue what had happened any further, because she knew the relationship would be a failure. Sipping her drink, she walked toward the rest of the group.

Ryan did not intend on sending the wrong signals to Julie, but this was his way of throwing Cassandra off and protecting his heart. He didn't mean to hurt Cassandra in any way; he just didn't want to get involved in anything right now. He knew if he continued kissing Cassandra, he would not have been able to stop. He wasn't even sure what Julie was talking about, but it was a good distraction.

"Are you going to take me up on the dance offer now?" Eric said looking at Cassandra intensely. Cassandra looked at Eric; she hadn't noticed how handsome he was before. He had intensely exotic features and a great body with broad shoulders.

She smiled at Eric, "Maybe later." Eric was the type of guy one needed to play hard to get. She could tell that he was used to getting a lot of attention. She walked away and toward the bar. She ordered another drink from the bar, looking around to see if there were any guys that were decent enough to talk to.

Julie came up running to Cassandra. "I think Ryan likes me! While he was talking to me, he had his hand on my back and then he told me the sweetest thing ever."

"Really. What?" Cassandra asked. "He told me that when he sent you the text message inviting you to the Marina, he was hoping you would bring me. Isn't that sweet? He wanted to hang out with me and was going through you." Cassandra stared at Julie. *Poor thing. Did she really believe him?*

"Wow, that's great," Cassandra replied.

"I am going to go dance with him now," Julie ran off into the crowd.

Cassandra thought to herself as she looked at Ryan and Julie on the dance floor. *What was Ryan up to? Why did he want to start playing this game? Didn't he know who he was playing with?* One thing was for sure: playing games with Cassandra was a deadly thing. On the upside, Ryan apparently didn't know Julie too well and couldn't see that she was somewhat unstable. That would become one of his problems to deal with.

Eric found Cassandra again at the bar. "Can you help me go to the men's bathroom?" Cassandra asked him, "There's too long a line at the women's bathroom."

"Sure, follow me," Eric said, taking Cassandra's hand and pulling her toward the men's restroom. While Julie was in the men's bathroom, Eric grabbed Cassandra and started kissing her passionately. Cassandra could not refuse his kiss and kissed him back. It was a short kiss, but it left her breathless. He looked at Cassandra and smiled, "Sorry, I have been meaning to do that since I met you." All Cassandra could do was smile. Julie finished using the bathroom and Cassandra ran in. She closed the door and stood against it. *What was going on? First, Ryan kissed her, and now Eric. Who did she like better? Now, Ryan was trying to put the moves on Julie?* The only answer she had was to get another drink.

35

Cassandra finished with the bathroom and followed Eric back to the bar. She waved for the bartender and ordered another vodka tonic. She started drinking. Eric said, "Hope you are not mad."

"No, why would I be?"

"I think you are very pretty," Eric stated.

"Thank you." Cassandra continued to sip her drink. *Now what?* she thought. She looked at Eric and he kissed her again. Alex noticed the two kissing and could not believe Cassandra would kiss Eric over him. He had wanted to talk to Cassandra all night, but he was probably too late. Eric and Cassandra kissed for some time. When they were done, he hugged her tightly and kissed her on the side of her neck. He had quickly developed feelings for her, without even knowing her at all! Cassandra enjoyed Eric's hug, more than she should have.

It was nearing 2:00 a.m. and Eric was getting tired. "Do you want to exchange numbers?" he asked Cassandra.

"Sure." Cassandra pulled out her iPhone and programmed Eric's number into it.

"Are you going to Rebecca's party tomorrow night in Long Beach?" Cassandra asked.

"I'm not sure. It's a long drive for me, and I already have plans to go to the W Hotel in Westwood tomorrow night."

"Are you going?"

"Yes, Julie and I will be attending." Cassandra had not been formally invited to the party; she actually did not know Rebecca at all. She had heard about the party from Ryan and had decided that it would be good to crash a party. She hadn't done something like that in a while.

"Give me a call tomorrow and I will definitely tell you if I am going or not."

"Okay." Eric kissed Cassandra and said goodbye and left the bar. She decided to hit the dance floor since now she felt like dancing. Julie and Ryan joined her.

The lights came on at the bar and Cassandra noticed how dark it had been. She was extremely buzzed from all the drinks she'd had through the night. The entire group walked to the parking lot, saying goodnight to each other.

Julie and Ryan were walking together. Cassandra did not care to look at Ryan. When they reached Julie's car, Ryan said, "I will be right back." Julie unlocked her car and Cassandra got in. Julie went to look for Ryan, who got into his car and took off. By the time she walked to where Ryan's car had been, he had disappeared. Julie looked disappointed and walked back to her car.

"He left!" Julie said.

"What do you mean *he left?*" Cassandra asked.

"His car is gone; it's not there," Julie exclaimed.

"That's weird. Why would he take off without saying goodbye?" Cassandra asked.

"I will try calling him," Julie said. Julie tried calling Ryan. His phone kept ringing.

Ryan heard his phone ring in the car and looked at it. Julie's name flashed on the caller id. He placed the phone back down on the passenger seat and continued driving home. He was beyond intoxicated and knew he should not be driving, but he only lived a couple of minutes away. His phone rang again, but he decided not to look at it. He could not believe the events from tonight. First, the kiss with Cassandra and then pretending to be interested in Julie. Why had he told Julie that lie? Because he'd had too much to drink? Hopefully, this will all be forgotten by the weekend and Julie would have forgotten the whole incident come Monday morning.

"He is not answering," Julie said.

"Maybe he can't hear his phone," Cassandra said.

"Maybe," Julie said. "I can't believe what happened tonight."

Me either, Cassandra thought to herself.

"Ryan totally likes me. Thank god I came tonight, otherwise, I would have never known. This whole time he liked me," Julie exclaimed.

"What am I going to wear to the party tomorrow?"

"Something nice," Cassandra said. "I have to go get something. Do you want to get a manicure and pedicure tomorrow and then go to the mall?"

"Sure," Cassandra replied. Julie drove on Sepulveda and got onto 10 going east. Cassandra looked out of the window, thinking about the next night and wishing that somehow it was already over.

Chapter 6

"*H*ow does the dress look on me?" Julie said looking in the mirror at Nordstrom.

"It looks nice," Cassandra said. Julie was trying on a black dress. She wanted to get a dress that would impress Ryan the best. She had started developing feelings for Ryan, even though it had been less than twenty-four hours since their first encounter. Julie thought this could lead to something long term. Ryan was not exactly Julie's type. Her type was more Hispanic, lower class— all the guys she had dated were from East LA. She also thought Eric was cute. Now, she had met a complete opposite of the kind she usually dated. *Maybe this guy is the one for me*, she thought.

"I think I will take the black dress," Julie said.

"That is a nice dress," Cassandra said, thinking of what she was going to wear. Cassandra had dozens of dresses at home and would look through them when she got home.

"I can't believe I am buying a dress. I usually don't wear dresses."

"Why not?" Cassandra asked. "All girls wear dresses. They're pretty and feminine."

"Well, I am more of a jeans and shirt type of girl," Julie said.

Julie paid for the dress and they hurried to the car; it was almost 6:00 p.m. and they had to head back to LA to get ready. They left South Coast Plaza and drove back to LA in a daze. Neither of them said much to the other; they were both lost in their thoughts.

I wonder if Eugene is home, Cassandra thought. She hated the fact that every time she headed toward Orange County she thought of Eugene. It had been weeks since she had last spoken to him. It was Memorial Day weekend, and she knew he would have gone away with his buddies to some place in Mexico. She decided to stop thinking about him; it would only make her sad.

Julie was thinking about what she could do to impress Ryan. She knew she wasn't pretty enough to keep him with her looks, but she might make it up in other areas. She did love sports and most guys love sports. Maybe she would buy him tickets to a game. Baseball? Basketball? Julie wasn't sure which one it would be.

Cassandra got out of Julie's car and went into her apartment. She was still tired from the night before and wanted to take a nap, but she had to get ready. She lay on her couch to relax for a couple of minutes before she had to get into the shower. Her phone rang and it was Eric.

"Hello."

"Hi beautiful. What are you doing?" Eric asked.

"Hi Eric, I am not doing much. Just got home and I am lying on my couch for a little bit."

"Where did you go?"

"Went to the mall with Julie. She needed something to wear for tonight."

"Have you decided if you are going tonight?" Cassandra asked.

"No, I am not going. I am going to the W Hotel instead. Do you want to join me? We have a table."

"I would love to, but I already told Julie I would go with her. All of a sudden she has taken a liking to Ryan."

"Okay, well, maybe we can meet up after."

"Okay, give me a call later."

"Have fun," Cassandra said. She hung up and thought, *Eric seems like a nice guy. Wonder what his story is.* She got up and went to the bathroom to start getting ready.

Driving down to Long Beach where Rebecca's party was going to take place took a while. Julie was extremely excited; she could not stop talking about Ryan.

"Do you think Ryan is already over there?"

"I am not sure; it's kind of early," Cassandra said. They reached their destination. The party was to take place in a restaurant on top of a hotel overlooking the water. Since they were not technically on the list to be let upstairs, Cassandra had to talk her way through, and the security guard let her and Julie through. As they made their way to the elevator, Cassandra noticed a guy who resembled Eric. Thinking it was Eric, she approached him.

"Change of mind?" Cassandra said. The man looked at Cassandra unsure of what she had just asked and said, "Yes, I did."

They all entered the elevator and rode to the top. Cassandra was not sure why Eric was so dry in his response, but after last night, she didn't know what to expect. After exiting the elevator, there was an additional set of stairs to the restaurant. Once they climbed the stairs, they entered the restaurant. The best part of the party was the open bar!

"I am not sure why Eric is being mean to me," Cassandra told Julie who was not really listening because she was looking for Ryan.

"Me either. Maybe he is just like that," Julie said. They walked into the bar and spotted JP and Stacey.

"Hey guys," Cassandra said.

"You look pretty, Stacey."

"You too, Cassandra and Julie, you look nice," Stacey said.

"Has anyone seen Ryan?" Julie asked.

"We were going to ask you the same thing," Stacey said. Julie found it weird that they were asking her if she knew where Ryan was. They had only really been dating a day, so she wouldn't really know his entire schedule.

Cassandra flagged down the bartender and saw Eric at the bar.

"Are you not speaking to me because you are here with your girlfriend?" Cassandra asked, assuming the girl standing next to Eric was his girlfriend. The man gave Cassandra a strange look and shrugged. Cassandra got her drink and walked away. She was still hungover from last night and really couldn't tolerate drinking again, but with Eric being here and Ryan on his way, Cassandra knew this was the only way she would make it through the night.

Cassandra went out to the terrace that overlooked the water and Julie spotted her.

"Where do you think Ryan is and don't you think it's weird that JP and Stacey asked me if I knew where Ryan was?"

"Why do you think it's weird?" Cassandra said.

"Well, maybe Ryan told them that he likes me, and they assumed I would know where he would be. I am going to call him again." Cassandra thought she must have heard incorrectly, but Julie was really crazy to think that Ryan would tell other people that he liked her. He did not even really like her. Julie needed to get a grip on herself.

"He didn't answer," Julie said. "I am going to send him a text message."

Ryan was passed out on his bed. He had gone out for an early dinner and had overdone the drinks. He was supposed to head straight from dinner to Rebecca's party, but had come home because he needed to sober up. He had to make it to Rebecca's party; she was Ryan's boss and would not forgive him if he didn't show up. He heard his phone ring a couple of times, but ignored it. Then he heard the text message alert and finally knew it was time to get up. Ryan looked at the phone and saw a missed call and text from Julie. *Why is she calling me?* He got up from the bed and headed to the party.

Julie was still wondering where Ryan was. She had dressed up for him and now he wasn't there. As Julie looked up, she saw Ryan walk in. He walked in a daze as if he was still half asleep; his suit was wrinkled from his nap. He said hello to everyone and then spotted Cassandra and Julie. Cassandra looked amazing he thought and hugged her. He then turned to Julie and gave her a hug as well and thought she looked pretty. Still feeling the alcohol from earlier that day, he went to get a drink. It would only be better if he kept drinking.

"Lady in Red" started playing over the speakers and to his own surprise, Ryan asked Julie to dance halfway through the song. Thrilled, she accepted the dance. Cassandra looked over and was surprised as well. Ryan took Julie's hand and led her through the dance. She was in a daze through the entire dance that lasted about three minutes. After, she rushed over to Cassandra. "Can you believe it? He asked me to dance! This is the best thing that has ever happened to me! I need a drink." Julie rushed to the bar and ordered her usual Jack and Coke. Ryan walked past Cassandra and smiled at her. It was then that he thought how much he would have loved to dance with Cassandra, but he was guarding his heart. He knew what he was doing.

Everyone gathered by a table outside on the balcony and started talking about where to go afterward. Cassandra turned to Alex. "What's up with your friend Eric?"

"What do you mean?"

"Well, I saw him inside at the bar, started talking to him, and he didn't say anything to me," Cassandra said.

"Eric isn't here."

"What do you mean? Eric is inside by the bar," Cassandra said.

"Are you drunk? I am telling you Eric is not here. Do you want me to call him on my phone?"

"Wait, are you for real? He is not here? Then who is the guy by the bar? I have been trying to talk to him all night!" Cassandra said.

"Well, whoever it is, it's definitely not Eric," Alex said.

"Oh god, I really need to stop drinking," Cassandra said as she sipped her cocktail.

They all decided to hit Pine Ave to see which bars looked good. It ended up just being Cassandra, Ryan, Alex, and Julie going out afterward. Each one had had several drinks and was beyond tipsy. They walked down Pine Ave and saw a Latin Club that was spilling out with people. They walked inside and went straight to the bar. Julie decided to order drinks; it was taking a while because there were a lot of people. Ryan finally had the nerve to talk to Cassandra who was standing in between him and Alex.

"Do you want to kiss me?" Ryan asked Cassandra. Cassandra looked at Ryan with a stern look.

"Are you kidding me? You clearly made a choice with Julie, so why would you ask me such a question?" Cassandra said.

"Because it's you that I want to kiss, not Julie. Plus we work together, so nothing will ever become of this. I am just being nice to her, because I need her on my team to help me make sales."

"Right, whatever you say."

Ryan leaned in and tried to kiss Cassandra. Cassandra quickly backed away and shot him an angry look.

"Seriously, you need to stop because Julie is going to see you."

"I don't care; I want to kiss you," Ryan said. Cassandra started to talk to Alex to distract Ryan from trying to kiss her. *What am I doing?* Ryan thought, *I truly like Cassandra, but I know how this is going to end up.* Julie came back with the drinks complaining about how long the bartender was taking. Cassandra grabbed her drink and started drinking it fast, hoping the night would end soon. She kept thinking about Ryan, trying to understand what he was doing, but decided it was not worth it. All of them talked and kept drinking, finally deciding to leave because the bartenders were taking too long to get their drinks.

Outside, they headed back to the restaurant because their cars were with the valet, and they decided to head to Ryan's house. Ryan drove with Julie, Cassandra drove Julie's car, and Alex drove by himself. After what seemed like an hour of driving, they finally reached Ryan's house in the Marina. They piled into the apartment, laughing, and decided to keep drinking. Cassandra, drunk as she was, called Eric to see what he was doing. "Hey sweetie," Eric said as he picked up the phone.

"Hi, what are you doing?"

"I am leaving the W Hotel in Westwood. Where are you?"

"We just got to Ryan's house. Where are you heading now?" Cassandra asked.

"I am going home. Do you want to come over?" Eric asked.

"Yes, can you come pick me up?" Cassandra asked.

"I am not driving. Let me get home, and I will call you back," Eric said.

"Okay," Cassandra said.

Ryan called Julie to his balcony. As they were talking, he tried to kiss Julie, but she was not ready to kiss him.

"What's wrong? Don't you want to kiss me?" Ryan asked.

"No, I am not ready yet," Julie responded. Ryan thought it was weird, but ignored the fact and went inside. Cassandra's phone rang, "Hello," she said.

"Hi, I just got home; I don't think I can drive all the way to the Marina. Is Alex there? Let me talk to him. Maybe he can bring you here and I will take you home tomorrow morning," Eric said.

"Hold on, let me get Alex,"

"Alex, Eric wants to talk to you." Alex grabbed the phone.

"Hey man, what's up?"

"Why don't you bring Cassandra over here for me? I can't drive right now because I had too many drinks at the club," Eric said.

"Man, I don't know about driving all the way over there."

"Drive here and you can crash on my couch," Eric said.

"I don't know about all that. Let me see how I feel."

"Come on and help a brother out. I have not had sex in a while and Cassandra is really pretty," Eric said. Alex gave the phone back to Cassandra.

"Hey," Cassandra said.

"I am not sure if Alex is going to bring you; if not, we can hang out tomorrow night."

"Okay," Cassandra said. They hung up and Alex and Cassandra sat on the couch watching TV, while Julie and Ryan lay together on the other couch. Cassandra didn't even notice them together because she was thinking about Eric. There was somewhat something attractive about Eric, and it would be a distraction from Ryan. Cassandra passed out on the couch in her thoughts and Alex also fell asleep next to her. Ryan went upstairs to his bedroom and Julie followed.

In the morning, Cassandra awoke to a huge golden retriever sniffing her face. Startled, she jumped up, and suddenly had the urge to vomit. *I can't handle this much drinking anymore.* She raced to the bathroom and passed by one of Ryan's roommates. Controlling the urge, she returned to the couch. She looked at her phone and saw that she had called Eric last night and he too had left a voice mail. Sometimes, Cassandra could not remember who she called or what she talked about when she had too much to drink. It was one of her flaws that she didn't like telling people.

Cassandra wanted to wake Julie up, but decided to wait. Finally, about an hour later, Julie came down and motioned for them to leave. On the drive home, Cassandra did not feel good and wished somehow, she could make it home faster. Once Cassandra reached her apartment, she took off her clothes and threw herself on the bed. She went to sleep for a while until her phone rang. It was Eric, "Hello," Cassandra said.

"Hi sweetie, what are you doing?" Eric said.

"Trying to recover from last night," Cassandra said.

"How much did you have to drink?" Eric asked.

"Way too much. I need to slow down. I just don't know how to have one drink without drinking the entire bar," Cassandra stated with a laugh.

"I am not feeling so good myself either. Had too much vodka last night," Eric said.

"I am just lying down on the couch watching TV. Did you want to get together later tonight?"

"Yes, I will give you a call later today, when I start feeling better," Cassandra said.

"Okay, talk to you then," Eric said. Cassandra hung up. She lay on the bed and thought about what had happened the night before with Ryan. How did she get into these situations? Cassandra always met nice guys, but they never wanted to pursue anything further with her. They would show signs of liking her and would do things for her, but it wouldn't go any further than that.

Julie had called Cassandra to invite her out for lunch. Still not feeling too good, Cassandra decided that eating would be a good thing for her. Julie picked her up in the afternoon and they headed to BJ's in Burbank to catch the Laker's playoff game. They walked into the restaurant and Cassandra cringed at the sight of alcohol at the bar. They sat down, ordered food, and sat in silence for the majority of the time watching the Laker's game.

"What do you think the situation is going to be like at work between you and Ryan?" Cassandra asked.

Julie shrugged. "I am not sure; I guess things will be the same. I don't know what to think."

Cassandra looked at Julie, unsure of how to respond to the situation. Right now, she did not care too much about anything because of the way she was feeling. When the game was over, they left the restaurant and headed back to downtown LA to drop Cassandra off. She entered her apartment and decided to call Eric. He didn't answer, so she left him a message. A few minutes later, Eric called Cassandra back. "Hi sweetie," Eric said.

"Hi, what are you doing?"

"I am about to go play cards with my friends. What about you?"

"I just got back from having a late lunch with Julie. What time are you going to be done playing cards?"

"Probably in about two hours. I really want to see you, so I won't take too long."

Cassandra smiled, "Okay, call me when you are done, and I will head over to your place."

"Okay," Eric said.

Cassandra hung up and smiled. She was starting to like Eric; he was a nice guy, but she wasn't too sure about him yet. Cassandra lay down on her bed and decided to take a nap until it was time to head to Eric's place.

As Cassandra sat in a taxi to go to Eric's place in the Valley, she wondered if he was thinking that she would have sex with him. Fortunately for Cassandra, it was her time of the month and she would not be doing anything of the sort. Cassandra's phone rang. "Hey, where are you?" Eric said.

"I am almost there," Cassandra said still thinking whether he was going to pressure her about sex.

"Okay, you can find parking on the street and call me when you park."

"Will do," Cassandra said.

Cassandra found Eric's place in Sherman Oaks. She had never been to this part of LA and was surprised to see how nice it was. After almost half an hour of trying to find parking space, she thought, *this is worse than downtown!* She walked over to Eric's building and rang for his apartment. He buzzed her in. Cassandra was a little nervous having somewhat forgotten what Eric looked like and remembering how she had mistaken him at the party the previous night. She hoped he was still handsome.

Cassandra walked down the long corridor to Eric's apartment, which was at the end of the hallway. She reached the door, knocked, and held her breath. Eric opened the door with a smile; to Cassandra's surprise, he was more handsome than she remembered. Relieved, Cassandra walked in and gave him a hug. "Hey sweetie." He hugged Cassandra tightly.

"Hi!" Cassandra said. They walked into the living room, which was nicely painted and decorated, which Cassandra found surprising for a single guy. *Was he single?* Cassandra asked herself. She had never asked him. She assumed that he was single since he was inviting him over to her place.

"Sit down. Would you like anything to drink?" Eric asked

"Water would be nice."

Eric got up and got her a bottle of water. Cassandra looked around the apartment. Everything was so neat. Cassandra took off her sweater; she was wearing tight black sweatpants and a black deep V-neck tank top. Eric sat down and handed Cassandra the bottle of water.

"Are you feeling better?" Eric asked.

"Yes, much better. How about yourself?"

"A lot better."

The conversation was short, and both Cassandra and Eric sat on separate sides of the couch and watched TV.

I wonder what she is thinking, Eric thought. *How do I make a move?*

Cassandra looked at the TV and wondered, *does he think I am going to have sex with him?* Cassandra started a conversation to break the silence. While watching TV, Cassandra noticed Eric staring at her, but not saying anything. *Why does he keep looking at me?* Eric kept looking at Cassandra, thinking how beautiful she was. There was something different about her. He had always dated pretty girls, but Cassandra was different. He couldn't stop staring at her! During their conversation, they talked about their families, work, and places they had been to. Cassandra was surprised to find out Eric has been to almost all of Europe. She didn't think he would be so cultural. She got up to use the restroom. When Cassandra was done, Eric showed Cassandra his room. She noticed a picture of Eric and two kids.

"These are my kids. I have a son and a daughter."

"Really?" Cassandra was taken by surprise. "How old are they?"

"My son is sixteen and my daughter is eleven."

"They are beautiful. Where do they live?'

"With their mom in South Pasadena."

"We have been divorced for about nine years," Eric said. He was nervous about telling Cassandra about his kids and his failed marriage. He usually didn't have a problem telling people about his kids, but he was not sure how Cassandra would react to the situation. She could not believe that Eric had been married and divorced and had kids. He was thirty-five and divorced; she thought—*a perfect example of her cookie-cutter men, except he didn't have blonde hair and blue eyes.* They left Eric's room and sat back down on the couch, this time closer than before. Cassandra was still a bit shocked about the information Eric had just given her. They sat in silence and watched TV.

Finally, Eric started playing with Cassandra's hair. He loved her long black hair and could not resist touching it. She enjoyed him touching her hair. She felt comfortable with him. It was strange; they barely knew each other, and it felt normal sitting on his couch watching TV with him. Eric continued staring at Cassandra and she could notice him staring at her, but did not say anything. After fifteen minutes of silence, Eric leaned in and kissed Cassandra. She did not refuse and gave in to him. He touched her face and then her hair. It was a soft and sensual kiss. He moved his hand from touching her hair to her arm and then started caressing her breast. He could feel her nipples getting hard and started playing with them. He then moved his hand down to her leg. Cassandra did not try to stop him because she enjoyed every minute of him touching her. She could feel his bulge getting bigger as he continued kissing her. They continued kissing for about twenty minutes. Eric could not take it anymore. He wanted to be inside of her, to taste her. He lay on the couch and motioned for her to lie on top of him. Cassandra seductively got on top of Eric. She could feel Eric harden by the second. Cassandra slowly began straddling Eric with his clothes on and she could hear him let out small silent moans.

Given her situation, Cassandra could not give in to him. Eric wondered how much longer until they moved into his bedroom and he could have Cassandra completely. He got up, grabbed her hand, and led her into his room. He placed her on the bed and took off his shirt, revealing tight abs and broad shoulders. Leaning down to kiss Cassandra, he started to take her pants off. Cassandra suddenly jolted up and stopped his hand. *Why is she doing this?* Eric thought.

"I can't do this," Cassandra said. "Not right now."

"Why, what's wrong?"

"Nothing, I just can't." Cassandra did not want to tell Eric the truth. She did want him badly, but she couldn't. Eric, disappointed and hurt, got off Cassandra and went to the living room.

Is she just playing games with me? Eric thought. He hated that she was hot one minute and cold the next. Eric sat on the couch and Cassandra followed.

"I am sorry, but I am not ready," Cassandra said.

"It's okay," Eric said, not believing himself. He was irritated and thought he was going to have Cassandra tonight.

"It's getting kind of late anyway. I have to go to bed soon," Eric said.

Cassandra thought she was going to stay the night, but given Eric's mood, she knew it was time for her to go.

"Okay," Cassandra said, confused and hurt. Cassandra got her sweater and her bag, and Eric said he would walk her out. Walking down the corridor to the elevator, Eric was confused. *What just happened?* He was sure Cassandra had come over to have sex. He wasn't mad that he hadn't had sex with her. He actually liked her, but he had also never been turned down and was angry at being rejected. *Who does she think she is?* Cassandra knew that Eric was mad given the change in his attitude. She then realized that maybe he was a jerk, and it was better off if she knew now.

They walked outside to Cassandra's car and Eric said goodbye and gave Cassandra kiss. She said goodbye and he promised he would call. She knew he wouldn't. She had thought Eric was a nice guy, but she knew that did not exist anymore—at least not in LA. Cassandra got in her car and drove away. Eric walked back to his apartment. Cassandra had been the first girl since his divorce nine years ago, whom he actually liked and was looking forward to get to know, but the frustration of not getting what he wanted took over his feelings for her. Since his divorce, he had kept women far away from him, just having the occasional one-night stand here and there. This way, he did not get tangled into something he didn't want, and he did not want to get hurt again. Entering his apartment, he knew that he would not call Cassandra. Maybe it was better off not starting something that he would get emotionally involved in. He did not need the headache or the heartache.

Chapter 7

On Memorial Day, Eugene woke up exhausted from drinking and partying all weekend. He was going to take it easy today. Since it was a holiday, he did not have to go to the office. Lying on his bed by himself, lonely, and listening to the cars drive by on Jamboree Road, Eugene thought about his failed marriage and how he was going to get past it. He wasn't upset about divorcing his ex-wife; he was more upset about the fact that he knew he had married the wrong person and now had a divorce on his record.

Eugene remembered his wedding day vividly. He was in his hotel room overlooking the Pacific Ocean from his balcony. This was supposed to be the best day of his life. The ceremony was set to take place on the beach of a five-star resort in Maui, somewhere Eugene had always dreamed of having his wedding. He had looked at his watch. "Thirty more minutes until the ceremony," he had said to himself. Eugene had taken as many deep breaths as he could while standing out on the balcony.

Then, he had walked back into the hotel room and gone into the bathroom. He had been sweating profusely while looking at himself in the mirror. He looked like a wreck. As he was staring at himself, he knew that he didn't want to do this. This was not the person he wanted to marry; he felt trapped given the fact that he had a three-year son with his soon-to-be wife and everyone including his family had pressured him into proposing to her. *It's too late to back down now*, he had thought. "I can't do this," he had said to himself in the mirror.

Eugene knew that he always did the right thing and in twenty-five minutes he would be walking down the aisle to marry someone he was not in love with. He thought about his son and decided that it would be best for Zachery if he married his mom.

Maybe it would work out? Maybe things would change?

As he adjusted his collar and bow tie, he knew that it wouldn't. He had been with Lisa for over five years and he had fallen out of love with her a long time ago. When he was ready to tell her, Zachary had come along and he was trapped. He would never change the fact of having Zachary; he couldn't imagine his life without him, but ever since then, he felt as if someone else was living his life and he was just a passenger. He had looked at himself in the mirror, taken one more deep breath, and known that his life would never be the same again.

That was over five years ago. Since then, he had divorced Lisa and now flew between Orange County, CA, and Scottsdale, Arizona, to see his son. What a whirlwind it had been from trying to make it work to realizing that he could not go on living with someone he was not in love with. He would always love Lisa because she was Zachary's mom, but it was a different kind of love now and had been for a long time.

He wanted to remarry, but with a woman he would be madly and deeply in love with. He wasn't sure when that would happen or if it would happen at all. The second time around would be harder; it would *have* to work out because he could not bear going through a divorce again, both physically and mentally.

Eugene had started casually dating since his divorce, but there was no one of real interest except for Cassandra. He knew that he was not ready to start anything, but Cassandra did not give up easily and had always managed to stay in his life one way or another. He estimated it had been over a year or so since he had met her, and she had always fought for their friendship. He was definitely flaky when it came to their friendship, but admired the fact that Cassandra always made it work. He wouldn't lie that he took her and their friendship for granted, knowing always that she would be there when he needed her. But how long would that last before Cassandra decided enough was enough?

He didn't want to lose Cassandra's friendship, but he knew he would have to make a decision soon or it would be over between them. He didn't know what to do; he was torn, but his heart was not ready to take anything on even the smallest type of relationship. Eugene knew that Cassandra thought that he didn't like her, but it was in fact completely the opposite. He liked her—a lot actually—and she had been the only girl in a long time to get as close to him as she did. He knew she would never understand given the circumstances. He had invited her over to his house several times and he never invited just any woman to his house. He always respected the fact that you just don't bring anyone home. He was actually ready and willing to bring Cassandra home the first night he met her. Cassandra probably didn't know—he never told her—but he still remembered the time they had first kissed on the dance floor of the Standard Hotel Rooftop Bar. Cassandra had been the first girl since his divorce that he had kissed so passionately for such a long time, never coming up for air. As much as he wanted to, he just wasn't ready for anything and he would have to make Cassandra wait for now. For how long, he wasn't sure.

Cassandra was happy she had the day off because of the holiday. This entire weekend had been a whirlwind, and she was glad to just stay home and recover especially from everyone. She thought about Ryan and his kiss, then what had taken place at Eric's apartment, and what Julie thought was going on between her and Ryan. It was all too much to think about and handle in one day.

She looked at her phone and saw she had a text message from Julie. She didn't respond because she did not want to be bothered with anyone today. She lay in bed wondering what had gone wrong with Eric. She liked him, but not enough to make the next move of calling him. She soon realized that she had not thought about Eugene for a couple of days, which was good because she always thought about Eugene and what he was doing or whom he was with. She wished she could pick up the phone and call him, but knew it was best not to. She hated the fact that their friendship was always so rocky. Some days she wished that they would never speak again, but knew that would be hard to do especially for her. Eugene was her world, but she had done that to herself and did not know why. Some days, she wished she could change the fact that she had ever met Eugene, but knew that would alter the course of the universe and she knew there was a reason Eugene was brought into her life. Cassandra's thoughts then drifted to something else, then to sleep again.

Chapter 8

*R*ested from her day off and ready to get back into the swing of things at work, Cassandra walked into the firm early in the morning to find Elizabeth making coffee.

"How are you? How was your weekend? Elizabeth asked.

"Full of drama, of course."

"Did you end up going down to the Marina to watch the game?"

"Yes, then we went to a bar in Santa Monica, ended up making out with Ryan and with Ryan's friend Eric, and then Ryan decided to hit on Julie."

Elizabeth just looked at her in confusion and amazement.

"I know . . . long story. This could have not been better written without people thinking it was not real," Cassandra said as they walked out of the kitchen. Cassandra gave Elizabeth a rundown of what had happened over the three-day weekend. It seemed more like an entire week than just a three-day holiday weekend. Once Cassandra was done, she was exhausted.

"I can't believe all this happened," Elizabeth said in awe.

"I know. I can't either."

"Seems like something that should be on MTV," Elizabeth stated.

"Maybe," Cassandra said.

Julie was making her way into work. She always ran late, and her manager would always chastise her about it, and then Julie would do it all over again the next day. This particular morning, Julie was excited to get to work. She had not spoken to Ryan since Saturday night and hopefully, he would be in her branch today.

What would she say to him? Or how should she act?

She was also leaving for Hawaii in five days, so she had to make sure they spoke before her one-week trip to the Big Island.

Ryan woke up and looked at his watch. He had five days before he had to move out of the apartment he shared with three other roommates. Their lease was up, and everyone had signed a new lease somewhere else. He had to still decide where to live. He had to get on it today; otherwise, he would be out in the cold. He got up and got dressed while on a conference call; Ryan was always one for multitasking. Once he was dressed and out of the door, his first stop would be the branch in the Aon building where Julie worked. He had forgotten what had happened between Julie and him—well, nothing really had happened. He was just trying to distract himself from Cassandra, and Julie just happened to be the closest person next to him at the time. Ryan hoped Julie had forgotten everything he had said to her. Moreover, he was drunk while he told her these things and technically it didn't count. Regardless, he had bigger things to worry about and finding a place to live was first on his agenda.

The first thing Julie did when she walked into the branch was call Cassandra.

"Hey, I sent you a text message yesterday and you did not respond."

"I was sleeping all day and was not near my phone."

"Oh, well, I was thinking all day yesterday about Ryan and me and our situation. What should I do about it?"

Situation? Cassandra thought to herself. *What situation? Nothing happened between the both of you.*

"Really and what is that?" Cassandra asked.

"Well, I thought I would approach him and just talk to him casually and see where the conversation goes."

"Maybe you should mention a casual lunch or something like that?" Cassandra said.

"Don't you think asking him out to lunch would be too forward?"

"No, not at all, I think it's a great idea," Cassandra said, thinking to herself what a crazy person Julie must be. Of course, asking him out to lunch would be too forward.

"Okay, I just might do that," Julie said.

"Great, let me know what happens," Cassandra said and hung up the phone. She really couldn't tolerate Julie right now.

An hour later, Ryan walked into the branch still thinking about how he was going to find an apartment. As he settled into an empty desk, he quickly got on the Craigslist website and started looking for apartments. He found several in the Marina. He wanted to stay in that area because he loved living next to the beach. There was one apartment of interest and the renter was looking for two roommates. *The renter will have to settle for one, for now,* Ryan thought. He quickly called the renter's number and set up an appointment for later that day. Hopefully, this would work out and he could move in the upcoming weekend. As Ryan was done with his phone call, Julie approached his desk.

"Hi Ryan," Julie said.

"Hey, how are you?" Ryan said looking at his laptop screen.

Julie sat down in the empty chair in front of his desk and asked, "Anything new?"

"Just trying to look for a place to live; I need to move out before the weekend is over."

"Really and you are just looking for a place now? It's already Tuesday," Julie said.

"I know, I have been busy, but I should find something. I have an appointment tonight. Hopefully, it works out."

"I hope it does too. I was wondering if you would like to go to lunch sometime this week?" Julie asked.

Ryan looked confused at the question, "Sure, I'll let you know."

"Okay," Julie said sounding disappointed.

Right then, Ryan's cell phone rang. He answered the phone and then mouthed to Julie "client."

Julie knew it was her cue to leave and smiled and walked back to her desk.

Had she done something wrong? Why hadn't Ryan accepted her invitation to lunch?

Well, he hadn't said no, but he hadn't said yes either. She thought she would try something different and she decided to call Cassandra.

Later that day, Ryan headed over to the Marina to see the apartment he had found on Craigslist. The apartment was on the second floor and only a couple of houses from the beach. The apartment looked older but doable as he needed a place to move into in four days. John, the renter and roommate seemed a bit off, but the house was only five houses from the beach. Ryan would have to find the third roommate soon. He drove back to his apartment, thinking about Cassandra and what she was doing.

Julie called Cassandra later that evening to invite her to dinner and tell her the events that took place earlier that day with Ryan. Bored, Cassandra accepted the dinner invitation. Julie decided on going to her favorite restaurant El Cholo in Los Angeles. Cassandra did not like the area, but decided to try out the place.

"I saw Ryan today and talked to him," Julie said as they sat down in a booth.

"Really, what did he say?" Cassandra asked not really interested.

"He said that he was trying to find a place to move into, and told me that he would let me know about my lunch offer."

"You did ask him out to lunch?" Cassandra inquired.

"Yes, I was scared to ask him at first, but I decided to try, and he said he will let me know. This is why I don't ask guys out because I am scared to hear their answer."

"Well, you tried."

"I guess," Julie said.

Cassandra thought, *Ryan had not directly accepted Julie's lunch offer; he really must not be into her.* Cassandra and Julie continued their dinner conversing over the events that took place during the weekend.

The next day, Cassandra headed down to the bank to see if Julie was available for a question about the law firm's accounts. She already knew Julie was not in the branch, but hoped she would run into Ryan. When she arrived at the bank, she was told that Julie had stepped out for an appointment. At that moment, she happened to see Ryan, and walked over to his desk.

"Hey Ryan," Cassandra said.

"Hey you, how are you?" Ryan asked with a big smile.

"Good, how about you?"

"Good as well. Where are you headed?"

"I was looking for Julie, but she is not here. Now I am going to get a sandwich from the shop next door."

"Let me join you; I need to get a cup of coffee," Ryan said.

Cassandra and Ryan walked out of the branch and headed to the coffee shop next door.

"Anything new?" she asked as if nothing had ever happened between her and Ryan.

"I was looking for an apartment and found one a couple of houses down the block from the beach. I need to be out of my apartment by this weekend."

"I didn't know you had to move? The new place is a couple of houses down the beach? How great is that!" Cassandra said.

"Yeah, it's great."

"I wish I could live by the beach. I have been living in downtown LA for over a year and sometimes I get bored with it."

"Well, if you are interested, we are looking for a third roommate. You should check out the place and see if you like it," Ryan said.

"You know what I just might. What are you doing later tonight?"

"I am actually going over there tonight to go over some details with John, the other roommate. I will text you the address, and then maybe we can get some drinks afterward." Cassandra could not believe that he was asking her to be his roommate.

Ryan was in shock too that he had invited Cassandra to come to check out the place and consider moving in. Ryan had had other women as his roommates before, but none that he was physically attracted too.

"Great, send me the address, and I will see you around seven tonight," Cassandra said.

They walked back toward the Aon Building and then went their separate ways. As soon as Cassandra got back to the office, she told Elizabeth what had happened.

"Are you serious? He asked you to be his roommate?" Elizabeth asked.

"I know. How random is that?"

"Wow, he must really like you or he's just plain insane. Have you told Julie yet?"

"No, I don't know how to tell her, but I have to because she is the one driving me down there to see the place," Cassandra said.

"Well, you better call her and tell her."

Cassandra dialed Julie's number and waited for her to pick up. How was she going to explain to Julie that Ryan had asked her to be her roommate? At least now, Julie would get the hint and realize that Ryan did not like her. Cassandra didn't really like Ryan either, but she didn't like losing and hated competition.

"Hello," Julie said.

"Hey, what are you doing?" Cassandra asked.

"Just finished seeing one of my clients regarding their accounts. What's up?"

"Well, I went downstairs to see if you were there and I ran into Ryan. He walked with me to get my lunch and told me about finding an apartment in the Marina, and they were looking for a third roommate. He told me I should go look at the place today."

"Really, he asked you to be his third roommate?" Julie asked.

"Yes, I know it was random; what do you think?" Cassandra asked.

"Sounds fun. Do you want to go tonight then?"

"Yes, after work. After we see the apartment, Ryan said we can get drinks," Cassandra said.

"Okay, I will pick you up at your place around 7:00 p.m.," Julie said.

"Great, see you then."

"What did she say?" Elizabeth asked.

"She sounded a bit shocked, but then agreed to go see the place with me. Whatever the case may be, I really don't care, I just need a ride down there," Cassandra said thinking that Julie must be a fool if she could not see or hear this. Cassandra had only known Ryan for about a week and now he was asking her to be his roommate. Who does that?

Julie hung up the phone and was a bit confused, but excited as well. First, she was not sure why Ryan had asked Cassandra to be his third roommate. Did he like Cassandra and not her?

Then she thought, maybe he asked Cassandra to move in so he could get closer to Julie. He knew that she would hang out with Cassandra all the time and maybe it was a way to get to know her better. Julie got even more excited at the fact that Ryan would go through all this trouble to get to Julie. He must really like her.

As Julie and Cassandra were driving down to the Marina, Julie was thinking how she should act toward Ryan. Should she play it cool or act like she was interested in him?

"Cassandra, do you think I should say something to Ryan . . . that I like him?" Julie asked.

Cassandra, lost in her thoughts, did not listen to Julie's question.

"Sure, tell him. What do you have to lose?"

Julie thought she would just play it cool and see where this goes. She parked the car and walked over to the apartment that Ryan was standing in front of.

"Hey ladies," Ryan said and gave them both a hug.

Ryan noticed Cassandra was wearing a short dress. He looked at her legs and wished he could kiss her again. They walked up the stairs to the apartment.

"Hey John, this is Cassandra and Julie," Ryan said.

"Nice to meet you both," John said.

Off the bat, Cassandra could notice that there was something strange about John. He seemed like he could be a bit crazy. The women walked around the apartment and surveyed everything. The apartment was a lot older than Cassandra's apartment in downtown LA, but it was only four houses from the beach and that could not compare.

"What do you think?" Ryan asked.

"It's nice," Cassandra said, lying. Julie was thinking how many nights she was going to spend here with Ryan, thinking she could alternate sleeping in Ryan's bed or the couch. Ryan was not sure what he was doing asking Cassandra to move in. He knew that it could be trouble, but he didn't care much at this point. He knew that Cassandra would be in the room next to his, and maybe something would come out of this.

"Is it a go or what?" John asked.

"I guess. Where is the application?" Cassandra asked.

John gave the application to Cassandra to fill out. Cassandra filled out the application and gave John the application and check for the application fee. Then they all headed to the bar a block over for dinner. Julie made sure she sat down next to Ryan at the table leaving, Ryan to sit across from Cassandra. Ryan tried not to keep looking at Cassandra; instead, he tried listening to Julie talk. He was not sure what Julie was talking about, but she did talk a lot.

They all ordered dinner and John kept to himself. Cassandra tried to make a conversation with him, but he was somewhat difficult to get to talk. As they were eating dinner, Cassandra felt her phone vibrate. She had received a text message from Eugene. She was a bit shocked that he had texted her. It was always when she was not thinking about him and moving on to something else that he came around. Wouldn't he get a kick out of this, if he found out that she would be moving to the Marina?

Cassandra chose not to text him back and enjoyed her dinner with the guy who she hooked up with, the girl who was madly in love with him, and the psycho who would not speak. Julie kept chatting with Ryan, and Cassandra noticed he was not listening. She decided to take part in the conversation. Once dinner was done, John said goodnight and the three of them headed to Cabo Cantina, which was located next door. They went upstairs and sat down at a table and ordered drinks. Cassandra was tired at this point and wanted to go home, but she knew Julie wanted to spend as much time as she could talking to Ryan. He did not like Julie because she acted stuck up and he did not like girls who acted that way. He was a simple guy who wanted a simple woman. Julie went on about her Louis Vuitton purse and how much she liked it and wanted another one. Cassandra looked at her and thought: *Julie is just crazy. No wonder she does not have friends. If she is trying to impress Ryan, she is going on about it the wrong way.*

An hour later, Ryan announced that he needed to head home to get some rest. He walked Cassandra and Julie to Julie's car and gave each one a hug. Julie insisted on hugging him again; he refused and walked away. *What is wrong with Julie?* Ryan thought. He hoped that she would not be hanging around the apartment too much. As soon as Julie and Cassandra got into the car, Julie started talking about Ryan and how much she could tell that Ryan liked her. She knew that he asked Cassandra to move in to get closer to her, just like the night he asked

Cassandra to come out hoping Julie would come too. Cassandra could not believe what she was hearing! She pretended she was listening, but was actually thinking about Eugene and his text. Maybe she should have responded? It wouldn't matter; it wasn't like he was sitting there waiting for Cassandra to get back to him.

As Cassandra walked into her office, Elizabeth bombarded her with questions. "Did you see the place? What did you think? Are you moving in?"

Cassandra laughed.

"Yes, I saw the place; it's a bit older, but right next door to the beach—literally four houses away. Ryan's room would be right next to mine. I didn't like the other roommate, John. He seemed a bit weird. I filled out the application and gave it to John so I should know by later today, if I am able to move in."

"Wow, that's quick. Are you excited?"

"A little bit. It would be a change of pace for me and being by the beach would be exciting. By the way, while we were eating dinner, Eugene sent me a text asking how I was. I didn't text him back. Maybe I will today." Cassandra said.

"You must be getting over him if you didn't reply right away. Maybe you are into Ryan," Elizabeth said.

"I am not sure if that is the case, but some days I wish I was over Eugene," Cassandra said.

Later that afternoon, Cassandra received a call from John, the psycho, telling her that her application to the apartment had been denied and she would not be able to move in. Cassandra was not sure what had happened, but she decided to call the realtor company to find out. Soon after, Ryan called and asked Cassandra what was going on. She called the realtors and they told her she did not have enough credit to move into the apartment. Cassandra was stunned. She was puzzled as to why she hadn't got approved; she was able to get a $2000 a month loft with no problem. Ryan called Cassandra again to find out the details. When she told him what the problem was, he said he would talk to John and try to work something out. A couple of minutes later, John called Cassandra and said that he did not appreciate her and Ryan talking behind his back regarding the situation and making their plan to move into the apartment. She knew there was something wrong with this guy and was relieved her application was rejected. She immediately called Ryan. "What is up with this guy? He just called and flipped out on me, telling me that we were plotting against him and we were making our own plans."

"I know, I just received the same phone call," Ryan said.

"I am glad that my application was rejected. He probably would have killed me in my sleep. I don't think I want to go through with the apartment."

"Me either," Ryan said. "I am also glad this happened now, instead of finding out after I signed a one-year lease. I just don't know what to do now."

Cassandra thought quickly. Maybe she should invite him to stay at her apartment until he found his place? Without thinking much, Cassandra said, "Hey, why don't you stay at my place. It's a block from the Aon Building and I have enough room for you." Ryan, shocked my Cassandra's offer, did not hesitate and accepted. "Sure, you wouldn't mind at all?"

"No, not at all. It will be fun, like a slumber party every night." Cassandra apparently was not thinking about the entire situation.

"Okay, then I will move in on Saturday," Ryan said.

"Great, call me later to go over the details."

Cassandra hung up and raced over to Elizabeth. Cassandra told her the entire story finally ending with Ryan's moving in on the coming Saturday.

"He is moving into your loft on Saturday?" Elizabeth asked puzzled.

"Yes," Cassandra said carefree.

"You don't actually have a bedroom because it's all open space, so that means you guys will sleep in the same bed?"

"Of course not, he will sleep on the couch or something."

"Right," Elizabeth said. "You guys are going to have a lot of sex, trust me."

"I don't think so, plus he is into Julie and Julie likes him a lot."

"Umm, Cassandra, he is moving into your apartment. It's like you guys are living together as a couple." Cassandra was not an idiot and knew exactly that Ryan was moving in with her and it wouldn't be as roommates, but more like a couple. Julie will soon learn her lesson.

"Did you tell Julie yet?" Elizabeth asked, bringing Cassandra out of her thoughts.

Damn, how am I going to explain this to her? Cassandra thought, although she really did not care.

Later that afternoon, Cassandra went downstairs to talk to Julie. She had figured it would be more fun to torture Julie with the Ryan situation in person. She also did not like the fact that Julie acted like she was better than everyone else because she had a Louis Vuitton bag. Cassandra laughed at the fact that she herself used to be a Louis Vuitton addict, but that was a lifetime ago. She walked into the branch and heads turned as always. She saw Julie at her desk and sat down. "How is your day going?" Cassandra asked with a smile.

"Horrible, I have so much stuff to get done before I leave for Hawaii in two days. How are you?"

"Good, nothing much going on."

"Did you talk to Ryan about the apartment yet? Did you get approved?" Julie asked.

Cassandra sat there and thought this should be fun to tell her about Ryan. She lived for moments like this; capturing priceless expressions was something she loved.

"I talked to Ryan earlier today and I didn't get approved for the apartment."

"What, are you serious? What is Ryan going to do now?"

"Well, we talked, John turned out to be a psycho and Ryan is not moving into the apartment either."

"Where is Ryan going to move?" Julie asked.

"He is moving into my apartment on Saturday," Cassandra said with a smirk.

Julie's face froze. She could not believe what she was hearing.

"What?" Julie said.

"We talked about it and since Ryan does not have a place to stay, I offered him to move in with me and he accepted."

"Where would he sleep?' Julie asked.

"He does have a bed. Maybe the couch? I am not sure," Cassandra said.

Julie was still in shock; she was not sure if she should be happy or upset. How would Ryan and Cassandra living together change the situation between her and Ryan?

"That's great! Now you will have a roommate and won't be lonely."

"Yes, now I will have a roommate," Cassandra said thinking that Ryan was not just a roommate. If he were a roommate, he would have his own room.

"I have to get back upstairs. Call me later." Cassandra said as she got up.

"Okay," Julie said.

Cassandra walked out of the branch feeling very happy. If priceless moments actually went for money, she would be filthy rich! Not like Cassandra wasn't. But with Julie's expression, she would be even richer. Cassandra got into the elevator, a big smile on her face.

Chapter 9

Cassandra woke up on Friday morning, realizing this would be the last night by herself in her apartment. She could not believe that Ryan was moving in. It had only been a little over a week since she had first set eyes on him, and here she was looking around her apartment thinking on how they were going to organize their stuff. Cassandra had only lived with one other guy, her then-boyfriend when she lived in Orlando, but that was short-lived and in another lifetime. At least, her and Eric had not worked out. It would have been weird if she was seeing Eric and Ryan had moved in. Eric and Ryan were not the best of friends, but they worked for the same company and occasionally had to be at the same meetings. They also shared the same best friend, but anyone could tell that they hated each other. No one knew that Cassandra had kissed Eric and been to his apartment.

Cassandra sat in her bed wondering what tomorrow would bring. She wished she could continue drinking the bottle of wine on her nightstand, but realized that she had to be at work soon. Did she really care? Cassandra didn't care about much these days; if it were up to her, she would let everything go. Her one dream that she had banked on was falling apart. She had gone to work drunk plenty of times. With that in mind, she grabbed the bottle and poured herself a glass. *Only one glass, I need to calm my nerves.*

Julie rolled over on her bed and shut off her alarm clock. She thought that she may have had a terrible nightmare about Ryan moving into Cassandra's apartment, but then realized it was a chilling truth that would unfurl the next morning—when she would be getting on a plane to go Hawaii for a whole week. *Why did this have to happen now, right before I have to go on vacation? Maybe I can cancel?* She knew her mother would kill her and that was not an option.

What would happen in the apartment with Ryan and Cassandra? Was Ryan attracted to Cassandra? Did Cassandra like Ryan? Too many questions flooded her head and she had no way of controlling it. She always liked situations that she could control because she was a control freak by nature. Perhaps that's why she did not have a boyfriend. She envied Cassandra with her carefree attitude. *Why couldn't I be more like that*, she wondered.

Ryan jolted awake and realized his head was pounding. Too many beers last night. He looked at his watch and realized that he needed to get some packing done before he left for work this morning. He put his head on the pillow and could not register that he was moving in with Cassandra the next morning. This whole situation had exploded. This was not his way of avoiding Cassandra. By moving in with her, things would only escalate. How he could resist being next to her and not kissing her? What was he thinking? He gave himself a deadline— just one week and he would find himself an apartment.

Two glasses of wine later, Cassandra left her apartment, a bit high. She loved the perfect high one got from drinking alcohol where you weren't drunk, but where nothing really mattered and your mind was not running at hundred miles per hour. She wished she could always be like this; not thinking or caring about anything— but who would want to go through life like this? She walked to work in a daze.

"What is wrong with you?" Elizabeth asked Cassandra noticing her eyes were sort of glassy.

"Nothing, just in a good mood," Cassandra responded.

Elizabeth did not believe Cassandra. She knew of Cassandra's drinking history. Day or night, Cassandra did not care. She had a reputation for always being at happy hour; as a matter of fact, that is how she got her present job at the law firm.

"I don't believe you, have you been drinking? It's only 9:00 a.m. Did Eugene call you and make you upset?" Elizabeth asked, with her arms crossed.

"No. Who cares about Eugene? I was a little nervous about Ryan moving in and I had two glasses of wine to calm my nerves down, that's all."

"I really admire you Cassandra, having the balls to drink before coming to work."

"Thank you," Cassandra said thinking that she did have balls. In fact, it was the only way to go through life, doing what you want; otherwise, life would pass you right by.

As the day went on, Cassandra's high wore off and she hated the feeling that came afterward: depression. At least moving forward, she would have someone in her apartment she could be with. But she had to realize Ryan was just a roommate and would only be there for a little while. She decided to make herself feel better, and called Julie. At least hearing someone suffering would make her feel better.

"Hello, Julie speaking."

"Hello Ms. Chow, how are you doing today?"

"Just looking at my computer screen, not being able to concentrate on any-thing. I have to finish work and I still haven't packed."

"Are you excited about Hawaii tomorrow?"

"I am. I wish I could stay and help you and Ryan tomorrow."

Cassandra thought: *For what? He's moving in with me, not you.*

"I know, I can't believe you are leaving when Ryan is moving in. What a shame," Cassandra said not meaning it at all.

"Weird how Ryan is moving in, and we just started hanging out with him last week."

"I know, I was thinking the same thing." What Cassandra was thinking was how long it would take before Ryan kissed her.

"Well, I have to go and try to get some work done; it's going to be a long day for me."

"Okay, call me later," Cassandra said.

She hung up and decided that since it was mid-afternoon and she'd had enough at work, she could go home for a nap. Cassandra loved the fact that she lived only a block from work. It made it convenient at times like this when she just wanted to go home and sleep.

Cassandra woke up from her nap later that evening to her phone vibrating on her nightstand. Ryan was calling her.

"Hello," Cassandra said in a sleepy voice.

"Hey, what are you up to?" Ryan asked.

"I just woke up from a nap."

"Awesome, do you want to come over and help me pack?"

"Not really, I am sure I am going to help you unpack tomorrow," Cassandra said.

"I knew you were going to say that. I figured that I would be there tomorrow afternoon. Say around 1:00 p.m."

"Sounds good to me. I will see you then."

"Okay, have a good night."

Cassandra clicked her phone off. How simple it was? Just like that and Ryan was moving in. Why couldn't it be this easy with Eugene?

Hey Eugene, can I move in with you?

Sure, why not?

Great, I will be there tomorrow afternoon.

Awesome, see you then.

If it were only that easy! She couldn't even get Eugene to answer her phone calls.

Julie called next. "Hey, I am on my way home to pack. What are you doing?"

"Just lying on my bed."

"Wish I were too. I just finished my entire paperwork and now going home to pack all my stuff. I have to be at the airport by 8:00 a.m. tomorrow."

"Sounds intense."

"I know, I will give you a call later when I am done."

"Sure thing," Cassandra said and hung up the phone and decided that she needed something to eat. She would not be going out tonight and downtown LA would have to go on without her.

After Ryan hung up with Cassandra, he realized he was not feeling like packing and decided to grab a couple of drinks with his friends who happened to call him to tell him they were at a nearby bar. A couple of drinks turned into more drinks and three hours later, Ryan looked at his watch. It was past midnight and he realized he still had to finish packing. Gulping his Jack and Coke, he threw a couple of twenties on the bar and said goodbye to his friends. He rushed back to his apartment. He could tell that he was drunk, because he was throwing everything into garbage bags without any order. He didn't feel like being alone, and Cassandra had obviously told him she didn't want to hang out with him. Julie came to mind. Without thinking, he called Julie.

"Hey, what are you doing?" Ryan asked.

"Nothing much, just getting ready for my flight tomorrow," Julie was shocked that Ryan had called her so late.

"Do you want to come over and help me pack?" Ryan said, immediately regretting the words as they were coming out of his mouth.

"Sure, I can come over and help."

"Okay, then get down here; see you soon." Ryan hung up the phone wishing he hadn't called her, but the alcohol had taken over. What the heck? He needed help packing and he didn't feel like being alone. As soon as Julie hung up with Ryan, she called Cassandra.

"Oh my God!" Julie yelled on the phone.

"What happened?" Cassandra said looking herself in the mirror admiring her long black hair that people hated her for.

"You won't believe who just called me? Ryan! He invited me to come over and help him pack. Can you believe it?"

Cassandra saw her own shocked reflection in the mirror. "Really, are you going over?"

"Of course, I am. Why wouldn't I? He must really like me if he is inviting me to help him pack."

"He really must," Cassandra said not revealing the fact that Ryan had called her earlier to help him pack as well and she had declined. This girl must live in some sort of bubble.

"You should totally go," Cassandra said in her most upbeat voice still looking at her hair in the mirror.

"I still haven't finished packing and I am leaving in eight hours. I have to go jump into the shower and get ready. I will call you on my way," Julie said sounding very excited.

"Okay, call me later, Cassandra said and hung up.

Cassandra looked in the mirror and said to herself: *What is Ryan up to inviting Julie over so late? Had he been drinking? I will find out tomorrow.*

As soon as Julie hung up the phone, she raced into the shower. Random thoughts flooded her head. *Does he really like me? Is he going to make a move tonight? Is he going to kiss me?* Hurrying, Julie threw on her favorite pair of jeans and a black shirt. She would do her makeup in the car on her way down to the Marina. She needed to look her best.

Ryan heard his doorbell ring and hoped that it was Julie and the alcohol he told her to bring when he called her while she was driving down to his place.

At least he would make use out of her trip, and he knew that he needed more alcohol in order to hang out with her. Ryan opened the door, happy to see the bottle of Jack Daniels in Julie's hand.

"Hi Julie," Ryan said excitedly.

"Hi Ryan,"

"Ready to start packing?"

"Sure, I am very good at packing!" Julie said with a smile.

They walked up the stairs to Ryan's kitchen and he made them drinks. Pouring himself more Jack than Coke, he took a long swig of his drink. Looking at Julie under his kitchen lights, he realized that she was cute, not pretty, but cute. He was not sure if it was him or the alcohol talking.

"Ready to go upstairs?" Ryan asked.

"Let's go, Julie said.

Julie looked around Ryan's apartment and realized that there was a lot to do; it would take hours before they were done. Julie got right into to work, folding clothes into the black garbage bags, then taking all the shoes from the closet and putting them into bags as well.

"You are going to Hawaii tomorrow?

"Yes, I have to be at the airport by 8:00 a.m. Hopefully, we will be done by then," Julie said joking.

"I am sure we will."

Several drinks later, Ryan starting realizing that he was deeply intoxicated and Julie was getting prettier by the second. Julie, herself, had had a couple of Jack and Cokes and was feeling loopy. Taking a break, they sat on his bed. Julie started getting nervous since Ryan was so close to her. He put his hand on her leg.

"Do you know why I invited you over tonight?"

"No, why?' Julie asked.

"I was hoping to see you one more time before you left for Hawaii. I couldn't bear not seeing you an entire week." Julie's faced flushed,

"Really, do you mean that?"

"Yes, I do." Without realizing it, Ryan leaned over and kissed Julie for a couple of minutes. When he was done, Ryan pulled back, smiled, and thought it was an okay kiss. Julie could not believe Ryan had just kissed her. He was the best kisser she had ever had. It was certain: she was falling for Ryan. Ryan got up, a bit dizzy, and continued packing. Julie did the same and asked Ryan,

"Do you think that you and Cassandra will get along living as roommates?"

"Sure, why not? She seems like a cool person."

"She is."

For some reason Ryan added, "Plus Cassandra is not my type so there won't be any messy stuff."

Julie was glad to hear those words. She knew now for a fact that Ryan was into her and only her. Happily, she continued packing. Somewhere in the middle of the night, they must have laid down on the bed and passed out.

Julie woke up and realized that the sun was out. She looked at her watch. It was 7:00 a.m. She jumped out of bed. She needed to get home, pick up her mother, and get to LAX by 8:00 a.m. She shook Ryan trying to wake him up. He didn't move.

"Ryan, wake up, I have to go."

"What?" he said. "What is going on?"

"It's 7:00 a.m. and I have to go home and then to the airport."

"So go, have a safe trip," Ryan said and rolled on to his side.

"Are you going to walk me to my car?" Julie said scrambling to get her things together. "Ryan!" she yelled, not getting any answer.

"Please, let me sleep. Call me when you get to Hawaii."

Why was he being so insensitive? He had kissed her the previous night and told her that he couldn't go an entire week without seeing her and now he couldn't walk her to her car?

"Ryan!" she yelled louder. "Please walk me to my car!"

Ryan tried to ignore her, thinking whether this girl was for real. *Does she really want me to walk her to her car that's a couple of houses away?* Finally, Julie gave up and left and simply said, "Goodbye Ryan," and stormed out of his room and out the front door.

Julie ran to her car, frustrated with Ryan. As soon as she sat in her car and put the keys into the ignition, she started crying. Not just a couple of tears, but a river of tears that left her gasping for air.

Why was she crying? Because Ryan wouldn't walk her to her car? It was more than that. Ryan had told her something special last night, something that no other guy had ever said to her. Looking at the clock in her car, she drove off speeding toward the highway wiping away the tears from her eyes. She thought about calling Cassandra, but it was too early and knew that Cassandra would be asleep. She raced home with all types of thoughts in her head.

Ryan woke up with a massive headache, trying to remember what happened last night. Julie must have left since he was lying alone in his bed. Then he remembered. Julie was trying to make him walk her to her car. *Was she insane? It wasn't like it was night or anything.* Then he went on to thinking about the kiss they had. It wasn't all bad, it wasn't great. Maybe that's what he needed in his life—a simple girl, like Julie. She wasn't pretty, but cute enough. Maybe he could become attracted to her and he knew that she would not break his heart, just annoy him. Then he realized that he was moving into Cassandra's apartment in a few hours. How was that going to work out? Being in Cassandra's presence will definitely bring on temptation? He dug his head into his pillow and decided to stop thinking and go back to sleep. Maybe he would wake up and this would be all a dream!

Cassandra stretched her long legs and arms as she woke up on Saturday morning, thinking, *today my entire life will change.* She still couldn't believe the fact that Ryan was moving in. If Eugene knew this, he would be upset. Who was she kidding? Eugene wouldn't even care; he probably would be happy to get Cassandra off his back. She got up deciding that she would wait for the cleaning lady and then head out for some breakfast. She hated the fact that on the weekends downtown LA was very isolated and the only good breakfast places were at the nearby hotels. She would have to settle for another breakfast at the Biltmore Hotel. Cassandra was very fond of that hotel; she could feel the history as soon as walked in. She needed as many mimosas as she could drink; today would be a long and challenging day. Shortly, she heard a knock on her door. With the cleaning lady here, she was ready to start her day.

Julie barely made it to the airport to catch her flight. She was excited about heading to Hawaii but was also disappointed that she would be leaving Ryan for a week, especially right after he told her that he would miss her. As she sat on the plane, she recapped the events from earlier that morning. Ryan had kissed her and it had been the best kiss she had ever had. His lips were soft and moist, and he knew how to maneuver his tongue as if he had done this a hundred times. Julie also remembered his words when it came to Cassandra: *she wasn't his type*—thank goodness for that. Julie was worried about how the living situation was going to work out. She knew once she came back that she would be spending a lot of time at Cassandra's place since Ryan lived there now and she and Ryan were now dating. With those happy thoughts in head, Julie dozed off in a nap exhausted from everything that had taken place that morning.

Cassandra was enjoying her mimosas and eyeing two businessmen at a table nearby. She liked the way the men looked in their suits. Cassandra was a sucker when it came to men in tailored business suits—it had something to do with money and power. Cassandra had grown up in Corporate America and spotting a man in a $2000 tailored suit was as easy to her as picking out ripped apples. She smiled at them and turned her attention to her iPhone that had started buzzing.

"Hello, are you done packing?" Cassandra said in a seductive tone.

"Hey, almost. The movers are here, and they are starting to load everything in the truck. I should be there by 2:00 p.m."

"Great, I will be waiting in the apartment for you," Cassandra said.

"Nice, see you then."

Cassandra clicked off her phone and thought about Ryan for a second and then turned her attention back to the businessmen who kept eyeing her.

Ryan stood out on his balcony just finishing his call to Cassandra. He was still confused about the feelings he might be developing for Julie and the existing feelings he had for Cassandra. He still remembered the night they had first kissed at the Circle Bar and how sweet Cassandra had tasted; it was all just a distant memory now. He made a pact with himself right there and then: he would not fall in love with Cassandra and that was a promise he was going to keep.

Ryan arrived at Cassandra's apartment around midafternoon and called her from the lobby. "Hey, I am downstairs," Ryan said. "What apartment number are you again?

"Hello, 1127, I am coming downstairs."

Cassandra hung up the phone and got into the elevator. She felt nervous and her stomach started to hurt. She wasn't sure if it was all the mimosas she had ended up having with the two businessmen at the Biltmore or whether she really was just nervous. Cassandra got out of the elevator and saw Ryan. He took one look at Cassandra and all his feelings started rushing back. She looked beautiful in her black sundress that showed off her curves. She was definitely not wearing a bra as he could see her hardened nipples through the fabric of the dress.

"Hi Ryan," Cassandra said with a smile.

"Hi babe," Ryan said as he went to hug her.

Cassandra could smell the liquor on him as she hugged him. He must have started drinking already.

"Ready to be my new roommate?" she asked.

"Absolutely," Ryan said.

The movers started putting all the furniture in the elevators, and Cassandra took Ryan up to the apartment. This was the first time Ryan set eyes on the apartment. It was more a loft than an apartment. It was an open space, with brand-new appliances and freshly painted walls. Cassandra had just moved in two months ago. Ryan walked into the apartment and was impressed; he hadn't realized that it would be so new and open. Cassandra showed Ryan around as the first part of his furniture arrived. She soon realized that Ryan had more stuff than the apartment could fit and once the movers were done she was left standing staring at all his stuff, wondering what to do with it.

"I have a lot of stuff, huh?" Ryan said.

"A little bit more than I expected."

"We have to think of how we are going to set up the apartment. We definitely don't have room for two beds. The walk-in closet is big enough for you to put your bed in there. Of course, if you don't mind sleeping in my bed with me or the couch, but the couch is not too comfortable."

"I don't mind sharing the bed with you," Ryan said, not realizing what was coming out of his mouth.

"Okay, then it's a plan," Cassandra said, realizing that this was more like a boyfriend moving in than a roommate.

She told the movers where to put Ryan's bed and then they started organizing the rest of the stuff into neat piles. Cassandra thought the best advantage was having Ryan's massive TV in the living area. Now she could sit on her couch and watch TV all day. Finally, the movers left and she and Ryan sat on the couch and just looked at all his stuff.

"I have to drive back to the Marina to get the last of my suits that are still in my old closet."

"Okay," Cassandra said, not really paying attention; instead she was thinking of what she had gotten herself into.

"I will go now before it gets late," Ryan got up from the couch and Cassandra handed him his set of keys to the apartment.

"For you," Cassandra said with a smile.

"Thank you. I will be back in an hour."

Ryan walked out the door and left Cassandra in the apartment with all his stuff.

Chapter 10

$\mathscr{D}$riving back down to the Marina, Ryan knew that this situation had trouble written all over it. How was he not going to fall in love with Cassandra while sleeping in the same bed with her? Was this insane? He knew his feelings would get stronger for her, but in the end she would break his heart. He was sure of it.

Back at the apartment, Cassandra tried organizing more of Ryan's stuff. It was just all too much to fit in one space. Some of his stuff would have to go to storage whether he liked it or not. After a couple minutes of fixing things, she gave up and opened a bottle of wine and waited for Ryan to return. *Was this how it was going to be from now on? Waiting at home for Ryan?*

Julie's plane landed on the Big Island in Hawaii and she rushed out of the plane to call Ryan. As she was walking down the runway that connected the plane to the airport, she turned on her cell phone and waited until she got service. As soon as she saw the bars on the phone light up, she dialed Ryan's number.

Ryan heard his cell phone ring and looked at it. Julie was calling; she must have landed in Hawaii. He chose to ignore the call. He couldn't deal with her right now. Ryan's phone went to voice mail and Julie was disappointed. *He must still be moving*, she thought. Julie left a message saying she just arrived in Hawaii and wanted to know how the moving day was going. She ended the call and headed to the luggage carousel.

About two hours later, Ryan walked into the apartment with his suits. Cassandra had happily made room for him in her walk-in closet: half for her and half for him. She had almost finished drinking the entire bottle of wine and was slightly nervous. Now that he was here, she wasn't sure how to act. Ryan himself was nervous as well and tried to act casual.

"What's up for tonight?" he asked. "Do you want to go out for drinks?"

"Sure, why not? Where do you want to go?"

"Well, this is your neighborhood, so you can show me around."

"Okay," Cassandra said thinking of places they could go.

It was already evening and she knew she needed more drinks to get her through this.

She realized that she had a new voicemail. Julie had left her a message; she had arrived in Hawaii safely and need to talk immediately.

Not now, Julie, Cassandra thought, *I can't handle any drama.* "By the way, Julie got to Hawaii. She called and left me a message," Cassandra said.

"I know, she called and left me a message too," Ryan said trying to find his clothes in one of the garbage bags.

"I heard that she went over last night to help you pack," she said casually.

"Yeah, I was a bit loaded and needed some help," he replied.

"You guys must have had fun. Did anything happen? Because Julie said she needed to talk immediately."

"Nothing out of the ordinary," Ryan said, lying because he was not sure what to do.

"Oh," Cassandra said. She knew there was more to the story,

"Listen, Ryan," she started. "I hope you know that we are friends and that you can tell me anything and I am always here for you, but there can't be any lies between us."

"I understand," Ryan said, not sure how to take what she had just said.

"I want us to be good friends, but our foundation can't be built on dishonesty."

"I want us to be good friends as well," Ryan said, and he gave Cassandra a hug.

"I have a present for you," Ryan told her.

"Really, what?" She was taken by surprise.

"Whenever we are bored, we can drink these," Ryan started, taking out all different little bottles of alcohol.

"With these, I can teach how to play poker," holding out a new deck of cards.

"And I want you to remember that you will always be number one in my book," holding a crystal figure shaped in the number "1."

"Aww, that is too cute," Cassandra said as she gave him a hug.

They got ready to go out for drinks, each changing their clothes separately in the bathroom, not knowing what were the boundaries yet. They left the apartment and headed to the Standard Hotel for drinks. They decided on the downstairs bar because neither of them had the energy for what upstairs had to offer.

At the bar, Ryan bought drinks for Cassandra and himself. They started talking about themselves and their families. Soon they were both on their third vodka and tonic and decided to sit outside. Both were tipsy with alcohol in their systems. Ryan started flirting with Cassandra. She was wearing a very short black dress that displayed her sexy long legs.

"Ryan!" Cassandra yelled.

"What, I just wanted to know how they feel."

"Whatever."

Ryan started spilling his guts to Cassandra; she was easy to talk with and anyone could get lost for days staring into her dark eyes. They were mesmerizing. Again Ryan, not being able to resist, went to touch Cassandra's leg. Only this time, he leaned in for a kiss, but Cassandra pulled back.

"Ryan, you know I can't kiss you. We live together now, and Julie really likes you."

She did not really mean what she said but was playing hard to get.

"It's okay. You know, I don't like Julie."

"Right, that is why you invited her last night to your apartment."

"I needed someone to help me pack and you turned me down."

Ryan, who had made the promise with himself of not falling for Cassandra, could not resist her lips any longer. He leaned in again, and this time Cassandra did not refuse. Their lips touched and it was like sparks were ignited. The kiss, same as the first time, was magical. This went on for about half an hour and finally, they both needed air.

"Let's get out of here," Ryan said breathlessly.

He grabbed Cassandra's hand and they left the bar.

They decided they were hungry and headed to the Ralph's Supermarket that was three blocks away.

"I notice we don't have any food in the apartment. Let's go grocery shopping."

"Now?" Cassandra said, wanting to go home and keep kissing Ryan.

"Yes." Ryan dragged Cassandra to the grocery store and along the way, they stopped every five seconds to kiss. At some point, they were huddled in the corner kissing each other hard, her one leg wrapped around his waist. Ryan couldn't help himself. Cassandra was too sexy and she turned him on. They finally made it to the grocery store, and Ryan threw anything he could get his hands on into the cart. Two hundred dollars and an hour later, they were sitting in a taxi on the way back to the apartment. As soon as they got home, Ryan put the groceries away and made grilled cheese sandwiches. Cassandra thought this might not be a bad idea after all. After they ate, they both lay on the bed and passed out.

With a two-hour difference between LA and Hawaii, Julie drove her and her mother to their hotel. On the hour drive, she wondered why Cassandra or Ryan hadn't called her back. They must be still getting everything situated. Julie thought about her kiss with Ryan, and it brought a smile to her face. It had been a long time since she had kissed anyone: two years exactly, since she had broken up with her ex-boyfriend. Julie had not been out on a date since then. Now, she had handsome Ryan who liked her and had just moved in with her best friend. Life was turning out to be great and she couldn't wait till Ryan and she would spend time together.

Sunday morning was Eric's best day of the week. After breakfast, he would get on his motorcycle and drive on the Pacific Coast Highway toward Malibu and sit on the beach for hours. He was content being by himself. He missed the company of having someone next to him, but it was hard to trust someone with his heart especially after having been through a divorce, but the divorce had been nine years ago and he still hadn't found a way to come out of it.

This particular morning, his heart felt different. Even though he and Cassandra hadn't really been close and had only exchanged a couple of kisses, she was someone he would have wanted to get to know, but his ego and issues got in the way. He remembered the conversation that took place last night when he and Alex had met up for drinks at a hole-in-the-wall bar in Culver City.

"You won't believe what Ryan told me today," Alex had said, eager to get rid of the information he had been holding on for hours.

"What?" Eric had taken a sip of his beer.

"He moved into Cassandra's apartment today."

Eric hadn't been sure if he had heard right, because that could not be possible. Could it be a different Cassandra?

"Cassandra, who? Cassandra, the girl I kissed, the girl that I let come over to my apartment?" Eric had asked shocked.

"Yep, that's the one. Now we know why she didn't sleep with you. She has been sweet on Ryan this whole time."

Eric had thought for a second. *Could that be true? Was that the real reason Cassandra didn't want to sleep with me?*

It couldn't be.

Cassandra was into him, he could tell. No wonder she hadn't called him.

"Eric, what do you think about the situation?" Alex had asked, noticing his friend lost in his thoughts.

"Whatever man, it is what it is. Good luck to Ryan," Eric had said, holding up his beer to do cheers. He had taken a big gulp of the beer, not sure what to think.

Remembering the conversation, Eric rolled over and looked at his ceiling thinking about the information he received last night. Was it possible that if he had called Cassandra after their first encounter in his apartment, would Ryan still have moved in? Did she always like Ryan and was just playing games with him? This is why he never liked getting involved with anyone. He had developed feelings for Cassandra, but now she was off-limits especially if Ryan was in the picture. He didn't like Ryan as it was, and this would only make matters worse. It was best to forget about Cassandra and just move on.

Cassandra woke up happily not having a hangover for once, and grateful for that. Cassandra rolled over to find Ryan sleeping soundly; he looked adorable, like an innocent little boy, which in many ways he might be. She smiled at him.

Was she falling for him?

She couldn't; it was not right.

It was new and exciting. Doesn't everyone like new beginnings?

Cassandra rolled over on her back. What was she doing? What about Julie? She really didn't care about Julie's feelings, but what about her feelings? She didn't want to get involved in anything that would cause her pain. She had been through too much in Manhattan before she had left over a year and a half ago. She cringed at the memories of Manhattan and quickly dismissed them. Ryan must have sensed that she was up and put his arm over her, indicating he wanted to cuddle. For once, she didn't reject Ryan's actions and she let him engulf her.

Later that morning, they were making breakfast as though it were a normal thing for them. They finished eating and decided to hit Target and Best Buy. Ryan wanted to buy a DVD of the Flights of the Conchords, a band that Ryan was going to see later that night. Cassandra liked this whole new experience of having someone to wake up to in the mornings, actually remembering their name, and they in return wanting to stay and hang out.

After shopping, they headed back to the apartment and watched the DVD. Cassandra thought the DVD was hilarious and watched it for hours. While watching TV, Ryan made it a point to hold Cassandra's hand and give her a kiss every now and then. She thought it was cute; he was very affectionate with her. Once the DVD was over, he started getting ready to head to the concert.

"Where is the concert?"

"In Pasadena. I am going with a bunch of friends. I won't be back tonight in case you wonder where I am."

"I wouldn't worry; I know you are a big boy."

Ryan smiled at her. *What I am doing? I am heading to watch the concert with another girl and staying at her house tonight, when really I just want to be with Cassandra.*

"What are you up to tonight?"

"Nothing much, just grabbing dinner and calling it an early night."

"Sounds relaxing."

"Yes," Cassandra said, secretly wanting Ryan to stay, but she didn't want to sound attached or clingy.

Ryan finished getting dressed, kissed Cassandra goodbye, and walked out the door. Cassandra, sitting on her bed, fell to one side.

What should she do now? She told herself not to become attached too quickly.

Ryan walked to his car that was parked in the garage a block away. He didn't know what to make of Cassandra and the apartment situation. He wanted to be with Cassandra, but he knew that his heart was at stake. Truth be told, he still hadn't fully recovered from his ex-girlfriend—the one who had made the move to LA with him and a year later decided to return to the East Coast. She had given Ryan an ultimatum and he had chosen to stay in LA. When she left, she took Ryan's heart with her and he had never been the same. Cassandra would just be someone who would dig that knife even deeper. He had to continue what he was doing by dating different girls to make him forget about the hurt. Once he got his car ready to pick up his date to take to the concert, Ryan put on his game face, something that he was getting used to doing.

Early next morning, Elizabeth—patiently waiting for Cassandra to come in and get the juicy details of the weekend—bombarded her with questions as soon as she walked in.

"So how did it go? Did you guys have sex yet? Was it good? Does Julie know?"

Dazed by all the questions, Cassandra sat at her desk and ignored Elizabeth for fun.

"Are you not going to tell me?' Elizabeth asked losing patience.

"Okay, so we didn't have sex. We made out a lot and went shopping for groceries and house stuff."

"So, you guys are like a couple?"

"No, not at all. Just roomies."

"Right, tell me that after you guys have had sex," Elizabeth asked with a smirk.

"We are not having sex. Remember Ryan and Julie like each other," Cassandra said with a face that no one would believe.

"Have you spoken to Julie?"

"No, she got to Hawaii and called me, but I was too busy with Ryan and didn't call her back."

"What a shame. She is going to miss out on the best week ever with you and Ryan," Elizabeth said.

"Like I said nothing is going on between us."

"Whatever you say," Elizabeth said

Cassandra thought about having sex with Ryan. Eventually, it would take place. How can two people that sleep in the same bed not be attracted to each other? Cassandra decided to go on with her day and deal with it when it happened.

Chapter 11

I t was way past 7:00 p.m. and Cassandra was not sure what to do. Should she go home?

Was she supposed to call Ryan?

What was the protocol for something for this?

Not sure what to do and not wanting to stay at work anymore, Cassandra decided the safest bet would be to go to the Library Bar. *Nothing better than a drink to help me through this situation*, she thought.

Walking into the Library Bar, Cassandra took a seat at the bar. It was somewhat dead for a Monday night, but she noticed one of the bar's usual patrons, Mark, who came over to keep her company. Talking with Mark was a distraction she needed. Once Cassandra had had two beers, she decided to go home and see what Ryan was up to. As she walked through the door, she was surprised that Ryan was not home. She looked at her watch. It was past 9:00 p.m. Cassandra decided to change into comfortable clothes and slipped onto the couch to watch TV. A few minutes later, she heard Ryan open the door and walk in.

"Hey, what's up?" Ryan said looking handsome in his suit.

"Nothing much, just watching TV. How was the concert last night?"

"Good," Ryan said as he sat down on the couch. "Did you eat yet?"

"No, I just got home a little while ago."

"Working late?"

"I had to stay and finish some paperwork."

"Do you want to make something to eat?" Ryan asked.

"We can make turkey burgers," Cassandra said.

"Sure, let me change and I will get started."

Cassandra was noticing how sweet Ryan was; he was polite and a real gentleman. He would make a great boyfriend. *Not yours, remember,* Cassandra said to herself, *this is strictly a friendship.*

Ryan cooked dinner while Cassandra watched TV. Once they were done eating, they sat and watched TV and barely talked. They were both not sure what to do or how to act.

"Ready for bed?" Ryan asked putting his hand on Cassandra's thigh and squeezing it.

"Yep," Cassandra said looking at Ryan thinking how long this stage of the friendship was going to last.

"Tomorrow, we start unpacking my stuff."

"Unpacking? Where? There is no room?"

"We will figure it out," Ryan said helping Cassandra up from the couch.

They both headed to her bed to lie on their assigned sides. In a few seconds, Ryan would be holding Cassandra until they both fell asleep.

This was the first time Ryan and Cassandra woke up to get ready for work. He had not come home after the concert till Monday morning, and by the time he had returned to the apartment, Cassandra had already left. His cell phone, which he used for an alarm clock, starting going off and woke Cassandra up.

"What time is it?" Cassandra asked groggily.

"Too early, only 7:00 a.m.," Ryan said. "What time do you have to get in the shower?"

"Around 8:00 a.m."

"Good, then we have time to get it on this morning," Ryan said as he hugged Cassandra from behind and made an attempt to touch her breast.

"Are you kidding me? Remember we decided not to have sex; it would be bad for our friendship and living situation. And Julie? She would be upset that you cheated on her."

"What are you talking about? Julie and I are not dating."

"Not according to her. She probably thinks you guys are a couple," Cassandra said laughing.

"Please, I am not interested in her that way. What I am interested is, is having you," Ryan said as he reached Cassandra's face to kiss her. Cassandra didn't resist Ryan's kisses anymore. She was enjoying herself and having Ryan around was good for her.

After their morning make-out session without sex, Cassandra hopped into the shower and got ready for work. She was already half an hour late, but she didn't care. She loved spending time with Ryan in bed. Cassandra left and told Ryan to have a good day. Ryan then proceeded to get ready. He had no set time to be at work.

As Cassandra was walking around downtown LA deciding if having a cocktail for lunch would be the best choice, she got a call from Julie. Wondering whether to ignore the call or not, she picked up.

"Hello, how is Hawaii?" Cassandra said, all chipper.

"It's amazing. I wish Ryan was here to share this experience with me," Julie replied.

Cassandra headed into the bar at the Sheraton Hotel to have her lunch: a vodka tonic. It was light on calories and in LA what else was there to do besides drink and get laid.

"I am sure Ryan would love to be there with you too," Cassandra said making a funny face.

"I know. How is it going with you two? I haven't heard back from either of you. Is everything okay? What are the sleeping arrangements?"

"Well, Ryan has just way too much stuff and we are trying to organize it. His bed is in the closet and we are alternating by having one sleep on the couch and one sleep on the bed," Cassandra said not telling her the truth because she did not want to hurt her feelings. She actually wanted to tell Julie because she always acted like a "know-it-all," but Cassandra knew it was not wise to let her know yet.

"Oh, how is that working out?"

"Okay. It's my turn to sleep on the couch tonight. Ryan didn't come home on Sunday night," Cassandra had to add that in to torture Julie.

"Where did he go?"

"To some concert in Pasadena and then stayed at a friend's house."

"A girlfriend's house?"

"I am not sure, I really didn't ask all the details," Cassandra said, signaling the waiter for another drink.

"Oh," Julie said somewhat disappointed.

"Don't worry; I am sure it was one of his male friends."

"Yeah, what are you guys doing tonight?"

"I am not sure. I am going home after work and just hanging out."

"Okay, tell Ryan I said hi and that I was thinking about him."

"Sure will," Cassandra said remembering to tell Ryan Julie's message while she was making out with him tonight.

"I'll call you later," Julie said.

"Okay, bye," Cassandra said, in between sipping her drink.

Cassandra hung up the phone somewhat annoyed. Was Julie really this dumb? Did she really believe they were alternating sleeping on the couch? She was a gullible one. Cassandra thought this might be fun after all. She signaled the waiter one last time for another drink before heading back to work. Cassandra noticed that her drinking was getting out of control: she was now having cocktails for lunch. She shrugged and thought she had been drinking plenty the last year and a half and she decided it was Eugene's fault. She had to blame *someone*, and who better than him? With that in mind, She got up from the bar, stumbled a little, and walked back to work.

"Are you okay?" Elizabeth asked noticing Cassandra's eyes were glassy once again,

"Of course, I am," Cassandra said sounding happier than usual. She loved the high that alcohol gave her when it was drunk the right amount.

"Where did you go for lunch?" Elizabeth asked curiously.

"Nowhere really, just around. While I was at lunch, I started thinking about my birthday party. I only have two weeks to decide where I am going to have it and I still have to send out invitations."

"Where do you plan on having it?"

"I am not sure; I had my birthday party last year at the Standard Hotel on Sunset in Hollywood and it was a blast."

Cassandra remembered her birthday party last year. Well, at least part of it and mostly through pictures she and her friends had taken. Everyone had a blast, including herself, and it had taken her two days to recover. Then, the memories that she had been trying to avoid about Eugene and her birthday came rushing into her head. Shortly after Cassandra had met Eugene, he had asked Cassandra if she would like for him to be her date to her birthday party. Cassandra, beyond words, had accepted Eugene's proposal. The day after her birthday party, Cassandra was supposed to take off to Paris for three weeks. She hadn't been able to believe what was happening. She had met the man of her dreams and he was going to be her date and then she was taking off to Paris for three weeks. What else could she ask for? Only, in the end, Eugene had never made it to Cassandra's party and she had been crushed.

Cassandra had left for Paris the next day with the thoughts of never speaking to Eugene again. A couple of days after Cassandra had arrived in Paris, Eugene had shown up at Cassandra's hotel in Paris. Cassandra had walked into the hotel lobby after a day of sightseeing and had spotted Eugene sitting in one of the vintage couches. Cassandra, not sure if she was imagining things, had approached Eugene wondering if he was real. Eugene had rushed to her and given her a big hug.

"I am sorry about your party. I have no excuse for not showing up, and if you never forgive me, I will understand, but I came here to show you how much you mean to me." Cassandra had not been sure what to say and had decided to kiss Eugene. After that, they had gone on to spend an incredible three weeks in Paris. When they had returned to LA, she had found out that she was two weeks pregnant and things had never been the same for Cassandra.

"Cassandra," Elizabeth shouted. "Where do you plan to have it this year?"

"Umm," Cassandra said coming out of her memories. "I think I am having it at the Standard Rooftop because my birthday lands during the week and I want to have it on the same day."

"Fun, my husband and I will definitely be there."

Cassandra quickly went to putting her list together and tried to forget about Paris. Over the course of the one and a half years that Cassandra had been in LA, she had managed to make a large group of friends. She started listing the names and made a mental note that Eugene would not be getting an invitation this year.

Cassandra decided that today she would go straight home instead of hitting the bar. When she walked into her apartment, she was surprised to see Ryan already home. He was watching TV, drinking a beer, and unpacking his stuff.

"Hey, how was your day?" Ryan asked.

"Good, how about yours?"

"Okay, didn't have many appointments and headed home early."

"That's nice."

"Grab a beer. They are in the fridge." "Thanks, do you want one?"

"Sure."

Cassandra sat down on the couch with the two beers and they watched TV for a while.

Again, they sat in silence and watched TV. Cassandra noticed that he did not talk too much and she was the complete opposite: a talker.

"What's for dinner tonight?" Ryan asked.

Was this going to be a regular question every night? Suddenly Cassandra felt like she was going to have a panic attack. She felt overwhelmed as if she was trapped in a relationship. *Calm down*, she told herself. *Just drink some more beer and it will be okay.*

"Well," Ryan said. "Did you decide?"

Cassandra had to get up and walk around. She headed to the closet in order for Ryan to not notice that something was wrong.

"How about ordering pizza?"

"Sounds good. Do you have the number? What are you doing in the closet?" Ryan asked confused.

Trying to catch my breath, she wanted to answer.

"Changing my clothes." Cassandra threw on a pair of shorts and tank top She came out of the closet, more relaxed, and went to grab another beer.

"The number to the pizza place?" Ryan asked again.

"Oh, yes. Here is it."

Ryan called and ordered dinner.

Later that night, Cassandra and Ryan were sitting on the couch in silence again. This time, Ryan motioned for Cassandra to come closer and he put his arm around her and kissed her on the forehead. Cassandra snuggled against his chest and enjoyed the affection. *Would things always be like this?* she wondered. In a strange way, they were both using each other in the sense of having someone there. An hour later, Ryan, motioned to Cassandra for bed. They both lay down on their assigned sides and for a second time in a row, Ryan fell asleep with Cassandra in his arms.

"How your new apartment and roommate? Have sex with her yet?" Alex asked Ryan at lunch the next day.

"You know, it's not like that. We are just roommates. It's a temporary situation until I find something in the Marina," Ryan said trying to harbor his feelings for Cassandra, which had been growing since he moved in.

"Yeah right. Come on, you are talking to me, man. Tell me the truth. Is she any good?"

"You are not going to give up? Huh? Like I said before, I don't like Cassandra in that way; she is not my type."

"A girl like that? Please, I would have made a move a long time ago."

"Exactly and that is why at your age, you are still not married and willing to sleep with anyone," Ryan said and flashed his famous smile.

"Did you and Ryan do the deed yet?" Elizabeth asked.

"No, I told you it's not like that. We are friends."

"Yes, friends that sleep in the same bed. Did you think Eugene would get a kick out of this?"

"Who cares what he thinks? He had his chance, but he is too busy chasing something that doesn't exist."

Cassandra realized that in many ways she was like Eugene: hungry for something that doesn't exist. That is why she knew they belonged together.

"I am sure he would get upset," Elizabeth said, not understanding the last comment Cassandra said.

"Whatever the case may be, Ryan is just a roommate and that is all. Plus Julie will be back in a couple of days, and then the real fun will begin," Cassandra said with a laugh.

Chapter 12

*I*t was the beginning of June, and Eugene enjoyed this time of the year, spending little time at the office and more time at the golf course.

"How was your date last night?" his cousin Sam asked.

"It was okay, another typical OC girl," Eugene said ready to take his swing.

"I thought you liked those kinds of girls?" Sam said.

"I did, and I married one, but it didn't work out. I need something different," Eugene said watching the ball he just hit fly across the course.

"Damn it," Eugene yelled. "Almost made a hole in one."

"Nice," Sam said.

"Not good enough," Eugene said disappointed at himself while taking a big swig of his drink.

"Do you have another date lined up tonight?"

"No, I am taking tonight off, keeping it low key. Do you want to go out to dinner?"

"Low key?" Sam replied, "Once you get a couple of drinks, there isn't anything low key about you."

Eugene laughed his famous laugh.

"We should make a trip out to LA this weekend. We haven't partied there in a while. I really like that rooftop bar. What's it called again?"

"The Standard," Eugene responded while trying to figure out how to make the next shot a perfect one.

"Yes, that is the name. I haven't been there since that night you met that pretty girl with the long black hair. Do you still remember her name?"

"Yes. Cassandra." How could Eugene forget? Cassandra never made him forget.

"Do you still talk to her? I can still remember you guys making out that night. Pretty intense."

"Yeah it was," Eugene replied not really paying attention and not wanting to get on the topic of Cassandra.

"Do you still talk to her?"

"From time to time," Eugene said.

"That was a long time ago. Did Scott . . . come with us that night?" Sam asked, his voice trailing off.

For a second, Sam forgot about the tragic accident that took his brother Scott's life right before Christmas last year. Eugene looked at Sam surprised that he would ask that question and he didn't know how to respond.

"Umm, I don't remember," Eugene, said hoping that his cousin would change the subject. Talking about his cousin Scott was not a pleasant topic for Eugene, and he really did not care to relive that day.

"I think I am ready to beat you right now," Eugene said. "And if I do, dinner is on you tonight."

After spending another night in the same routine with Ryan, Cassandra decided that tonight she was going out. It was Thursday and it was the best night at the Standard Rooftop. After work, Cassandra headed over and called a few of her friends to join her.

"Hi sexy," said her friend Oscar.

"Hi sweetie."

"Isn't today gorgeous? And the men here are to die for."

"Where is Lila?" Cassandra asked.

"On her way. Look at him over there . . . isn't he yummy?!"

Cassandra laughed at the fact that her friend wanted every guy at the bar. This was Cassandra's favorite place in LA. Forget all the Hollywood bars, there was nothing like the Standard Rooftop. This had been the bar that Cassandra visited on her first night in LA. The friend that she had made at the hotel bar had brought her here. She remembered looking at the sky and thinking anything was possible in LA and feeling happy that she had escaped Manhattan. Now, well over a year later, so much had changed, and every day had become one big drinking party.

"Penny for your thoughts?" Oscar said.

Cassandra smiled thinking how great it had been to meet Oscar and his sisters. They were her family in LA.

"We are not thinking about Mr. Conrad, are we now?

"Who? I don't even know that name," Cassandra said with a laugh.

"Well, forget him, and look at the handsome man walking our way."

Cassandra realized that it was a famous defense attorney who couldn't get enough of her.

After several drinks—seven to be exact—Cassandra stumbled home. Almost forgetting that Ryan lived with her, she opened the door to find Ryan still unpacking his stuff.

"Hi," she said somewhat slurring.

"Hey, what were you up to tonight?" Ryan asked, trying to not sound like he was prying, but surprised that Cassandra had taken this long to come home.

"Met some friends for drinks at The Standard."

"Fun." He wondered why she hadn't invited him.

While Cassandra was getting undressed by the bed, Ryan tried not to watch her and concentrated on the TV. Not realizing what she was doing, Cassandra now stood in just her lacy underwear, wondering if Ryan was watching her. Due to the amount of alcohol in her system, she decided to walk to the closet practically naked. Ryan tried as hard as he could to *not* look, but it was too late. He was turned on and he could feel his bulge getting harder by the second. Cassandra, knowing that she was somewhat teasing Ryan, decided to stay naked for a couple of more minutes. Finally, she threw on a pair of skimpy shorts and a short T-shirt and joined Ryan on the couch, who now had a complete hard-on.

"Is there any more beer left?" Cassandra asked.

"Yes, in the fridge," Ryan said.

Cassandra got up to get a beer and Ryan watched her walk to the fridge. He wanted her so bad at this point. He did not know what to do. When she returned to the couch, Ryan who was a bit loose after drinking a few beers himself asked Cassandra, "Are you ready to have sex and get it over with?"

"What? I thought we decided not to."

"I thought it would be easier if we just did it to get it out of the way."

"Really?" Cassandra said. "You think we should do this to get it out of the way?"

"Yes," Ryan said wanting to kiss her moist lips.

Cassandra was not sure if it was the alcohol or the fact that she liked him, but she got up and headed to bed.

"Well, are you going to join me?" Cassandra said.

Ryan walked over and without saying anything started to kiss her softly.

I am a sucker when it comes to kissing Ryan, she thought.

He then started kissing Cassandra's neck and touched her nipples as they hardened. Cassandra let out a little gasp. She started moving her hands down to Ryan's pants and undoing the button and zipper. Cassandra really didn't care about anything anymore, not even Julie. Ryan peeled off Cassandra's shorts and underwear and lay her on the bed. He took off his pants and that revealed his package. Cassandra, impressed with what she saw, starting touching it slowly. Ryan, liking the touch of Cassandra's soft hands, found it hard to resist anymore. He reached over for a condom and entered Cassandra in pure passion. Through the latex, Ryan could feel how hot her vagina was and let out a big gasp. He moved slowly, kissing Cassandra on her mouth and neck. Before they knew it, they had both climaxed and Ryan lay on top of Cassandra not moving an inch.

"Are you okay?" Ryan asked.

"Yes," Cassandra said gasping for air.

Ryan rolled off of Cassandra and onto the bed, still thinking how good it felt to do what they just did and the connection that was there. He held her hand, unsure of what she was thinking. Cassandra, a bit shocked that she had just had sex with Ryan, decided to blame it on the alcohol. She did not lie to herself. She had enjoyed Ryan taking her body into his; there was something there.

"Aren't you glad we got this over?" Ryan said laughing.

"Yes, I am sure. Are you?" Cassandra said feeling quite dizzy from all the alcohol she'd had earlier that evening.

Ryan got up and dressed himself. He gave Cassandra his hand to help her up and gave her a kiss when she stood up. He told himself that he was in trouble now, having slept with Cassandra and it having felt this good only meant that he would want more.

Immediately, Cassandra said, "We are not going to tell anyone; this is between you and me, right?" She was not sure why she said that.

"Of course, no one is to know," Ryan was taken aback by her comment. *Was she ashamed to let anyone know they slept together?* At least she wasn't clingy and he didn't have to worry about her thinking they were an item. Cassandra told herself that she could do this: have sex with Ryan and not get attached. Who was she kidding? She was already attached.

Julie was sitting in the jacuzzi at the resort she and her mother were staying at. It was a beautiful night in Hawaii, and she would have given anything for Ryan to be here sitting in the hot tub with her. She thought about their kiss and the many more that were to come. *Wonder what he is doing now? Probably hanging out with Cassandra.* She was very happy that Cassandra and Ryan were becoming friends. This way, she would have a boyfriend and a best friend who got along. Julie thought about how weird it was that neither of them had called her even once. In fact, she was the one to reach out to Cassandra and Ryan; they had not returned any of her calls. She put those thoughts aside and told herself that she would be home in two days and then she would be with Ryan. She went back to gazing at the stars and thinking about Ryan.

Cassandra walked into the office and passed by Elizabeth in the kitchen.

"Cassandra," Elizabeth yelled.

"Hey, I didn't see you there."

"Well, any new developments?" Elizabeth asked smiling at Cassandra.

Cassandra looked at Elizabeth not sure what to say to her. Elizabeth looking at Cassandra's face and knew that something had happened.

"OMG, did you sleep with Ryan?" Elizabeth asked.

Not sure how to answer, she replied: "Yes, I did." She had to get it out.

"How was it? How big is it?"

Laughing Cassandra said, "It was good, I was surprised that we had somewhat of a connection there. To be honest, I had a few drinks at the Standard and then went home and not thinking about it too much, we went at it."

"Are you going to tell Julie?" Elizabeth asked in a more serious tone.

"Of course not, It's just a one-time thing between Ryan and me."

"Right, you will be at it again tonight?"

"I don't think so. He is going to a baseball game, probably won't be coming home tonight. Which reminds me that I should get tickets for tomorrow's game. The Cubs are Ryan's favorite team and I should surprise him with tickets."

"Right and you are not into him," Elizabeth said.

"I am not," Cassandra said with a serious face.

Cassandra walked over to her computer and looked at tickets for the Saturday's game. She bought two tickets for Ryan and her. *He will totally like this idea,* she thought to herself, sounding very proud. Cassandra also realized that she needed to get her invitations out for her birthday party. She decided on the Standard Rooftop where she had realized many things about herself and life in LA.

Walking home later that night, Cassandra realized that Ryan probably wouldn't be home and tonight she would be alone. Typically she would go out, but she still felt a bit queasy from drinking the night before. She was excited to surprise Ryan with tickets to the Cubs game. She decided to call him and tell him before he made any plans.

"Hi, what are you wearing?" Cassandra joked to Ryan.

"A Cubs jersey, why?" Ryan responded, not getting the joke.

"Are you on the way to the game?" Cassandra asked.

"Yes, picking up some friends from the Marina and then heading over to the stadium."

"Cool. Guess what? I have a surprise for you?"

"Really, what?"

"You have to guess," Cassandra said seductively.

"Umm . . . you are going to cook me dinner?"

"Yeah right, better than that. I just got us tickets to the Cubs game tomorrow!"

"Really?" Ryan sounded surprised and shocked that Cassandra would get him tickets for the game.

"Yeah, do you not want to go?"

"No, course I want to go. It's going to be fun; I can't wait."

"Good, tomorrow, game three of the series or something like that," Cassandra said.

"Yes, something of that sort," Ryan said, still taken aback by Cassandra's surprise.

"Have fun at the game, see ya later," Cassandra said and hung up, not giving Ryan a chance to say goodbye. *I would have thought Ryan would be more excited about the game*, she thought. Maybe he was upset about something, but tomorrow will be different.

Ryan was driving to pick up his two male friends. *What is Cassandra doing? Was she falling for him?* As much as he liked Cassandra, he didn't need the drama of a woman starting to like him and worse still, he was living with her. Maybe she is just cool and got tickets for fun. Cassandra didn't seem like the clingy type, but always had her own agenda, which he thought might be the problem.

Back in the apartment, Cassandra made herself comfortable on the couch glad to have some time to herself, and knew that Ryan wouldn't be coming home tonight. She put her phone on vibrate because she did not want to be disturbed by any calls. Tonight was just going to be about her. She needed her rest for tomorrow afternoon.

"Hey, what's going on?" Eugene answered his phone with an upbeat tone.

"You tell me?" the sexy female voice said on the other end.

"Nothing much, just at home relaxing."

"Are you taking me out to dinner tonight?" she asked

"Where would you want to go?" Eugene asked sounding uninterested. He hated girls who were pushy and demanded things.

"Where are you willing to take me?" the female voice said.

"How about this? Let me call you back in a couple of minutes and you figure out where you want to go," Eugene said, not having the intention of ever calling her.

"Promise?"

"Most definitely," Eugene clicked the phone off before she could say goodbye and called his buddies.

"Yard House tonight?" Eugene said. "Meet you there in an hour."

Dealing with a pushy OC woman was the last thing Eugene needed.

On entering the Yard House restaurant, Eugene noticed his friends sitting at a table near the bar.

"Hey guys," Eugene, said.

"Conrad, what's up dude?" said Brad, Eugene's friend and coworker.

"Nothing much, same ol same ol."

"No hot date tonight?" asked another one of Eugene's friends, Matthew.

"No way, no more dating for me. Too much of a hassle. I just had one girl call me to ask me if I could take her out to dinner. Very un-classy."

"At least you would have gotten laid," said Brad

"Not worth it, to deal with someone who speaks of nothing but themselves all night."

"You are not getting any younger, Conrad, and you have to have one more baby before you hit forty," Matthew said smiling.

Eugene thought, *Will I ever meet someone? Or will it just be endless nights of worthless dinners and sex?*

Chapter 13

Saturday morning Julie woke up, excited to know that in less than twenty-four hours she would be back in LA and able to see Ryan. That thought made her get out of bed and start packing her suitcases. Julie had enjoyed her time in Hawaii, but now it was time to get back and be with Ryan. She carefully packed the souvenirs that she had purchased for Cassandra and Ryan on her trip. She wondered where Ryan was this morning and whether he was thinking about her.

Cassandra opened her eyes, surprised to see Ryan lying next to her. She looked at him and realized that he must have come home drunk and passed out, because he was still wearing his clothes including his sneakers and baseball cap. Cassandra thought about undressing him, but did not want to disturb him. She just took his baseball cap off, gave him a kiss on the forehead, and left the bed.

Cassandra was not sure if she should cook breakfast. She was actually a good cook, but no one knew that because she never cared to cook for anyone. She decided on watching TV for now. An hour later, Ryan stirred from his sleep and sat up on the bed.

"Good morning, what time is it?" Ryan asked

"About 11ish. How was the game last night? I didn't hear you come home."

"It was great, even though the Cubs lost. I did, however, chip one of my back teeth on a nacho at the game last night."

"Ouch, are you okay?" Cassandra asked concerned.

"Yeah, I am okay. I am going to call my dentist in Glendale to see if she can take me. Do you want to come?"

"Umm, no that's okay, I am going to get ready while you go," Cassandra said.

"Aren't you going to come over and give me some this morning?" Ryan asked with a smirk.

"You wish. I don't feel like it," Cassandra said not paying attention to Ryan.

"Are you rejecting me?" Ryan asked pretending to be hurt. He got up from the bed and took his clothes off from the night before and walked over to Cassandra just wearing his boxers and bent down to give her a kiss.

"That is not I what I said. I am just not in the mood."

"I thought you enjoyed having sex," Ryan said as he started to push Cassandra over to make room for him on the couch.

"I do, but I am tired this morning"

"Right, well, maybe later,"

Ryan and Cassandra lay on the couch watching TV for a while and then Ryan got up.

"I am going to take a shower, head to my dentist's office, and then pick you up for the game," Ryan said giving Cassandra a kiss.

"Okay," Cassandra said thinking how great it was to have Ryan around.

On a beautiful Saturday morning in Newport Beach, Eugene Conrad had yet another hangover. Eugene woke up yet again with his head pounding. He didn't have to get out of bed to realize that he would be spending all day in his house due to the fact that he had drank extensively the night before. He sat upright in his bed, trying to open his eyes and accept the fact that he had overdone it, yet again. He didn't remember much from last night's events at this point. He didn't care to remember much. *Why do I do this to myself*? Eugene wondered to himself as he rubbed his head. Suddenly, Eugene heard a noise from downstairs; he realized that some of his friends must have stayed over. He threw on a pair of sweats and a T-shirt and headed downstairs as his head pounded insanely.

"Hey Brad, how are you feeling?" Eugene asked as he descended the stairs and found Brad trying to get up from the couch.

"Man, I am hurting. How about you? You must feel the same?"

"Yeah. I can't even see straight. Do you want some water? "Eugene asked.

"Please! Enough to get rid of this headache."

Eugene went into the kitchen, grabbed two Fiji bottles of water, walked back into the living room, and threw one to Brad.

"Man, what was up with you last night? For someone that didn't want to date anymore, you sure got a lot of digits."

"I did?" Eugene sounded surprised, because he couldn't remember much of last night.

"You were relentless in your pursuit. No stone left unturned," Brad said with a laugh.

"Really?" Eugene said with a huff wishing he could remember something from last night, but all that came to mind was when he first arrived at the bar, and him talking to his friends and immediately taking shots of SoCo and lime. He had lost count after his fifth one. He immediately realized that he couldn't keep going through life like this—a series of drunken nights that came with massive headaches the next day. *At least I didn't sleep with anyone, but I am guessing I must have kissed someone.*

Ryan walked into the apartment happy because he was able to see the dentist who was able to fix his tooth.

"Are you ready?" Ryan called out to Cassandra as he entered the apartment.

"The car is double-parked downstairs."

Cassandra walked out of the closet dressed and ready to go,

"Yes, I am."

"Okay, let me put on my jersey and we are out of here. By the way, we are going to pick up one of my friends, Amy, and then head to the Saddle Ranch to have endless mimosas."

Cassandra was surprised that he wanted to include another friend. "No problem."

They approached Ryan's car and he opened the door for Cassandra. Cassandra loved the fact that Ryan was a gentleman. *Must be the mid-west thing.*

They drove off toward I-10 West to pick up Ryan's friend.

"You don't mind if Amy comes along? You are going to love her." "I don't mind, but we only have two tickets to the game."

"I know, but maybe we can scalp them for three tickets. Would you mind?"

"No, not at all," Cassandra said wondering if this girl Amy was someone Ryan was seeing. They never did have the discussion about whether or not each one was dating anyone, not that they needed to because they were just roomies.

As they approached the Robertson Ave. exit off of I-10, Ryan called Amy.

"Hey, I am getting off the exit now. Which way do I turn?" Ryan asked.

"Oh, okay, be there in five minutes." Ryan hung up the phone and squeezed Cassandra's leg and smiled at her.

They approached the street indicated by Amy, and Ryan parked the car and got out, and went to get Amy. He had to go around the corner to get her, which Cassandra thought was weird. On turning around the corner, he had to come up with a quick story about Cassandra. Most of his friends didn't know that he had moved in with her and he didn't want them thinking that Cassandra was his girlfriend.

"Hi Amy," Ryan said giving her a tight hug.

"Hi Ryan, how are you?" Amy said. "Where is your car?"

"Around the block," Ryan said quickly, "My friend Cassandra is in the car. I happened to move in with her last Saturday, but we're just friends, nothing else. Don't worry about her."

Amy, surprised by the information, just nodded and said, "Okay."

As they were walking to the car, Amy wondered who this girl might be— the girl that Ryan had moved in with because, according to him, he was not ready to be in any type of relationship. There was no type of physical attraction between Ryan and Amy, but Amy had always had a secret crush on Ryan. She got into the back seat and he into the driver's seat.

"Cassandra, this is Amy. Amy, this is Cassandra."

Cassandra turned around and extended her hand and flashed her million-dollar smile.

"Hi Amy, nice to meet you," Cassandra said as she shook Amy's hand.

"Likewise," Amy said noticing how beautiful Cassandra was.

"We are heading to the Saddle Ranch and then to the game," Ryan said.

"Sounds good to me," Amy said as she started to text her friends about Cassandra.

Ryan merged into the street, somewhat relieved that Cassandra and Amy were getting along.

On arriving at the Saddle Ranch, Cassandra, Ryan, and Amy walked in and took seats at the bar. They immediately ordered drinks; Cassandra and Ryan opted for the bottomless mimosas and Amy chose beer. Amy and Ryan started talking about her roommate, John. Apparently, Amy was trying to be a good roommate to John, but John was not returning Amy's gestures. Cassandra sat there patiently and listened to her talk, wondering if Ryan and Amy had ever kissed. After listening, Cassandra decided to interject and become part of the conversation. Cassandra thought Amy seemed nice, and there was no threat to her at all. Not that anyone was much of a threat to Cassandra. As the conversation progressed as well as their alcohol intake, Ryan started paying more attention to Cassandra. Ryan was the kind of guy who always thought a lot and when he drank, he was able to put his thoughts to the side and let his feelings go. Amy soon noticed that Ryan was into Cassandra, *but who wouldn't be*, she thought. Cassandra was gorgeous. They all decided to stay at the restaurant to watch the game instead of going to the stadium. After countless mimosas, Cassandra started getting the itch to call Eugene. This always happened whenever she drank too much. They left the restaurant and decided to head over to the Barney's Beanery. When they got in the car, Cassandra without thinking dialed Eugene's number. It rang and rang, but he didn't pick up. *Typical Eugene*, she thought. She tried one more time because at this point Cassandra couldn't feel anything and anything was a go. Cassandra loved this feeling where nothing mattered. They all got into the car and drove to the next location.

While they were all sitting down in a booth ordering drinks, Cassandra decided to text Eugene about her birthday party. Cassandra's initial plan was not to invite to Eugene, but after numerous drinks everything usually changes.

Cassandra typed the message, "Hey, want to invite you to my birthday party on The Standard Rooftop, next Tuesday the 17th. Hope you can make it."

Eugene responded, "I am glad you sent me a text. I lost my phone last week and didn't have your number. I am going to Cabo San Lucas for Father's Day weekend, but I can definitely make it to the party."

Cassandra, annoyed and drunk, knew that Eugene was lying about losing his phone and replied, "You don't have to lie to about losing your phone. I understand that you don't want to be my friend."

At the local bar in Newport Beach, on Saturday afternoon, not fully cured from the previous night's hangover, Eugene looked at his phone and read

Cassandra's text message. "Why would I lie to her about my phone?" he said out loud. Cassandra always knew how to push his buttons and this was just another time of her doing so, but he wasn't in the mood for it.

Annoyed, he responded, "Why the hell would I have to lie to you about my phone? I lost it and that's the story." He slammed the phone down at the bar and took a swig of his drink. Why did Cassandra always have to get him mad? Granted he had always flaked out on Cassandra, but there was no reason not to believe him when he was telling the truth.

"What's wrong?" Brad said as he noticed Eugene was upset.

"Nothing, just dealing with something that is not important."

Eugene thought that sometimes it was too much to deal with Cassandra. Yes, he admired her sarcastic charm and unwillingness to give up on him, but some days he just wanted to be free from everyone.

Back at Barney's, Cassandra looked at the incoming text message from Eugene while Ryan and Amy played pool. *What a jerk*, Cassandra thought. *Why should I believe you? It's not like you haven't lied to me before.* She decided not to write another sarcastic message. Now, he was aware of Cassandra's birthday party and it was up to him to decide if he was going to attend. Cassandra quickly remembered her last birthday party and all the memories that came with it—Paris, her unexpected pregnancy, and everything else that tumbled afterward. How vivid the memories were to her as well as the pain she still felt. She quickly changed gears and started downing her vodka tonic. *Thank goodness for alcohol*, she thought.

Cassandra got up and joined Ryan and Amy at the pool table.

"Who were you texting?" Ryan asked surprised that he asked that question.

"No one important," Cassandra said.

"I am next, Ryan. Me and you at the pool table," Cassandra said looking intensely at him.

After they finished playing pool, Ryan contacted some of his friends in the Marina and everyone was heading to Cabo Cantina in Santa Monica. Instead of heading straight there, Ryan decided he wanted to stop at his old apartment in Marina Del Rey to pick up his mail. On the ride there, Amy passed out in the back seat and Cassandra was starting to black in and out. While driving to the Marina, Cassandra decided to call Julie.

Julie, sitting in the main airport on the big island in Hawaii waiting for her flight to LA, felt her phone vibrate. She looked at the phone, saw it was Cassandra, and quickly picked it up.

"Hello," Julie said excitedly.

"Hello, where are you?" Cassandra asked.

"At the airport on The Big Island waiting for my flight. What are you doing?"

"Ryan, Amy, and I are headed to Santa Monica. We just went to the Saddle Ranch and Barney's Beanery in Hollywood and drank way too much."

"Oh, how fun," Julie responded wishing she was there.

"Totally," Cassandra said.

"Oh, by the way, I have invited Eugene to my birthday party and Ryan invited us to Vegas next weekend."

"What?" Julie said shocked by all the information she was receiving.

"Did Ryan invite you and me to Vegas or just you?"

"He invited both of us silly. Why wouldn't he invite you?" Cassandra asked knowing that Ryan had only invited her.

"I am not sure, because he has not called me all week. Maybe he doesn't want me to come?"

"Oh, stop it, of course, he does."

"Is he next to you?"

"Yes, he is driving."

"Oh, can you tell him I will be back tonight?"

"Sure thing."

"Hey, did you want to go get a manicure and pedicure tomorrow morning?" Julie asked hoping Cassandra would say yes and she could head over to the apartment early in the morning to see Ryan.

"Sure, what time?"

"9:00 a.m."

"9:00 a.m.? That is too early. How about 10:30 a.m.?" Cassandra responded knowing it was going to be a long night ahead and she was going to be regretting all the drinking tomorrow morning.

"Okay."

"Great, have a safe flight and I will see you tomorrow morning."

"She is so into you," Cassandra said to Ryan as she hung up with Julie.

"No, she is not."

"Yes, she is. Julie can't wait to see you tomorrow."

"Please, I am not paying any attention to her."

Cassandra smiled to herself. *Of course, you are not. You are into me and no one can compare.*

They drove to the Marina and came upon Ryan's old apartment. Ryan, just wanting to check the mail, realized he needed to use the bathroom. He announced in the car that he was going to use the bathroom and both Amy and Cassandra decided that they too needed to use the bathroom. Not thinking too much about it, they all got out of the car and headed into Ryan's old apartment, thinking it was vacant. Making their way upstairs to Ryan's old room, he first used the bathroom and then left and Amy went next. As Cassandra was on the phone talking to an old friend, a woman approached her and asked, "Who are you?" Stunned by the appearance of this stranger, Cassandra did not want to say anything.

She yelled, "Amy we need to go."

Amy not realizing what was going on, was taking her time looking at herself in the mirror.

"Amy, we have to go," Cassandra said again.

"I was thinking, should I wear my hair up or down?" Amy asked Cassandra.

"Amy, the new tenants in the apartment are asking what we are doing here. We need to go now."

"What are you doing in here?" the woman asked again.

"Sorry, I thought my friend still lived here," Cassandra said running down the stairs.

"No, I live here now," the woman said angrily.

"Sorry," once again Cassandra said, continuing down the stairs with Amy right behind her.

They both ran out of the apartment and into Ryan's car.

"OMG, let's go," Cassandra said laughing. "The new tenants just saw us. I thought the place still had your old roommates."

"Apparently not," Ryan said laughing.

"I can't believe that just happened," Amy said laughing in the back seat.

"I know. I was trying to tell you that there was someone here and you kept talking about your hair," Cassandra said in between laughs.

"Oh my," Amy said. "Too much for one afternoon."

Everyone agreeing that they were hungry headed to Cabo Cantina to meet up with Ryan's friends.

It was early evening and the sun was starting to set along the beach in Santa Monica. While Ryan was driving on Ocean Blvd., Cassandra started looking at the sunset thinking how beautiful it was. Even though her thoughts were inhibited with alcohol, she still thought about Eugene and wondered what he was doing. Was he thinking about her?

Standing on the patio of the bar in Newport Beach, Eugene was looking at the same sunset as Cassandra, wondering if he would ever find his true love. Or had she already found him? Eugene didn't want to be alone anymore; he was ready to share his life with someone. He just didn't know where to begin or who to trust with his heart. He kept looking at the sunset, while different thoughts filled his head.

Julie's plane started approaching LA. She could see the sun setting on the horizon and admired the shades of red, orange, and yellow. Julie thought about the days to come with Ryan. Would he kiss her again? Ask her to be his girlfriend? She couldn't help smiling to herself about Ryan. He was the first guy in a long time whom she really liked and had let in. Granted it had only been a couple of days, but those days had been a whirlwind. She closed her eyes and thought about Ryan and their first kiss.

"What's up, Ryan?" Alice said in her husky voice as Ryan, Cassandra, and Amy walked into Cabo Cantina.

"Hey Alice, what's going on?"

"Nothing much, this is my friend Michelle. She's visiting from out of town."

"Hi Michele, Alice, this is Cassandra," Ryan said.

"Hi Cassandra," Alice said remembering what Amy had said in her text message earlier that day. *Ryan definitely has hooked up with this girl,* Alice thought.

"Hi Alice," Cassandra said politely.

"Okay, it's two for one margarita," the young waitress said.

Everyone looked at each other and nodded in agreement about ordering margaritas.

"Margaritas for everyone," Alice said.

"Salt or no salt," the waitress asked.

"Everyone," Alice said. "Salt."

The waitress smiled and left menus on the table.

"Be back with the drinks."

Soon after, Alex walked into the restaurant and said hi to Ryan, Amy, and Alice. Surprised to see Cassandra seated behind Ryan, he greeted her as well. Alex took the seat next to Cassandra.

"Hey Cassandra, how are you?" Alex said.

"Good, how about you?"

"Hanging in there."

"That's good," Cassandra said noticing some tension from him.

"How is the roommate thing going between you and Ryan?"

"Great so far; it's only been a week, ask me when more time has passed," Cassandra said with a laugh.

Not knowing what else to say, Cassandra started talking about Julie and her obsession with Ryan. It was not the right topic of conversation, but Cassandra had started drinking one of the margaritas in addition to everything she had already had earlier. Alex was surprised to hear her speak about Julie and how much Julie liked Ryan, leading him to believe that Cassandra was into Ryan. *How weird,* he thought. Instead of saying anything, he stood quietly and listened. He couldn't wait to tell Eric everything he had heard.

Cassandra, knowing that Eric and Alex were best friends, continued talking about Julie and Ryan. Having heard herself talk too much, she stopped and started paying attention to Ryan.

Quickly, Alex took his phone out and texted Eric, "I came to hang out with Ryan and found Cassandra here as well. You wouldn't believe the words that came out of Cassandra regarding Ryan. Good thing you never called her back. Tell you more later!"

Cassandra glanced over in Alex's direction and noticed him quickly typing away on his phone. She knew that he was sending Eric a message and smiled to herself.

This particular Saturday night, Eric was at home with kids. It was his weekend to have them and he chose to be at home with them. He and his daughter were sitting on the couch watching TV, while his son was at the computer. Eric heard his phone beep once, indicating a text message. He contemplated looking at his phone. He was in one of those moods where he did not want to be bothered. Regardless, he decided to look at his phone. There was a message from Alex. He read the message and looked annoyed. Why was he telling him about Cassandra? Eric had decided that he didn't want anything to do with Cassandra.

Now, Alex had just opened a whole new can of worms, and Eric did not want to be bothered with it. He knew that Ryan had moved in with Cassandra, but now they were hanging out as well.

Wait, why did he care?

He tried paying attention to the TV, but now was consumed with questions about Alex's text message.

What did Cassandra say to Alex about Ryan?

Was Cassandra really into Ryan?

How could she have done this to him? He never should have kissed Cassandra. Now he was angry. The last thing he was going to do was lose to Ryan.

Ryan started grabbing Cassandra's thigh under the table. Cassandra looked at him with glassy eyes. She was on her third margarita and he on his fourth beer. Neither had eaten much since that morning. Ryan was now in a state of confusion, but all he wanted to do was kiss Cassandra. While everyone was busy, engaged in their own conversation, Ryan grabbed Cassandra's hand and said, "Let's go."

She followed him out of the restaurant. As soon as they were outside, Ryan immediately kissed Cassandra. Not refusing, she returned his passionate kiss. Cassandra loved the way Ryan kissed and could have stood there all night. Coming up for air, he grabbed her hand and they started walking toward the parking garage.

"Do you remember what floor we parked on?" Ryan asked.

"Not really. I don't even remember what parking garage we parked in," Cassandra said slurring.

"We can just press the button for the car alarm to see if it's in there."

They walked to two different parking garages and didn't find anything. Walking through one alleyway to the next garage, Ryan grabbed Cassandra and pushed her against the wall and started kissing her. Not resisting his kisses, she felt his hand brush against her nipples and then up her skirt through her underwear. He felt her wetness and instantly grew hard. Cassandra not thinking twice grabbed his waistband and undid the button, pulling down the zipper and exposing his hard-on. Unable to resist her and remembering how wonderful the first time felt, he picked her up and put her legs around him and entered her with force, not caring that there was no condom involved.

"Oh Cassandra, you feel so good," Ryan gasped.

"Ryan," Cassandra moaned.

He went in and out of Cassandra hard and fast for a couple of minutes. Then, no longer being able to hold it, he pulled out and released himself. Out of breath, Cassandra unwrapped her legs from his waist. They both stood next to each other, trying to catching their breaths.

"That was great," Ryan said kissing her on the lips.

"It was," Cassandra said thinking that she was indeed falling for him.

He gave her one more kiss and put his pants back on. Realizing for the first time that he was in public, he asked, "Do you think anyone saw us?"

"I don't think so," Cassandra said with a laugh.

Both, high on alcohol and sex, stumbled to the next parking garage where they were able to find Ryan's car.

"Can you drive?" he asked Cassandra.

"I think so."

"Good, because I can't"

Cassandra laughed, took the keys, and got into the driver's seat. She pulled out of the garage and headed to her apartment. She had to drive on the highway with caution because she was extremely intoxicated, and Ryan had passed out in the passenger seat. Somehow she made it home, woke him up, and passed out on the bed as soon as they entered the apartment.

Alex, wondering where Ryan and Cassandra were, went to ask Amy and Alice.

"Hey, do you know where Ryan and Cassandra went?"

Both Amy and Alice shrugged.

"Not sure," Alice said, wondering the same.

"I think I saw them go outside but they haven't been back since."

Alex decided to call Ryan, but his phone just kept ringing until the voice-mail picked up. He left Ryan a voicemail, "Hey man, where are you? Are you skipping out on the bill? Call me back?"

Alex tried his cell phone a couple more times and then gave up.

Back in the apartment, Ryan's phone rang, echoing in the apartment. Cassandra and Ryan were both soundly asleep.

Julie, excited, woke up early on Sunday morning. She looked at her alarm clock and snuggled under her covers. It was 8:00 a.m. Time to start getting ready to see Ryan. *What should I wear?* Julie always decided on a pair of jeans and a black shirt. Still sleepy, she got out of bed and proceed to the bathroom. Julie looked at herself in the mirror. *I am pretty*, she thought, *but is that why Ryan likes me?*

Chapter 14

*D*azed and confused, Ryan woke up early on Sunday morning. It took him a second to realize what had happened the previous night between him and Cassandra. *Did I actually have sex in the middle of an alleyway?* He was not sure if he had dreamt it or not, but the jackhammer pounding in his head was an indication that indeed it had taken place. He looked over at Cassandra more confused than ever. He had promised himself in the beginning that he would not fall in love with Cassandra, but given the circumstances, there was nothing he could do. The heart wants what the heart wants, and he was in love with her. She was sexy, fun, carefree, and emotionally unattached. If anything, he didn't need anyone clinging on to him, creating something more than it was. He wasn't sure what was to be done at this point. He couldn't just leave or pull himself away from her. They lived together, and it would be hard to try to be cold and distant to her. Ryan would just have to start paying more attention to the other girls he was dating and start spending nights at their places. He smiled to himself thinking about the great time he had with Cassandra. If ever, having sex with her was something he had never experienced. Cassandra indeed was a great lover. As much as he tried to resist, he rolled over and hugged Cassandra. He might as well enjoy her as much as he could.

Cassandra felt Ryan's arm around her and she cuddled with him. She also started remembering the previous night and laughed to herself. She turned over and faced Ryan.

"I can't believe we did that last night."

"I know," he responded. "But it was fun."

"Yes, it was."

"I have to check my phone and see if Alex or Amy called me," Ryan said getting up from the bed.

"I am sure, since we didn't go back. They must be mad about the bill."

"I have over twenty missed calls and five voicemails!" Ryan said shocked.

"Really, what did they say?" Cassandra said as she sat on the bed.

"Four are from Alex and one from Amy asking where did we go," Ryan said laughing.

Ryan walked back into bed and lay down with Cassandra in his arms.

"I can't believe we left without saying goodbye."

"I know. I hope they are not mad at you?"

"No, Amy said that the guy who likes her paid the entire bill."

"What? Serious? Whoa, he must really like her!"

"Yeah," Ryan said.

He then turned over and started kissing Cassandra. He couldn't resist not kissing her and soon he found himself inside of Cassandra, enjoying every minute of it. There was a force that drew him to her that he could not explain. As he was moving back and forth inside of Cassandra, they heard a knock at the door. They looked at each other, having forgotten that Julie was going to come by early that morning. They both laughed and hoped that they weren't making loud moaning sounds that she might have heard.

"I don't want to stop," Ryan said kissing Cassandra.

"Me neither, but we can't stay like this."

Ryan, realizing he had to get off of Cassandra, enjoyed his last second in her and got up. Suddenly, Ryan's cell phone rang.

"It's Julie," Ryan said in a whisper. He ignored the call and then Cassandra's cell phone rang. "Julie," Cassandra mouthed in case Julie could hear them.

Outside Cassandra's apartment, Julie heard shuffling sounds when she arrived at the door. Not paying too much attention to the noises, she started knocking on the door, expecting Cassandra to answer the door immediately. It was past 10:00 a.m., the time they had agreed to meet. Julie had been out there for at least a minute and decided to call Ryan's cell phone first. She could hear Ryan's cell phone ring through the door and then go silent. Next, she decided to call Cassandra and she could also hear her phone ring too. Julie wondered if they were still asleep. Not knowing what to do, she knocked on the door again— this time she knocked harder.

"She is not going to go away, Ryan," Cassandra said.

"I know. I am going to jump in the shower and then you can open the door."

"Okay," Cassandra said somewhat disappointed that their morning had been cut short and now she had to deal with Julie. Ryan walked slowly to the bathroom trying not to making a lot of noise. Once Ryan was in the shower, Cassandra got up and adjusted her clothes and made her way to the door.

Cassandra carefully opened the door, acting like she had just woken up.

"Hello Julie," Cassandra said in a sleepy voice.

Julie, somewhat frustrated that she had been waiting, said,

"Hey, I have been knocking and called you and Ryan."

"I just saw you called. I thought I was dreaming when I heard the knock on the door and my phone ringing," Cassandra said as she let Julie in.

"It was my turn to sleep on the couch and didn't realize what was happening, but it's good to see you," Cassandra said as she gave Julie a hug.

"Where's Ryan?" Julie asked.

"In the shower. He must have gotten in while I was sleeping."

Cassandra forgot about Ryan's silk sheet she had placed on her bed. She hoped Julie wouldn't notice. "Wow, there is a lot of stuff here," Julie said.

"I know, this is all of Ryan's crap. I don't know what to do with it. I am thinking of putting some stuff in storage."

"Yeah, you should," Julie said sitting down on the couch. She didn't want to say anything. She felt that something wasn't right but chose to ignore it.

In the shower, Ryan was wondering what he was doing. Things were not the way they were supposed to be. Everything was just out of control. There was something that people didn't know about Ryan; he wanted to have a wife and kids more than anything else. He had grown up in a broken home where he never knew what it meant to be a family. He wanted at least four kids and a dog—the complete storybook family. It was what he craved the most. Ryan hated being with different women and playing the field while his heart still felt the pain from the ex-girlfriend who had left him. He let the hot water hit his face, and then decided to step outside and face the music.

Ryan walked out, a towel around his waist, and saw Julie. He knew he needed to act surprised.

"Julie!" he exclaimed, "How are you? I've missed you!" He did not believe the words he was saying.

Excited to see Ryan, Julie jumped up from the couch and walked over to give him a hug, saying, "Hi stranger, it's good to see you."

Ryan gave Julie a hug and knew he wanted to get out of there.

Cassandra was wondering why the hell Ryan came out of the bathroom in a towel. *Is he trying to prove something?*

Cassandra shrugged and decided that today was going to be a long day. Ryan walked toward the dresser to get a change of clothes and went back to the bathroom. Cassandra started texting Elizabeth about what was taking place.

Julie sat back down on the couch. "He comes out in his towel? What was that about?" "I don't know," Cassandra said shrugging not really listening to Julie and wondering what Eugene was doing right now or more like *who* he was doing.

After dressing up, Ryan came out of the bathroom and sat down next to Julie.

"How was your trip?"

"It was good and relaxing," Julie said, really wanting to say *it was good, but better if you were there*, but decided to keep her thought to herself. In the meantime, Cassandra was in the shower wondering what Ryan and Julie were talking about. She started to feel jealous now that Julie was back. Was she being territorial? She couldn't be. Ryan was just someone to pass time with so she would not feel lonely. She rushed through her shower and threw on a dress. She didn't want to leave Ryan and Julie by themselves for too much time. Once Cassandra was done, she came out and noticed that Julie had downed a Jack and Coke and Ryan had had a beer.

"So, what are we doing today?' Cassandra asked everyone not sure what to think anymore.

"I am not sure, but I am hungry. Did you girls want to go eat?" Ryan asked hoping they both would say they had other plans.

"I am hungry. I really didn't eat since yesterday," Cassandra started to say but decided not to continue because she remembered what had taken place between her and Ryan in Santa Monica.

"I am hungry, and this Jack and Coke is making me even hungrier," Julie replied.

"I am actually in the mood for Applebee's," Ryan said. "I know it's random, but I remembered it from the commercial I just saw."

"I know where there is one," Julie announced.

"Well, let's go!" Ryan exclaimed.

"Well, I have no choice in this matter," Cassandra whispered to herself.

Cassandra, Julie, and Ryan left the apartment and headed to his car. Since he was driving, Julie declared that she would sit in the passenger seat and Cassandra in the back. *How did I get to the back when I was in the passenger seat with Ryan last night?* Cassandra thought to herself. Cassandra knew that she had to revert to the old person she was used to being, someone who did not have feelings, but how could she, when she was falling for Ryan.

On arriving at the restaurant, Julie and Ryan sat on one side of the booth and Cassandra on the other side by herself. She decided on ordering the biggest size of beer available because she knew that it was going to be a long day and didn't care that it was only 11:00 a.m.

"Miller Lite draft large size, please," Cassandra ordered.

"Sure thing," said the waitress. "And you for you two, what will it be?"

"Margarita on the rocks with salt," Julie said.

"Blue Castle for me," Ryan said.

"I'll be back with your drinks."

The waitress left and Julie looked at Ryan and then at Cassandra. "I can't believe we are drinking this early," Julie said

"I know, I am not even over last night's hangover," Cassandra said looking at Ryan thinking not less than twelve hours ago they were having sex in an alleyway in Santa Monica.

"You are hungover?" Ryan asked as if he had not been with Cassandra the night before.

She decided to ignore his comment and looked at Julie.

"So, Hawaii. Tell me about it," Cassandra said and soon remembered the moments of when she and Eugene were supposed to have headed to Maui earlier that year. Why couldn't she get him off of her mind? Will she ever be able to?

"Hawaii was great!" Julie announced. "The weather was amazing, and the sunsets were incredible. Have you ever been to Hawaii, Ryan?"

"No, I haven't yet, but plan to soon. I have a friend who goes every three months," Ryan said referring to the friend as a woman he was currently seeing.

"You should go sometime. It's breathtaking!" Julie said.

"Are you guys ready to place your order?" the waitress said as she put down their drinks.

"Guys, ready to order?" Cassandra asked.

After placing their orders, the conversation continued between the three of them with Julie and Ryan doing most of the talking. Cassandra sat back and did not say much. She was observing Ryan and Julie. Did he really like Julie? Or was she imagining it? Unsure what to think anymore, she decided on drinking more beer. She knew it was the only to deal with this situation. Cassandra realized more and more that she was reverting to alcohol as her drug of choice in dealing with situations that were hard. *Well, it's better than doing actual drugs*, she thought to herself.

Suddenly while Cassandra was having a conversation in her head, she heard Ryan ask Julie if she was a virgin.

"Okay, so are you a virgin?" Ryan asked Julie out of the blue.

Julie, shocked, did not know how to answer the question. "Of course, I'm not a virgin! Why would you think that?"

"I am not sure . . . because you act like a prude sometimes," Ryan said thinking back to the first time he had tried to kiss her, and she had refused.

"Well, I am not a prude. Sorry, I am not jumping on you to kiss you like the other girls," Julie said.

"I was just curious because I really thought you were one," Ryan concluded.

Julie thought to herself. She had actually slept with three other men before, so she was definitely not a virgin.

"OMG Ryan, why would you ask that?" Cassandra said acting surprised and knowing that Ryan was going to ask that question.

When they had been seated earlier, Julie had gone to the restroom and Ryan and Cassandra had discussed about Julie.

"Do you think Julie is a virgin?" Ryan had asked Cassandra.

"I am not sure. Why do you care?" Cassandra had asked.

"I don't know. Whenever I try to kiss her, she pushes me away."

"So, then you like her?" she had asked.

"I am not sure, Maybe." Ryan had said to intentionally hurt Cassandra's feelings.

Cassandra, trying not to look hurt, had responded, "Well, then you should ask her if she's a virgin and if she responds no, then maybe she just doesn't like you."

"I will ask her and let's see what she says."

Cassandra, being the one to set up and start this game, was growing tired of it real quick. Was she falling for Ryan or was he just a distraction to help her get to the next part of her life? They had stopped the conversation when Ryan had spotted Julie returning from the restroom.

Julie, still shocked, from Ryan's questions, decided not to give in to him and act as if everything was okay. When they were done eating, Ryan asked, "Should we go see a movie?"

"What movie would you like to see?" Cassandra asked, thinking about how much she was starting to hate Ryan.

"I am not sure what is playing. There's a movie theater next door. We should check out the movie schedule.

"I have a better idea. Why don't we go play golf instead?" Cassandra suggested.

"Really? And you know how to play golf?" Ryan asked

"Of course, I used to play in the summers back East," Cassandra said remembering the summers in the New York where she would pretend to need help playing golf only to flirt with the instructors.

"And how good are you?" Ryan asked.

"Not that good, I am sure you can beat me," Cassandra said knowing that she was better than most guys out on the golf course: Cassandra had been playing since she was three.

"There is a golf course a couple minutes away from here," Julie interjected, feeling left out from the conversation and never having played golf.

"Great, let's go!" Ryan said looking at Cassandra with a glimmer in his eye.

At the driving range, Julie kept flirting with Ryan and Cassandra tried to ignore them both.

"I don't know how to hit the ball," Julie said.

"Let me teach you," Ryan said as he went behind Julie, putting his arms around her and his hand on top of hers.

"Thank you," Julie said enjoying every minute of it.

"This is how you stand, bring your feet closer to the ball, your shoulders together, and take a swing at the ball," Ryan instructed.

Cassandra looked at Ryan, wondering what he was doing. Maybe he did really like Julie, but Cassandra knew she couldn't lose, not to someone like Julie.

"Your turn, Cassandra," Ryan said.

"Let me teach how a real pro plays golf," Cassandra said as she brushed past him.

She took her place and prepared herself and took a swing at the ball and it went flying hitting the four-hundred-yard mark.

"Impressive," Ryan said not knowing that Cassandra did indeed know how to play.

Cassandra, proud of herself, remembered the summers when her father would teach her how to play golf. "If you master the game of playing golf, you can have any man's heart," she remembered her father's words. Cassandra smiled at herself and threw the golf club at Ryan, "Beat that," Cassandra said. Ryan, even more attracted to Cassandra, thought how dangerous she was now that he knew that Cassandra did, in fact, possess what every man wanted.

"I am not sure if I am getting the hang of this," Julie said looking at Ryan hoping that he would come over and help her.

"You are doing well," Ryan said as he sat down, not wanting to get up and help Julie again.

Cassandra looked over at Ryan and saw him smiling at her. She chose to look at Julie trying to hit the ball. *Why is he trying to be nice now?* Cassandra thought.

After Julie missed a couple of times, she came over to where Cassandra and Ryan were sitting, "Do either of you want a drink?"

"Sounds like a good idea," Cassandra said noticing that she was coming off her high.

"I would like a beer," Ryan said.

"Okay, I'll get one for you, and Cassandra what would you like?"

"A beer too, Miller Lite," Cassandra said thinking back to when she had started liking Miller Lite. Her brother was dating a girl from Michigan and Miller Lite is the beer for the Midwest.

"Okay, I'll be back," Julie said.

Julie left and walked to the bar on the other side of the golf course.

"I didn't know you were so good at golf," Ryan said.

"You never asked," Cassandra said as she was getting ready to take a swing.

"I guess you surprise me more and more," Ryan said as the sun hit his face making his brown eyes glimmer and making him more handsome and desirable.

Julie returned with the drinks, excited to get back to Ryan. *Maybe he will hold me again and try to kiss me?* Julie thought to herself. She found Cassandra hitting the ball and Ryan watching.

"Here are your beers," Julie said to Ryan and Cassandra.

"Thanks," Ryan and Cassandra said in unison.

"Cheers to Sunday," Cassandra said.

"Cheers," Ryan and Julie responded.

After they all took a sip of their drinks, Cassandra said, "Okay, let's make a bet and see who can hit the ball the furthest."

Alex picked up his cell phone as he just received a text from Ryan: "Ready for Vegas this weekend?"

"Definitely, I am still waiting on Eric's response to see if he's going," Alex responded.

"Okay, let me know. I need a break and need to get away from LA for a couple of days," Ryan replied.

Alex wondered what Ryan was up to that he needed a break.

"I knew I should have bet more money," Cassandra said.

"You just got lucky," Ryan said.

"Yeah right, there is no such thing as luck. Luck is when opportunity and preparation meet," Cassandra said remembering the quote from some movie she had watched.

"Right, whatever you say," Ryan said, a bit agitated. Like Cassandra, he hated losing.

"Pay up," Cassandra said.

"How about double or nothing?" Ryan said. "If you can get into the bucket that's in the middle of the range. Are you in or out?"

"I am in," Cassandra said, confident.

Julie sat in the chair and observed Cassandra and Ryan interact. She wondered if there was anything going on between them. She knew that Cassandra would never do anything to her and Ryan had told her that Cassandra was not his type. She smiled to herself thinking how he really liked her; she could already picture the holidays together.

"I hope you have cash," Cassandra said as she took her first swing.

Cassandra, upset that she missed the first opportunity, hit the turf with the club.

"Your turn," Cassandra said.

"Please pay attention to someone who truly knows how to play golf," Ryan said with his killer smile. He too missed his first opportunity.

"Right, when did you start playing golf?" Cassandra asked sarcastically.

Ryan just looked at her and handed her the golf club. Cassandra, knowing that this was going to be the winning swing, got in position and with all her energy hit the ball that went right into the bucket.

"Yes!" Cassandra said out aloud. "I told you! Pay up, please."

"You were just lucky," Ryan said.

"I was born lucky," Cassandra said

"Wow, I can't believe you made it," Julie said standing up and joining them.

"I know, that was awesome!" Cassandra said, still shocked by the play.

"Well, I think I have had enough golf for one day. What do you think about watching the Lakers playoff game?" Ryan asked.

"Sure, where do you recommended?" Cassandra asked.

"Let me call Alex and ask him where he thinks is a good place to go," Ryan said.

"Hey man, how's it going?" Alex was lying on his couch watching TV.

"I just finished playing golf with Cassandra and Julie and we are going to watch the Lakers game. Do you want to come?"

"Ah, Cassandra and Julie! How's that going?"

"I don't want to get into right now."

"So, it's going good huh? Wish I was that lucky having two girls after me."

"Not even like that. Do you want to come or what?"

"Where are you guys heading to?" Alex asked with no intention of leaving his couch today.

"That is why I was calling you, to ask you where we should go."

"How about City Walk? They have a lot of good places there."

"Sounds good to me."

"I will call you once we get there to let you know what restaurant we are at."

"Sounds good, stay out of trouble."

"Right, you know me. Bye."

Ryan hung up the phone thinking about what Alex had just said and smiled to himself.

"Let's head to City Walk at Universal to watch the game."

"Great," Cassandra said.

"Sounds good to me too," Julie said.

They all piled into Ryan's car and drove to City Walk. Cassandra was thinking how bad this day was going, especially the fact that Ryan was paying attention to Julie. Julie was thinking of how great it was to be back and be with Ryan. *Can life be any better?*

All three were seated at the bar at Jillian's watching the Lakers game; Ryan was in the middle with Cassandra and Julie on either side of him.

"This seems like a great place," Cassandra said wondering how this night was going to turn out.

"Have you been here before?" Ryan asked.

"No, not at all."

"I like this place too," Julie interjected, trying to steal the attention from Cassandra.

"What are we drinking?" she asked after getting no response for her earlier statement.

"Okay, guys," said the handsome bartender, "What's it going to be?"

After drinks were ordered, they all sat watching the game and started making bets on who was going to win. Ryan, after drinking his fourth beer, was now leaning toward Cassandra. He wanted to grab and hug her, but knew it was not possible because of Julie. He needed Julie to stay on his good side. Instead, he decided to keep grabbing Cassandra's thighs.

"Ryan, please stop grabbing me. Julie is going to start to notice something."

"What? We are roommates and I am just being nice."

Ryan, hurt, started paying attention to Julie. She, of course, loved the attention and knew he was into her. Cassandra noticed that he was giving Julie attention now and she started to get jealous. Then she thought to herself: *Why should I care?* It was more about winning and Cassandra never liked to lose. That was a big problem with Cassandra. Losing was not part of her vocabulary and she would go to great lengths to make sure she didn't lose. She started remembering her conquest in New York and decided that those memories should be left as memories. Cassandra had lost big in New York by risking everything, but to her, a true risk would be not betting at all.

"I have to go the restroom," Julie stated.

Once Julie left, it was Ryan and Cassandra. "So you like Julie or what?" Cassandra asked, already knowing the answer, but she just enjoyed teasing Ryan.

"I am not sure," Ryan said answering the question with some truth.

"Well, you know that she is into you and likes you a lot. Maybe too much," said Cassandra knowing that she had to continue throwing in the fact that Julie may like Ryan a little bit too much too quickly.

"Well, I am not ready to be in any type of relationship, and I'm dating other girls."

"Then you need to tell her that because she thinks that you like her and by hanging out with her, she thinks she is your girlfriend."

"Yeah right!" Ryan said not really wanting to believe Cassandra.

"I'm telling you the truth. Why would I lie to you? We are roomies."

Maybe she's telling the truth. Why would Cassandra lie to me when I know she has feelings for me? he thought.

"Did I miss anything?" Julie said as she approached the bar.

"Nothing much," Cassandra said, wishing somehow she could get rid of her jealousy.

After the game was done, they decided to go upstairs for bowling.

"How about we make a bet and see who bowls the better score?" Ryan said knowing that he would be the better bowler.

"Sure, why not," Cassandra said, knowing that this was going to drag on longer than expected.

"That will be fun," Julie said, knowing that any extra time hanging out with Ryan was always great.

They all got their bowling shoes and bowling balls and decided on a $20 bet for the winner. Ryan knew he had it in the bag. They took turns bowling: Ryan first, Cassandra next, and then Julie. When it was Cassandra's turn, she took the ball and threw it with all her strength and managed to get a strike. When she turned around excitedly, Ryan was kissing Julie. Shocked, Cassandra did not know how to react and turned back to look at the lane. *What the hell*, she thought. She felt a mixture of hurt and jealousy. She didn't know how long to wait before she could turn around again. This time, she waited and right when she was about to turn, Ryan yelled, "Awesome strike!" She turned around with the fakest smile, "Isn't it great? I think I might win."

"Maybe," Ryan said brushing past Cassandra, because it was his turn to bowl. As he took his place ready to bowl, Julie went up to Cassandra.

"Did you see Ryan kiss me?" Julie asked giggling like a schoolgirl.

 "No, I didn't. I must have been bowling when it happened," Cassandra said trying to hide the jealousy from her face.

"It was great. He held me and kissed me; I think he's starting to change his feelings toward me. Maybe I will become his girlfriend soon."

"Yes," Cassandra said, thinking of a way to make sure that didn't happen.

"Damn," Cassandra heard Ryan said. He was only able to knock down half the pins.

"Better luck next time. It's your turn, Julie."

Julie happily took the ball and approached the lane. She thought she could ask Ryan to help her. "Ryan," Julie said, "Is it possible to teach me how to bowl correctly?"

Cassandra was amazed—more embarrassed for Julie and the idiotic question she had just asked.

Ryan, reluctant to help her, knew he had to because he had just kissed her.

"Sure," Ryan said, not being sure of anything at this point.

Cassandra watched as he walked over to Julie and showed her how to hold the ball and throw it down the lane. Julie looked happy as he showed her the technique. Unimpressed, Cassandra knew that she would have to work harder.

For the rest of the evening, while bowling, Ryan and Julie would exchange kisses and hugs as each would get a great score. Cassandra, like a trooper, took the sidelines and watched them interact. Finally, the game was done and they all headed over to Howl at the Moon for more drinks. Each one, more drunk than the next, stumbled toward the bar. Sunday night was the best night at this bar. On entering the bar, it was crowded, noisy, and high on energy.

They walked up to the bar and Julie placed the order for their drinks. Since it was Sunday, drinks were two for one. "Awesome," Julie told the bartender. Julie picked the chips for their free drinks.

They all stood against the bar: Julie and Ryan close together and Cassandra next to Julie thinking how quickly she could drink her drink in order to get another one. Ryan, now uninhibited with the alcohol, started flirting with the other girls that were near him. Julie noticed this and started to get mad.

"What is he doing?" Julie whispered to Cassandra trying not to let Ryan notice.

"I guess he's talking to other girls," Cassandra said with a smile. Cassandra did not care that Ryan was talking to other girls as long as it wasn't Julie. Now, Julie was the one who was upset.

Which of course made Cassandra intensely happy.

Ryan, not sure what he was doing, spotted a group of young girls that were pretty.

"Hi, what are you going doing here? Celebrating a birthday tonight?" Ryan asked.

"No, one of my friends is visiting me from out of town," said the girl with the short blonde hair and sparkling blue eyes.

Ryan immediately took a liking to her.

"And where is your friend from?" Ryan asked

"From Minnesota."

"Minnesota. And how are you liking it here in CA?"

"I like it. I live in Santa Monica."

Cassandra approached Ryan while he was talking to the girls. "Julie wants to leave. She's had enough to drink. Frankly, she is upset that you are talking to those girls."

"Why is she upset? It's not like we're together."

"I told you that she's started thinking you guys are together, but of course you don't listen to me."

"Maybe I should start listening to you," Ryan said.

"Right. Anyway, I want to go to; it's getting late." Ryan looked at his watch.

From far away, Julie was watching Ryan and Cassandra interact. How easy it was for Ryan to listen to Cassandra and do as she said. Julie knew nothing could happen between them because they were just friends.

Cassandra didn't know why she worried so much when she knew that at the end of the night, Ryan was going home with her. They both walked toward Julie who had a look of annoyance on her face. "What's wrong?" Ryan asked her.

"Nothing," Julie said with an attitude, putting her drink down at the bar. "I want to go home."

"Well, let's go," Ryan said trying to reach for Julie's hand as she pulled away.

"Okay." He shrugged. They all started walking out of the bar. Ryan tried giving Julie a hug, but she was upset and kept pulling away.

"Julie, why are you mad at me?" Ryan asked casually.

"No reason; I am just tired and want to go home."

"We are going home, don't worry."

They all reached the car and Julie knew that Ryan was in no condition to drive. "Give me your car keys," Julie told Ryan.

"For what? I am going to drive."

"There is no way you are driving. You can't even walk straight."

"Of course, I can," Ryan said.

Cassandra just looked at the two bickering. Finally, Ryan gave in and handed the keys to Julie. Julie happily took the keys and got into the driver's seat.

I can't believe I am driving his car, Julie thought to herself, *he must really like me.*

Julie headed on the 101 South toward downtown LA. Cassandra, in the back, just thought about reaching home and getting done with this day. *Boy, am I going to have a story to tell Elizabeth tomorrow!* Julie headed into the parking garage and parked the car. Ryan and Cassandra immediately got out, Cassandra quicker than Ryan because she just wanted to get home. Julie locked the car and gave Ryan his keys. Julie was waiting for some kind of hug, but instead Ryan put his hand up for a high five. Shocked, Julie returned the high five and walked toward her car. She was expecting Ryan to follow her to her car to give her a proper goodnight, but instead Ryan walked with Cassandra toward the elevator. "Julie, I will see you tomorrow," Cassandra said walking with Ryan. "Okay," Julie called out.

Ryan and Cassandra got into the elevator, onto Wilshire Blvd., and then toward their apartment. "What a night," Cassandra said.

"It was fun," Ryan said still drunk. Cassandra laughed and grabbed Ryan's hand as they walked toward the apartment.

Julie got into her car, confused by the whole situation. Upset, she drove home. She wasn't going to cry, she told herself, but she couldn't help it. Tears were rolling down her cheeks before she even approached the highway. Why did Ryan act hot one second and then cold the next? She couldn't take his ups and downs. She just wanted to be with him.

Cassandra and Ryan entered the apartment, and he immediately took her into his arms and kissed her long and hard. He knew that it was the alcohol that made him act this way. Cassandra, not refusing his kisses, enjoyed every minute of it. They both threw themselves on the bed and let passion take over. Soon after, they were both in each other's arms fast asleep.

Chapter 15

"Tell me, how was your weekend? Aren't you happy to have Julie back?" Elizabeth said, smirking to Cassandra.

"Thrilled to have her back," Cassandra replied sarcastically.

"Did you tell her that Ryan and you have already had sex?" Elizabeth questioned.

"Um, no, why would I tell her that?"

"Because she should know! Wouldn't you want to know?"

"It's better that she doesn't know. I don't want her to get hurt," Cassandra said knowing that she didn't mean it at all.

"Right, if you didn't want her to get hurt, you would have never had sex with Ryan."

Maybe Elizabeth was right, but the connection was there with Ryan and her. Then she thought she really didn't care about Julie's feelings anyway.

"Whatever the case may be, I have bigger things to worry about. My birthday party is next week, and I have to send out invitations today."

"Okay, but I think you should still tell her."

As Cassandra wrote out her guest list, she thought about Julie and Ryan and if Cassandra really told Julie, would things change? Would Ryan still live with her? Cassandra decided to keep her thoughts focused on her invitations.

"Are you still leaving for Vegas on Thursday?" Cassandra asked, sprawled out on the bed. Ryan had just arrived from work and was changing into his outfit to play softball.

"Yes, I am seeing a couple of buddies and play in the poker tournament."

"Should be fun," Cassandra said thinking about how going to Vegas could be fun. "Don't forget about my birthday party on Tuesday; it's going to be fun."

"Of course not, how would I ever forget?" Ryan said as he gave Cassandra a kiss on the forehead.

"I have to run or I'll be late for my softball game."

"Okay," Cassandra said as she lay on the bed thinking of what to do next. Soon she received a text message.

"We are at the Library Bar," said her friend Michele.

That should be fun, Cassandra thought to herself. She decided to get dressed and head to the Library Bar.

On arriving at the Library Bar, Cassandra called Julie to join her. "Hey, I'm at the Library Bar, come join me!"

Julie replied, "On my way, let me just finish up and I will head over."

"Okay," Cassandra said and hung up.

Cassandra sat down with Michele and her friends. They were all drinking and talking.

"How are things going?" Michele asked.

"Okay, for now," Cassandra replied rolling her eyes.

Michele laughed slightly and continued drinking.

As Cassandra was listening to the conversations around her, she thought of an idea. Maybe she could convince Julie to go to Vegas? Julie would totally fall for the bait that Ryan would love to see her there. Cassandra made a plan in her head and waited for Julie to arrive.

Julie walked in and spotted Cassandra. She thought to herself that Cassandra always looked pretty no matter what. She saw an empty chair and sat down across from Cassandra.

Cassandra smiled to herself and put her plan into action.

"Hi Michele," Julie said.

"Hey girl, how is it going?"

Julie sighed, "Well, you know the banking industry, it never stops. I am going to get a drink; does anyone want anything?"

"I will take another vodka tonic," Cassandra said.

Julie got up and headed to the bar.

"When was the last time you went to Vegas?" Cassandra asked Michele.

"I was just there a couple of months ago with some girlfriends. I don't remember what happened half of the trip," Michele said laughing.

"I am sure you don't."

Julie returned with the drinks.

"What are you guys talking about?" Julie asked

"I was just asking Michele when was the last time she was in Vegas."

"Oh, Vegas. I love Vegas," Julie replied.

"I have an idea. We should fly to Vegas this weekend. We can leave Saturday morning and fly into Vegas, get some lunch, go shopping for a dress, party all night, have some brunch Sunday morning and then head back. What do you think?" Cassandra said.

"That sounds great," Michele said before Julie could reply.

"Isn't Ryan going to Vegas this weekend?" Julie asked.

"Yes, but he doesn't own Vegas; we can go too. Plus like I said, I need a dress for my birthday party. And if we run into him, we do. I think it will be a great surprise for Ryan. I won't say anything until we land in Vegas Saturday morning and then you can call him."

"Are you sure he won't mind us going to Vegas?" Julie said with a worried look.

"No, not at all. If anything, Ryan would be surprised. And then we can hang out with him and gamble. I mean come on, how many times are you going to be able to hang out with Ryan in Vegas?" Cassandra said excitedly.

"I would go if I were you Julie. It sounds fun." Michele interjected.

"Okay. I am in." Julie said. "I will look into the flights."

"Perfect," Cassandra said with a smile.

Cassandra thought to herself, *this was easier than I thought. Wait till I tell Ryan that Julie came up with the plan.*

Everyone continued talking and drinking. Finally, Cassandra had enough, and she couldn't wait to run home and tell Ryan.

Cassandra entered her apartment. Ryan was not home yet. She decided to wait for him and fell asleep doing so.

On her way home. Julie thought about what Cassandra said about Vegas. Should they really go? What was Ryan going to think? She knew that going to Vegas the same weekend as him would like just plain crazy. But Cassandra did have a valid point. *How many times will I be able to hang out with Ryan in Vegas?* It was worth a risk and Julie did not like taking risks, but decided that it might not be that bad after all.

The next morning, she felt Ryan next to her. Cassandra looked at the clock on her cell phone. It was 7:00 a.m. He must have come home sometime during the night and hadn't woken her up. She turned over and saw him sleeping. She didn't want to wake him and slowly got up from the bed heading to the bathroom to take a shower. When she was done with her shower, Cassandra walked into the kitchen to find Ryan making something to eat.

"How was the softball game night?" she asked.

"It was good. My team won, and then we headed to a bar by the beach for some beers."

"Nice," Cassandra smiled.

"What about you? What did you do last night?"

"I just went to the Library Bar for some drinks, nothing major. Oh, but before I forget to tell you. Your girlfriend Julie asked me if I wanted to go to Vegas this weekend. Can you believe her? I said, 'You know Ryan is going this weekend?'"

"What? Are you serious?" Ryan said stopping what he was doing. "What did you say?"

"I told her that you were going this weekend and it would look bad if she decided to go to Vegas as well. She replied by saying, 'Ryan doesn't own Vegas, I can go if I want.' I told her she should reconsider. Then she went on about how I need to buy a dress for my party and Vegas would be the perfect place for it."

"No way; are you guys really going?" Ryan asked again surprised.

"I think so. When we left, she was going home to buy the tickets. I haven't heard anything yet."

"Wow, that would be insane if she did go. This girl must be really crazy."

"Tell me about," Cassandra said walking away, a big smile on her face.

Cassandra walked into work, thinking how well her plan had worked. Neither Julie nor Ryan had any clue of what had just transpired. Cassandra knew that at any moment she would be hearing from Julie about the tickets she had purchased for Vegas. Cassandra sat at her desk and checked her emails. She always wondered what she was supposed to do at work.

"It's about time you came into work," Elizabeth said sarcastically.

"If you must know, I was busy taking care of business."

"Oh, and what business might that be? If you mean having sex with Ryan, I already assumed that is what you were doing."

"You wish. Not this morning. I came up with the best plan ever. You know how Ryan is going to Vegas this weekend?"

"Yes," Elizabeth responded, looking at her monitor.

"Well, I really want to go too, but I just can't show up there because Ryan would think it crazy. So, I talked Julie into going to Vegas by telling her how what a great surprise it would for Ryan if she showed up there."

"O-M-G, are you for real?"

"Of course, I emphasized to Julie that if she went to Vegas this weekend, Ryan would be so excited to see her there. Then I also made up something about buying a dress for my party."

"You are crazy; that poor girl is going to go insane and you are going to hell," Elizabeth responded shaking her head.

"Well, if I go to hell, at least I will do so by having a great time in Vegas and I also get to spend time with Ryan," Cassandra said smiling.

Just as soon as Cassandra was done with the sentence, her cell phone rang.

"It's Julie," Cassandra said and walked away.

"Hey Cassandra,"

"Hi Julie, what's up?"

"I looked at tickets and they are not too expensive. We can leave Saturday night and return Sunday afternoon; I just don't know what time."

"Well, how about we leave Saturday morning from LAX and return on the same flight with Ryan Sunday night at Burbank. He is parking his car at the airport and he can give us a ride back."

"Are you sure that we should fly back together?" Julie asked.

"Of course," Cassandra said reassuring Julie. "Plus, I am his roommate. He has to give us a ride back." Cassandra thought to herself, *This is working better than I thought.*

"Okay," Julie said sounding doubtful. "I hope Ryan doesn't get mad. I am purchasing the tickets right now."

"Perfect," Cassandra said. "I will call you later today to talk about more details. Vegas here we come!" Cassandra hung up.

She looked outside the window. She loved the view she had working in one of the tallest buildings in downtown LA. As she smiled to herself, Cassandra thought what a great weekend this was going to be. *Julie will make a fool of herself by going to Vegas and Ryan will realize that Julie is crazy and he should just stick with me. It's not like he is going to forget me. I left him with a smile on his face this morning as I left for work and he was still lying in bed, naked.*

As the plane descended on the tarmac in SDJ Los Cabos International Airport, Eugene leaned back in his chair, closed his eyes, and gripped the armrests of his chair. Eugene had a fear of heights and flying. Even though it was a private jet, the fear still haunted him. Once the plane came to a complete stop, Eugene was able to relax.

"Hey buddy, relax, we made it in one piece," Brad said as he finished sipping his drink. "It's time to party!"

"For sure," Eugene replied still trying to compose himself.

They all exited the plane on the runway exclusively for private jets. Eugene loved flying private versus commercial and in recent years, it had become a priority for him. Being as successful as he was, it allowed him the perks of flying private and spending on lavish vacations whenever his heart desired. As they approached the limo, Eugene still knew that all these material things didn't fill the void of his empty heart, but the only way he knew how to avoid it was by drinking. As soon as he entered the limo, he popped a bottle of champagne.

"To Mexico," he yelled to all the guys and drank from the bottle.

"To Mexico and a wild weekend," all the guys responded.

Eugene's head filled with thoughts of what was to come this weekend.

Cassandra always loved sitting next to the window when flying so she could look at the view. It was moments that took her breath away that she cherished the most. She was now looking out the window and the Las Vegas strip was coming into view. *What a great weekend this was going to be*, she thought to herself. She looked over at Julie who had fallen asleep during the flight. How peaceful she looked, but then Cassandra decided to shake her shoulder to wake her up.

"What is going on?" Julie said with her eyes closed.

"We are here. I can see the strip." Cassandra said enthusiastically.

"Really? Great, now I am getting nervous," Julie said.

"Nervous about what?"

"That I have to call Ryan and tell him we are here."

"That will be easy; just send him a text message saying we just landed in Vegas and want to know what you are doing tonight."

"You think I should send him a text message instead of a call?" Julie asked, her eyes wide.

"Yes, it will be simple and to the point," Cassandra said looking out the window.

Julie thought to herself: *Should I call Ryan or send him a text? What would be better?* She better listen to Cassandra; she knew Ryan better than her since they were roommates.

"Okay, I will send him a text."

"Yes, as soon as the plane lands, text him and see what he responds," Cassandra said not looking at Julie.

The plane hit the runway with a jolt and everyone on board gasped.

"What the hell!" Julie said.

"I know," Cassandra said, a little shaken up.

The pilot's voice came on over the speakers, "Sorry folks for the rough landing, but there were some birds in the way and had to go over them."

"Whatever," Cassandra said, thinking how she should be flying private and not commercial, like Eugene does. Oh, why did she have to think about him? Now, her thoughts were going to be filled with him. She decided not to think about Eugene this weekend as she had some damage to cause. Plus, by now, she knew Eugene was drunk at some pool in Cabo.

Ryan barely stirred when he heard his phone ping, signaling the arrival of a new text. He tried looking for his phone without opening his eyes. He was lying on the floor of one his friend's apartments still dressed from the night before.

There were beer cans, half-eaten pizza, bags of potato chips, and plastic cups all over the place and somewhere in between the mess was Ryan lying face down. His phone beeped again and he still tried looking for it without opening his eyes. With no luck, he finally opened his eyes. For a moment, he looked at the cups that were in his line of sight and wondered, *Where am I and why am I lying on the floor?* He tried picking up his head and the thought of it made it hurt more. *What the hell, man. What happened to me last night?* His memories were not that vivid; all he could remember was playing poker and drinking, after which everything went blank. He was finally able to turn himself over and now he was staring at the ceiling. Before he could think further, he heard his phone again. Annoyed and without sitting up, he turned his head around for the phone. He finally saw it and reached for it. He saw one new message from Julie, "Hey, we just landed in Vegas. What are your plans for tonight? Maybe we can all get together."

"This girl is insane," Ryan said out loud.

He decided to text Cassandra to see if they were really here. He waited for a response. For a moment, Ryan was startled because he wasn't sure where his wallet was. Hurriedly, he started checking all his pockets and finally found it in his back pocket. Sighing with relief, he saw that Cassandra had responded.

"Yes, we are here. I told you Julie is nuts, but you wouldn't listen to me. I guess I will see you later. We are staying at the Paris Hotel."

Ryan thought to himself, *Cassandra must be right; Julie is definitely nuts!*

Cassandra leaned back into her chair and smiled.

Julie asked, "Was that Ryan that texted you?"

"Yes, it was. He just wanted to know what hotel we are staying in. I told him Paris."

"Oh," Julie wondered why he hadn't texted *her* back.

They both got off the plane and made a plan. They were to check into their hotel and take a nap because of the early flight they had taken into Vegas. Then they would get something to eat and check in with Ryan to see what his plans were.

Ryan called Alex immediately to tell him the news. Alex and Eric had flown in the night before and were staying at Caesar's.

"Hey man, what's up?" Alex said as he rolled over on to his back.

"Listen to this. I just received a text message from Julie. She and Cassandra just landed in Vegas. Can you believe that?"

"Seriously?" Alex said knowing that Cassandra had something to do with the sudden surprise.

He had an idea of what was going on between Cassandra and Ryan. It was impossible for two adults to live under one roof and not be having a sexual relationship.

"Insane. What should I do?" Ryan said as his head began to throb even more.

"Just let it be. If you have time later tonight, then meet up with them."

"You're right. Right now I am too hungover to think about it."

"Okay. Call me later. Eric and I are going to get some breakfast and then hit the casino."

"Okay, man, talk to you later."

Still lying on the floor, Ryan didn't want to move or think about Julie and Cassandra—as if he needed the additional stress. He was going to be playing in a poker tournament later this afternoon and that was his main focus for now.

Alex laughed to himself as he ended the call with Ryan.

"What's up?" Eric said in a muffled voice with his head in the pillow.

"Your girlfriend is here!" Alex said with a smirk.

"What do you mean?" Eric, confused, raised his head from the pillow.

"Cassandra and Julie just landed in Vegas this morning."

"Really?" Eric sounded interested. "What are they doing here?"

"I am pretty sure they are here because of Ryan. Why else?"

"You think they both came for Ryan?" Eric said laughing. "He is going to have his hands full!"

"I know. I can't believe they came. I am sure that this was all Cassandra's idea." Alex said, sounding sure.

"I wouldn't put it past Cassandra," Eric said putting his head back onto the pillow.

For a second, Eric wondered if Cassandra knew he was here. Maybe she came to see him as well. Eric wasn't sure, but he didn't want to find out. Getting caught in this drama was not his idea of a fun weekend.

Cassandra and Julie opened the door to their suite. Cassandra looked around in amazement. It was a two-bedroom suite. The living room was filled with modern furniture, all in dark red tones. Each girl walked into their respective bedrooms to keep their luggage away, and then met back in the living room.

"Let's relax for a while and then get something to eat," Cassandra said.

"Good idea!" Julie replied.

They took opposite sides on the couch and turned on the TV. As Cassandra watched TV, her thoughts starting drifting to Eugene. She didn't mean for it to happen, but her mind had a mind of its own. Cassandra would have loved for Eugene to be with her, and she wouldn't have had to worry about tearing Julie and Ryan apart. *But* that wasn't the situation and in order to make herself feel better, she would go along with her plan. Cassandra closed her eyes and let her thoughts take control of her.

People were laughing and yelling all around him. Eugene stood at the bar, lost in his thoughts. This weekend was Father's Day and instead of being with his son and father, he was in Cabo drinking and trying to forget the thoughts that always over took his mind. On most days, Eugene wished for the peace and tranquility a marriage brought to him, but he had to be honest with himself before he could be honest enough to be with someone else. He knew his marriage was bound to fail the minute he said: "I do." Then there were days where all he could think of were drinking and partying. Yes, he did enjoy being free, but what price was he willing to pay?

"Hey Conrad, what are you thinking about?" Brad said as he walked up to him.

"Nothing much, just going over some things in my head."

"Listen buddy, we are in Cabo. Time to forget everything and party." Brad said putting his arm around Eugene. "I have some pretty ladies that are dying to meet you. So bring your A-game and let's do this!"

"For sure," replied Eugene.

Eugene let Brad led the way to a group of young women in bikinis, drinking the afternoon away.

Maybe this trip will not be bad after all, Eugene thought to himself. *I can be a good boy when I get back home.*

Cassandra and Julie walked into the Hard Rock Café to grab an early dinner.

"Do you think there's a wait?" Cassandra said, looking around to see if there were any cute guys.

"I hope not," Julie replied checking her phone to see if Ryan had texted her.

"How many?" asked the hostess standing behind the hostess desk.

"Two, please," replied Cassandra.

"Follow me."

The hostess sat Julie and Cassandra at a round table in the middle of the restaurant.

As Cassandra turned to look around, she noticed groups of tourists. Every other table seemed to have a groom and a bride, dressed in wedding attire.

"Did you notice all the brides and grooms?" Cassandra asked Julie

"Yes, I did!"

"Seriously, who has their wedding reception at the Hard Rock Café?" Cassandra said with a smirk.

"I know! I wouldn't," Julie said, thinking about where she and Ryan may have their wedding reception.

A waiter approached their table. Cassandra quickly surveyed him, noticing his dark eyes and dark hair that accompanied his medium height and built. Before the waiter could say anything,

"I will have a strong margarita on the rocks with salt, please," Cassandra said.

"Okay," the waiter said, confused.

"Me too," Julie said

Cassandra thought to herself that she would need all the alcohol in the world to get her through this dinner with Julie and to listen to her talking about Ryan. *Maybe if I pretend to laugh and smile, Julie will think I am listening.*

Julie started talking about Ryan and never stopped to take a breath. Cassandra sat there listening, but her thoughts were flitting about. Finally, Cassandra had had enough.

"Maybe you should text Ryan and see what he is doing," Cassandra said as she finished her margarita, looking for the waiter.

"Do you think I should?" Julie asked looking at her phone.

"Yes, let's see what he's up to?" Cassandra said, silently pleading to herself. *Please! Before I drink myself to death!*

"Okay," Julie replied as she started texting Ryan.

Cassandra finally caught the waiter's attention and signaled for another margarita.

Ryan looked around intently at the other players at the table. He wanted to see which man was flinching. Ryan was down to his last bet and he knew his cards would not take him to the next round. He looked at his cards one more time, in case they may have changed, but they stayed the same. Then, he looked around and saw the same stares—they hadn't changed either. What was he to do now? He had no choice but to go all the way. He looked one more time at his cards and said: "All in." Some players folded, but two continued staring intently at Ryan. In the background, Eric and Alex looked on, waiting to see if Ryan was to win the pot. Finally, the dealer called, "Cards down," and everyone threw in their cards. Ryan's face went blank. He had just lost thousands of dollars. He silently got up from the table, put his hat on, and took his glass of Jack and Coke.

"That was harsh," Alex said as Ryan walked toward him. "Are you okay?"

"Yeah, I am okay; at least I got to the last round," Ryan said, feeling his phone vibrate in his pocket.

"That's true. Where to next?" Alex said.

Ryan looked at his phone and saw an incoming text from Julie. "What are you doing? We're having dinner at the Hard Rock Café. What are your plans?"

Ryan was in no mood to hang out with Julie and Cassandra after losing such a big pot. Instead he decided on telling her. "Heading to Planet Hollywood."

"Hey, Ryan just texted back saying he's heading to Planet Hollywood. Want to go?"

"Sure, let's get the check."

Julie signaled to the waiter to get the check.

After paying, they got up and headed outside to get a taxi.

"Planet Hollywood," Cassandra said looking out her taxi window.

"The casino or restaurant?" the driver asked.

"Hmmm, not sure," Cassandra said. "Let's go with the casino." "Are you sure, Cassandra?"

"Yes, Julie. It's Ryan. I'm sure he's gambling his heart away."

The taxi drove off toward the strip.

Cassandra and Julie walked into the Planet Hollywood Casino and went straight to the game tables to find Ryan. Looking at each table one by one, they couldn't see any sign of him.

"Do you see him, Cassandra?"

"No," Cassandra replied. "Why don't you call him or text him?'

"Okay," Julie said as she took out her blackberry and called him. "No answer, let me text him."

Cassandra was starting to get frustrated. She was not going to spend all night looking for Ryan. Suddenly her phone pinged with a text. "Hey, I told Julie I was at Planet Hollywood, but I am not. I am at Harrah's, but don't tell her. I need time to drink and gamble." Cassandra smiled to herself.

"Hey. I texted Ryan, but he hasn't answered yet."

"Give him a second," Cassandra said. "Why don't we go get a drink and wait for his response?"

"Are you sure?" Julie asked still looking for a sign of Ryan.

"Why don't you check out the poker rooms and I will meet you at the bar," Cassandra said already thinking of what she was going to order.

"Okay, I will be right there," Julie said taking off toward the poker rooms.

Poor Julie, Cassandra thought. *How naïve can she be?*

Cassandra headed over to the bar and sat on a stool.

"What will it be?" asked the young handsome bartender

"Grey Goose tonic, please," Cassandra said, flashing her killer smile. She decided to read the text message from Ryan again and decided to let Julie wander all over the casino before telling her that they should go back to their hotel to change and then head to Harrah's. In the meantime, Cassandra noticed the attractive gentleman sitting next to her. He had stared at her when she'd entered the bar. He winked at Cassandra and she knew it was a win.

"Why do you think Ryan would lie to me and tell me he is in one place and not be there?" Julie asked confused.

Cassandra, who had had too many drinks at the bar with the unknown gentleman, really didn't have an answer because she couldn't think straight.

"Why don't you call him and ask him?" Cassandra said not really knowing what was coming out of her mouth.

"I have, but he doesn't answer."

"Let me try," Cassandra said and scrambled through her purse to find her phone. Once she finally got it, she dialed his number.

"Hello," Ryan said.

"Hey Ryan, where the hell are youuuuuu . . ." Before Cassandra could finish, Julie had snatched the phone from her hand. Cassandra just looked at her and then out her window.

"Ryan! Where the hell have you been?!" Julie yelled.

"Hey baby, why are yelling at me?" Ryan asked.

"Because you told us you were going to be at one casino, and you weren't there and we spent two hours looking for you!"

"I am sorry. Listen, babe. I am at the Harrah's poker room, come meet me here."

"Are you sure you are there?" asked Julie.

"Yes baby, and I can't wait to see you," Ryan said.

"Okay, we are heading back to our suite to change and then we will head over."

"Great, see you soon."

Julie hung up and gave Cassandra her phone back. She took it without looking at Julie because she didn't want to laugh at her.

"Okay, he is at Harrah's casino. We will change and then head over," Julie said looking at Cassandra.

"Okay," Cassandra said with a smile, knowing all along that Ryan had been there. Then she started hiccupping and couldn't stop, and then she began laughing uncontrollably.

"What is wrong with you?" Julie angrily asked.

"Nothing, just remembering something funny," Cassandra said in between laughter.

Julie ignored Cassandra and looked out her window, thinking how good it felt that she was on her way to see Ryan.

"Ryan, who were you on the phone with?" Alex asked as he took a swig from his drink and looked at himself in one of the casino mirrors.

"I was just talking to Julie," Ryan said with a smile because he was already drunk and was swaying back and forth.

"Man, you are too much. What are you going to do? Are you staying here or coming with us to dance the night away?"

Ryan just looked at Alex. He needed a second to digest what he had just said.

"Are you listening to me, ryan?" Alex asked.

"Yes. I am staying here and playing more poker."

"Suit yourself. Eric and I are going to hit the club to get some action tonight. In case you forget, I am going to write our room number on your arm. This way you will remember where to go when you are even more drunk than now."

Ryan laughed at Alex as he watched him write the room number of their Caesar's room on his arm.

"Don't forget. 417 is the room number. Be careful!" Alex said as he and Eric walked away.

"You think he will be okay?" Eric asked, not really caring because he didn't like Ryan that much—actually, not at all. To even think he was in Vegas with him. The only reason Eric was in Vegas with Ryan was because he had a free room and airline ticket that he needed to use.

"Yeah, he is old enough to take of himself," Alex said

Ryan still stood in the place Alex had left him, swaying. For a second, he thought of what to do next. Then he turned around and saw the closest poker room and headed in that direction.

Cassandra looked at herself in the bathroom mirror. Even though it had only taken her a second to get ready, she looked beautiful. Her reflection looked a bit fuzzy because of all the drinks she had had before, but it didn't bother her because Cassandra had that natural beauty that most women die for. She sat on the living room couch, waiting for Julie, and wondered whether her body could get up to get another drink from the minibar. Her mind saw her reaching it, but her body was still sitting on the couch. Cassandra laughed for the most part. She was always a happy person, but lately with all the drinking and messing with others, it had taken a toll on her. Like most people, she just wanted to be happy. To her, it was not the monetary value of life, but the real sweet part of it, which was having someone who stood by her and loved her unconditionally. That was part that everyone craved but few people had. Cassandra knew from an earlier age the difference between loving someone and unconditionally loving someone, and she couldn't even count on one hand how many people she knew who had that. *Of course,* she said to herself. *I would want only the impossible.*

"Are you ready?" Julie asked as she walked into the living room, wearing her "going out uniform" yet again: jeans and a black top.

Again, Ryan found himself amongst men who were all staring at him intently waiting to see if he was lying about his hand. This time, he stared back without looking at his cards. Finally, everyone folded and Ryan took the pot. "It's about time," Ryan said as he leaned into the poker table and gathered all the chips toward him. As he was counting, he heard a knock on the glass window. He turned to look and saw Cassandra and Julie standing there and smiling. He smiled to himself for a second and saw how different the two women could be. Cassandra had exotic features that automatically made her sexy no matter what. Then, there was Julie—no matter how much makeup and designer clothes she put on, she lacked the appeal. She was just plain and ordinary, like someone who was trying too hard to make herself look good.

Ryan motioned for them to enter the poker room.

"Hey Ryan," Cassandra said in her sexy voice as she came close to him for a kiss. She really wanted to kiss him on the lips but opted for the cheek instead.

He hugged Cassandra tightly inhaling her scent that smelled sweet and fresh.

"Hi Ryan," Julie said looking at him hugging Cassandra.

"Hey baby," Ryan said and gave Julie a hug and held her hand when he was done hugging her. Julie smiled and couldn't be happier.

"What are you guys doing?" Ryan asked looking at Julie.

"Nothing, just came to see what you were doing?" Cassandra asked noticing how he was holding Julie's hand.

"Well, I have an idea. Let me cash out and then we can hit some of the tables," Ryan said.

"Okay," Julie said letting go of Ryan's hand so he could cash out his chips.

Immediately, Julie rushed to Cassandra and asked, "Did you see Ryan holding my hand?"

"Yes, that is sweet. He must really like you!" Cassandra said with a fake smile.

"I know, I am so glad we came to Vegas."

Cassandra just looked at Julie, not sure whether or not she wanted to choke her.

Moments later, Ryan walked over, "Ready, girls?"

"Let's do this," Cassandra said.

All three walked toward the roulette table. Midway Ryan stopped and grabbed Julie and started kissing her. Cassandra looked astonished and wondered, *why is Ryan kissing Julie in the middle of the casino floor?*

Once Ryan stopped kissing Julie, he smiled at her and said, "Let's get a drink."

"Okay," Julie smiled.

Cassandra, still confused, grabbed Ryan as Julie walked to the bar.

"What was that about?" Cassandra asked him angrily.

"Nothing, I just wanted to kiss her. It meant nothing," he explained leaning close into Cassandra.

Cassandra pushed him away before Julie could see.

"What's your problem? Don't you see Julie is crazy and that is why we are here in Vegas this very moment."

"Yes, I do, but I just wanted to kiss her. I am really confused right now and don't want to do."

"Right, well, that is your call. If you keep kissing her, she is only going to think that you like her."

"I know. I won't kiss her anymore," Ryan said as he leaned in to try to kiss Cassandra. Cassandra pushed him back and realized he was more drunk than her.

"Seriously, behave. I am not dealing with this right now," Cassandra said,

Julie walked toward them with drinks in her hand wondering what was going with those two; they seemed to be arguing but she wasn't sure.

"Hey guys, here are your drinks. Is everything okay?" Julie looked back and forth between Cassandra and Ryan.

"Yes, everything is fine," Cassandra said taking a big swig from her drink.

"Babe, everything is okay," Ryan said hugging Julie again.

"Let's go play some roulette," Cassandra said as she started walking toward the roulette table.

"Let's go!" Ryan exclaimed holding on to Julie.

As the night progressed, the three of them played roulette with Julie chasing after Ryan and Cassandra chasing after Ryan. Cassandra didn't like to lose and this game was becoming more of a loss for her; she did not like that. Finally, toward the end of the night, Cassandra noticed a number written on Ryan's arm.

"Why is there a number written on your arm, Ryan?"

"I am not sure, someone wrote it for me. I don't know where it is to."

"Okay, is it your hotel room?"

"Maybe."

"Where are you staying anyway?" "I don't remember," Ryan said drinking his beer.

"You don't remember?" Julie asked.

'Nope," Ryan said again.

"I think it's time for you to go to your hotel room," Cassandra said unamused.

"What? I don't think so. I am okay," Ryan said not able to stand straight.

"Yeah, I think it's time."

"What hotel are you staying at?" Cassandra asked.

"I don't remember," Ryan said. In reality, he was trying to not tell them where he was staying because he knew Alex and Eric didn't want them there, so he pretended to be forgetful. Cassandra noticed something was up and didn't say anything.

"Okay, why don't you come back to our suite instead?" Cassandra suggested.

"Yeah that is a good idea," Julie concluded.

"Okay," Ryan said.

They left the casino and headed toward the taxi stand. Cassandra just wanted to get back to the hotel and lie down. In the cab, Ryan sat between Julie and Cassandra with this head on Julie's shoulders. Cassandra just turned the other way and ignored the situation. Once they arrived at the hotel, they walked through the casino and to the elevator banks that took them up to the suite.

"Finally, we are here," Cassandra said as she took off her heels.

"Yes," Julie said.

Cassandra headed straight for the minibar.

"Would either one of you like something to drink?"

"No, I am done," Julie said.

"Julie, where is your room?"

"That way," Julie pointed toward the room on the right.

"Good, I am going to bed," Ryan said, and Julie followed right behind him and closed the door.

Suddenly Cassandra found herself alone, something she was used to. Not that she cared. She poured herself a vodka tonic, left the room, and headed to the casino.

Julie lay next to Ryan as he slept. Nothing happened between them. When Julie had followed him into her room, he had immediately laid on the bed and fallen asleep. She decided to just lie next to him. *I wonder why he didn't make a move.* She heard Ryan's cell phone ringing but couldn't reach it because it was in his front pocket and he was lying face down.

Cassandra woke the next morning with a massive headache. *Why do I drink so much?* She rolled on to her back and thought about last night. She really wanted to know if anything had happened between Ryan and Julie. But why did she really care. Again, it wasn't like Cassandra really liked Ryan; she just didn't like to lose. Her head started pounding even more as she started to think more.

"Ugh, I hate this feeling," Cassandra said out loud.

She rolled over to her side and heard a knock on the door.

"Yes?" Cassandra managed to say without making her headache anymore.

"Can I come in?" Julie asked innocently.

"Sure."

Julie sat on Cassandra's bed. "What's up?"

"Well, Ryan is passed out on my bed and he won't wake up. I tried jabbing him in the side, but he only makes noises."

Cassandra laughed, "Must have been a fun night if he won't wake up."

"I wish. He immediately passed out when he slept on my bed," Julie remarked.

"Oh," Cassandra said thinking to herself that Ryan always tried to have sex with her before they went to sleep—drunk or not.

"Just give him more time and he will wake up."

"His phone keeps ringing and I can't reach it to see who's calling," Julie said.

"Why don't you just roll him over?" "Didn't think of that."

"Come on, I will help you," Cassandra said wondering who was calling Ryan.

Cassandra approached Ryan to make sure he was asleep and carefully rolled him over and waited to see if he woke up. Once she knew he was still sleeping, she dug into his pocket and took out his cell phone. She sat on the floor and Julie joined her.

"Okay, let's see who's been calling him," Cassandra said, her eyes sparkling.

"Apparently, Alex has been calling him a lot. Wonder why," Julie said.

"Me too," Cassandra said more interested in checking his text messages.

She navigated herself into Ryan's inbox of text messages and then started reading them. There were multiple text messages from different women stating how much fun it had been to hang out with Ryan. Text messages from one woman especially caught their attention. Ryan and this mysterious woman had been texting back and forth for a couple of weeks, even indicating that she could be Ryan's girlfriend. Both women were in shock as they continued reading the messages. Finally, when they had had enough, Cassandra carefully put the phone back in Ryan's pocket. They left the room closing the door behind them and heading into the living room.

"Interesting messages, huh?" Cassandra said.

"Yeah, who is that woman who keeps texting him?" Julie asked

"I am not sure who that is. Maybe someone he is dating?" Cassandra had to say this with a straight face.

"Listen we are not sure who this woman is so there is no need to worry," Cassandra said reassuring Julie.

"You are right."

"Plus, I will get to the bottom of it," Cassandra said as she heard the door to Julie's room open. Ryan walked out talking on the phone.

"Okay, I will see you in a bit," Ryan said as he ended his conversation.

"Who are you talking to?" Cassandra asked feeling hurt and angry knowing Ryan was speaking to another girl.

"I was talking to Alex; he wanted to know where I was and if I was coming back to the hotel room to get my stuff."

"Wait, Alex is here?" Cassandra asked surprised.

"Yes, Alex and Eric are here. The number on my arm is the number to our room in Caesar's."

"I didn't know Alex and Eric were here," Cassandra said. "If I would have known, I would have totally hung out with them."

"Oh, I guess I failed to mention it," Ryan said.

Cassandra looked at Julie with a confused look.

"Why would you forget to tell us something like that?" Julie asked.

"I don't know why. I mean why are you guys here right now?" Ryan asked with an attitude.

"Where are Eric and Alex staying?" Cassandra asked knowing that if she knew Eric was in Vegas, she would have spent time with him, instead of chasing Ryan around casinos.

"At Caesar's. And the number on my arm is our room number," Ryan replied annoyed and wanting to leave their suite. Cassandra immediately called Alex.

"Hello," Alex said.

"Hey Alex," Cassandra said. "I didn't know that you and Eric were here. Can I speak to Eric?"

"Sure, hold on," Alex said.

"Hello," said Eric.

"Hey, I didn't know you were in Vegas!" Cassandra said confused.

"Yeah, I got here Friday night and checked in. When did you get here?"

"Saturday morning. When are you flying out?"

"I am leaving for the airport right now."

"Really? Because Julie booked us on the same flight as Ryan."

"Oh, I have a much earlier flight."

"I wish I had known you were here. I would have loved to hang out with you! Regardless, I am having my birthday party on Tuesday at the Standard Rooftop. Can you make it?"

"I will see, maybe," Eric said in disbelief.

"Okay, hope to see you there," Cassandra said disappointed.

Once she hung up, Cassandra knew that the reason why Eric had never called her back was because she hadn't slept with him that first night. But she didn't care for just a one-night stand. Cassandra wasn't that type of girl. Plus sleeping with Eric would just cause trouble.

Eric hung up the phone in disbelief. He remembered the first night that he and Cassandra had spent together. Nothing had happened between them besides some kissing. After that everything was vanilla. So why did he still have feelings toward her? He would have enjoyed spending time with her in Vegas instead of chasing something that was never meant to be. He decided to leave back in Vegas what did happen. It was better than having his heart broken, and Eric could not deal with that.

"So, Ryan, anything else you want to tell us?" Cassandra smiled with attitude.

"No," Ryan replied with the same attitude.

"Okay, then," Cassandra said as she sprawled out on the couch.

"I am heading back to my hotel room. I will see you guys later," Ryan said,

"Okay," Julie said. "I will call you later."

"Weird why Ryan didn't tell us Eric and Alex were here with him," Cassandra said flipping through the channels.

"Yeah, I wonder why he didn't."

"Oh well," Cassandra said.

Cassandra stared at the TV not really paying attention, but lost in her thoughts. She wondered what she was doing with Ryan and Eric. Did she even like any of them? She knew the real reason she was doing this was because she couldn't be with the person who owned her heart. Instead of dwelling on the situation, she shut off the TV.

"Ready to get some breakfast? I was thinking champagne," Cassandra said as smiled at Julie.

Brunch was one of Cassandra's favorite meals. She wished she could eat brunch every day. The champagne, of course, was the best part and not to mention French toast. Julie and Cassandra sat in a café inside the Paris Hotel. It reminded Cassandra of her time in Paris and brought a smile to her face with an immediate tinge of sadness.

"What's wrong?" Julie asked as she noticed Cassandra's expression change.

"Nothing, just remembering when I traveled to Paris."

"How was it?" Julie asked sipping her champagne.

"Pretty much like this. Sitting at cafés drinking wine and champagne and eating all day."

"Nice, how long were you there?"

"Three weeks."

"Ever plan on going back?"

Cassandra thought for a second. Paris held the best memories for her, but she had no plans on returning. "I don't think I will be returning any time soon." Cassandra wanted to change the subject immediately and asked Julie a question about Ryan, knowing she was going to regret asking the question.

"Where do you think you and Ryan stand?" Cassandra asked.

"I am not sure. Last night he was great, and I truly enjoyed kissing him, but this morning things were weird. It was as though nothing happened."

"Don't worry. You know how Ryan can be sometimes," Cassandra said. What she really wanted to say was *the real reason why Ryan flirts and kisses you is because he is drunk beyond belief.* Seriously, didn't Julie see how drunk he was last night? He couldn't even stand, let alone know what hotel he was staying in.

"I guess. I just have to wait and see," Julie said, and Cassandra just smiled at her.

"My man, did you have a threesome?" Alex asked Ryan as he walked in.

"Wouldn't you like to know," Ryan said throwing himself on the empty bed. "Where is Eric?"

"In the shower. What's up for today?" Alex asked as he put his shirt on.

"I want to take a shower and then we can head to the ESPN to get lunch and watch some of the games."

"Sounds good. Eric is leaving for the airport; he has an earlier flight."

"Okay," Ryan said kicking off his shoes.

"Hey Eric," Ryan said.

"Hey, what happened to you last night. Get lucky?" Eric said walking toward his suitcases.

"You know, a little of this a little of that."

"You are insane," Eric said knowing that Ryan probably drank too much and passed out immediately.

"Cassandra was kind of upset that she didn't know you were here," Ryan said, a big smile on his face.

"Really?" Eric said trying to find clothes to wear. He really didn't want to hear about Cassandra. He felt as though he were in competition with Ryan and he knew Ryan loved to win. Ryan knew that it killed Eric that he was better at everything, especially work, and Ryan was not going to back down. "What time is your flight? We are going to the ESPN Zone."

"In about two hours. I am going to get dressed and then head to the airport."

"Okay, it was great hanging out," Ryan said as he got up from the bed to shake Eric's hand. "I am going to get into the shower. Are you going to Cassandra's birthday party?"

"Not sure. I have to check if I have any plans."

"Okay, have a safe flight."

Ryan walked into the bathroom and smiled to himself in the mirror. *Score two for Ryan*, he thought.

Eric finished dressing and then got his luggage together.

"You out of here, man?" Alex asked, knowing that something was not right with Eric.

"Yeah, I am heading to the airport."

"Call me when you get home," Alex said.

"Sure," Eric said as he gave Alex a hug.

Cassandra was admiring her reflection in the mirror as she tried a dress for her party. Suddenly her phone rang, bringing her out of her reverie. She noticed it was Ryan calling her.

"Hey," she said.

"What are you doing, sexy?"

"Trying on a dress."

"I am sure it looks great on you," Ryan said.

"Maybe."

"Why don't you come over to the ESPN and help me eat my food."

"I'll be right over," Cassandra said, still admiring her reflection.

"Who was that?" Julie asked from outside the dressing room.

"It was Ryan. He is at the ESPN Zone. He asked for us to come over."

Cassandra thought that he had really just asked her to come over, but she would have to take Julie too.

"Oh okay," Julie said disappointed.

Julie stood against the wall wondering why Ryan had called Cassandra instead of her. She convinced herself it was because they were roommates. Cassandra thought how funny it was that every time Ryan called, she would run to him. Maybe she did like him?

Entering the ESPN Zone, Cassandra surveyed the room looking for Ryan. She found him and Alex sitting at a table that was facing the TVs. Cassandra didn't really like Alex, but she knew she had to tolerate him.

"Hey guys," Cassandra said taking a seat next to Alex, since Julie immediately jumped at a chance to sit next to Ryan.

"Hey girls," Alex said.

"Where's my food, Ryan?" Cassandra asked.

"Right here," Ryan said as he pushed his half-eaten plate to Cassandra.

"Whatever," Cassandra said taking the drink menu from the middle of the table.

"Did you find a dress?" Ryan asked.

"Yes," Cassandra said not looking at him.

"Can I see it?"

"No, it's a surprise."

During the conversation, Alex just smiled to himself knowing that each of them held the secret that they were sleeping with each other. The waiter came and took Cassandra's and Julie's order for drinks.

"Where is the bathroom?" Julie asked.

"I think they are by the entrance," Alex said.

"Okay, I will be right back," Julie said.

Julie got up from her chair and headed to the restroom. As soon as Julie walked away, Cassandra started shaking her head.

"What's wrong now?" Ryan asked.

"Nothing. You just never learn."

"Learn about what?" Ryan said drinking his beer.

"About Julie."

"What about her?" Ryan asked

"Last night—your kissing her makes her think that you like her. Which will only make her go even more crazy."

"I think you're just jealous," Alex said looking directly at Cassandra.

"I am not jealous. I am just trying to help Ryan."

"Well, to me, it sounds like you're jealous," Alex said again.

"Whatever," Cassandra said taking a sip of her drink.

Ryan got up and said, "I am going to the restroom."

He walked away hoping he would run into Julie. Ryan did like Julie somewhat, but was not sure whether what Cassandra was saying about Julie was true. She did decide to show up in Vegas and that was kind of weird. Ryan ran into Julie getting out of the bathroom. He took her hand, pulling her toward the craps tables.

"Let's gamble some money away," Ryan said.

"Sure," Julie said enjoying Ryan holding her hand.

They arrived at a craps table and Ryan pulled out hundred-dollar bills and exchanged them for chips. He started placing chips all around the table and he started winning. He soon doubled his betting amount. Julie loved being next to Ryan. She thought it was so cool to be his girlfriend.

"You must be good luck because I keep winning," Ryan said to Julie.

Julie smiled and said, "I guess I must be."

Back at the ESPN Zone, Cassandra and Alex sat watching the TVs wondering what had happened to Julie and Ryan. They must have bumped into each other and gone off somewhere.

"You know that Ryan likes Julie and you should just let them be," Alex said to Cassandra.

"I am not doing anything wrong."

"You are getting in the way."

"In the way of what? I don't even like Ryan," Cassandra said.

"Sure."

Alex's phone rang and he answered it. "Hey, you got home? Ryan, Cassandra, Julie, and I are at the ESPN having drinks. Our flight leaves at 8:00 p.m. Okay. Talk to you later!"

"That was Eric; he reached home."

"Why did he not leave with you guys?" Cassandra asked, trying to sound uninterested.

The travel deal he secured only allowed him to take a certain flight time.

"Oh," Cassandra said, thinking she needed to make the best of this conversation.

"So, are you coming to my birthday party on Tuesday?"

"Yeah, maybe, I will drop by. You have any single friends?"

"Of course, I do. I have the prettiest single friends. Whatever type of ethnicity you like, I have."

"Cool. I will definitely come by."

"I will be right back. I am going to the restroom."

"Okay," Alex said and laughed to himself.

Cassandra walked by the restrooms and looked outside the restaurant to see if she could spot Ryan and Julie, but didn't see them. She decided to head back and just wait. A couple of minutes later, Ryan and Julie walked back to the restaurant.

"Where did you guys go?" Alex asked.

"We hit the craps table and I won some money!" Ryan yelled.

"He did; it was fun," Julie said.

"Hey guys, we have to be heading soon. Julie and I need to get our bags from the hotel and then head to the airport."

"Yeah," Julie said looking at her watch.

Julie and Cassandra finished their drinks and headed back to their hotel to get their bags.

On the way to the airport, Julie pulled out hundred-dollar bills.

"Look, Ryan gave me his money at the craps table, and he forgot I have it."

"What?" Cassandra said looking at Julie as if she was crazy.

"He forgot I have his money."

"Why didn't you give it back to him?"

"This way he has a reason to call me when we get back to LA."

"Are you serious? You need to give him his money back."

"I will."

The taxi pulled up to the airport.

Cassandra saw Ryan and Alex get out of their taxi. Cassandra got out of their taxi and yelled, "Hey Ryan!"

Ryan turned around and looked at Cassandra. He marched over and leaned into the taxi. He looked at Julie. "Where is my money? I was going to pay for the taxi, and I realized you have my money."

"Oh yeah, here it is," Julie said as she pulled his money out of her pocket.

"Thanks," Ryan said and walked away.

Julie paid the taxi driver and she and Cassandra walked into the airport with Ryan and Alex trailing behind. After they had all checked in, they still had an hour before departure. They headed to a Mexican restaurant and sat down at the table.

"So, Ryan, when are you going to buy something?" Julie asked.

"What? What are you talking about?"

"I would like for you to buy me a purse," Julie stated.

Cassandra looked at Julie and wished she would just stop talking.

"Why would I buy you something?" Ryan asked bewildered.

"Why not? If you buy me something, I will buy you something."

"I really don't want anything," Ryan said.

"Please, Ryan," Julie pleaded.

"Wow, Julie, you are really too much," Alex said exasperated.

"Why do you mean?" Julie asked naively.

"You need to stop asking Ryan to buy you something. It's annoying!"

"Thank you, Alex," Ryan said.

Cassandra decided not to respond because she didn't know what to say.

Finally, it was time to board the plane. The flight was half full so Ryan and Julie sat in one aisle and Alex and Cassandra sat in the other aisle. During the flight home, Julie and Ryan talked the whole way and Cassandra tried to listen, but really couldn't hear anything. Cassandra sat next to Alex and for a second thought about making a move, but decided not to. Kissing all three friends would have been a record for her, but she decided it was not classy. Also, she wasn't attracted to Alex. Cassandra continued looking at Ryan and Julie. It didn't seem like they were into each other but were in a deep discussion. The plane landed at Burbank airport and Cassandra was glad to get up and walk out.

"Hey, how are you and Julie getting home?" Ryan asked trying to catch up to Cassandra because she was walking fast.

"What do you mean? You are our ride home. We live together. How else would I get home and Julie's car is parked in the garage."

"Oh, you just assumed I would drive you home?" Ryan asked Cassandra, teasing her.

Cassandra didn't respond and kept walking outside because she needed fresh air.

"Where are you parked?" Cassandra asked throwing her bag on the floor once she reached outside.

"I really don't remember. I think we have to take one of those buses to the parking lot," Ryan said looking confused.

"Okay, then," Cassandra said, agitated.

"Alex, do you remember where he parked?"

"No, because I didn't fly with him."

"I think we take this bus," said Ryan walking toward the bus stop sign.

"Okay, let's go."

During the bus ride to the parking lot, Cassandra didn't say much. She was tired of dealing with Ryan and Julie's chatter and Alex in general. Once they got to the parking lot and found Ryan's car, Ryan could not find his keys. He searched through his luggage and had to empty the contents of his bag. After thirty minutes of searching, he finally found the keys. Julie immediately rushed to the front seat of Ryan's car. Cassandra just shook her head in disbelief and got in the back with Alex.

Once they reached the outskirts of downtown LA, Alex said, "Hey, don't forget my car is parked in the Wells Fargo parking lot."

"Okay," Ryan said and headed in that direction.

Once they arrived at the building, Alex got out and said goodbye to everyone.

At that point, Ryan decided to get out of the car and told Julie to drive.

Delighted, she got out of the passenger car and into the driver seat.

"I always end up driving," she said.

Cassandra just looked out of the window.

Julie drove the car to the apartment's parking lot.

It was a short three-minute drive, but to Cassandra it felt like a lifetime with Julie chatting away. They drove into the garage and parked next to Julie's car. They all got out and Julie leaned against Ryan's car, waiting for him to give her a hug goodbye. Cassandra started walking toward the elevator. Ryan got his luggage out of the trunk and asked Julie for his keys.

"So, I guess this is goodbye," Julie said.

"Yeah," Ryan said hauling his bag on his shoulder. "Have a good night!"

"That's it?" Julie asked with a shocked look.

"What else would there be?" Ryan asked confused.

"I don't know. Maybe a hug?!" Julie said.

Reluctantly, Ryan gave Julie a hug and started walking away. Cassandra was standing at the elevators watching this unfold. She just wanted to go home.

Finally, Julie got into her car and watched Ryan walk away. Tears started rolling from her eyes.

"Can we please go?" Cassandra asked as Ryan walked toward the elevator.

Julie watched Ryan and Cassandra enter the elevator and disappear. How she wished she was Cassandra. When the elevator doors open on the ground floor, Cassandra and Ryan walked outside.

"Do you want to get something to eat? Maybe a sandwich?" Ryan asked.

"Sure, why not. The sandwich shop is open around the corner by the apartment."

They both started walking, noticing Julie's car disappears as it turned around the corner.

"What did you and Julie talk about on the plane? It seemed like an intense conversation."

"It was nothing; she asked me if I was dating anyone and I told her yes."

"Hmmm and what did she say?" Cassandra asked wanting to know who he was dating.

"Nothing, she was upset and left it at that."

"You know when you were sleeping in her room, she went through your text messages and contact list on your cell phone."

"Wait, are you serious?" Ryan asked, stopping dead in his tracks.

"Yes, why would I lie to you."

"I can even tell you some of the text messages."

"She really is crazy," Ryan said. "I guess I am lucky I didn't start anything with her."

"I told you, but you never listen."

Ryan thought to himself for second, *maybe Cassandra was right; she did have my best interests at heart.*

Ryan and Cassandra got their sandwiches and headed up to the apartment. As soon as Cassandra walked inside and put her bag down, Ryan walked behind her, grabbed her hand, and pulled her toward him. Without hesitation, he kissed with such force it took her breath away. *What was Ryan doing?* But she didn't stop kissing him back. They walked toward the kitchen counter without unlocking their lips. Ryan picked up Cassandra and put her on the kitchen counter. Reaching under her skirt, he peeled off her panties. Then, he undid his belt and pulled down his zipper. His pants fell to the floor. Without a second thought, he entered Cassandra with force, still enjoying her sweet lips.

Cassandra gasped and moaned with delight. He remembered how great she felt and could not stop himself from moaning aloud. Their passionate lovemaking continued for several minutes. At the same time, Cassandra received a text from Julie: "I am not sure what I did to Ryan for him not to like me. Can you please talk to him for me and tell me what he says?" Julie had pulled over on her way home, because it bothered her so much that Ryan was not responding the way she had wanted him to. She put her phone down and started driving, thinking about Ryan and wondering why Cassandra hadn't answered back.

Ryan pulled out of Cassandra with much delight. They were both gasping for air.

"That was incredible!" Ryan remarked.

"Yes," Cassandra said as she jumped off the counter. Ryan walked toward the bathroom to clean up, and Cassandra walked to her purse to check her phone. She read Julie's text message. For a second, Cassandra felt remorse, but what was she to do? She couldn't change Ryan's feelings toward Julie. Cassandra walked toward the living room and looked out of her window. The view at night was amazing, given that she was in between all the buildings in downtown LA. She stared at the building lights, thinking about Julie and Ryan. Then she reminded herself she really didn't care who got hurt as long as she got what she wanted.

Chapter 16

Eugene stood on his balcony overlooking the ocean. He loved the view at night and the sounds of the crashing waves. He held on to the railing, closed his eyes for a couple of seconds, and felt different memories flash through his head. He opened his eyes, but the loneliness he felt before he closed his eyes was still there. As much as he had enjoyed partying in Cabo and meeting different people, coming home to an empty home was his biggest fear. He did not enjoy being alone at all, but that was the price you paid for getting a divorce in the hopes of finding your soul mate. Once more, Eugene closed his eyes and took a deep breath of the ocean air. He knew that once he opened his eyes, he would still be alone and kept them closed for a few more seconds. His thoughts wandered to what the future was going to offer. He looked out to the ocean one last time before he headed back inside. He entered his living room and closed the sliding door behind him, heading to his bedroom for a restless night of sleep.

Cassandra walked into work the next morning knowing that Elizabeth was going to have questions about her weekend. She thought about avoiding her altogether but knew that Elizabeth was very persistent. The only thing that made Cassandra happy was knowing that her birthday and party was tomorrow.

"Good morning," Cassandra greeted.

"Hey," Elizabeth said. "Tell me what happened now."

"Nothing much, we ended up going to Vegas on Saturday."

"Yes, I know. What happened in Vegas?"

"Well, you know, a little of this. Ryan kissed Julie in front of me. Eric was staying in the same hotel room as Ryan and never told me until he was about to leave. Julie cried on the plane on the way back and then, when Ryan and I got home, we had amazing sex. How was your weekend?" Cassandra smiled.

"I love that you are such a slut," Elizabeth said, not holding back.

"Well, thank you. I did find a dress, which was the best part!"

"Are you excited?"

"Yes, I cannot wait for the drama tomorrow night. It's going to be amazing."

"How many people are going?"

"Just fifty of my closest LA friends."

Elizabeth smiled and went back to work.

Cassandra walked into her office, sat in her chair, and turned around to stare out of her window.

Later that day, Julie called Cassandra to talk about the previous night.

"Hey, where have you been? Did you talk to Ryan?"

"Hello Julie, how is your day going?" Cassandra asked sipping her vodka tonic for lunch.

"Great, did you talk to Ryan? I haven't seen him today." Julie whispered into the phone.

"I didn't have a chance to talk to him last night. When we got home, I went to sleep and he sat on the couch watching TV," Cassandra offered, remembering the amazing sex they had had.

"Oh really?"

"Yes, sorry, I will talk to him tonight."

"Okay, I am worried. I really want to know why he doesn't like me."

"Okay, I will find out.

"Where are you?" Julie asked curiously, hearing noise in the background.

"Just shopping and heading back to the office now."

"Okay, call me later."

Cassandra hung up the phone and had no intention of heading anywhere until she had had another cocktail. She loved drinking her lunches; it was the best way to save on calories.

The next morning, Cassandra woke up to someone knocking on her door and realized that Ryan had not come home last night. *How weird,* she thought getting out of bed and heading toward the door. *Who is knocking this early in the morning?* Cassandra found a delivery man standing outside her door with an enormous bouquet of floors and balloons.

"Delivery for Cassandra Zea," the middle-aged delivery man said with a smile.

"That's me!" Cassandra said excitedly.

"I am guessing today is your birthday?"

"Yes it is," Cassandra said grabbing the flowers.

"Please sign here and have a happy birthday."

"Thank you," Cassandra said, closing the door behind her.

She put the flowers on the kitchen counter and the balloons rose to the ceiling. She saw the card and opened it. She didn't bother reading the card because as soon as she opened it, she saw a check and dropped the card. Cassandra knew it was from her beloved mother back East. She looked at the check and said, "Happy Birthday to me!" The amount on the check was $5,000. Cassandra had an estranged but loving relationship with her mother, who did not agree with the way Cassandra lived her life. She thought about calling her to thank her, but she would wait till later. Having forgotten about Ryan for a second, she realized that he had not come home last night. She wondered where he had spent the night, but decided not to care because it was her birthday today. Cassandra skipped to her closet to decide on what to wear. She wondered where she would be able to get a drink this early in the morning.

Ryan looked at his watch while he was driving back to Cassandra's apartment. Ryan had spent the night with one of the girls he was currently dating. He thought that Cassandra may be mad since it was her birthday and he wasn't there in the morning. He reached the garage and realized he should have stopped to buy her roses.

Cassandra got ready and headed out the door. It was only eight o'clock in the morning, but she was ready to start her day. She walked outside her apartment building and decided on where to have breakfast. Then she remembered The Biltmore Hotel, one of her favorite places and it reminded her so much of New York City. She walked the two blocks to the hotel and took a seat at their indoor café. The waitress approached Cassandra and asked, "What would you like this morning?"

"Is it too early for champagne?" Cassandra said with a smile.

Ryan opened the door to the apartment slowly and walked in, not wanting to wake Cassandra. He noticed the huge bouquet of flowers on the kitchen counter and all the balloons clinging to the ceiling. He read the card: "Happy Birthday to my darling daughter. Love, Mommy." Ryan smiled to himself and, when he turned to the bedroom, noticed that Cassandra was not in bed. He walked further down to the closet—still nothing. He went to the bathroom and she was not there either. *She must have left for work already.*

He decided to take a shower and get ready for work.

Cassandra was sipping her glass of champagne when her cell phone rang.

"Hello," Cassandra said.

"Happy Birthday!" Elizabeth yelled. "What are you doing?"

"Thank you!" Cassandra said. "I am having breakfast. What are you doing?"

"Heading to work. Are you coming in today?"

"I don't think so. I did start the day with the intention of going in, but I don't think I am. You are coming to the party tonight, right? "Of course, I would not miss the drama."

"Great! Then I will see you later. I have to get back to my champagne," Cassandra said.

"Oh no, already?" Elizabeth said with a smirk.

"Yes, what can I say. I'm celebrating another year that I am alive."

"Have fun, I'll call you later."

As soon she had finished speaking to Elizabeth, her mom called. Cassandra hesitated for a second but took the call anyway.

Eugene opened his eyes and his alarm went off. He rolled over, turned the alarm off, and looked at the ceiling. He reached for his cell phone and looked at the time: 8:00 am. He stretched and thought about not going to work. He then thought, *what will I do if I don't go to work?* For a second, he contemplated the idea, but instead got up and headed to the kitchen for some water. As he sipped water, he stood looking around the enormous kitchen. He felt as if there was something he had to do today, but wasn't sure what. He returned to his bedroom to look at his cell phone. *Maybe I have a meeting?* he thought, but the calendar was empty today. He sat on his bed knowing that there was something today, but could not figure it out. He decided to forget about it and head for the shower. As the hot water hit his face, he suddenly remembered that it was Cassandra's birthday party today. Eugene sighed and closed his eyes and thought about Cassandra and her birthday last year. Eugene could not believe it had been a whole year since her last birthday. A year ago, Eugene had been in a different place in his life. Everything in his life had been jumbled and then this gentle, adorable woman had walked into his life. He was absolutely not ready for some-one—it was Cassandra, then—but when is someone ready for anything?

It was last June. Eugene had been partying like crazy. He hadn't wanted to remember his divorce and the fact that he no longer lived with his son. He used to party every night and before he could nurse his hangover, he would be already hitting the bottle. During one of his many evenings, he had encountered Cassandra and her amazing eyes. He had assumed his meeting with Cassandra was just for that one night. He enjoyed the drinking, dancing, and kissing on the Rooftop Bar at the Standard Hotel. When the night had ended, he had driven Cassandra home even though she lived across the street. When they had reached the front of her apartment, he had wanted to ask her if she would come home with him all the way to Orange County, and that had scared him because he was thinking of doing it with someone he had just met. He had continued kissing Cassandra in the car and just when he had been about to ask her, he had caught himself changing his mind and had instead said goodbye. His cousin had even mentioned that he had never seen Eugene into someone the way he was into Cassandra. Eugene had pulled away and driven home, thinking of Cassandra and her sweet kisses. After that night, Cassandra had sent him a text message and he had been in touch with her through texts and calls, which he did not do with other women. A month later, he had driven down from San Francisco and stopped in downtown LA to see Cassandra. He had admitted, only to himself, that he missed her. They had agreed to meet at the same bar they had first met at. When he had walked in, Cassandra was standing there looking even more beautiful then he could remember. He had walked quickly and given her a hug. Her smile had melted his heart and he had never wanted to leave her again, but his typical way of torturing himself would make him choose otherwise. They had walked into the bar and ordered cocktails, enjoying each other's company. For Eugene, it had been easy to open up to Cassandra and he hadn't had to bother being anyone but the imperfect person he was. As the night had progressed in laughter and smiles, they had decided to get a room. Walking to the lobby, Eugene had thrown his card on the reception desk and booked a room. Eugene and Cassandra had entered the elevator, kissing as the doors closed. He didn't remember much of what had happened the rest of the night in the room after they had taken their fifth tequila shot. The next day, he had woken up with a jolt and looked at Cassandra sleeping next to him. He had smiled to himself and rubbed his head. He lay looking at Cassandra, running his hand through her long shiny hair. Then, he had thought he shouldn't be having such feelings and had wanted to turn them off, but he hadn't been able to.

They had spent three days locked up in the hotel room, laughing, eating, and watching TV. He had told Cassandra all his secrets and stories about his family and she had listened attentively, taking in every word. He had enjoyed talking to her and the way she listened to him. He had even discussed how their wedding would be in Maui. At that point, he had been ready to take her to Maui. Although the one thing he had never told Cassandra and what she did not know to date was that at that time, his divorce had not yet been finalized. It was in process, and the court had not sealed the papers.

Eugene continued to let the water run down his face, as he remembered the rest of those memories.

Finally, after having spent three days together, Eugene had realized that he had to return to reality. He had been away from the world for three days, but he had never been happier. He had told Cassandra that it was time he returned to Orange County. He had seen the sadness on Cassandra's face, but he had promised he would be at her birthday party in three weeks. He had asked her if he could be her date and she had been delighted. He had been happy to accompany her. They had left the hotel room and he had driven her home, which was across the street. He had given her a hug and a kiss goodbye. As he had driven home, he had thought about everything that Cassandra and he had done and it had brought a smile to his face. Once he had returned to Orange County, he had gone right to party without taking a breath. Cassandra had tried calling him several times, but he had ignored her, sending her sporadic text messages. He knew he was hurting Cassandra, but at the time the only person he could think of was himself. He had also remembered that her birthday party was approaching and on the night before he had the option of heading toward Los Angeles or San Diego—and had selected San Diego for a two-day drinking binge. When he had woken up, it had been Sunday morning—Father's Day and Cassandra's actual birthday. He had missed her party the night before. He had looked at his phone and thought about calling her, but he didn't know what to say. As his head had started to clear later that day, he had started thinking about checking himself into rehab to seek help for his drinking, but knew he could change by himself. Then, he had thought about Cassandra; he hated himself for what he had done to her the night before. He knew she had been counting on him and he had made a promise to her. He had then remembered that Cassandra was leaving for Paris the following day for three weeks. By the time he had built enough courage to call Cassandra, her voicemail had stated she was on her way to Paris for three weeks. Eugene hadn't slept the whole night, thinking about Cassandra and how he had lost the chance to apologize to her. As soon as the sun had risen, he had got up, gone to his closet, and reached for his luggage that was on the top shelf of his closet. He had started packing his clothes with no set plan. Once he was done, he had closed his bag, grabbed his passport and keys, and got into his car. He had driven to the airport, parked his car, and walked into the Air France terminal. It was still early and only one person was working.

"Good morning, I need a ticket to Paris, France."

"For today?" the gentleman had looked at him strangely.

"Yes, when is the next flight leaving?"

"Well, sir, there is no direct flight to Paris from the John Wayne Airport. You have to fly on a Delta to Houston, Texas, and there you will transfer to an Air France flight."

"Okay, please book me a ticket on the next flight to Houston and then on to Paris," Eugene said as he took out his Platinum Credit Card and placed it on the check-in desk.

"I can get you to Houston on the 9:00 a.m. flight and then on the 12:00 p.m. flight to Paris non-stop."

"Perfect and please make sure it's first class for both flights."

"Will there be a return date?" the check-in attendant had asked Eugene, already hating him.

"No, just book me one way," Eugene had said, checking his pockets to make sure he had everything.

"Okay, with the times of the selected flights and first-class cabin, the ticket will be $4,520.

"Fine, just put it on this credit card."

The check-in attendant had taken his credit card with annoyance and run it through the system.

"How many bags will you be checking in?"

"One bag."

"I also need your passport."

"Yes, it's right here. Also, there is internet access in the first-class lounge?"

"Of course, along with a continental breakfast."

"Thanks," Eugene said as he waited to get back his credit card and passport.

Once the check-in attendant had given him his ticket and items back, he had headed to security and then to the first-class lounge. He still had no plan for when he arrived in Paris. He had sat down at one of the computers and started researching the hotels in Paris. He hadn't fully remembered the hotel name that Cassandra mentioned she was staying at, but knew that once he started looking at hotel names, he would remember. He had found two hotels with similar names, and they were in the same arrondissement. He had looked at his watch and headed for the flight gate. Eugene hated flying, but he had sat down and looked out the window. Finally having a moment, he had asked himself, "What am I doing? Am I this crazy to get on a plane to Pairs for a girl I barely know?" But before he could answer, his heart had answered for him. He had known this was what he wanted and he was following his heart.

It was a warm, sunny afternoon when he had arrived in Paris. He loved Paris and everything that it offered. Yes, it truly was the city of love. Eugene had taken a taxi and told the driver the name of the first hotel. On arriving, he asked the driver to wait to make sure this was the correct hotel. He walked into the tiny, but glamorous lobby and found someone to help him.

"Bonjour monsieur, is there someone here staying by the name of IsaCassandra Zea?"

"Monsieur, let me check, one moment."

The receptionist had started typing and Eugene's heart had begun racing, as if Cassandra were to appear from behind the desk.

"Ah, yes, Ms. IsaCassandra is staying with us. She is on a tour right now scheduled to be back in two hours. Would you like to leave a message for her, sir?"

"No, no. I will wait for her to return."

"Yes, sir. There is a café in the hotel and some others around the corner."

"Thank you." Eugene had walked outside to pay the driver and take his luggage.

He had decided then on getting a much-needed drink at the café in the hotel and wait for time to pass by.

After an hour, he had headed back to the lobby with his luggage and had sat on the couch near the hotel entrance. He had wanted to make sure he wouldn't miss Cassandra. When he was in the hotel, he had thought about what he would say to her. He tried to practice a speech, but couldn't come up with anything. Moments later, Eugene had noticed a bus pull up to the hotel and a group of people got off and headed into the hotel. He had looked in between the group, hoping to see Cassandra but the group was huddled very close together. They had passed him by and at the end, Cassandra had walked by without noticing Eugene.

"Cassandra," Eugene had called.

Cassandra had slowly turned around, now seeing Eugene. He noticed her shocked and confused expressions but she ran to him and hugged him. He had hugged her back, taking one look at her and then kissed her.

"What are you doing here?" Cassandra had asked catching her breath.

"I wanted to apologize for missing your birthday party." Eugene had smiled.

"A phone call would have been sufficient."

"Yes, but I thought saying it in person would be better," Eugene had said and kissed her again.

Cassandra had grabbed Eugene's hand and taken him to the elevator and then to her room. Eugene had been nervous, knowing they were going to make love. They had spent the whole afternoon in bed. The next three weeks had been magical for him and Cassandra. They had gone sightseeing, eaten at every café in sight, drank every kind of champagne and wine, and he had bought Cassandra anything she desired.

He had left a day before Cassandra. She had accompanied him to the airport. He had not wanted to say goodbye, but he had to get back to CA for business. He had promised her that once she would return, they would get together and talk about what the future held for them. He had made many promises to her, kissed her, and said goodbye.

When the plane had landed in Orange County, he had immediately tended to business matters. He hadn't felt sure of what was to become of him and Cassandra. He had failed to make on his promise. He hadn't answered any of Cassandra's calls and text messages for about three weeks. He just hadn't known what to do about them or what he would be able to offer her emotionally. He had known that Cassandra was seeking something long term, and that he wasn't capable of that, not at that point. When he had finally responded to her text message, he knew that something had changed, but he wasn't sure what.

Eugene turned off the shower and knew he would not be attending Cassandra's birthday party tonight. As much as he knew it would hurt her, he just couldn't give in to her—not yet, he wasn't ready. He got ready for work and decided to push back the thoughts he had dug up deep into the back of his mind, where he wanted to leave them.

Chapter 17

Cassandra ignored the phone calls on her cell phone, because she was getting ready for the party. She was applying her makeup when she heard someone knock. She opened the door and Julie was standing outside the door, holding bottles of champagne.

"Happy Birthday!" Julie said.

"Thank you," Cassandra said and gave her a hug.

"Let's open a bottle," Cassandra said, taking one from Julie's hand.

Julie looked around the loft.

"Where is Ryan?"

"I am not sure, probably on his way home," Cassandra said ignoring the fact that Julie was here because she wanted to be with Ryan.

"How was your day?" Julie asked, accepting the champagne glass Cassandra gave.

"Cheers!" Cassandra said.

"Cheers!" Julie said.

"Today has been good. Had breakfast, went shopping, came home, took a nap, and started getting ready."

"Nice. I brought my clothes to change."

"Good," Cassandra said refilling her champagne glass.

Cassandra's phone kept ringing, and she walked toward it to see who was calling. In the back of her head, she was secretly wishing that one of the callers was Eugene. He should have remembered it was her birthday.

"Who keeps calling?" Julie asked.

"Different people."

"Do you want more champagne?" Cassandra asked Julie.

"Sure," Julie said.

Cassandra was pouring more champagne into Julie's glass when the door opened, and Ryan walked in.

"Hey birthday girl," Ryan said, walking over to Cassandra to give her a hug and a kiss.

"Thanks."

"I came home this morning, but you were already gone."

"Yeah, I started my day early."

"Hi Ryan," Julie said in case he hadn't noticed her.

"Hey Julie," Ryan said as he walked over and gave her a hug.

"Ryan, would you like some champagne?" Cassandra asked.

"Sure, pour me some."

Cassandra walked toward the counter, reached for a champagne glass, and grabbed the bottle of the champagne. Just as she was about to pour the champagne, she had a flashback of Eugene.

Eugene had surprised her in Paris after having completely let her down at her birthday party. She had been devastated, but when he had appeared in Paris, she knew that he loved her, but he needed to take his time. You couldn't force someone like Eugene; he did things on his own time. After having spent those three magical weeks, she couldn't have been happier. Cassandra remembered having said goodbye to Eugene at the airport, while being scared that everything he was promising would not be delivered. She had left the airport in tears not knowing what to expect when she returned to CA. She had decided to go back to the hotel room. A couple of days before Eugene was to leave, Cassandra had started feeling sick every day, but hadn't thought anything of it. She assumed it was from all the drinking and eating they had been doing. On that particular day when Eugene left Paris, she had felt more nausea than the other days, and had vomited when she returned to the hotel room. She thought it was from the nerves of watching Eugene leave and the uncertainty of when she would see him. She was still sick when she had returned to CA and decided to go to the hospital. It was there that she had learned that she was two weeks pregnant. Cassandra had not been able to believe what the doctors were telling her. She had left the hospital numb because she knew that there was no future for this baby. She could never tell Eugene that she was pregnant because she already knew what his response would be. He was definitely not ready to have another child and she was not ready to bring a child into this world alone. Cassandra hadn't slept for days after getting the news, wondering what to do. She had decided on telling Eugene that she was pregnant but her decision was to not keep the baby. It would not have been fair to bring another human being into this world if the parents were not ready to give it everything they could. It was the best option. For two weeks, she had tried getting hold of Eugene. She had called him, texted him, even called him at work, but Eugene hadn't returned any of her calls. She had known a little over a month ago that she was pregnant and couldn't wait anymore. She had tried one more time, and with no response, she had given up. The next day she had booked an appointment at the health clinic for her abortion. She had chosen not to tell anyone and had gone by herself. She had been terrified, but knew it was the right decision. When she was done, Cassandra had walked with an empty feeling and a blank look. While in the taxi, on the way home, her cell phone had started beeping with an incoming text: "Sorry, I have been extremely busy playing catch up at work. Hope you are well and will call you when I get my head above water - Eugene" Tears had started pouring from Cassandra's eyes. She had lost feeling in her body and wasn't sure how she would ever feel again. Till this day, she hadn't told Eugene or anyone about that day.

"Cassandra, Cassandra," Ryan yelled.

Cassandra, still holding the champagne bottle, realized she had been lost in her thoughts.

"Yes," Cassandra said, turning around with a smile.

"Are you going to pour me some champagne?"

"I'm sorry, I lost track of my thoughts for a moment," Cassandra said as she turned back to the pour the champagne hoping they hadn't noticed the tears that had started trickling down her face.

After an hour of indulging in drinking and eating, the three of them headed out the door to the Standard Hotel. The Standard Hotel was a landmark for Cassandra. Everything always happened to her at the Standard Hotel. They breezed by security and headed upstairs to the rooftop bar where Cassandra secured the center couches in the middle of the floor and ordered bottles of champagne for her guests. In the beginning, it had only been Cassandra, with Julie clinging onto the Ryan the whole time. Cassandra just ignored her and kept drinking her champagne waiting for the other guests to arrive. Finally, Oscar and Lizzette had arrived with the other friends. Cassandra was thrilled to see them because she was bored of Julie gazing into Ryan's eyes the whole time ignoring Cassandra. As soon as Lizzette arrived, Cassandra sat next to her and narrated the story of what was transpiring between her and Ryan and then Ryan and Julie. Lizzette just sat there in awe looking at Cassandra as if she was making this story up.

"Wait, you and Ryan are sleeping together, and Julie has no clue?"

"Yes," Cassandra said sipping her champagne.

"You are truly unbelievable."

"Thanks. Oh, I see some more friends; be right back!"

Cassandra approached her friends who just arrived. Her friends were always beautiful and tall just like her. Two of them were bombshell knockouts at five feet ten inches with figures other women would die for. They greeted Cassandra with hugs and kisses, and she brought them over to where her friends were sitting. The girls knew some of the other guests. Then, Cassandra's favorite person walked in: Downtown LA's famous defense attorney—the buzz was that he was only famous was because he had never lost a case. He had become good friends with Cassandra.

"Cassandra, you always look so beautiful."

"Thank you."

"Come let's go to the bar, I will buy you and your friends anything you and they want."

He pulled Cassandra toward the bar and signaled the bartender.

As the night progressed, more of Cassandra's friends arrived—those whom she had not seen in a while and those she had met just the previous day. Then she noticed Alex arrive and was surprised to see him there.

"Happy birthday, Cassandra."

"Hi Alex, thanks for coming!" Cassandra was happy to see him and hugged him. She introduced Alex to some of her girlfriends that she knew he would like.

An hour after Alex arrived, Cassandra was standing by the bar talking to some friends when she noticed Eric walk by. At first, she thought she had made a mistake, but then realized that it was indeed him. Excusing herself, she walked over to him.

"Hey, you came after all."

"Yes, I wouldn't miss your birthday for the world."

Eric gave Cassandra a big hug and kiss. She was ecstatic. She then walked him over to where the others were sitting and Eric saw Ryan and Alex. Soon after, they all walked to the bar and had birthday shots with Cassandra. Without her knowing, a cake had been brought out and everyone started singing happy birthday. Then, everyone hit the dance floor. As Cassandra was dancing with everyone, one of her friends came up behind Cassandra and started grinding with her. Seeing this, Eric got jealous and pushed Cassandra's friend. Her friend responded and pushed Eric back. This caught the attention of the security and they rushed over. Cassandra got in between to stop them and assured the security that it would not repeat.

"If it does, we are kicking both of them out of here."

"Understood," Cassandra said and looked at Eric.

"If you push him again, the security is going to throw you out."

"Fine," Eric said visibly upset.

They continued dancing. In the midst of the party and drama, Cassandra did not notice that Ryan and Julie had left the party and headed downstairs to play pool.

"I bet you a hundred dollars I win," Ryan said to Julie as he racked up the balls.

"You are on," Julie said with a big smile.

"Okay, but if you lose you can go back on your word."

"I won't," she looked at Ryan with a very loving look.

Upstairs, Cassandra sat down on the couch and drank some champagne. It was the first time all night that she had thought about Eugene. She didn't want to ruin her night by thinking about him, but it was the first moment she had alone to herself since arriving at the bar. She grabbed her glass of champagne and walked toward the railing, staring beyond all the buildings and their twinkling lights. She started remembering what had happened after her visit to the clinic.

Eugene had finally responded to her numerous calls and texts. At this point, Cassandra had not been sure if she should tell Eugene. She had already taken care of the situation and telling Eugene would not change the outcome. Different types of emotions were running through her and she hadn't known how to respond to his text message. Part of her wanted to tell him and send him to hell, and the other part wanted to tell him that she loved him and to forgive her for what she had done. She knew at the time it was the best option for them. Then, she had finally decided if she ever wanted Eugene to be part of her life at all, she would have to play his game and give him time. She knew that as time went by, he would come around. She had finally texted him back, "Glad you are okay. I am doing fine. I am sure you are backed up at work since we spent three fabulous weeks in Paris. Call me when you get a chance." Cassandra had left it at that and waited for Eugene. It had taken him a month to actually call her back and by then Cassandra had not cared about anything and would spend her days drinking and trying to forget.

Cassandra hated thinking about the previous year. She had come a long way in some ways and still needed help in other ways. Chills ran up her spine just thinking about last summer. She was in a different place now, but a better place—somewhere in between. Then, Cassandra felt a hand on her shoulder.

"Are you okay?" her friend Lizzette was asking. "You seem to be somewhere else. When I called your name you didn't respond."

"I am okay. I was just thinking about last summer."

"Oh gosh, that was an intense summer."

"Tell me about it," Cassandra said still staring at the buildings.

"I don't mean to bring anything up, but has Eugene called or texted you?"

"No, he knew about the party, but he hasn't called. I pretty much doubt he's coming or even remembers."

"I am sorry."

"It's okay; I expected nothing less from him," Cassandra said still trying to shake off the memories.

"Well, enough talk. Let's go take some shots of Patron!" Lizzette yelled.

Cassandra and Lizzette walked to the bar and started drinking more.

"Hey, by the way, where is your boyfriend and his stalker?" Lizzette asked biting on a lime.

"I don't know." Cassandra looked around for Ryan and Julie who were nowhere in sight. She shrugged and went back to drinking.

"I told you I would win," Ryan said to Julie as he walked by her.

"I am over this," Julie said looking for a hundred-dollar bill in her purse. "Here, don't spend it all in one place." "Thanks," Ryan said taking the hundred-dollar bill and putting it in his pocket. "Are you ready to go back upstairs?"

"Let's go," Julie said, agitated.

Ryan and Julie exited the elevator upstairs and headed toward the bar. Cassandra spotted them both and walked over. At this point, she had consumed a lot of alcohol and she was starting to feel it.

"Where have you guys been?" Cassandra asked defiantly folding her arms across her chest.

"We went downstairs to play pool," Ryan asked matching tone for tone.

"The party isn't downstairs, it's up here," Cassandra said looking straight at Julie. Then she turned around and walked away.

"What's her problem?" Julie asked Ryan.

"I am not sure, and I don't want to find out," Ryan said as he walked toward the bar. Julie followed one step behind him.

"What was that about?" Lizzette asked Cassandra as she walked toward her.

"Nothing, all Julie wants is Ryan to herself and doesn't even hang out with me when it's my birthday! Whatever, I am over it. Let's dance!" Cassandra said and she grabbed Lizzette's hand and pulled her to the dance floor.

As it was getting close to last call, Ryan found Cassandra, "Are you ready to go?"

"Yeah, let's head home," Cassandra said.

She started saying goodbye to the few guests that were still there. In the meantime, Ryan had gathered Alex and Eric to come back to the apartment with him. They all met at the elevator and Cassandra spotted Eric and walked toward him. She was a bit intoxicated by now and was being very flirtatious with Eric. He loved it and reciprocated.

"Are you coming back to my apartment?" Cassandra asked looking directly into his eyes.

"Of course," Eric said, wanting to kiss Cassandra.

The elevator doors opened and they all got in.

Eric grabbed Cassandra's hand and waited for the elevator to reach the ground floor.

They exited the hotel and started walking toward the apartment. At this point, Julie had started talking to Alex and Eric about Ryan. Cassandra let go of Eric's hand and caught up to Ryan.

"Did Julie suffocate you enough tonight?" Cassandra said

"Maybe," Ryan replied.

"I guess you like it," Cassandra responded. "By the way, I believe she may be under false pretenses because she believes she is staying and sleeping with you. I just don't know where this is going to take place."

"She is not staying over," Ryan said.

"Well, you tell her that," Cassandra said smiling to herself.

"Do you think Ryan likes me?" Julie asked Alex and Eric.

"I am not sure if he does. Why don't you ask him?" Eric responded.

"Listen Julie, he doesn't talk about anyone else besides you. You can pretty much say he does like you," Alex replied.

"Really, you think?" Julie was excited.

"Yes," Alex said starting to get annoyed. "Also, just give him time, don't pressure him into anything. Guys don't like that."

"Okay," Julie said making a mental note to herself.

Cassandra and Ryan reached the apartment first and the rest of the group was close behind them.

"Wait for us," Alex called out.

Cassandra walked into the apartment without waiting for anyone. Ryan held the door open for the other three. Cassandra started eating pizza because she was hungry from all the alcohol she had drunk. When Julie entered, Cassandra turned around and looked at her angrily. She was upset at Julie for not being a good friend and trying to spend all her time with Ryan. Ryan and Julie sat on the couch and watched highlights from that night's basketball game. Alex and Eric joined Cassandra in eating pizza.

"I don't think I can eat anymore." Cassandra was starting to feel nauseous.

"I would feel that way too if I drank as much as you," Eric replied.

"Will you hold my hair if I have to vomit?" Cassandra asked Eric.

"Of course, sweetie. I would do anything for you."

Cassandra smiled and kissed Eric on the mouth. Then she looked over at Ryan and Julie and noticed how close Julie was to Ryan. Cassandra walked over to the living room.

"By the way, Julie, you suck as a friend. You just wanted to spend the whole night with Ryan instead of hanging out with me at *my* birthday party. And Ryan you suck too. Both of you suck!" Cassandra said walked back toward the kitchen. Ryan and Julie looked at each other blankly and continued watching

TV. Eric and Ryan laughed because they knew Cassandra was too drunk and didn't know what she was saying.

"So, Eric," Cassandra started, "Do you want to lie down on my bed?"

"I am out of here," Alex said. Knowing he was the odd man out, he left the apartment.

Eric followed Cassandra to her bed, passing by Ryan and Julie who were now trying to fit themselves on the couch to try to sleep. Eric sat on the bed, as Cassandra stood in front of him, took off her dress, and threw it on the floor. Eric smiled as he admired Cassandra's body, her red lacy panties, and no bra. He grabbed and pulled her toward him and they started kissing. He ran his hands down Cassandra's back while feeling her nipples harden. At the same time, he was feeling aroused. He gently lay her on the bed next to him when all of a sudden they heard Julie yell, "Ryan," followed by a thump on the floor. Ryan had pushed Julie off the couch! Eric and Cassandra started laughing uncontrollably and Julie tried to reposition herself on the couch again. Eric went to Cassandra's side again and wanted her right there, but he knew that Julie and Ryan were still there and he couldn't do anything. Instead, he noticed Cassandra starting to fall asleep and decided to leave. She felt Eric leave and covered herself and went to sleep. Shortly after, Julie could no longer sleep on the couch and saw space on the bed, and came to sleep in Cassandra's bed.

Chapter 18

*T*he next morning, Ryan woke Cassandra.

"Cassandra, Cassandra, wake up. Are you going to work today? It's 9:00 a.m."

It took Cassandra a moment to wake up and realize where she was. She opened her eyes and tried to focus on Ryan.

"What's going on?" she asked Ryan trying to get him to stand still.

"It's 9:00 a.m. Are you going to work? If yes, you are going to be late."

Late, Cassandra thought to herself. *She didn't even know where she was.*

"Okay, thanks," Cassandra said and went back to sleep. Then, she noticed Julie was sleeping next to her and wondered how she got there. She nudged Julie because she knew she had to be at work in forty-five minutes. Julie didn't move so Cassandra nudged her harder this time.

"What? What is happening?" Julie said slowly opening her eyes.

"Ryan said it's 9:00 a.m. and something about work," Cassandra mumbled with her eyes closed.

"Oh really?" she sat up on the bed with the biggest headache ever.

Ryan was rushing around the loft because he was going to be late for a meeting.

"Good morning," Julie said to Ryan.

"Hey," Ryan said and he put on his jacket and adjusted his tie. "I am running really late this morning."

"Do you have a meeting?" Julie said.

"Yes, and it's half an hour away."

Ryan threw his stuff in his briefcase and headed toward the door. He yelled "Bye" and closed the door behind him. Julie replied "Bye" knowing he wasn't going to hear her. She looked over at Cassandra who was sleeping and decided to start getting ready for work. She showered, changed, and put her things together from the night before. How weird last night had been for her. She recapped the moments from where Ryan had started indicating that he liked her, then playing pool together, and then Cassandra yelling at them because she was not a good friend. Cassandra woke up when she heard Julie close the door behind her. She tried lifting her head, but it hurt immensely. It even hurt to think. She tried getting out of bed, but decided it would be easier to just lay there and not move. Cassandra thought how much she had enjoyed her birthday party. *Another success,* she told herself. Cassandra reached for her phone and started looking through her missed call log and text message. *Thankfully,* she thought, *she didn't drunk dial anyone.* By now, it was 10:00 a.m. and too late to go to work. Plus she knew it would take all day to get rid of her headache. She sent Elizabeth a text: "Not coming today, call you later." She put her phone away, rolled over, and went back to sleep.

Some days had passed since Cassandra's birthday party and she had confronted Julie about her behavior during her party. Julie had apologized about it, but Cassandra was still angry and in time she would make Julie pay for her little episode. It was now Saturday morning and Cassandra had woken up to not find Ryan next to her. The last few days Ryan had been spending his nights elsewhere—not that it mattered to Cassandra, but it did make her feel lonely at night. Cassandra was lying on her couch watching TV when she received a text message from Ryan, "Have you eaten lunch yet?"

Cassandra read the message twice and wondered about what to respond.

It took her a couple of minutes; then she texted, "No, I have not."

Ryan replied, "Don't. On my way home."

Cassandra read the message and put down the phone.

She wondered what he was up to but continued watching TV.

An hour later, he showed up at the apartment.

"Hey sexy, how's it going?"

Cassandra looked at Ryan and turned back to the TV.

"Ignoring me?"

"No, just watching this show."

"I stopped at the store to get some food to BBQ on the rooftop."

"What did you get?"

"Steak and chicken—because I know you don't eat red meat—and potatoes and corn. Let's go upstairs and cook food."

"Okay, I am going to take a shower. I will meet you up there."

"I have to prep the food first."

Cassandra got into the shower and took her time. She got out of the shower, and wrapped herself in a towel, and walked outside. Ryan was prepping the meats.

He looked at Cassandra in her towel, feeling aroused. He tried to concentrate on the meats.

She walked toward the dresser to find something to wear. She knew Ryan was staring at her the entire time, and she let her towel fall accidentally. She bent down to reach for it and noticed Ryan walking toward her. Unable to resist himself, he pulled the towel away from her and placed her on the bed. He unbuckled his pants and entered Cassandra with sweet passion. She smiled to herself as she watched him enjoy himself.

Ryan was barbecuing the meats as Cassandra sat on a barstool drinking a beer. Outside, it was perfect Saturday afternoon in downtown LA. The sky was blue with no clouds, a view that could be seen for miles away.

"What's up with you and Julie?" Cassandra asked not looking at Ryan but admiring the view.

"Funny," Ryan remarked.

"Just asking, since we are friends and all."

"Right, she has been quiet for a couple of days."

"That is because I yelled at her for her behavior at my party."

"Interesting."

"Yes, anyway, what else is new?"

"Nothing much, talked to my mom in Vegas."

"How is she doing?"

"Good."

"How come you never mention your father?" Cassandra asked, looking at Ryan for his reaction.

"I am not sure; we grew apart years ago."

"I am sorry," Cassandra said remembering her own family problems.

When they started eating, Ryan got into a deep conversation about his father and mother and how his parents had got divorced at an early age. During his childhood, Ryan's dad would always take him to the Chicago Cubs baseball games because he would have season tickets. As Ryan grew older, his father started distancing himself more and more and his grandfather took over the "dad" role. In the last couple of years, Ryan's grandfather and grandmother had passed away leaving him with his mother and estranged father. Ryan didn't know why he was telling all this to Cassandra, but he felt comfortable with her.

"Have you tried contacting your dad?" Cassandra asked, in between bites of chicken.

"No, not really. I tried a couple of times many years ago, but nothing came out of it."

"I am sorry. Do you plan to try again?"

"I don't think so. The relationship is dead . . . has been dead for many years."

"Well, I think you should try, you never know, and it's not too late."

"Okay, enough of this talk. How is your food?"

"It's good," Cassandra said as she smiled at Ryan knowing she had broken through the first and most important layer of ice that he had built around him.

When they returned to the apartment, Ryan noticed how he was enjoying his time with Cassandra and wanted to continue spending the afternoon with her. She had received a couple of text messages from Julie, but chose to ignore them. "Hey, do you want to learn how to play poker?" Ryan asked putting the leftovers in the refrigerator.

"Sure, why not!"

"Great," Ryan said as he got his poker chips and cards.

They both sat on the floor in the middle of the loft. Ryan opened up his poker case and took out his chips and started shuffling the cards. Cassandra observed Ryan's intensity, admiring his focus on shuffling and counting the chips. Cassandra thought to herself for a second, *maybe I can see myself with someone like Ryan or Ryan himself.* They continued playing poker with Ryan showing Cassandra every step and Cassandra picking it up quickly.

"Maybe I should head to Vegas and start playing professionally."

"You should. You are good despite having just learned today!"

"Yes, I am," Cassandra said, knowing that she had learned to play poker before she could write. It was one of the many things one learns when growing in a large city like NY, *but I can pretend,* she thought.

After an hour of playing, Ryan and Cassandra were done with the game.

"What are your plans for tonight?" Ryan asked Cassandra as they sat on the couch. "Hanging out with Julie?"

"Funny! Probably."

"I have to get ready to head out," Ryan said. "I have a date with Hermosa girl tonight."

"Cool," Cassandra said trying not to sound too jealous.

Ryan got into the shower and Cassandra looked at her phone. She had numerous texts from Julie. She decided to just call her.

"Hey," Cassandra said not really paying attention because her mind was focused on Ryan.

"Where have you been?"

"I have been hanging out with Ryan all day; we were having a 'roomie day,'" Cassandra said making sure that Julie got jealous.

"Great, what did you guys do?"

"Ryan barbecued and showed me how to play poker. Now, he is getting ready for a date with Hermosa girl," Cassandra said smiling to herself.

"Oh, who is this Hermosa girl?" Julie asked holding back her tears.

"Some girl he met who lives in Hermosa. I don't know all the details. Anyway, what are you doing tonight?"

"Nothing. Want to get some drinks?"

"Sure, why don't you come over in a couple of hours?" Cassandra said making sure she and Ryan didn't meet.

"Okay, see you soon," Julie said and hung up. As soon as she did, tears started rolling down her cheeks. *Why was Ryan going out with another girl? Was he just playing with her feelings?* Julie composed herself and got ready to head out to Cassandra's for, hopefully, some excitement.

Cassandra woke up on Sunday morning and hated the fact that Julie was spending the night only in the hopes of seeing Ryan. The downside, for Julie, was that Ryan was not coming home anytime soon. He enjoyed spending his time in the South Bay area. Cassandra lay in her bed annoyed with Julie. She then thought of an idea. The night before, Julie had mentioned that she was going to an LA Dodger's game mid-week but would be sitting in one of the suites. *What if,* she thought, *I told Julie that it would be great if she invited Ryan to the game? Next, I'll tell her to buy three tickets one each for me, Ryan, and her, even though Julie would be sitting in the suite. Then, I'll tell Ryan that I've bought two tickets to the game and if he'd like to go. On the other hand, I will tell Julie that Ryan agreed to go to the game knowing Julie was going to be there, but only I will know that Ryan does not know. Next, I'll tell Julie to come down during the third innings to join us, but I'll act as if I have no clue and Julie had tricked me into buying the seat next to me. It was going to be perfect. I will set both Ryan and Julie up for failure.* Cassandra stretched her long body and smiled to herself. *Time to wake up Julie,* she thought.

It was mid-week and Cassandra's plan had unfurled and fallen into place by itself. Cassandra, for added drama, said that she bought the two tickets from Julie because she was going to sit in the suite all night. It was horrible to play with people's feelings and emotions, but at the end of the day, it was all in good fun. Ryan and Cassandra met up at the apartment a couple of hours before the game and started drinking some beers.

"Excited about the game?" Cassandra asked.

"Yeah, always happy to see a baseball game."

"Cool."

"Just to make sure about tonight. Julie is not sitting with us, right?"

"No, she and I were going to the game, but received an invitation from a client to sit up in one of the suites and sold me the tickets."

"Okay, do you want to get going?"

"Sure, let's go see some Dodgers."

Entry into the stadium was clogged with traffic and Julie had purchased special parking for Ryan and Cassandra. Cassandra had smiled to herself remembering about that. Once they were able to park, they walked toward the stadium and headed to get some beers.

Julie had texted Cassandra, "Are you guys here?"

"Yes, on our way to our seats."

"See you soon," Julie texted back.

After purchasing some beers, Ryan and Cassandra found their seats and waited for the game to start. They casually talked about work and their weekend plans. Cassandra thought sometimes she wanted Ryan all to herself, but it was more of just getting what she wanted and she was one to always get what she wants. Around the third innings, Julie made her way down to the seats where Ryan and Cassandra were sitting. Julie was nervous to see Ryan because she wanted him to like her. She walked down close to the field and found Ryan and Cassandra drinking beer.

"Hey guys," Julie said.

"Hey Julie," Cassandra said surprisingly.

"Hi Ryan," Julie said nervously.

"Hey Julie," Ryan said sounding awkward.

Julie proceeded to pass by Ryan and Cassandra and took the empty seat next to Cassandra. Cassandra smiled at herself because her plan was working better than she thought. Ryan now knew he was trapped and didn't know what to do. He decided to run up to the stands and get more beer.

"Anyone want some beer?"

"Yes, one for me please," Cassandra said.

"Julie, would you like one?"

"Sure, thanks."

Ryan left.

"See Julie, he was nice to you. You have nothing to worry about. The only piece of advice I am going to give you is not to act too clingy like you usually do. Just pretend you don't like him, and give him space to breathe."

"I know, aren't I doing good?"

"Yes, so far you are," Cassandra said. What she really wanted to say was *you will be okay as long as you keep your trap shut.*

Ryan returned with the beers, passing one to Cassandra and one to Julie. They all sat and watched the game with Cassandra just talking and neither of the other two saying much. Once the game was done, the three of them walked out of the stadium.

"Do you guys want to get more drinks?" Ryan asked the girls.

"I am up for it," Cassandra said really wanting to go home and make out with Ryan.

"Sure," Julie said, "But where?"

"How about Casey's next to our building?" Ryan suggested.

"Okay. Julie, you will meet us there?" Cassandra said as she started walking toward Ryan's car.

"Yeah," Julie said and walked toward her car.

Ryan and Cassandra got into Ryan's car.

"I can't believe she tricked me," Cassandra said angrily. "She told me she only bought two tickets."

"Really?" Ryan said not fully believing Cassandra.

"Yes, she told she only had two tickets; she must have set the whole thing up."

"Well, we will only have a drink or two with her and call it a night."

"Okay," Cassandra agreed.

Ryan drove out of the garage thinking to himself, *did Cassandra really plan this whole situation or was it Julie? What would Cassandra get out of this if she did?* He decided to stop thinking and just try to make the best of the situation.

Julie met Ryan and Cassandra at the underground bar, which was dimly lit and had no air conditioning. They all sat on barstools and ordered their individual signature drinks: Cassandra, vodka tonic; Julie, Jack and Coke; Ryan, beer.

They sat and talked for a while, Julie trying to get Ryan's attention and Cassandra looking around the bar trying to find someone decent to pass time with. In between, Ryan left for the restroom.

"How am I doing?" Julie asked.

"You are doing great, Cassandra said sounding bored with her already.

"Do you think he likes me more today?"

"Maybe, just make sure to get the tone low and act like you don't like him," Cassandra said wishing Julie would leave because there was no other man that looked promising other than Ryan.

"After you finish your drink, you should leave before Ryan and I do. This way you look less desperate and don't care about being here."

"Really?" Julie asked not wanting to leave until Ryan and Cassandra left. She wanted to spend time with Ryan.

"Trust me, it will look good," Cassandra reassured her.

"Okay," Julie replied.

When Ryan returned, Julie did not heed Cassandra's advice and ordered another drink because she wanted to spend time with Ryan. Ryan instead said he was going upstairs much to her disappointment.

"I'm going upstairs. Bye Julie, I had fun. Cassandra, I will see you in a bit."

"Bye Ryan," Julie said.

Cassandra just nodded.

Once Ryan walked up the stairs of the bar, Cassandra scolded Julie.

"I told you to be the first one to leave. It would have looked great. What were you thinking?"

"I know, I just couldn't leave. I really like Ryan."

"Well, you will never get him like this."

"Okay, I will listen to you from now on."

"I would not give you advice that would ruin your chances with him."

"I know," Julie replied, wishing Ryan would have stayed for another drink.

After Julie finished her drink, they said goodbye. Julie headed for her car looking disappointed and trying to not cry, but the first two tears had already escaped. She got into her car and drove off the in hope that her mistake at the bar would not cost her.

Cassandra pushed the elevator button and waited. Once it arrived, she entered the elevator and headed to the top floor of the building where her apartment was located. Cassandra's apartment took almost the entire floor of the building. It was a magnificent 2,000 square feet loft with floor-to-ceiling windows. All the kitchen appliances were stainless steel and her furniture was a modern dark brown color. People had always questioned how she paid for such a pricey apartment knowing that she didn't have a well-paying job. She had brushed off the questions and kept the information secret. She entered the apartment and admired the view from her living room windows. Setting her purse and keys on the kitchen counter, she noticed Ryan in bed watching TV.

"Hey," Cassandra said walking to the closet to undress herself.

"Did Julie go home?"

"Yes," Cassandra said exhausted. She quickly changed and headed to her side of the bed to lie next to Ryan. Cassandra sometimes wondered why they played all these games. If they were a couple, the relationship would have its ups and downs, but it would be fun too.

Cassandra turned on her side and wished Ryan goodnight.

Ryan replied with a "Goodnight" but instead of turning away from Cassandra, he hugged her from behind and they fell asleep.

Chapter 19

July marked the middle of summer for many. For Eugene, it was another reminder of how fast time was passing by and yet not much had changed in his life. His partying ways were supposed to decrease in the last year; if anything, it had stayed the same and also elevated to another level. Eugene sat in his office chair, staring out the window that overlooked Fashion Island. He remembered the first incident that should have been a wake-up call to his drinking. *It was last November and Eugene had been on his way back from visiting friends in the northern part of Orange County. It was close to midnight and he had had too many glasses of chardonnay. He had got behind the wheel, never thinking about the dangers to his life or others. He knew he had control. As he had exited the residential streets and onto the main streets that would lead him to the highway, he had been pulled over by the city police. Eugene had been terrified because he knew that he had consumed a lot of wine and might have been weaving in and out of traffic. When the officers had approached, he'd tried to act calm and sober. Unfortunately, the officer knew all too well that Eugene was intoxicated and asked him to step out of the car.*

"Have you been drinking, sir?"

"I had a glass of wine at my friend's house."

"It seems like you may have had more than just one glass. Please walk a straight line for us."

He had tried his best to walk a straight line but could not hold his balance. The officer then knew that his conclusion was right.

"Please blow into the alcoholometry test."

Eugene had done so without objecting and was found to be way over the drinking limit. He had then been placed under arrest. Mortified and humiliated, he had called his sister to bail him out of jail. In the process, he had had to spend the night in jail before he was released.

Eugene continued thinking about the situation because every month there would be a constant reminder of how he had to be in court to try to fight the charges. He could not let anyone at work know about this; it would ruin his wholesome imagine. Just then he received a text about his Fourth of July plans, and he was ready to party again without hesitation.

"What are your Fourth of July plans?" Elizabeth asked Cassandra since she wasn't sure when she would be at work again.

"Well, I have planned this pool party at the Ritz-Carton in Marina Del Rey."

"Nice."

"Is Julie going?"

"Yes, she thinks it's a party that we both planned, but in reality it's all my friends who are invited because she doesn't have any!"

"Horrible person you are."

"Me? No! I am just telling you how it is. The party is on Saturday and then Sunday we are heading over to Alex's place for his birthday party."

"That should be fun."

"I know."

"What is going on with Ryan and Julie?"

"They are no longer are on speaking terms. Ryan wants nothing to do with her and Julie still loves Ryan. He is always sick of Julie talking about him as if they are going out—wonder where he got that idea."

"Me too," Elizabeth said knowing it was Cassandra who was giving Ryan the wrong information.

"Anyway, Ryan is coming to the party because my girlfriends are going to be there and I think he likes one of them, but he said he isn't talking to Julie."

"Great, more drama."

"No, at least this time, I told him Julie was going to be there,' Cassandra said as she smiled and walked away.

On Saturday? morning, Julie picked up Cassandra to head to the pool at the Ritz-Carlton in Marina Del Rey. Cassandra had been receiving text messages all morning updating her that some of her friends had already arrived at the pool. Cassandra told Julie to hurry because her friends were waiting for her.

"Hey, we need to get there ASAP. A couple of friends are there."

"Okay, we'll be there in about half an hour." Cassandra also enjoyed the view while heading toward the South Bay. Looking at the crystal blue water gave her warmth.

Julie pulled up to the valet, got out of the car, and handed the keys to the attendant.

Cassandra got out of the car; grabbing her bag from the back, she headed toward the pool.

Julie checked in and then they headed outside.

Walking outside, Cassandra looked at the amazing view. The marina was behind the pool and you could see the boats and yachts. Blocking the sun with her hand, she started looking for her girlfriends. She found all them by the poolside.

"Sorry girls," Cassandra said as she approached everyone and gave them each a kiss.

She loved all her girlfriends, because they were fabulous like her.

She placed her stuff on one of the empty lounge chairs and spread her towel. She took her dress off and applied oil all over her lean body. Julie took the lounge chair next to Cassandra and took out her things. Julie did not dare to take off her dress. She was somewhat embarrassed by her body compared to Cassandra and her friends. Cassandra flagged down a waitress, "Hi, please bring out a few bottles of champagne and glasses for everyone. Thank you!"

Cassandra then lay back on the chair and started gossiping with her friends.

About an hour later, Cassandra's other group of friends arrived.

"Darling!" Cassandra ran to Oscar and gave him a hug.

"Hi gorgeous," Oscar replied.

"Hi sweetie," Lizzette chimed in.

"Hi!" Cassandra gave her a hug and kiss.

"Come, let's go over here and have some champagne."

They all sat down and dipped their feet in the pool. Out of nowhere, Ryan showed up.

"Hey," Cassandra said with a smile.

Ryan ran from behind and gave Cassandra a big hug, almost pushing her into the pool.

"Ryan!" Cassandra yelled.

"You know I wasn't going to push you in."

"Hey, you remember everyone and of course Julie," Cassandra said, her smile devilish.

"Yes, hi Julie!"

Julie's heart was racing, as she said, "Hi Ryan."

The only space open was next to Julie and Ryan sat down next to her. Julie unable to cope with the situation started drinking more and more.

Ryan ordered a drink from the waitress and took part in the conversation with Cassandra and her friends. Julie tried to chime in, but was always talked over. Cassandra got up to get something from the bar and Ryan followed her.

"Are you enjoying yourself?" Cassandra asked Ryan, sipping on her champagne.

"Yes, it's nice out here. By the way, are you coming to Alex's birthday party tomorrow?"

"Of course, Julie and I are spending the night here and then heading over after spending some time by the pool in the morning."

"Wait, Julie is coming?"

"Yes, Alex invited her. Didn't you know?"

"No, I had no clue. I don't want her to come."

"Well, you don't have much choice in the matter. It's Alex's party and his house," Cassandra said sitting on one of the bar stools. Ryan sat next to her. "Plus, I need a ride to Alex's house."

'Great, what am I going to do?"

"Just ignore her, she won't bother you."

"Then, I am going to bring one of my girlfriends."

"Sounds good to me," Cassandra said ignoring Ryan because she really could care less. She wanted a stronger drink.

Ryan was truly annoyed with the whole Julie situation.

"What are you guys doing?" Lizzette asked as she approached Ryan and Cassandra from behind and took the other stool next to Cassandra.

"Nothing, we were just discussing Julie, not a new topic."

Lizzette laughed, "Leave that poor girl alone. She looks so sad in the corner. No one is really talking to her."

"Oh well," Cassandra said and started looking for the waiter.

"I could care less too," Ryan chimed in.

"Oh Ryan," Cassandra laughed, "When will you learn?"

They headed back to the pool area where everyone else was still sitting and Cassandra took her spot in the middle of everyone and started talking. Cassandra did love being the center of attention. She enjoyed the looks and stares of envy from others.

A while later, Ryan announced that he was leaving.

"Hey, I am out of here," Ryan said.

"Leaving so soon?" Cassandra said jokingly.

"Yes, I am heading to meet some friends."

"Okay, see you tomorrow," Cassandra said as Ryan leaned down for a kiss. Ryan gave all the girls kisses goodbye—even Julie.

As Ryan walked away, Julie thought in her head: *Why was Ryan nice to everyone else but me?* She thought about it for a while and decided perhaps changing her attitude would work. Being less needy and more fun would make Ryan like her better.

As the sun started setting, the group decided to head back to Julie and Cassandra's room to change and head over to the pier area for the fireworks later that day. Everyone was pretty intoxicated at this point, and they were all jumping on the bed and running wild in the penthouse suite. Cassandra loved being with her friends because it brought her so much joy. Oscar was running up to all the girls, hugging them and patting their butts. Julie walked over to Cassandra. "Isn't Oscar gay?"

'Yes, why?" Cassandra asked.

"Because he keeps patting my butt."

"Yeah, that doesn't mean he likes you. He is totally gay. He does that to everyone," Cassandra said frustrated and walked away.

Julie thought to herself, *I think he likes me more than anyone. No one pats your butt unless they like you.*

"What's wrong?" Lizzette asked Cassandra in the bathroom.

"Julie annoys me. She thinks Oscar likes her because he patted her butt."

"Wait, are you serious?" Lizzette said looking at Cassandra.

"Yes, imagine that."

"Oh gosh, she needs help with that *and* her makeup."

Cassandra and Lizzette both looked at each other and laughed.

They all finished getting dressed and headed to the front of the hotel to hail a taxi. They managed to fit in one taxi while Cassandra's other girlfriends were already waiting for her at the Cabo Cantina by the Pier in Hermosa.

On entering the bar, Cassandra spotted her friends and everyone joined the table.

They started ordering drinks and foods and once the food arrived they all started devouring the food. After everyone had food and drinks, they noticed it was time for the fireworks and started walking toward the pier. The pier extended outward onto the Pacific Ocean. Cassandra walked onto the pier thinking about what a beautiful summer night it was and that she was going to be watching the fireworks with no one by her side to hold or kiss. She snapped out of her thoughts when the first firework hit the air and made a boom sound. The sky lit up. Cassandra loved the firework display because of the colors and how it illuminated the sky.

Sitting on the sands of Laguna Beach, Eugene stared into the sky watching the fireworks display. He could also see every firework display up the Pacific Ocean light the sky. Lost in his thoughts, he could still hear his family and friends enjoying the show. Eugene's sister sat next to him in the sand.

"What are you thinking about?" his sister asked, as she put her hand on his back.

"Nothing much, just watching the firework show."

"Really, because you look like you were in deep thought."

Eugene's sister had always been a strong person in his life. Even though she was younger than him by six years, Eugene looked up to her for a lot of advice. Her opinions mattered a lot to him.

"I don't know, I was just thinking about the last couple of years and my life now." "Are you happy with your life now vis-à-vis two years ago?"

Eugene thought for a second. Two years ago he was married and was living with his son and wife, but unhappy. Now two years later, he was single, living by himself, but still something was missing from his life.

"Work-wise, I am happy, extremely happy, but there seems to be something missing from my life. I am just not sure what that is."

"Maybe it's because you are single?"

"I do want to be with someone, but just not anyone. It has to be the right person, but at the same time, I have this feeling as though I had something but lost it. I am not sure what that is."

"Do you think it's Lisa?"

"No, I stopped being in love with Lisa many years ago but will always love her because of Zachery."

"Well, the only thing I can advise is that you find what is missing or has been misplaced in your life. That is the only way you will be truly happy."

"I guess," Eugene said looking up at the sky. He wondered what was "missing" in his life.

The next morning, Cassandra woke up early and headed to the pool. She wanted to get a pool chair before the rest of the hotel guests invaded the area. She found one by a tree with some shade and sun. She spread her towel and lay down reading a magazine. She ordered some water and took in the sun. During her sunbathing, Cassandra decided to give Elizabeth a call and catch her up on the gossip.

"Hey, what are you doing?" Cassandra asked her face tilted up to the sun.

"Just at home, what about you?"

"Lying by the pool, taking in the sun."

"Really, how was yesterday?"

"Insane! Everyone came by and we sat and drank by the pool. Ryan came by for a couple of drinks, ignored Julie, told me he loves me, you know the usual."

"Right, where is Julie now?"

"I left her sleeping in the room. I need time by myself. We are going to Alex's party in the afternoon. The only catch is that Ryan does not want her there, but I told him I need a ride and he has to deal with the situation,"

"Does she know Ryan doesn't want her there?"

"No, but I am not going to tell her. I don't think it's my responsibility," Cassandra said. She realized that since it was already 10:30 a.m., she was allowed to have a drink. Then Cassandra noticed Julie walking around looking for Cassandra. "This girl does not leave me alone."

"What is going on?" Elizabeth asked.

"I just spotted Julie walking around the pool looking for me. I will call you tomorrow. Let you know what happens."

"Okay, call me."

Cassandra hung up and wondered how long she should let Julie look around for her. Just then, Julie spotted her and Cassandra waved reluctantly. She needed a drink quickly.

"Hey, I was looking all over for you!" "Oh, I didn't see you till just now," Cassandra lied.

"It's such a great day out." "Totally," Cassandra said.

"Do you want to get some champagne to start our Saturday?"

"Sure," Cassandra said knowing that any type of alcohol would be very good right now.

As they sat on the chairs by the pool, drinking champagne and eating, Julie started to ask questions about Ryan.

"When we reach Alex's apartment this afternoon, do you think Ryan is going to talk to me?"

"I am not sure. He hasn't said anything to me about you. Remember, like I said before, just act civil and as if you don't care. It will make him talk to you."

"Okay, I will try. Is Eric going?"

"Apparently he is, with his two kids."

"Oh my, are you ready to meet the spawns?"

"I am not sure; I guess if they are there, why not?" Cassandra said thinking that she really hadn't given much thought to Eric since her birthday. She had tried to contact him, but he was always busy or taking care of his kids. Eric was an amazing father who took his kids every weekend and was at every practice.

Cassandra did enjoy his company, but knew in the long run, his schedule would not allow the time she needed from him.

"I am looking forward to Alex's party."

"Me too," agreed Cassandra, faking a smile.

Julie and Cassandra returned to the room and finished getting ready while drinking more champagne. Julie dressed into her uniform outfit of jeans and a black shirt, while Cassandra looked stunning in a black short summer dress. The tan that she had gotten earlier was an accessory to the dress.

"Ready?" Cassandra said looking herself in the mirror on more time. She really just wanted to admire herself one last time.

"Ready," Julie repeated.

Julie checked out of the hotel and Cassandra walked over to the valet to get Julie's car. Cassandra had already consumed two bottles of champagne and was quite buzzed that when she got into Julie's car.

"Let's stop and get something to bring to the party. We cannot go empty-handed."

"Right," Julie said, wondering why she hadn't come up with the idea herself.

"I think there is a store around here somewhere."

If Cassandra was going to get through this party, she needed all the alcohol she could get.

They arrived outside Alex's apartment and Julie took in a deep breath. She was preparing herself to walk into the apartment and act as if Ryan meant nothing to her. Cassandra noticed Julie was breathing harder than usual.

"Are you okay?" Cassandra asked as she gathered the bags from the store.

"Yes, just preparing myself for this.

"Don't worry, remember to just act cool."

"Okay," Julie said as she opened her car door.

They walked toward Alex's apartment, and found his apartment door open. Cassandra and Julie walked in. Cassandra saw some of her girlfriends from the day before.

"Hey girls," Cassandra walked over and gave them a hug and kiss. Then she saw Ryan and walked over and kissed him on the cheek. Ryan tried to intercept it with a kiss on the mouth. "Watch it, Ryan, your girlfriend is here," Cassandra said laughing.

"Whatever," Ryan said as he went back to handling the BBQ.

"Hey Cassandra," Stacey called from behind.

Cassandra turned around and saw Stacey, "Hi, how are you? I have not seen you since that party in Long Beach." "I know seems like forever. I saw Julie."

"Where is your boyfriend?"

"Around here somewhere. Come we are going to make mojitos!" Stacey yelled.

Cassandra followed Stacey into the kitchen where Julie and JP, Stacey's boyfriend, were talking. "Hi JP!" Cassandra gave him a kiss.

"Hi, how are you?"

"Not drunk enough," Cassandra giggled.

"Well, let's take care of that and start on the drinks."

Stacey started mixing the drinks while Julie started talking casually about Ryan. Cassandra's ears were not sure if she heard right? *Why would she start talking about Ryan to his own co worker JP? She never learns.* Stacey started talking about Ryan too, thinking the conversation was going to be short.

"JP and I have not seen Ryan around lately. Do you know what he has been up to?" Stacey asked Julie.

Julie shrugged, "Not sure, I see him at work sometimes, but that is about it."

"Oh, maybe he has a new girlfriend?" Stacey said as she crushed the mint for the drinks.

Julie blushed wondering if "the new girlfriend" might be her.

When Stacey and JP were done making the drinks, they went to the living room to hand them out.

"Cassandra, do you think Stacey asked me about Ryan's whereabouts because she thinks that we are together, and she probably thinks I am the new girlfriend?"

Cassandra just looked at Julie and wanted to slap some reality into her. Sometimes Cassandra just wanted to yell at her and tell her that she and Ryan were sleeping together and how stupid she was not to realize it.

"I don't think she thought that," Cassandra said as she turned around and left the kitchen.

Cassandra walked outside to the balcony where Ryan and Stacey were having a conversation. "What are you guys talking about? Me?" Cassandra said flashing her famous smile.

"You wish," Ryan said. "Stacey was just telling me how Julie was talking about me and asking Stacey questions about whom I was dating."

"That is true," Cassandra said with a smirk. "Stacey, I told Ryan that Julie was trouble, but he doesn't listen to me."

"I don't even want her here," Ryan said.

"She did start asking all these questions about you. It seemed kind of weird, if you ask me," Stacey said looking back at Julie.

"I am going to tell her to leave," Ryan said.

"You can't; it's not your house." "I don't care. They are my friends."

"Do whatever you want. I am going to the ladies room," Cassandra said and walked away. As she walked to the bathroom, she noticed that Eric had arrived with his son and daughter in tow. Cassandra was just going to walk past them when Eric stopped her.

"Hi Cassandra, how are you?"

"Good, thank you. How are you?"

"Great, this my son and daughter."

"Nice to meet you," Cassandra said wondering how old they were compared to Eric's age.

"Did you guys go swimming?" Cassandra asked, wanting to get away.

"We were by the pool for a while and came in to grab some hot dogs and burgers."

"Ryan is cooking up a storm out there. I will be back in a couple of minutes."

Cassandra walked to the bathroom hoping she could hide there for the rest of the afternoon.

"By the way, Ryan, I think Cassandra is one of the most beautiful women I have seen," Stacey told Ryan. "You should be with her."

"I know, it's complicated, but she is beautiful."

Just then Eric walked out to the balcony.

"Hey guys. Ryan, do you mind if I get some burgers for my kids?"

Ryan looked at Eric for a second. He really didn't like him at all—even more because he knew there was something between him and Cassandra.

"Sure, how many?"

"Three is good."

Ryan handed Eric a plate of burgers and he went back inside.

As Cassandra was walking out of the bathroom, Julie pulled her to the side.

"Did you meet Eric's kids?"

"Yes," Cassandra said already looking bored with this conversation.

"What did you say to them?"

"Nothing, I said hi and that was about it. They really don't talk too much."

"They are older than I thought."

"Tell me about it," Cassandra said wondering what her next drink would be.

Cassandra started walking to the kitchen and passed Eric on the way, who smiled at her. She wondered why he was acting strange; usually, he would be very affectionate with Cassandra and now he was acting like they had just met.

"Hey Alex, how are you enjoying your party?" "Good, getting my drink on!" Alex said with excitement.

"What's up with Eric? He seems to be acting different."

"Yeah, that is true. When his kids are around, he is not allowed to talk to other women because they go back and tell their mom and that creates problems for him."

"Oh, baby! Momma drama."

"Yep."

"Too bad for him," Cassandra made a mental note to cross him out of her top three because he was worthless anyway. She made herself a drink and joined Ryan out on the balcony. Some time had passed and everyone had consumed a lot of alcohol.

"Have you greeted Julie yet?" Cassandra asked with a smirk.

"No, I really don't want her here." "What are you going to do about it?"

"I am going to ask her to leave."

"Really? You don't have the balls," Cassandra said instigating him.

"Watch me," Ryan said as he entered the living room.

Julie was sitting on the couch talking to Stacey and JP about Ryan when Ryan approached her. Julie's heart stopped when she saw him walking toward her.

"May I talk to you for a second?" Ryan asked Julie. Cassandra was watching from the balcony quite impressed that he was actually going to do it.

"Sure," Julie said and got up.

Ryan headed for the apartment door, opened it, and they both headed outside.

"What is going on with them?" Alex asked as she noticed them walking outside.

"Ryan is about to kick Julie out."

"What? Are you sure?"

"Yes," Cassandra said looking at the door wishing she could be witnessing it.

Outside, Ryan walked to the stairs and turned around to face Julie.

"Why are you here?" Ryan asked almost yelling.

"What do you mean? I was invited," Julie answered in almost the same tone.

"I am not sure who invited you, but I have been hearing from people that you are talking about us as if we are a couple."

"Who told you that?" Julie said thinking about throwing her drink on Ryan.

"Don't worry about it, but I just want you to know that all we did was kiss and there is nothing going on with us. Got it? And I think you should leave because these are my friends, not yours," Ryan said and started walking back to the apartment.

Julie stood for a moment, trying to calm herself because she didn't know if she wanted to scream or cry. After a couple of minutes of composing herself, she marched back into the apartment, got her purse, and left without saying goodbye to Cassandra but just giving her a look. She didn't want to cry in front of everyone. She then ran to her car where she started crying hysterically wondering what she had done to Ryan to deserve such treatment.

Cassandra noticed Julie but did nothing to stop her. If anything, she thought *Now I have Ryan all to myself.* She went to the balcony to look for Ryan who was talking to Alex.

"You can't just tell her to leave!" Alex told Ryan, "It is my party."

"I know, but I didn't want her here and you are my friend."

"I am going to call her to tell her to come," Alex said as he left.

"Wow, I can't believe you did it. I guess I was wrong about you." Cassandra said.

"Of course, I am truly annoyed by her and her trash talking."

"What did you say to her?"

"That I heard from some people that she was talking about us as an item and to stop because nothing was going between and to leave because she was not invited."

"Nice, I will call her in a little bit, because I cannot deal with her drama right now."

Cassandra went inside to enjoy the rest of the party with her friends and continued to have more alcohol. By the end of the night, Cassandra was drunk and the only ones who were left were her, Ryan, Alex, and his roommate. Ryan and Cassandra were sitting outside on the balcony and Cassandra brought up her favorite subject: Eugene.

"Why do you keep talking about this guy who does not give you the time of day?"

"Because I love him and it's hard to let go when you have so much faith in something."

"You need to let go of someone like that because they are just holding you behind."

"I know you are right, Ryan, but sometimes it's just hard," Cassandra said looking at Ryan as tears streamed down her cheeks. It was the alcohol that was making Cassandra emotional. Ryan leaned in and kissed her and the tears that had made their way down to her mouth. Cassandra knew that she had to let go of Eugene, but she wasn't sure how. Ryan continued kissing Cassandra and then came up for air and smiled at her.

"I am going to start working on it," Cassandra said and right then and there she took out her phone and erased Eugene's number and all the text messages she had been saving for almost a year. At the same time, she wished she could have easily erased Eugene from her memories.

"Are you ready for me to take you home?" Ryan asked worried that Cassandra was still crying.

"Yes, I am ready," Cassandra said as she dried the tears from her face.

Ryan and Cassandra said goodbye to Alex and left.

Ryan dropped off Cassandra at the apartment and made sure she got in okay because she seemed to be wobbly.

"Are you going to be okay?" Ryan asked Cassandra as she sat on the couch.

"I am okay, don't worry."

"Okay, I am going to go back out. I will see you tomorrow."

"Okay," Cassandra said not really sure what was going on. All the alcohol had made her mind go numb. Ryan left the apartment and she sat staring at the TV for a second. Then looking for her phone, she decided to call Julie.

"Hey, where are you?" Cassandra asked.

"At home, hating life and hating Ryan."

"What happened? I tried to call you, but I couldn't find my purse in the apartment." Cassandra lied.

"Ryan told me he heard some rumors, but I told him they weren't true, and he wouldn't believe and told me to leave the party because I wasn't invited."

"Wow, that's harsh," Cassandra said not really listening, partly because she was drunk.

"And I called Eric to see what he was doing and if he had heard what happened at the party."

"What do you mean?" Cassandra became more aware, trying to clear the fog from her head.

"I called him because I wanted to know if he knew what Ryan was talking about."

"How did you have this number?" Cassandra said getting angrier by the second.

"Remember last month you called Eric from my phone, so I saved the number."

Cassandra thought, *this girl must be crazier than I thought. Why would she save Eric's number?*

"Oh, what did he say?" Cassandra said sobering up.

"Eric said that he hadn't heard anything and would let me know if he does. Then it was weird because an hour after I spoke to him, he texted me and invited me to go bowling."

"Interesting. Did you respond?" Cassandra said drinking water.

"I did. I thanked him for the invite but have decided to stay home tonight. Then he responded, 'okay maybe next time.'"

Cassandra was now furious and thinking of yet another way to get back at Julie. *Doesn't this girl learn her lesson?*

"Well, I am glad you are okay. Call me tomorrow so you can drop off my bag I left in your car."

"Okay, goodnight," Julie said, and Cassandra hung up without saying anything.

Cassandra stood by her kitchen counter, deciding what her next plan of attack should be. But she decided to wait until tomorrow because she was too exhausted and her brain wouldn't let her think.

Chapter 20

A couple of days passed since the Fourth of July fiasco, and Cassandra was now deciding what to do to get back at Julie. She had realized the best way to decide this would be over lunch—more like a liquid lunch. She headed to the restaurant below her office and slid into a booth to start thinking of a plan. As Cassandra sipped her lunch, it came to her. She remembered that Ryan had mentioned that he was interested in one of her friends, Lyn, and Alex had also mentioned that he was interested in Lyn's roommate, Jackie. Cassandra decided to put together a happy hour evening, only inviting Ryan, Alex, Eric, and her two friends. She would brag to Julie about the get-together, but not invite her. That should make her realize who she was messing with! Cassandra smiled to herself, took her phone out, and started contacting her new happy hour group.

Cassandra had set everything up with everyone involved. The plan was set for the following evening. Jackie and Lyn were more than happy to meet up with the boys. After spending two hours at lunch. Cassandra headed to the bank to tell Julie. Cassandra walked into the bank and it was the same scene every time. Every single male in the area turned his head to look at her. She ignored them all and headed to Julie's desk. Julie was on the phone and it seemed like she was toward the end of the conversation. Cassandra smiled and waited.

"Hey, how are you today?" Julie said as hung up the phone.

"Good, just on my way back from lunch and wanted to stop by and see what was going on."

"Nothing much, just working and dealing with annoying customers," Julie said rolling her eyes.

"Right, has Ryan been in today?" Cassandra asked, knowing that Ryan was at a different branch this particular week.

"No, I haven't seen him. How are things at home with him?"

"Good, he has been bothering me about hooking him up with Lyn. He just wouldn't leave me alone about it. Then Alex wants me to hook him up with Jackie. The only good thing is that they are both roommates!"

"Really?" Julie said, annoyed that Cassandra would mention something like that.

"Yes, so I decided to have a happy hour tomorrow night. This way I can have both Jackie and Lyn there with Alex, Ryan, and Eric. Everyone can mingle with whomever they want."

"Oh," Julie was puzzled why she was not invited.

"It should be fun. Anyway, I must go and get some work done," Cassandra said she got up and grabbed her purse. "Call me later."

Julie looked on as Cassandra walked away. She sometimes wondered why Cassandra was so spiteful toward Julie. She had never done anything wrong with Cassandra.

Cassandra smiled to herself as she walked away. *Hope Julie learns her lesson now.* Instead of getting into the elevator, she decided to head home and take a nap. It was already mid-afternoon and there was no point heading back to the office.

The next evening Cassandra reached the bar and looked around to see if anyone had arrived. She realized that she was the first one there and took a seat at the bar. Her favorite bartender, Carlos, saw Cassandra and walked over.

"What can I get you, beautiful?"

"Hello, how are you?" "Good and you?"

"Surviving," Cassandra said flashing her smile.

"Vodka tonic?" "You know me so well," Cassandra said, "Don't forget the lime."

"Never," Carlos said giving her a flirtatious look.

Cassandra wished he would stop flirting and hurry up with her drink. As Carlos left to make her drink, Alex walked in and spotted Cassandra. He went behind her and put his hands over her eyes.

"Let me guess . . . who this is?" Cassandra smiled and put her hand over Alex's hand and then proceeded to move her hands down toward his pants. Alex jumped.

"Hey, what are you doing?" he laughed.

Cassandra turned around on her barstool. "Well, you wanted me to guess who you were. I thought I'd reach down there and recognize who you were," Cassandra said with an impish smile.

"You are too much! Where is everyone else?"

"I just got here a couple of minutes ago."

"What are you drinking?" Alex asked Cassandra.

"Vodka tonic, what else?"

Alex took the stool between Cassandra and another patron and ordered himself a beer. Cassandra realized her phone was beeping, and she had received several text messages while talking to Alex.

"Jackie and Lyn are on their way and Ryan is running late."

"Cool. Is Julie coming?"

"No, why do you ask? Ryan doesn't want her here. Plus he wants his space to get to know Lyn."

Alex just stared at Cassandra and she responded with a *"this girl is some piece of work; she will do anything to get Ryan"* look.

Lyn was not a threat to Cassandra because Lyn was her friend and if Lyn did like Ryan, Cassandra would tell her awful things about Ryan, and she would no longer be interested in him.

As Cassandra was completing this thought, Lyn and Jackie arrived. Jackie, at five feet ten inches, with long hair and never-ending legs, had spent about two years in America—having come from Korea. She enjoyed living in California. Her counterpart, Lyn, was just as gorgeous, but shorter. She still had the features and flawless skin of an Asian girl. Both had been roommates since they had arrived in America. Cassandra waved to them.

"Hey girls," she greeted them with hugs and kisses. Cassandra loved these two out of all her girlfriends because they were still humble and not jaded from what LA had to offer.

"What do you girls want to drink?" Cassandra asked them as they were finishing greeting Alex.

"I will have a Mai Tai," Jackie said first.

"Just a beer for me," Lyn said, her voice soft.

Cassandra ordered their drinks and once they were served, the four of them walked over to a corner booth and sat down. Everyone started talking. Before they realized it, an hour had gone by and then Ryan finally arrived. He looked around inside the bar. Because it was dimly lit, it was almost impossible to see toward the back of the bar. He finally saw Cassandra and walked toward their table.

"Sorry, everyone, I got stuck at work and had to finish with a customer," Ryan said as he greeted everyone. "What is everyone drinking? This round is on me."

When Ryan returned with the drinks, he sat next to Lyn and casually started talking to her. Alex continued talking with Jackie. Cassandra just sat looking at the two couples. She then realized that Eric had not shown up yet and decided to call him. Her call went to voicemail, which upset her. Instead of dwelling on Eric, she headed to the bar to order another drink and decided she should make the best of this situation.

Cassandra sat down at the bar and ordered her drink. There was a gentleman sitting next to Cassandra who had noticed her from the moment she had walked into the bar.

"You have amazing hair," he said.

Cassandra, wanting to be alone, looked at him sourly, said "thanks," and looked away. She was not in the mood to be bothered.

The man noticed Cassandra's reaction, took out one of his business cards, and placed it on the bar.

"I am a hairdresser and I would love to cut your hair."

Cassandra looked at the card and then at the man, still wondering why Eric had sent her to voicemail.

"Thanks, I will think about it. Where is your salon located?"

"We just opened up a month ago, around the corner."

"Okay, I will give a call soon," Cassandra said as she grabbed her drink and left the bar. She dropped off her drink at the table and headed to the ladies room. She thought about trying Eric one more time. Cassandra was not the desperate type, but hanging out with the four of them was starting to drive her crazy.

Finally, Eric answered the phone, "Where are you?" Cassandra yelled into the phone.

"What do you mean? I was at the gym, now I am home. Where are you?"

"Wait, you're home? I thought you were coming!"

"I was, but it got late and so I decided to stay home." Annoyed, Cassandra hung up on Eric and stormed out of the bathroom. As she turned around the corner, she saw Eric standing beside Alex.

"Wow, you just hung up on me?" Eric said with a grin.

Instead of responding, Cassandra hugged him and gave him a kiss.

They all continued drinking. Ryan was the first to leave; he had enough of trying to understand Lyn's foreign accent and watching Cassandra and Eric have a good time. He said goodbye to everyone, got into his car, and headed for South Bay. Judging by the way Eric was flirting with Cassandra, Ryan knew they would want the apartment to themselves.

After everyone left the bar, Eric and Cassandra stayed behind and had another drink. By this time, Cassandra had drunk a lot of alcohol without eating and she was starting to feel the effects, because she was blabbering nonsense.

"So, why did you and your wife get divorced?" Cassandra asked not realizing the question was slightly personal.

"Well," Eric began, "we fell out of love and then there wasn't much after that. We were always fighting and thought it was better for the kids."

"Have you dated anyone after?"

"Yeah, a couple of people."

"Seriously dated. Long-term?"

"Yes, one woman, but after two years it wasn't going anywhere, so we broke it off."

"Sounds like you are still in love with your ex-wife," Cassandra said as she started getting hiccups.

"I don't think so. Hey, why don't we get out of here and head back to your apartment?"

"You got it," Cassandra said trying to hold her breath so the hiccups would go away.

They both left the bar hand in hand and headed toward Cassandra's apartment.

As soon as they entered Cassandra's apartment, Eric started kissing her and would not stop. Cassandra unable to resist the force of his tongue returned his kiss. Before she knew it, they were both lying naked on her bed, exploring each other's bodies. She enjoyed the way Eric touched her without hesitation. She lay back and enjoyed the moment. After an hour of exploring each other, they were exhausted, unable to move. The lay there, holding hands and laughing.

"That was amazing," Cassandra said.

"I know," Eric remarked.

Eric then looked at the clock and announced it was late and he had to leave.

"Why are you leaving?" Cassandra asked as propped herself on her side.

"It's getting late and I have to head back home, I have an early start tomorrow."

Eric started getting dressed and Cassandra watched. Eric had an amazing body. *He must work out every day,* she thought to herself.

Eric leaned down to Cassandra and gave her a kiss. "I will give you a call tomorrow."

"Okay," Cassandra said accepting the kiss.

She watched Eric walk away and turn the corner for the door. Cassandra lay on the bed for a couple of minutes thinking about Eric and why she liked him. She really didn't find any solid reasons except for tonight. She knew what he was capable of in bed and that was reason enough. Cassandra laughed at herself, walked toward the closet, and threw on some clothes. Heading to the kitchen, she realized that she was extremely hungry and had not eaten all night. As she was in the kitchen, she heard the door open and Ryan walked in.

"Hey," Ryan said.

"Hey, what's up?" Cassandra said as she started making a sandwich.

"Nothing much. How was the rest of the evening?"

"Everyone stayed a little bit longer and then left."

"Cool."

"Anything good happened between you and Lyn? Did you get lucky?"

"No, not really. It's hard to understand what she is saying."

"Oh," Cassandra said.

"I am going to change and hit the bed," Ryan said yawning.

"Okay," Cassandra said thinking to herself that had Ryan walked in ten minutes earlier, he would have caught her and Eric in the act. She smiled to herself as she ate her sandwich.

"Anything good happened last night?" Elizabeth asked from her desk.

"Not really, just happy hour," Cassandra answered back, distracted. She noticed the new Heath Ledger movie was about to release and she wanted to attend the midnight screening.

"Really? That's hard to believe. Something always happens when you go to happy hour."

Cassandra didn't want to get into all the details since she was already plotting how to make Julie want to pull her hair out. Cassandra immediately called Julie, sounding chipper, "Hey, how are you?"

"Good, how was last night?"

"The usual, everyone showed up, drank, and talked."

"Oh, that's nice," Julie said remembering that she had spent the previous night upset at home thinking of Ryan and Lyn at the bar.

"Anyway, the new Heath Ledger movie is coming out this Friday and there's a midnight screening. How about we get everyone together and go?"

"Everyone like who?"

"You, Eric, Alex, Lyn, Jackie, Ryan, etc.," Cassandra said annoyed, because it was always the same group of people. *Why did she need to ask?*

"Ryan too? Do you think he will be okay with me going?"

Cassandra thought, *this girl is getting more pathetic as days go by.*

"Who cares what he thinks. We are all going to watch a movie; it will be dark."

"Okay, if he doesn't mind me going."

Sometimes, Cassandra wondered why she bothered with Julie at all.

"Okay, I have to go and will call you later about the details," Cassandra said and hung up.

"What now?" Elizabeth asked standing at her door.

"Julie! She annoys me by just breathing," Cassandra said and turned to her computer screen. She purchased ten tickets for the new movie and started to text everyone.

Chapter 21

Eugene was back at work after his long Fourth of July break and with the realization that something was missing from his life, but he wasn't sure what. After the Fourth of July, Eugene hopped on a plane and headed to Costa Rica by himself for a couple of days. It was unusual for Eugene to take trips by himself, but he needed time away from everyone and everything to just think about himself. During his week's stay in Costa Rica, Eugene sat on the beaches and thought long and hard on what he was doing with himself and what he was trying to accomplish. He didn't have a privileged life growing up. He thought that hard work always pays off and it did just that for him. He had started working at the age of eleven delivering newspapers and then onto other jobs he could find. His parents divorced before he had become a teenager and it was mostly him looking out for his mom and younger sister. He had become the man of the house overnight and it might have been there when he lost sight of where he wanted his life to head. Since that day, he just did as he thought he had to do, never taking a moment for himself. It had taken him a failed marriage to realize that he was unhappy and something had to change. As he sat on the beach, looking out to the ocean, he wasn't sure what that *something* was yet.

His thoughts were interrupted by his cell phone buzzing. A text from Cassandra that said, "Hey, I have tickets to the midnight screening of Heath Ledger's new movie. Would you like to join?"

"What day is it?" Eugene texted back.

It took Cassandra a couple of minutes; she replied, "Thursday night."

Eugene looked at the calendar on his phone screen and realized he would be in San Francisco that evening.

He wrote, "I am sorry, but I'm going to be in SF that night. You always give me little notice."

Cassandra waited for the incoming message, holding her breath and hoping he would say *yes*. She heard her phone beep, looked at his reply, and threw the phone on her desk. She thought, *he always has an excuse whenever I invite him* and Cassandra was starting to get sick of it. She turned her chair around to look at the view, thinking about Eugene. It had been some days that she had not thought about him. As she was thinking of why she still liked him, she remembered the connection that they had. It wasn't by choice that they were connected. Cassandra, to this day, remembered that one day that she'd like to keep hidden away in her memory. A year had almost gone by since the death of Eugene's cousin, Rob.

That particular Saturday, Cassandra had woken up extremely early for a Saturday. It was 8:00 a.m. and she could not sleep any longer. She had gone into the living room, lay down on the couch, and tried watching TV in order to fall asleep again. It was then that she had started getting a strange feeling as if something was wrong. She had tried shaking the feeling, but it was there creeping about her. Since she couldn't fall back asleep, she had decided to get ready to run some errands. Cassandra had gotten in her car and <u>driven</u> *toward Hollywood. It was her friend's birthday party later that night and she needed to look good. She had started the day with a manicure and pedicure and then had her eyebrows threaded, which was the trend. As she had continued her day, the strange feeling that she was trying to avoid had started becoming stronger. She had ignored it and decided to go tanning and grab some lunch. By the time she was done with lunch, it had been around 2:00 p.m. and when she got on the highway to head back to downtown there had been bumper-to-bumper traffic. She had remembered that the big rival college football games took place every December in LA. To California, these were bigger than the Rockets during Christmas in New York. Then, she remembered that Eugene was going to the game because he had attended one of the rival colleges. She had thought about Eugene as she sat in traffic, thinking of calling him since he was going to be in the area, but then decided not to. She would probably call him and he wouldn't answer anyway, so what was the point. She had thought about it again as she was still in traffic. Maybe they could meet up after the game for a drink, but she knew if he really wanted to hang out with her, he would have called her by now. He was only a few blocks from where she lived. She* had decided to stop thinking about it and continued sitting in traffic until she reached home. An hour or so later, she had finally got home and decided to take a nap because she knew she had a long night ahead of her. She had laid on the couch watching TV, but could not sleep, because the strange feeling she had was getting worse. Cassandra couldn't describe the feeling, but it was like a premonition that something bad was going to happen. An hour later after a restless nap, Cassandra finally had decided to get up and find something to wear for tonight. It was around 6:00 p.m., and she kept trying dresses in her closet but nothing seemed to be right. Finally, after an hour of trying on clothes, she had decided to walk over to the department store to find a new dress for tonight's party. As she had left her apartment building, her gut feeling had started getting stronger and it was scaring Cassandra, but she didn't know what to do. As she had started walking, she made sure to look all around her because she didn't know if something was going to happen to her. When she had stopped at the crosswalk waiting for the light to change, she had stood far away from the corner because she thought she could get hit by a bus. At this point, Cassandra was having a hard time breathing. She had literally darted across the street into the department store because she felt unsafe outside. Once in the department store, she had found she could breathe a little bit better, but the strange overwhelming feeling was still lingering. She had tried a couple of dresses, chose one, and paid for it. During that time, the feeling had not gone away. She had tried to ignore it, but it wouldn't let her. As she was leaving, she had started looking for her phone but couldn't find it. She still had to stop at another store, but needed her phone just in case something was about to happen. As she had stepped outside, the feeling got stronger again. Cassandra had just decided to run and ran the two blocks to her apartment without looking back. Once she had gotten inside her apartment building, she felt safe and ran to her apartment. She had found her phone and it had no missed calls. Not knowing what to do, she had decided on going back out to the store. It was 7:30 p.m. and the feeling she was experiencing returned with such force that Cassandra had to stop. It was almost as though the wind had been knocked out and she had to calm down to catch her breath. The feeling had immediately disappeared. She had started breathing normally again and the strange feeling that had lingered all day was now gone. She had stood on the sidewalk for a minute while people passing her by looked at her strangely. She wasn't sure what just happened, but whatever it was had now left. It was the first time all day she had felt okay. She had continued walking to the drug store and then headed home to get ready for the party. It wasn't till *three weeks later that Eugene had called her to tell her about his cousin's tragic death the night of the big college rival game. He had explained to her that they—Eugene and his two cousins—had attended the game in LA and after, headed back to Newport Beach. Around 7:30 p.m., his cousin Rob had left to meet some of his friends at the nearby bars and restaurants and as Rob had crossed one of the major streets he was hit by a car and had been instantly killed. Cassandra could not believe what Eugene was telling her. It had taken Cassandra a few days to put the two events together. When she finally realized what had happened, she couldn't believe it. She had researched the story and found an article that read "young man killed instantly by car when crossing major intersection in Newport Beach. It is said to have happened at 7:30 p.m." Cassandra had immediately started crying because it was that same day and that same time that she had felt an awful strange feeling that she would never forget. At the same time, she had found it difficult to breathe, Eugene's cousin had been killed.*

Cassandra felt goosebumps all over her body and had to get out of her office. She remembered that story all so well and had never told Eugene about it and wasn't sure if she ever would. Not a day had gone by where she didn't blame herself for Eugene's cousin's death. If she had just picked up the phone and called him, maybe they would have met Cassandra for drinks and his cousin would have never died. As much as she blamed herself, there was no way of knowing if Eugene would have picked up the phone or met her for drinks. It would always be one of those "what if" situations. Cassandra grabbed her phone and decided she needed a drink immediately.

Eugene waited for a text back from Cassandra, but never received one. He leaned back in his chair and thought about the new Heath Ledger movie. It instantly reminded him of his cousin Rob—how young he was and how tragically he had died. A year had barely gone by and he still missed Rob every day. He blamed himself for his death every day. If only he had driven Rob to meet his friends instead of him deciding to walk, Rob would have still been here. Eugene realized that he couldn't keep reliving the past. What had happened was done and now it was a matter of dealing with it. This was one of the many things he was dealing with on the beaches of Costa Rica. His cousin's death should have been a wake-up call for him, but if anything it dragged him down further and deeper to a place Eugene had never been and simply couldn't get out of. He decided it was better to get back to concentrating on work because it was all he had right now.

When Cassandra walked into her apartment, Ryan was already there watching baseball.

"Hey, how was your day at work?" Ryan asked.

"Good and yours?" Cassandra asked

"Okay, what's for dinner tonight?"

"Dinner? You mean what are you cooking?" she replied jokingly.

"Right. Do you want to order something?" he inquired.

"Sure, whatever you like. I am going to change out these clothes."

Ryan watched as Cassandra walked away and emerged from the closet wearing nothing. She walked up to him and asked, "Hungry?" She sat on top of him and kissed him before he could even answer. A little later, as they lay in bed next to each other, sweat trickling down their foreheads, Cassandra brought up the topic about the movie.

"Did you get my text about the midnight showing?" "Yes."

"Well, are you going?" "Of course, it's supposed to be the best movie of the year. How many tickets did you get and who is going?"

"I bought ten tickets and so far, it's me, Julie, Jackie, Lyn, Alex, Eric, maybe Julie's brother, and you. Why?"

"Julie and her brother are going?"

"Yes. Julie made a whole big fuss about her and you going. I told her to get over it."

"If she is going, then I am bringing Hermosa. Is that okay?"

"Fine with me. Maybe that will make Julie realize that she doesn't stand a chance with you," Cassandra said as she gave Ryan a kiss on his forehead and left the bed to get some water. *This is actually working better than I thought*, she said to herself.

Chapter 22

The day of the movie premiere, Cassandra had to break it to Julie that Ryan was bringing his current girlfriend. It was early in the morning and the bank was not yet occupied with customers. Cassandra walked into the bank and spotted Julie at her desk. She sat down on one of the chairs in front of her desk.

"Hello Ms. Chow, how are we this doing this morning?"

"Good, I didn't hear back from you last night. Hope all is well with your roomie?"

"Ah yes, everything is well. We spent some time hanging out last night," Cassandra said as she replayed the scene of her walking up to Ryan naked.

"What did you guys do?"

"Watched baseball and drank some beers."

"Nice," Julie said wishing it was her and not Cassandra hanging out with Ryan.

"Yes, anyway, I came here to tell you that Ryan informed me last night that he was bringing Hermosa to the movie."

Julie was shocked and could not believe what she was hearing. "He is?"

"Yes, I am sorry. I guess that's an indicator that there is no chance between you and him," Cassandra said making sure it stabbed Julie in the heart.

Julie immediately starting crying. "I can't believe it. Did he say anything about me?" She started wiping the tears away.

"No, he didn't. He asked me if there was an extra ticket for her and I said yes," Cassandra said trying not to show her smile.

Julie thought that Cassandra was a complete bitch for letting Ryan invite that girl.

"Well," Julie said composing herself since she was in public and at her office. "I am fine with it. I tried to show him I like him, but I guess it's not going to work out. I mean things were good for a while and then it went bad. I am not sure how it happened."

Cassandra thought for a second. *Things were good? When were you ever together?*

"But you and Ryan were never together as a couple."

"Well, in the beginning, we were dating, and things went sour."

Is she serious?

"Wait, I am confused, are you talking about the same Ryan?"

"Yes, why?"

"I didn't know you guys were together?"

"You know what I mean," Julie said, getting frustrated with all her questions.

"All right then. I have to get going. I will call you later," Cassandra said and got up she walked away, not caring if Julie continued crying or not.

Cassandra reached her office floor and walked into the reception area. Elizabeth greeted her with a smile, "You are here early," she remarked.

"Well, I have a busy day of planning on destroying Julie's life and I have the movie tonight."

"Poor girl, I am surprised she has not turned psycho on you yet!"

"She is torturing herself. I just left her crying at her desk. Who really cries at work?" Cassandra said as she walked off.

Elizabeth was left behind shaking her head.

Cassandra worked later than she thought she would that night. She looked at the time and rushed home. Living two blocks from work was convenient. She got into her apartment, took off her clothes, and changed into something more comfortable. Julie and Julie's brother were on their way to pick her up. Cassandra got ready and looked at herself one last time before she ran out the door. In the elevator, she wished she had taken a drink for the ride. As she got into Julie's car, she met Julie's brother for the first time. "Cassandra, this is Mark. Mark, this is Cassandra." 'Nice to meet you," Cassandra said surprised that Julie's brother was handsome. Julie had always spoken about him as if he wasn't, but now she could see that she was just jealous.

"By the way, would you like a drink?" Julie said holding a bottle of vodka.

"Absolutely," Cassandra said surprised that Julie had thought of something like that.

"I need alcohol to get through this night," Julie said as she poured Cassandra a drink in the plastic cup.

On the ride to the movie theater, Cassandra received a text from Ryan, "Where are you? Everyone is here."

Cassandra replied, "On my way, running a little late."

"Ryan just texted me. He wants to know where we are."

"Whatever," Julie said.

"Okay," Cassandra said sarcastically.

"All I know is if Ryan even tries anything tonight, I will jump on him," Mark said.

Cassandra thought to herself, *where am I and who are these people?*

Finally, they arrived at the movie theater and found everyone waiting by the door.

"Sorry, I am late," Cassandra announced. She walked in with the tickets. "I have the tickets, let's go."

They all walked into the movie theater and tried to find a row that fit them all. Ryan pointed to one toward the front of the theater. They sat down in an order to try to avoid each other. Ryan and Julie sat on both ends. He had brought his Hermosa girl, but had not introduced her to Cassandra. Cassandra sat in between Julie and Jackie. She then noticed that Eric was not there. She quickly asked Alex, "What happened to Eric?"

"He couldn't make it; he had the kids tonight," Alex explained.

Cassandra just smiled at Alex. *He didn't even call to tell me*, she thought. She decided to ignore it and enjoy the movie.

After the movie was over, everyone spilled into the lobby of the movie theater and started talking about how good the movie was. Cassandra noticed that Ryan had not yet introduced her to Hermosa girl, so she decided to go up to him.

"Hey, how did you enjoy the movie?" Ryan asked Cassandra.

"It was better than expected."

"Yeah, I thought too," Cassandra said waiting for him to introduce Hermosa, but he never did and someone else came along and interjected.

After a couple of minutes of talking, everyone said goodbye and parted ways.

"Well, that wasn't so bad after all," Cassandra told Julie.

"If you say so. Ryan didn't even look at me or say anything to me and his Hermosa girl is absolutely not pretty."

In Cassandra's head: *Are you serious? She is prettier than you!*

They continued walking to Julie's car and then they drove off to Downtown LA.

"The movie—how was it?" Elizabeth asked Cassandra over the phone. Cassandra had decided that it was Friday and it was pointless to go to work.

"Good, not too much drama. Everyone got along. Ryan brought his girl-friend and Julie was jealous."

"Is she pretty?" Elizabeth asked curiously.

"Prettier than Julie, but not prettier than me." "Oh gosh," Elizabeth said rolling her eyes, "What are your plans for today?"

"Going to lie in bed for a bit longer, then get some lunch and see if I meet anyone who is decent enough."

"In other words, you are looking for a one-night stand,"

"I am just trying to keep my options open," Cassandra said with a smile.

"Good luck, I will talk to you later." "Thanks, bye," Cassandra said.

Cassandra lay in bed, remembering how Eric had been a no show for last night and he still hadn't called her. Not that it really mattered because they weren't together, but he should have had at least sent her a text message. Cassandra decided to forget about it and go back to resting.

A week went by and Cassandra was yet to hear from Eric. She decided to give him a call since it was Friday night and maybe they could get together.

"Hey, what's with you?" Cassandra asked Eric.

"Nothing much, just busy working and taking care of the kids. I have them for two weeks because their mom is on vacation."

"Oh, where did she go? Off to Paris on your dime?"

"Aren't we funny today? She went to some island and probably with my money. What have you been up to?"

"Same. Working, trying to cause trouble," Cassandra said laughing. "I am guessing that you will not be free tonight to come over?"

"I would love to, but I can't leave my kids."

"No, problem. Give me a call when you are off babysitting duty."

"I will, promise."

"Bye," Cassandra said and actually felt bad for a moment because she did have some feelings for Eric, but it lasted only for about a second and then she switched it off and decided to see who was out tonight and ready to play.

Eugene loved waking up to Saturday mornings in Orange County. The sun was shining, bringing a day full of fun and promises. Eugene got up from the bed and walked outside to the adjoining balcony from his master bedroom. He loved the sounds of the waves crashing and the salty air hitting his face. *How can anyone not want to live by the beach?* Eugene thought to himself. It was barely 9:00 a.m. and his phone was already ringing constantly regarding what today's plans would be. Eugene took a deep breath, and headed inside to make some coffee and to see what the day would hold for him.

Last night had been very successful for Cassandra. She had hit a few of the bars around downtown LA and made very interesting friends: the usual lawyers, real estate developers, and more. She already wondered where were the men in suits—like she found in NYC. She lay on the couch watching TV. Ryan had not come home the night before and Cassandra had slept by herself—not that she would have noticed either way because she had quickly passed out on returning from the night of bar hopping. As she was switching channels, her cell phone rang, "Hello," Cassandra did not bother to see who it was.

"What are you doing, sexy?" Ryan asked.

"Nothing, what are you doing?"

"On my way to the apartment. What are your plans for today?"

"Nothing yet."

"Well, don't make anything. Maybe we can grab some breakfast/lunch."

"Sounds good to me."

"See ya soon."

About half an hour later, Ryan walked into the apartment and immediately joined Cassandra on the couch. He started caressing Cassandra's leg, but she was not in the mood for it.

"What's the matter?" Ryan asked confused.

"Nothing, just not in the mood," Cassandra said flipping through the channels.

"Okay, well, do you want to do something?"

"Like what?" Cassandra asked not looking at Ryan.

"Ever been to Tijuana?"

Cassandra immediately looked at Ryan, "Seriously?"

"Yeah, why not. We have nothing to do today. Where is your passport?"

Half an hour later, Cassandra was in Ryan's car and they started the trip down to TJ. Cassandra had never been to TJ and Ryan had been there numerous times.

"This is the plan. We will head to TJ, pick some pills, get some drinks, party, and spend the night there."

"Sure," Cassandra said. She was the type of girl who loved adventure and this seemed to be one of them.

As Ryan was driving, Cassandra's phone started receiving text messages from Julie. "Hey, what are you doing? Do you want to grab some lunch?"

"I can't. On my way to TJ," Cassandra replied.

Julie read Cassandra's messaged and was confused. *Who is she going to TJ with? That is strange. She never mentioned anything to me.* Julie texted back: "Wait, who are you with?"

Cassandra looked at her phone and smiled to herself. She would make Julie wait a little to annoy her because once she found it was with Ryan, she would be devastated. After a few minutes, Cassandra texted back. "Ryan and I are going to have a roomie weekend in TJ."

Julie waited patiently for the incoming text, and once it arrived she read it with tears streaming down her face. *Why does Cassandra get to spend time with him? Why doesn't he want to be with me?* Immediately, Julie went nuts throwing everything everywhere as feelings of confusion and jealousy took over. After a few moments, she calmed down, took a deep breath, and decided if she couldn't be there, she would be sure to text Cassandra every minute. This way they would not be enjoying their time alone.

Cassandra looked at her phone, surprised to see Julie texting her as Ryan drove down the freeway that led them to Mexico. Cassandra noticed that the Newport Beach exit was approaching and she thought about Eugene. She had not responded to his text when he had told her that he couldn't go to the Heath Ledger movie. She thought it would be fun to rub it in his face that she was heading to TJ without inviting him, and decided to send him a sweet message.

"Hi, heading to TJ, hoping to have a blast. Passed by your exit on the freeway, so thought about you." Eugene and his buddies were having a late breakfast at a restaurant overlooking the ocean, when Eugene felt his phone vibrate in his shirt pocket. Eugene read it, surprised that it was a text from Cassandra. "Why is she going to TJ?" Eugene said out loud, shaking his head.

He immediately wrote back, "TJ is not safe, you really should not be going!"

"Who is going to TJ?" Brad asked.

"Cassandra just texted me saying that she is headed to TJ."

"Today?" Brad asked, confused.

"Apparently," Eugene said, getting kind of worried. "I guess she doesn't know TJ isn't safe right now."

Brad looked at Eugene and remembered the first time he met Cassandra. A few months ago, Eugene and Brad had been partying pretty late and Cassandra had called Eugene. Eugene had invited Cassandra over, but since it was late, he had doubted Cassandra would drive all the way down to Newport Beach. Brad had fallen asleep waiting to meet Cassandra. The next morning, he had awoken to find Cassandra had made it after all. He first remembered seeing Cassandra coming down the stairs in Eugene's house. She was wearing her dress from the night before, but still looked gorgeous. Even though it was morning, he had noticed how much of a natural beauty she was. He had been amazed that Eugene had not taken the chance to be with her. Brad and Cassandra had spoken for a while that morning and he had enjoyed the conversation. Then, she had driven Brad and Eugene to their cars at the bar, where they'd been drinking the night before. He had thought about all of them going to get breakfast, but Eugene seemed to want for Cassandra to leave and Brad had got the hint. He always wondered why Eugene didn't like Cassandra. From what he saw, she would be number one in his book.

Cassandra received Eugene's text and was surprised to see him say that TJ was dangerous. *Maybe he is just making it up.*

"Hey, my friend just said that TJ is dangerous right now and we should reconsider going. Do you think that is true?" Cassandra asked Ryan.

"I don't think it's that dangerous. If anything, we can check it out, get some pills, and head back to downtown San Diego to party."

"Sounds good to me," Cassandra said and texted Eugene back, "Weren't you just in Mexico?" Cassandra asked Eugene.

Eugene looked at the text and replied, "Yes, but is a whole other area of Mexico,"

"This girl is too much," Eugene said to Brad.

"Is she still going?" Brad asked.

"Yes, you know, Cassandra works on her own terms."

"What is going on with you guys anyway?" Brad asked, curious.

"We are still friends. In reality, she is probably the only girl that I have let so close to me since my divorce. But I still need time and I don't think she understands that," Eugene said staring into the ocean. Eugene started thinking about Cassandra and how much she really did mean to him. He knew she was frustrated because he was not giving her what she wanted. But he was not ready for that. He really did enjoy their friendship, but he still needed time for himself. He smiled to himself remembering the first day they had met and how fun Cassandra had been that night, and decided to send her another text message.

"If you do decide to head to TJ, call me if you need any help."

Cassandra received his texts and was surprised to read them. *Wow, Eugene must care after all,* she thought. *How strange their relationship was.* She would take whatever she could right now, as long as she had him in her life. That was all that mattered. She would keep working at their relationship; maybe one day he would realize how much she loved him.

Chapter 23

*R*yan and Cassandra approached the Mexico border. Cassandra was excited since she had never been to the border.

"Are we driving in?" Cassandra asked

"No, I want to park and then walk over, but I think I missed the exit. They will strip my car in two seconds if I park it anywhere in Mexico."

By the time they had figured out where to park, it was too late and they'd already crossed the Mexican border. Cassandra looked outside her window and saw how poor TJ was. She had always heard what a great party place it was, but from the looks of it, it seemed more like a forgotten place.

"We will have to turn around and head back to California and park the car," Ryan said.

"Sounds good to me."

As Ryan made a U-turn to the U.S. border, Cassandra sat in the car amazed at all the little children running up to the car asking for money or selling food and every knickknack possible. After an hour of sitting in border traffic, they were finally back in the United States.

"Make a next right and park in that parking lot," Ryan said directing Cassandra where to turn. Cassandra did as Ryan said and pulled into the parking lot. She started driving slowly until she found a spot all the way in the back of the parking lot. Cassandra said, "Well, we are finally here after sitting in that traffic forever." They both got out of the car and started walking toward the entrance of the parking lot. Ryan noticed that Cassandra had on a sexy black summer dress that was blowing in the wind. Without hesitation, Ryan grabbed Cassandra and pulled her behind the abandoned train that was next to the parking lot and started kissing her. "What are you doing?" Cassandra yelled as she pulled away from Ryan.

"Sshhh," Ryan said. "Just come here and let me kiss you."

"We are in a parking lot!" Cassandra exclaimed.

"We are behind a train; no one can see us and being outside has not stopped us before!" Cassandra let herself fall into his arms and he started kissing her. Within minutes, Cassandra's legs were wrapped around Ryan's waist and they were moving like two waves crashing against each other. Once they were done, Cassandra stood next to Ryan thinking how great that had been.

"Ready to go to Mexico?" Ryan asked Cassandra, flashing his killer smile.

"Yes," Cassandra said, feeling lost in his eyes.

They walked hand in hand toward the Mexican border. Being in a car crossing the Mexico border was one thing, but actually walking into Mexico was another. Cassandra was a bit nervous. She moved cautiously staying very close to Ryan and observed all the people running around and yelling different things: "Taxi!" "Buy one, get one free!" "Tacos!" Cassandra looked in amazement; she had never seen anything like this. Ryan looked around for the nearest pharmacy; he too wanted to leave the area. After roaming a couple of blocks and never leaving the site of the Mexico/U.S. border, Ryan found exactly what he was looking for. This pharmacy had the specific pills he wanted. These pills gave you a feeling of numbness while still trying to cope with life.

"How much for the white ones?" Ryan asked the man behind the counter.

"$5 each," the man answered looking at Cassandra.

"Okay, give me fifty pills all white and no substitutes."

The man nodded and went around the corner to a little window where he knocked and it opened. He slipped the order and the money to the person behind the window. Moments later, the pills were produced in a small plastic bag.

"Here, count if you want," the man said as he slammed down the bag.

"No need. Where is your bathroom?" Ryan said as he took the pills.

"Through there." The man indicated behind the doors made out of curtains.

Ryan walked through the curtains and into the dark little bathroom, which could not fit two people at the same time.

"Hey mamacita, is there anything you like?" the man said to Cassandra, and she threw him a dirty look. As Cassandra was about to say something,

Ryan walked out of the bathroom. *Finally,* she thought to herself and turned around to walk out of the store. Ryan nodded at the man and the man waved. "Hope to see you again."

"What were you doing in the bathroom?" Cassandra asked Ryan.

"I put the pills inside my pants."

"What?" Cassandra said not sure she had understood Ryan correctly.

"Yes, I put the bag of pills down my pants, in case the Border Police search me."

Cassandra was surprised and really just wanted to be back on American soil.

"Well, do you want to stay here or hit the Gas Lamp District in San Diego?"

Cassandra took one look around and said, "Let's go to SD."

Ryan and Cassandra walked to the U.S. border with their passports in hand. The line was rather long but moved quickly.

"What was the purpose of your visit?" the border policeman asked Cassandra in a strong voice.

"To get something to eat," Cassandra responded without flinching.

"Are you bringing anything back?" the policeman asked, looking her straight in the eyes.

"Nothing at all," Cassandra said looking back into his eyes, her black eyes gleaming.

"Okay, welcome back," the policeman said as he stamped Cassandra's passport. Cassandra took the passport, smiled, and walked away. She saw Ryan was a couple of steps in front of her.

"That was intense," Cassandra said.

"Tell me about it!" Ryan said, relieved to be back in the United States. Cassandra thought *I couldn't be more grateful.*

Ryan drove the car toward San Diego as Cassandra listened to music.

"What bar do you want to hit first?" Ryan asked Cassandra.

"Any would be great. I really need a drink after being in Mexico."

"Okay, the first one we see is where we'll stop."

As Ryan approached downtown San Diego, Cassandra admired all the buildings that were starting to appear over the highway. She always loved the view of any city's downtown; it reminded her of home. Cassandra had grown up in the heart of Murray Hill in New York City, with her workaholic father, ambiguous mother, and a younger sister who would send Cassandra postcards from her most recent adventure, one being from Alaska. "Wish you were here" was all it read along with Cassandra's infamous signature of a lipstick kiss on the postcard. *She must have inherited it from Mom,* Cassandra thought to herself.

"Hey, how about that bar on the corner?" Ryan asked Cassandra.

Cassandra looked at the bar. It was crowded with no name on the front. "Sure, let's go for it," Cassandra said not certain what the inside held.

Ryan parked his car in a nearby parking lot and got out of the car.

"Let's go," Ryan said to Cassandra.

Cassandra got out of the car happy to finally be heading to a bar to grab a drink, hopefully, more than one. Cassandra and Ryan entered the bar, which was crowded in every direction. They both squeezed their way to the front of the bar.

"What do you want?" Ryan asked.

"Vodka and soda," Cassandra said without a second thought.

Ryan ordered the drinks from the bartender who could barely hear him. The bartender nodded his head and went to work. Cassandra started surveying the room and noticed some nice-looking men but decided to stay away from any trouble tonight, since Ryan could get out of hand when he started drinking. The bartender brought their drinks and Ryan paid for them.

"Do you want to find a place to sit?" Cassandra asked looking around.

"I think I see an empty booth in the corner," Ryan remarked.

Cassandra followed Ryan to the empty corner booth that had all types of glasses and beer spilled on the table. Cassandra sat down and moved the glasses to the other side of the table.

"So . . ." Ryan started.

"Yes?" Cassandra sipping her drink, enjoying the taste.

"What do you want to do after this?" Ryan asked.

"Not sure, I'm up for anything." "Good, let's have some more drinks here and then head to the casinos."

"Okay," Cassandra said, thinking how much she loved to gamble.

They each had three more drinks, left the bar, and started asking people on the street if they knew how to get to the closest casino.

"Take Highway 79 and it will lead you to the nearest casino, Harrah's," a young woman said, slightly slurring her words.

"Thanks," Ryan said while Cassandra wondered how many drinks she had had. They headed to the car.

"Can you drive?" Ryan asked Cassandra.

"Okay," she said. She really wasn't in any condition to drive, but she realized that Ryan had popped one of his pills before they had started drinking and she was in a better condition than him. Cassandra pulled out of the parking lot and headed toward the highway. As she drove, Ryan fell asleep. She looked over and smiled thinking what a lightweight he was. Cassandra drove for over half an hour and eventually, the road ran out. She didn't know which way to turn and decided to take a left, hoping it was right. She started going up winding roads, until she started seeing casinos of sorts all over the place. *I must be going the right way,* Cassandra thought to herself. She continued driving and finally saw the signs to Harrah's casino. "Great," Cassandra said out loud, hoping to wake up Ryan, but he didn't budge. After another ten minutes of driving, Cassandra pulled up to the casino.

"Ryan, we are here," Cassandra said as she nudged Ryan.

"What?" Ryan said as he started to open his eyes. It took him a second to realize where he was and looked around and then at Cassandra.

"We are at the casino, sunshine. The valet is waiting for us to get out of the car."

"Okay," Ryan said with his eyes still slightly closed.

They both got out of and walked into the casino. The lobby was done in white and tan marble. Cassandra was impressed for a casino in the middle of nowhere. They walked up to the reception.

"Do you have a room?" Ryan asked the receptionist leaning against the counter.

"Let me check," responded the receptionist without looking at Ryan. "We have one room, but check-in will have to be in thirty minutes."

"Fine," Ryan said and placed his card on the counter.

The receptionist swiped the card and took Ryan's information.

"Come back in thirty minutes to get your room keys."

"Okay," Ryan said and started walking toward the casino.

Cassandra looked at her watch and realized that it was later than she thought. It was 3:00 a.m. *I must have been driving for a while*, she thought. They walked around the casino and Cassandra realized that she had not eaten in a while.

"Let's get something to eat," Cassandra said to Ryan.

"I am not hungry."

"I am. I will be at the restaurant," Cassandra said and walked away.

Cassandra sat down at a booth and took her phone out of her purse and realized it had died sometime during her drive here. She looked at the late-night menu and didn't know what to order. Nothing looked good. She started looking around at the people in the restaurant and they were all older couples eating soup or drinking coffee after having spent hours at the penny and dime machine. Cassandra decided to skip the eating part and went to the casino floor to look for Ryan. She found him standing behind the poker players at a poker table. "Let's go check if our room is ready," Cassandra said hoping Ryan was not going to join the table because that would last all night.

"Okay," Ryan said wondering if he should start playing.

They walked toward the reception and waited for someone to attend to them. It was a couple of minutes before the rude man from before walked out of the back office.

"Yes," he said as if they were infringing upon him.

"Is our room ready?" Cassandra said with an attitude.

The man looked up at Cassandra and said, "Yes," and then looked back down. He swiped two room keys and programmed them with the room number.

"Here you go," the man said, placed the room keys on the counter and walked away.

"Thank you," Cassandra yelled after the man who ignored her. "Wait till morning until I speak to the manager." Ryan barely heard her because he was already asleep in his head. They walked into the room. It was just a regular king-size room with outdated draperies, bed covers, and furniture. Cassandra threw her purse and clothes in the room and got into bed. Ryan had already fallen asleep, clothes and everything.

Julie tossed and turned in her bed. She looked at the clock on her nightstand: 3:00 a.m. *Why can't I sleep?* She tried to close her eyes and turn to her side. She finally landed on her back and opened her eyes. Her immediate thought was about Cassandra and Ryan: *Where are they and what are they doing?* She hadn't received a response from the text she'd sent Cassandra over five hours ago. She thought that Cassandra would never do anything with Ryan, or anything to hurt her. She turned to her side and tried closing her eyes, but she ended up with her eyes open and random thoughts running through her head.

Chapter 24

Cassandra woke up to see the sun coming through the outdated draperies. She looked at the clock on the old furniture. "7:00 a.m.," Cassandra said out loud and rolled over to look at Ryan. He was still asleep and in last night's clothes. She could hear her belly making noises. She thought about waking Ryan up, but decided not to bother him and instead turned on the TV. She flipped through the channels, decided on the news, and wondered what city she was actually in. She wished she had brought her phone charger; she felt cut off from the world.

Julie woke up after a short nap. She had barely got an hour of sleep, but that was sufficient as her body would not let her sleep anymore. She looked at her cell phone and had no new text from Cassandra. She thought about calling Cassandra but that might be too crazy since it was only 7:00 a.m. Julie then got out of the bed and headed for the kitchen. Maybe something to eat would help calm her nerves.

Cassandra awoke again from a short nap and now it was 11:00 a.m. She could not stand being hungry anymore and started pushing Ryan to wake him up. He didn't move at her first attempt and Cassandra tried harder. Nothing happened. Finally, Cassandra had to use both her hands and feet to move Ryan.

"Wake up, Ryan!" Cassandra yelled in his ears.

"Hmmm," was all Ryan managed to say.

"It's morning!" she said as she sat up on the bed.

Ryan looked around as if had no clue where he was and finally remembered that he was in a casino. "What time is it?" he asked.

"11:00 a.m. Let's get some breakfast. I'm starved," Cassandra said jumping out of the bed.

Ryan looked at the ceiling waiting for his head to stop spinning.

"Are you hungry?" she asked him.

"Yeah a little bit," he said holding his head. He finally got up and sat in bed, but the room was still spinning.

"Get up and let's go," Cassandra said moving around in the room trying to find her clothes and shoes.

Ryan knew better than to start arguing with Cassandra and got up and saw that he was still dressed. "Let me take a quick shower, then we will head out."

"Okay," Cassandra said. "Can I join you?"

"Sure," Ryan said grabbing her hand and heading into the bathroom.

Julie was not sure what to do with herself this particular morning. She had been up for hours now, thinking about calling Cassandra just to see what she and Ryan were up to. It was 11:00 a.m. *A decent time to call, no?* she asked herself. Finally, she grabbed her cell phone and pushed talk on Cassandra's name. Julie held her breath; it rang once and then went straight to voicemail, "Hey, you reached Cassandra, leave me a message and I will get back to you." Julie let the air out of her mouth and hung up. *Cassandra's phone must have died; it's always running out of battery,* she thought. *What to do now?* Julie walked back to her room and got dressed. She could no longer stay in the house and decided to go out. She didn't know where, but it was better than sitting at home waiting for Cassandra to call her.

Ryan and Cassandra roamed the casino floor looking at the tables, Ryan surveying which table he would like to join and Cassandra looking for her favorite game, roulette. They walked side by side when Ryan finally found the poker section. "Hey, I am going to take a seat here, where are you going to be?"

"I am going to walk around and see what there is to play."

"Okay, come get me in half an hour," Ryan said taking money out of his pocket.

Cassandra smiled at him and walked away. *Right, half an hour. More like two hours,* she thought to herself and went on to find her favorite game.

Eugene had made it home early last night—more like he passed out early since his drinking started pretty early the morning before. He lay in his bed, one hand over his right chest. For some reason, his chest was hurting this morning. Eugene started getting worried because he never felt his heart hurt in this way. He tried massaging the area that hurt, but it didn't help. He tried to breathe slowly because he didn't want to agitate his heart anymore. *What's wrong with me?* Eugene thought. He decided to just lay still and wait for the pain to stop. *Maybe I should cut back on the drinking.* He knew that his partying ways would eventually take a toll on his body, but this was ridiculous. Closing his eyes, he started thinking about something else to take his mind off the pain. He started thinking about Maui, his favorite place in the world. He thought about the beaches, the sun, the amazing sunsets, and then Cassandra. He remembered the trip he had planned for them to Maui. After several months of pursuing Eugene to take another trip together, Eugene had decided on surprising Cassandra with a Maui trip. She had known nothing about the trip and it had been almost a year since his surprise trip to Paris. Eugene had researched some dates and booked two tickets for an entire week. He had then called the favorite house he liked to stay in and booked it too. The house was set on a semi-private island and included everything from its own swimming pool to jet skis and a boat. Eugene had been excited as he had made the plans. Finally, when he was done, he thought for a second on what he had just done. He knew this trip would bring him and Cassandra closer together and that scared him completely. He had looked at the email he received from his travel agent: "The airline tickets have been purchased and confirmed. Have fun!" It was like Eugene had frozen after reading the email. He had never brought anyone to Maui besides his ex-wife; this was something special. He had decided to stop being scared and picked up the phone to call Cassandra. Her phone had rung and rung and then gone straight to voicemail. He had left her a message asking her to call him back, and then hung up and stared into the phone. She had called back the next day, but by then it was too late. Early the next morning, Eugene had canceled the plane tickets and the reservation on the house. He wasn't ready to let anyone into his heart. He didn't talk to Cassandra for weeks after that.

As Eugene was remembering, his cell phone rang and brought him out of his thoughts. He moved over a little bit on the bed, his hand still on his chest. He looked at his phone and it was a call from one of his clients. He was about to pick up the call, but the caller had already hung up. Eugene remembered he had a meeting with the client this morning, even though it was Sunday. The client was only available to see the property where he wanted his new development to take place. Eugene started taking deep breaths and realized the pain had subsided. He still waited a few more minutes, hand still on the chest. He now wished he had taken Cassandra on that trip; she probably would have been lying next to him helping him cope with the chest pain. He knew he needed to start his day. Lightheaded, he got out of bed and called his client back.

Cassandra was still wandering through the casino trying to find a game to play. The roulette game was a bust because it was a different type of roulette. Instead of a turntable spinning the ball, it was a ball full of air with different numbers flying inside the ball waiting for the button to be pushed for the number to come out. Cassandra had never seen anything like this and walked away before she placed any bets. She walked by the table Ryan was at and he was intensely staring at the other players. Cassandra decided to keep walking and find something else to play.

Julie drove for miles and miles that afternoon thinking to herself on what was to be done about the situation. It was not like Ryan and she were together, but she liked him a lot. He was the first guy that was interested in her, who was actually a great catch, educated, successful, and fun to be with. Every other man Julie had dated always had issues, had no job, or was just plain ordinary. Ryan was different and it was hard to let him go. Lost in thoughts she had driven far and didn't realize she was on the county border of LA and Orange County. She stopped at the coffee shop she spotted off the highway and decided to take a break for coffee.

Exhausted from walking around and finding nothing to play, Cassandra finally went back to the table where Ryan was still playing. *I don't care if he is done or not, we are leaving,* she thought. She walked over to him carefully trying not to disturb the other players. She tapped his shoulder. He looked at up and noticed her face that read *let's go.* He got the hint, played his last hand, cashed out, and walked out of the poker pit. "Did you win?" Cassandra asked Ryan.

"No, I am down a hundred bucks."

"Oh, so where are you taking me for lunch?" Cassandra said.

"Anywhere your heart desires," Ryan said as he put his hand around Cassandra and they walked toward the lobby. The found the valet and Ryan gave him the ticket for his car. They walked outside and waited for the car. It was a beautiful Sunday afternoon and the sun was gleaming through. Cassandra closed her eyes and took a deep breath. The air was thinner up in the mountains where the casino was located. Ryan's car came around the bend and stopped in front of the casino. Ryan tipped the valet and they both got into the car. He drove away from the casino and Cassandra looked at it from her rearview mirror knowing she would probably never visit again.

"You drove all of this last night?' Ryan asked as he drove down the winding roads.

"Yes, while you slept," Cassandra said.

Cassandra started noticing the fruit vendors on the side of the roads. There were different vendors selling strawberries, raspberries, and cherries. Ryan stopped when he saw a vendor who sold different types of beef jerky meats. He pulled over and got out; Cassandra opted to stay inside because she had no taste for beef jerky. She watched Ryan talk to the man and pay for what he bought. Ryan got back into the car. "Want to try?" Ryan said as he pulled out a slice of the beef jerky.

"Ugh, no way," Cassandra said as she squirmed. "Get that away from me!"

Ryan laughed, "You are so cute."

Ryan continued driving and saw an orange orchard and pulled over.

"Let's get out and walk through the trees."

Cassandra didn't object and got out of the car. They both walked through the enormous trees that had oranges growing on them. Cassandra had never seen anything of the sort and, excited, started pulling oranges from each tree. The ones that she couldn't reach, Ryan reached for her. Cassandra thought, *wouldn't it be great if Ryan and I were always like this? A couple.* Just then Ryan grabbed Cassandra's hand, looked at her, and smiled. They continued walking through the orchard talking and laughing. Ryan enjoyed spending time with Cassandra and mostly liked enjoying talking to her. She had a knack for listening to others and especially making them feel comfortable about themselves. Ryan let himself go and enjoyed the time with her. After a long walk, they walked back to the car and headed to the freeway.

Julie continued driving through Orange County after her coffee break. She didn't know where she was heading, but she needed to clear her head and decided to drive along the Pacific Coast Highway. As she drove, she looked over to the ocean and wondered when she would find someone who truly loved her and wanted to spend time with her. Just then, tears started rolling down her face, and Julie wiped them away from her cheeks. She tried to stop herself from crying, but the tears started to fall uncontrollably. There was nothing she could do now. She pulled over on the side of the road and let the tears flow. She missed Ryan terribly and there was nothing she could do to stop her heart from wanting him.

Eugene drove to meet his client at a restaurant across the street from the Pacific Ocean. It was the best steakhouse in the County and one of Eugene's favorites. His heart and chest were feeling better now and he was grateful that the pain had gone away. As he drove along the coast, he noticed a car pulled over to the side with a woman in it. He really couldn't see what she was doing, but it looked like she was crying. He felt bad for a moment and thought about turning back to help her, but knew it wasn't his place to do so. He pulled into the parking lot of the restaurant and headed straight for the valet. Eugene put his car into park. The valet opened his door and Eugene got out. *It's game time*, Eugene thought to himself. He knew this was another deal he was about to close and make a huge commission, and then head home to his empty house. Eugene walked into the restaurant and cleared his head of any thoughts. When it came to business, nothing stood in the way.

Ryan and Cassandra talked all the way as they drove back to Los Angles. As they started entering the outskirts of Orange County, Ryan remembered a promenade mall located at the beginning of the County from the south side.

"Hey, do you want to get something to eat?" Ryan asked Cassandra.

"Yes, please! We have not eaten at all since yesterday," Cassandra responded patting her belly.

"Okay. I know there's a promenade mall a few miles ahead. After we eat, maybe we can watch a movie?"

"Sounds good to me," Cassandra said wishing this day would never end.

Ryan continued driving and Cassandra just gazed at his face.

Julie was finally able to control her tears and she pulled back on to the road. She continued driving through Orange County. Realizing that she had driven too far, she decided to head back. She made a left on a road that would bring her back to the main highway. As she was driving, she realized that she was running low on gas and thought of stopping at the next gas stop before merging onto the main highway that would take her home. She looked at her phone. Still no text or call from Cassandra. What was she to do?

"Is that the promenade?" Cassandra asked as the promenade mall started appearing on her left. "Looks nice."

"Yes, there is a sports bar and restaurant. We can go and watch the games."

"Of course, there is." Cassandra knew that with Ryan no one could escape sports.

Julie reached the end of the road that was going to take her back to the main highway, when she spotted the promenade on her right. She had not been there in a long while, and thought about going to take a walk around, but then instead it was better to just go home. She pulled into the gas station and parked her car next to a pump and got out.

"Should we stop for gas?" Cassandra asked Ryan as they exited the main highway to the street that was going to take them to the promenade.

Ryan thought about it at the red light; the gas station was to his right. He looked at his tank and had enough gas to get home. "No, we don't need any right now."

"Okay," Cassandra said as she turned her head away from the gas station.

At the same gas station that Cassandra and Ryan had just driven past, Julie stood next to her car, with swollen red eyes, filling gas into her car.

Eugene and his client got into Eugene's car and headed to the site where the client was to build a state-of-the-art office space. "Do you think the vacant area next to the promenade will be a great location?" the client asked Eugene.

"Yes, of course, especially being next to the promenade it will draw great traffic," Eugene responded.

"Yes, that is what I was thinking. Do you mind parking at the promenade first and taking a walk around? We should enter the movie theater."

"Of course," Eugene said, knowing he had to make the client happy.

Ryan and Cassandra drove through the parking garage, trying to find a place to park.

"I think there is one up ahead," Cassandra remarked.

"I see it."

"I am famished," Cassandra said. "If I don't eat, I am going to disappear."

"Funny!" They both got out of the car and entered the promenade by the movie theater.

"Let's see what is playing first and the timings," Ryan said.

"Okay."

They walked up the steps to the screen that displayed the movie and times and they read the movies.

"Which one?' Ryan asked

"Doesn't matter," Cassandra said.

"How about the new action movie with Will Smith?"

"That looks good," Cassandra said not knowing what movie it was.

Ryan searched for the showtime, as Cassandra looked around the area.

"This is going to be a great place for my clients and workers to come to," Eugene's client remarked, as he stood in front of the movie theater surveying the area. "They have so many restaurants. I think it's an amazing place."

"Yes, sir, it is," Eugene said not looking all that happy.

"Let's walk around some more and see what else is here."

"Sure," Eugene said with melancholy.

They started entering the promenade.

"Ready to eat now?" Ryan asked Cassandra.

"Yes, already," Cassandra pleaded. Ryan grabbed Cassandra's hand and they walked toward the sports restaurant passing the backs of Eugene and his client, each one not noticing the other.

After getting gas, Julie merged onto the highway; she was still visibly upset and lost in her thoughts. She needed a way to handle the situation when he saw Cassandra and Ryan tomorrow. *What would she say? What would she do?* She decided to clear her head and just drive; she was yearning for her bed and the comfort of sleeping.

Ryan and Cassandra ate their meal, giggling and feeding each other. Anyone who saw them would think they were in love. Maybe they were, but neither would ever admit it.

"Would you like anything else?" the waitress asked them with a jealous look, wishing she was with her boyfriend instead of serving this couple.

"Do you want anything else, Cassandra?"

"No, I am okay."

"We are good, please bring us the check. We have a movie to catch," Ryan said. The waitress smiled, said, "No problem," and walked away rolling her eyes without them seeing her.

"What is this movie about again?" Cassandra asked finishing her pasta.

"I thought you knew," Ryan asked smiling.

"I did, I just forgot," Cassandra said looking down at her plate.

"It's a good movie; don't worry about it," Ryan said and winked at her.

The waitress brought over the check and Ryan immediately gave her his credit card. The waitress took it and left.

She came back with the receipt and his card. "Thank you, please come again."

Ryan signed the receipt and said, "Ready?" "Yes, let's go," Cassandra said.

They walked out of the restaurant diagonally to the movie theater. Ryan bought the tickets for the movie and they walked inside.

"Hope this is a good movie," Cassandra remarked.

"It will be," Ryan said confidently.

"Great job son," said Eugene's client to Eugene.

"Thank you, sir. You will be very happy working with our firm," Eugene replied.

"I'm sure, I will. Please send over all the contracts to move office tomorrow."

"Will do first thing in the morning," Eugene said.

Eugene had driven his client back to his car and he had closed the deal. A deal that would increase his back balance with another six figures.

"Have a great evening. The wife and kids are waiting," the client said as he got into his car and waved.

"Good night," Eugene said and waved back, watching his client drive away. Eugene stood in the parking lot for a couple more minutes. The sun was starting to set behind the Pacific Ocean and the sky was lit up with reds, oranges, and yellows. He stared at the sky dreading the fact of getting into his car because he knew that he wouldn't be driving to his waiting wife and kids. His house was as lonely as he was. He finally got into his car and drove off toward home with no one to celebrate his new deal. It felt like he had not accomplished anything.

"The movie was so so," Cassandra said to Ryan as they walked to the car.

"You didn't like it?" Ryan asked.

"It was okay."

"Okay, I think it was great," Ryan said.

"Great? I think I saw you fall asleep," Cassandra remarked.

"Yeah, I am kind of tired. Ready to go home?" Ryan asked as he turned to look at Cassandra.

"Yes, ready to go home," Cassandra said grabbing his hand.

Ryan drove off as the last of the sun was setting. Cassandra looked into the sky and enjoyed how this felt: being with someone, enjoying the day with him, and then going home. She knew that she liked Ryan, and her feelings had started escalating the past couple of weeks. She had started feeling something she didn't know was there. She wasn't sure how long Ryan would stay with her. That was one of her greatest fears. She didn't want to let Ryan in because if she did then he might hurt her and she couldn't handle any more pain. She would just have to enjoy the moments she had and hoped he felt the same because she didn't know when they could end. No one could predict the future or what was about to happen.

Chapter 25

A few days later, Cassandra was sitting in her office. It had been some days since the trip to Tijuana and Ryan had started acting distant. He was coming back to the apartment at night and when he did, he actually slept on the couch. Cassandra didn't want to make a big deal about it and didn't bother asking questions. She had a feeling that he might be spending time with Hermosa or whatever her name was. Cassandra's phone rang, interrupting her thoughts.

"Hello," she said. It was an unrecognized number.

"Hi, is this Cassandra Zea?" the woman on the other end asked.

"Yes, this is she. Who may I ask is calling?"

"My name is Elaine Robinson and I am with Beach Realty. Ryan put you down as a reference for the new apartment he is renting in Manhattan Beach. May I ask you a couple of questions about him?"

"Yes," Cassandra said barely recognizing her own voice. She was in utter shock.

"How long have you known Ryan?"

"Over a year," Cassandra said not really thinking, but just blurting answers out.

"Is he reliable?"

"Yes," Cassandra said.

"Do you know him to be late on any payments or rent in the past?"

"No."

"Thank you so much, have a nice day."

"Yes, you too," Cassandra managed to say as the tears were starting to form in her eyes. Putting down her cell phone, she could not believe Ryan was leaving her and hadn't even bothered to say anything, not even on their weekend trip, where Cassandra thought things were actually moving to another level. Not knowing what to do and not wanting to cry, Cassandra immediately called Julie.

"Hello," Julie said in her usual monotone.

"Hey, it's Cassandra."

"What's up?"

"I just got a random call from Beach Realty. They wanted to check Ryan out before they let him move into his new apartment in Manhattan Beach. I was his reference," Cassandra said trying to hold back the tears.

"Are you serious?" Julie asked, just as shocked. "Wait, when is he moving?"

"I am not sure. It's already mid-July so I am thinking August. It's two weeks away."

Julie was just as shocked as Cassandra, so she didn't know what to say. If Ryan left Cassandra's apartment then she surely knew Ryan would never be with her. Him staying at Cassandra's apartment was the glue that was holding them together.

"I am utterly shocked!" Julie finally said. "Are you going to confront him? Say something to him?"

"I don't know what to do. It's not like he signed a lease with me. I always had this feeling in the back of my mind. I just didn't know when it was going to happen and if it was going to happen. I just don't know what to do."

"Me either. Do you want to get some drinks after work?"

"Yes, that would be great, I will meet you in the lobby at 6:30 p.m. sharp."

"See you then," Julie said and hung up.

Julie sat at her desk unable to think straight. She sort of felt bad for Cassandra, but also for herself. If Ryan was gone, what was she going to do?

Cassandra leaned back in her chair, unable to think clearly. She never imagined Ryan leaving her apartment without saying anything to her. She had been kind enough to open her apartment to him when he had had nowhere to go and now he was repaying his kindness by betraying her. Cassandra was upset for a few minutes, but then the anger set in. As her mind started to clear, she was already thinking of a plan to get back at him. No one was going to treat her the way he did and get away with it. Payback was one of Cassandra's specialties.

Cassandra walked into her apartment later that evening. She had gone out for drinks with Julie and drank way too many margaritas. She had a hard time opening the door and spilled into her apartment making noise with her shoes and purse. She took her shoes off and threw her purse on the kitchen counter. She turned the corner, walking toward the end of the apartment where the bed was. She noticed that Ryan was not home. Angry and drunk enough to think about calling Ryan, but before she did, Cassandra lay on her bed and fell asleep, dreaming a wonderful dream of her and Ryan.

The next morning Cassandra woke up to noises in the walk-out closet. She lifted her head and tried to open her eyes, but it was usual. The pain in her head was too intense and it made her put her head back on the pillow without bothering to open her eyes. She attempted to roll over, but was unsuccessful.

"Long night?" Ryan asked, coming out of the closet, knotting his tie.

Cassandra didn't want to answer because a wave of anger swept over her, but she remembered she had to play it cool.

"Yes" was all she managed to say because her throat was dry.

"Would you like some water?"

"Please," Cassandra said and thought, *don't try to be nice to me.*

Ryan walked over to the water cooler and got Cassandra water.

"Where did you go out last night? I am guessing you went out with Julie?"

"Yes, and I really can't remember where we went."

Ryan sat on the bed and waited for Cassandra to sit up to drink water. She tried her hardest and finally had enough strength to sit up and remove her hair from her face. She finally opened her eyes halfway.

"Thank you," Cassandra said as she took the glass of water from Ryan.

Ryan looked at Cassandra. Even though she had just woken up, she still looked beautiful.

"Are you going to work today?" Ryan stood up and continued to knot his tie.

"I think I am still drunk," Cassandra said sipping her water.

"I can make you something to eat before I leave," Ryan said looking at himself in the full-length mirror.

"No, I am okay. I am just going to sleep it off," Cassandra said putting the glass of water on the nightstand and lying back down. *Don't try to play your games with me, Ryan. I am on to you,* Cassandra thought.

"Okay, I will be home after work," Ryan said as he grabbed his jacket and suitcase and started walking out the door. "Hope you feel better."

Cassandra heard the door slam and she stared at the ceiling. *Was I imagining the call from the realtor yesterday? Why is Ryan being so nice to me? If only he knew what was coming for him.*

Later that afternoon, Cassandra's cell phone started to ring. She was still lying in bed and had just started feeling better. She looked at the phone. It was Julie.

"Hello," Cassandra said, her voice scratchy.

"Are you okay? Are you at work?" Julie asked annoyed.

"No, I am in bed," Cassandra said.

Julie was always annoyed by Cassandra and her constantly skipping work. *Doesn't she have to be at work? How does she pay rent? Or her bills?* Julie really never asked Cassandra about her financial situation because that was a personal topic.

"Oh, well, I have great news."

"Really, you won the lottery?" Cassandra said skeptically.

"No, better. You remember the college games that Ryan keeps talking about, that are played in September in Los Angeles?"

"Yes," Cassandra said, as she thought to herself, *how can I forget that Eugene attended the school that one of the teams is playing.*

"I was able to purchase four tickets to the game," Julie said, excited.

"Really?" Cassandra said thinking of how she now may run into Eugene at the game. Eugene was the biggest supporter of his alma mater.

"Yes, isn't it great? Now, we have to think of whom to invite. Or I can just resell the other two tickets at a higher price."

"How about Eugene? Maybe he can bring a friend?" "Really, you think Eugene would want to go?"

"I don't see why not," Cassandra said wondering whether Eugene would really go to the game with her.

"Let me send him a message and see what he says," Cassandra said now moving herself from the bed to the couch to watch some TV.

"Okay, let me know what he says."

"Okay, call you later."

As soon as Cassandra hung up, she started feeling even better. She knew Ryan's heart was set on going to his game and that is why he was dating Hermosa. Her family held season tickets to all the games at Los Angeles State University. If Cassandra found a way for Hermosa to break up with Ryan before the game, he would be left without a ticket and since they would already be sold out, and there was no way he would get a ticket to sit by himself. Also, Ryan had attended the other team's school and wished nothing more than to go to the game. Cassandra smiled to herself and knew this would hurt Ryan more than anything, but first she must text Eugene and tell him about the game.

Eugene was in his office writing emails to his good friend in Arizona.

"Hey, did you hear about the big game between Los Angeles State University and Cleveland State University?" his friend had written in the email.

Eugene responded, "Yes, I am trying to find tickets, but it's difficult and they are already sold out."

"I have been searching too; let me know if you find anything."

"Will do."

Eugene continued searching the internet for the tickets, but when he did find them the bidding price had escalated and they were sold out even before he could place a bid. All of a sudden, he heard his cell phone beep indicating a new message. Eugene grabbed his phone and looked at the message.

"Have two extra tickets for the LASU v. CSU game in September. Interested? You can bring a friend."

Eugene smiled ear to ear and could not believe Cassandra was sending this message. He immediately responded, "I was just literally talking to a buddy of mine about the game. I would love to go with you. May I bring my friend from Arizona? He attended CSU."

Cassandra waited for Eugene's response and was surprised to see that he responded so quickly. Cassandra read the message and smiled. "Of course you can bring your friend. The only problem is that you have sit to next to me during the game." She always loved teasing Eugene; she knew better than anyone how to push his buttons.

Eugene read the new message that just came in and got annoyed. *She always finds a way to be sarcastic toward me.* It bothered him a lot, but it bothered him even more that he let Cassandra get to him. "I knew it was way too easy to have a conversation without you lowballing me."

Cassandra looked at her phone and smiled even more. "You know I am joking. Can't wait for the game and see your team lose. Let your friend know he is in!"

Eugene looked at his phone, still annoyed, but happy. *I can't believe Cassandra came through. I could always count on her.* It was something Eugene was starting to realize. No matter what Eugene did to her, she never left his side.

"You will not believe this, but my friend Cassandra just sent me a message that she has two extra tickets to the game. So we are in!!"

His friend responded, "Awesome. Do you know where the seats are? By the way, who is Cassandra?"

"I am not sure where the seats are, but I am sure they are not in a bad location. Cassandra—long story, tell you when I see you for the game."

Cassandra, happy than ever about Eugene coming to game, now needed to get her plan ready to hurt Ryan, just as he had hurt her.

Later that evening, Cassandra, having still not moved from the couch, heard the door open.

"How are you feeling?" Ryan asked Cassandra.

"Better, thank you for asking," she replied, not even looking at Ryan.

"Have you eaten?' he could clearly see that she had not moved from the couch.

"Not really, didn't have much of an appetite."

"I am going downstairs to get some sandwiches. Want one?"

"Yes, turkey."

"Okay, will be right back."

Cassandra just smiled at him as he walked out. As soon as Ryan left the apartment, Cassandra noticed that he had left his cell phone on the kitchen counter. She grabbed it, quickly unlocked it, and started reading his text messages. She found the ones from Hermosa, then clicked on her contact number. Cassandra quickly jotted it down on a napkin and put the phone back in its original place. She was unsure how she was going to handle the situation, but it would come to her.

The next morning, Cassandra was sitting in her office looking at the napkin, thinking of what she could do. She clearly could not call from her phone or send her a message because Hermosa would be able to see the number. She thought about sending her a message from Julie's phone and this way she would get both Julie and Ryan into a fight. That would be fun, but it somehow would lead back to her. Then, she remembered one of the girls Ryan was dating before he moved into Cassandra's apartment and thought about using her name. Cassandra tried remembering the name: *Sammie, Samantha, Rebecca—that's it, it was Rebecca.* Cassandra blocked her number and dialed Hermosa's number. She didn't know what she was going to say, but let the phone ring.

"Hello," Hermosa answered out of breath.

"Hi," Cassandra started to say and stalled for a second.

"Hello," Hermosa said again.

"Yeah, this is Rebecca. I am not sure if you know me, but I am currently dating Ryan and I noticed you have been calling him."

"I am sorry, who are you again?"

"Rebecca. Can you not hear me? I am dating Ryan and would appreciate you not calling anymore. We got back together a couple of weeks ago and I notice that you are calling him. Can you please stop?"

"I am not sure who you are, but Ryan and I are together. Don't ever call me again." Hermosa said, with tears rolling down her face as she hung up.

Cassandra smiled to herself and knew that the plan worked. From what she could tell, Hermosa was a fragile one and this would definitely make her break up with Ryan.

Cassandra had decided to go home after work instead of hitting the bars. She was still recovering from the night before. When she walked into the apartment, she noticed Ryan was home and sitting on the couch.

"Hey," Cassandra nonchalantly.

"Hey," Ryan said softly.

She noticed that he was upset, but chose to ignore the situation and acted as if nothing was wrong.

"It's a miracle you are home," Cassandra said looking around the fridge for something to eat.

"Yeah, had a tough day."

"Oh," Cassandra said as she walked by Ryan and further down the loft to the closet they shared. Cassandra walked into the closet and changed her clothes. She thought about what Ryan and she were going to do all night together. She had already let go of the feelings that she had harbored for him. She just wanted him to leave! Cassandra walked back into the kitchen and decided on making some dinner. She didn't bother to ask Ryan if he wanted some. It's not like it was a fancy dinner, but she did love eating turkey burgers. Cassandra decided that she would first announce that Julie had bought tickets to the game.

"Guess what?" Cassandra said without trying to laugh. "Julie got tickets to the LASU v. CSU game. She bought for tickets and me, her, Eugene, and his friend. Where are you sitting again?"

Just then, Ryan's face went blank, "Wait, you got tickets?"

"Yep, Julie got them yesterday."

"Where are the seats located?"

"Only ten rows from the fifty-yard half mark."

"Really?" Ryan said intrigued that Julie had got tickets. He still had not told Cassandra that Hermosa canceled his ticket and told him never to call her again.

"Yes, I can't wait. Sounds like it's going to be lots of fun."

"Yeah, it is," Ryan said as he devised his own plan to get Julie on his good side to get the tickets instead of Eugene and his friend.

The morning after, Julie called Cassandra.

"Hey, I told Ryan about the tickets and his jaw almost dropped."

"Good, that is what he gets for choosing that Hermosa girl over me. Has he said anything about moving out?"

"No, I am not sure what he is waiting for."

"Me either," Julie said as she noticed him walking in. "I have to go, have a customer."

"Okay," Cassandra said and hung up.

Julie watched Ryan walk across the lobby and hoped he would come by her desk and talk to her. She watched him talk to the other bankers and finally saw that he was walking toward her desk. Julie quickly started pretending like she was working and looked at her computer.

"Hi Julie," Ryan said with his killer smile and sat down in one of the chairs in front of her.

"Hi," Julie said visibly shaking.

"How are you today? Anything new?"

"I am good, what about you?" Julie said finally looking at Ryan.

"Good. How are your sales?"

"So so. Working on them."

"Do you have any plans for after work? Maybe you want to get some tickets and watch the game?"

"I don't have any plans," Julie said trying not to look too excited. "Drinks sound good."

"Great, let's meet across the street at the bar, say 7:00 p.m.?"

"Sure," she said.

"Good, we have lots to catch up on and I hope you know that we are still friends."

"Of course," Julie said smiling at Ryan. She thought to herself, *he looks so handsome.*

Ryan smiled and walked away. Julie immediately called Cassandra to tell her about the news.

"I can't believe he asked me out for drinks."

"Me either," Cassandra said thinking to herself. *Something must be up.* "Where are you guys going?"

"Just across the street. I hope I look okay."

"You look fine," Cassandra said knowing that Julie needed a lot of help in the makeup and fashion departments. "Let me know the details."

"Okay, by the way, my dad gave me tickets to the baseball games for this weekend. Want to go? I have four tickets. Should I ask Ryan?"

"Um, no, are you crazy? That would be too soon, makes you look desperate," Cassandra said annoyed.

"Who can we get to go?"

"Don't worry, I will take care of filling the seats," Cassandra said thinking, *don't I always? It's not like you have any friends.*

"Okay, I will call you later. I am so excited."

Cassandra hung up thinking about Ryan and what he was up to. *He just wouldn't have drinks with Julie for no reason, unless Hermosa dumped him.* Cassandra was getting frustrated over Julie's excitement and would have to take care of that part later. Once again, when she thought about the tickets, she thought about Eugene.

Chapter 26

Eugene arrived at the airport half an hour early. He was waiting for his son Zachery's plane to arrive. Eugene was granted access to the arrival gates since Zachery was a minor. He looked at the empty row of seats near the windows that faced that runway. He took a seat and looked at his watch again. He had half an hour till the plane touched ground. Eugene started thinking about how this flying back and forth may be taking a toll on Zachery. His son was just eight years old, but had been put through an ordeal that may have made him grow up a bit sooner and for that Eugene would never forgive himself. He started remembering the day his ex-wife had told him that she was six weeks pregnant. They were living together at the time, having been dating for just less than three years. Eugene had come home that evening after a long day of work. He had walked into the kitchen to find Lisa leaning against the counter in tears.

"What's wrong?" Eugene had walked over to give her a hug. "Come here, tell me what is bothering you."

Lisa had just kept sobbing and couldn't get the words out. Finally, after Eugene had continuously asked her, she had blurted out, "I am pregnant," and continued crying even harder. Eugene had just stared at her, not knowing what to say. Those were the last words he had expected her to say. They had always been so careful. His first reaction had been "Are you sure?" Eugene had sounded cold.

"Yes," Lisa had yelled. "You don't have to be insensitive."

"I am sorry, it's just that I am in shock right now. When did you find out?"

"This morning. I thought I was just late, but I took a test and then another to make sure and they both had the same result: positive."

Eugene had continued staring at her not knowing what to say. Lisa continued crying and he had hugged her.

"What are we going to do?" Lisa had asked in between sobs.

"I am not sure. What do you want to do? We should sit down and think of all our options."

"What do you mean options?" Lisa had asked angrily.

"We should talk about this and weigh our options."

"There are no options, Eugene," she had said walking away. "I am having the baby whether you want to or not."

"Don't I have a say in this?" Eugene had yelled back.

"Are you honestly thinking we should consider having an abortion?" Lisa had asked, unable to fathom the idea.

"I am not sure what I am saying, I need time to digest the news."

"Digest the news. Let me tell you something. We are having a baby and you are going to be a father, end of case. I thought you would be happy," Lisa had said as she walked away and slammed the bedroom door. Eugene had sat down at the kitchen table and was still in shock over the news Lisa had told him. Him a father? He was in his mid-twenties but still, he and Lisa were not married, and bringing a baby into this world in that type of situation was not ideal. Financially, he was secure—always had been. But he wasn't ready yet. There were other things he wanted to do with his life, but being the honest and reliable man he was, he knew that he had to be there for Lisa and ultimately had no choice. He had walked into the bedroom and found Lisa lying on the bed crying uncontrollably.

"I am sorry if I acted insensitively. I was in shock."

"I understand," she had said. "I am just as scared as you, but we are in love and that is what this baby needs."

"Yes, I know."

"I love you," Lisa had said.

"I love you too," Eugene had given her a hug.

Eugene remembered that day vividly as though he would never forget it. What he had never told anyone was that on his drive home that night, he was starting up a dialogue in his head to tell Lisa that he was no longer in love with her, that they should take time apart, and that he was going to move out to another apartment he had found. Only he never had the chance to tell her because she had surprised him with her own news before he could ever utter a word.

Eugene's cell phone had been vibrating in his pocket for about a minute before he realized it was ringing. He finally took the phone out and answered it without looking at it, "Eugene Conrad."

"You have such a sexy voice," Cassandra said as she sipped her martini at the rooftop bar.

"How sexy?" Eugene joked with Cassandra. He could always recognize her voice for some reason.

"It's so sexy that you just made me wet right now," Cassandra purred into the phone.

"Really?" Eugene smiled. Her words actually got him excited.

"Yes, do you want to come over and play?" Cassandra said taking another sip.

"I wish I could, but I am at the airport waiting for Zachery's plane to arrive."

"Cute, how long will he be staying?" Cassandra asked thinking about her and Eugene's first time together.

"For a week. I was thinking about hitting the beaches with him."

"Sounds like a great father and son week. And here I was calling asking you if you wanted to go to a baseball game. I have two extra tickets."

"Who is playing?"

"How should I know? I know there are two teams with balls and bats."

"Funny!" Eugene was always amused by what Cassandra had to say.

"Well, I would be interested in going, if you don't mind hanging out with my son and me?"

Cassandra thought to herself, *really, he would like me to meet his son?*

"Of course, I don't mind. It will be fun."

"Who else is going?" "You know Julie?"

"Have I met her?" Eugene asked watching Zachery's plane land.

"No, she is not important. Anyway, the game starts at 7:00 p.m. Meet you at the stadium?" Cassandra asked signaling the bartender for another drink.

"Yes, definitely. Zachery's plane just landed; I have to go. See you Saturday."

"Okay, bye," Cassandra hung up, surprised and excited that she was going to meet Zachery. She knew Eugene never introduced his kid to anyone. This meeting would be a huge step in their non-relationship.

Ryan and Julie were at the bar having drinks without talking much to each other. Ryan stared at the TV and Julie stared at Ryan. This went on for about half an hour when Ryan started easing his way into Julie. "I just want you to know that I completely blew the whole situation at Alex's party. I hope you know that."

"Yeah, I was a little hurt by your actions and what you said to me that day."

'Well, just know that I overreacted. Friends?" Ryan said holding his hand out.

"Friends," Julie said with a smile and shaking Ryan's hand.

They continued to watch the game. Julie was in heaven. Thoughts were running through her head. She now knew that Ryan and she were going to be together. She was so excited she could not wait. Meanwhile, the thought that was running through Ryan's head was *how long do I have to be friends with her?* He felt Julie looking at him and turned and smiled at her. He would have to play nice long enough to get his hands on the tickets.

Cassandra got bored at the rooftop bar quickly and started looking through her contacts. She knew Ryan and Julie were having drinks, which of course, annoyed her and she needed a distraction. She came across Eric's name and realized that she had not spoken to him in a while. She dialed his number.

"Hello," Eric answered on the first ring.

"Hi, what are you up to?" Cassandra asked sipping the last of her drink.

"Nothing much. At home. What about you?"

"At home too," Cassandra said lying. "I was thinking I haven't seen you in a while. Maybe you can come over?"

"Sure, where is your roommate?"

"With Julie, probably reproducing ugly babies as we speak," Cassandra said enjoying talking bad about them both.

"Funny, I will head over in five minutes. Call you when I get there."

"Okay," Cassandra said and hung up. She told herself, *I have to keep myself busy; otherwise I get into trouble.*

It was Saturday morning and Cassandra was starting to get nervous about the ball game later that evening. She didn't know how to act or what to say in front of Eugene and his son; it was a first for her. Julie had spent the night at Cassandra's apartment waiting for Ryan to get home. Unfortunately, she was still waiting. Ryan must have found a new girl because he had not come home the night before.

"Did you want to get some breakfast this morning?" Julie asked from the couch.

"Sure. Where?" Cassandra answered staring at the ceiling thinking about the great night she had had with Eric in her bed. Of course, he had to leave because she hadn't been sure when Ryan may get home.

"How about the Pantry?"

"Sounds good," Cassandra said getting up from the bed and walking to the bathroom.

"Do you want to take a taxi or drive?"

"Let's drive. Hailing a taxi in downtown LA is hard."

"Okay by me," Julie said getting ready herself.

Cassandra looked at herself in the bathroom mirror. She wondered sometimes why she just couldn't be in a committed relationship with someone that cared about her. Some days she was tired of playing all these games with these people who didn't mean anything. She wished she had the stability of someone always being there no matter what, but that was the hardest part for Cassandra. She never had trouble getting or having what she wanted. It was the unconditional love she couldn't buy and Cassandra had earned that at an early age.

"Should we get some snacks for the Conrad's son?" Julie asked as they were eating their breakfast at the Pantry.

"Snacks? What do you mean?" Cassandra asked Julie, thinking she was talking crazy again.

"You know snacks, candy, chocolate, maybe drinks for your future stepson?"

"Funny! I guess so."

"It will keep him entertained and you and Eugene can catch up."

"Yeah," Cassandra said. "Time to catch up."

Cassandra started thinking when was the last time she had seen Eugene. It seemed like their meetings were spreading further and further apart. They always stayed in touch through the phone and text messages, but the last time they were together was before the summer started and Cassandra had planned an elaborate surprise for Eugene's birthday. He had driven to LA for the weekend and stayed with Cassandra. Cassandra had taken him for drinks and dinner and then surprised him by taking him to see the Los Angeles basketball team play. It was the best gift Eugene had ever been given and it left quite an impression on him. They had spent the weekend talking, laughing, and making love. When the time had come to say goodbye, Cassandra was a wreck inside because she didn't know when she would see Eugene again. All his promises were full of nothing. She had kissed him goodbye and watched him disappear in the elevator. Her heart had hurt for days because she yearned to touch his face again.

"Cassandra!" Julie yelled. "Cassandra!"

"What?" Cassandra said looking at Julie.

"I was calling your name. Did you go to outer space or what?"

"Sorry, I was just thinking. Let's head to the grocery store down the street to get some stuff for the junior mint."

Julie and Cassandra walked into the store and headed for the candy aisle.

"What kind of candy should we buy?" Cassandra asked Julie.

"I don't know. A little of everything. All kids love any type of candy."

"Okay, let's get everything," Cassandra said as she started grabbing all the different bags of candy and throwing them in her basket. "Let's not forget the bottle of vodka. I am going to need it for tonight."

"You sure are," Julie said trailing behind Cassandra.

Back at Cassandra's apartment, there was still no sign of Ryan. When Julie entered the apartment, she had hoped Ryan was there, but her bubble of excitement was deflated because there was no sign of Ryan ever having come home. Cassandra also noticed that Ryan had not been home yet.

"Where do you think he is?" Julie asked nonchalantly, trying not to make a big deal.

"Who knows? I personally don't care!" Cassandra said knowing that she was lying. She did care and thought she had fixed the situation between Ryan and Hermosa, hopefully breaking them apart for good.

"Yeah. Anyway excited about tonight?"

"Kind of, not sure. Maybe I should start drinking. Ask me in about an hour."

Cassandra started making herself a drink. *This will help calm my nerves.*

They started getting ready. Cassandra needed to look her best when seeing Eugene to make sure he knew what he was missing. *Not like it mattered,* she thought, *he surely didn't care.* Cassandra heard her phone ring and saw that Eugene was calling her.

"Yes," Cassandra said as she picked up the phone.

"Hi, I am on my way to the stadium. Where should I meet you?"

"We are sitting in section seven. Park in the parking lot that corresponds with that section."

"Are you headed that way yet?"

"In a couple of minutes. See you there," Cassandra said grabbing her drink.

"What did he say?" Julie asked applying her makeup.

"That he was on his way to the stadium and now I think I am starting to get nervous."

"Don't worry, you will be fine. Are you almost ready?" Julie asked looking at Cassandra and admiring and hating her for her beauty. Cassandra really never had to do much to make herself look pretty. Cassandra was just that beautiful.

"Yes, let's drink on the way," Cassandra said grabbing a plastic cup to put her drink in.

"Definitely," Julie said doing the same thing Cassandra just did.

They headed out of the apartment and walked toward the garage where Julie's car was parked. This was the first meeting between Julie and Eugene. Julie had heard a lot about Eugene and she felt as if she knew him. Julie pulled out of the garage and headed toward the stadium, Cassandra's apartment was only a few minutes from the apartment, but with traffic it seemed forever.

Eugene arrived with Zachery at the stadium and found parking. They got out of the car and walked toward the closest entrance to the stadium. He thought that was the first time he was going to introduce his son to a woman who was interested in him. He looked at Zachery and could not believe how big he had gotten. Since his visits with Zachery were far and few in between, he felt like his son grew an inch taller every time. Eugene smiled to himself and remembered the first day he had met Zachery when his mom had delivered him. He was a complete mess drinking during the nine months of the pregnancy and even worse on the day of the delivery. Lisa was in labor for almost nine hours and Eugene had paced the floors of the hospital like a madman thinking to himself whether he was anymore ready for this than he was when Lisa had broken the news. Finally, the doctors had called Eugene because Lisa was ready to push. He had run to Lisa's side and held her hand and she had yelled and cried. Eugene had just stood there as her pillar, never showing how scared he was. Finally after a few minutes of pushing, he had heard Zachery cry and moved toward the end of the bed where the doctor had Zachery in his hands. "It's a healthy baby boy," the doctor had said as the nurse had handed the scissors to Eugene to cut the umbilical cord. Eugene had cut his son's umbilical cord and the baby was taken, wrapped, examined, and handed back to Eugene. When Eugene had held his son for the first time, his entire life changed and he felt it. He had been so happy that tears were coming down his cheeks. He had walked over to give the baby to Lisa. Lisa had been extremely happy to see Eugene admire his son and she could see the instant connection between them. Eugene had handed the baby to Lisa never taking his eyes off of him. That was eight years ago and he could still vividly remember that day. Eugene patted Zachery's head.

"Dad, you are going to mess up my hair," Zachery said, and Eugene just smiled.

Then, he felt someone tap his shoulder and he turned around to see Cassandra. He looked at her and took her in. Cassandra smiled at him. He realized he was staring and gave her a hug, "Hi!" Cassandra said.

"Hi!" Eugene replied. "This is my son, Zachery. Zachery, this is Cassandra."

Cassandra extended her hand and looked at Zachery. He was truly the spitting image of his father with bright blue eyes, an amazing smile, and matching facial features.

"Sorry. Eugene, this is Julie, Julie, Eugene and Zachery."

"Nice to meet you," Julie said to both Eugene and Zachery.

"Hi," Zachery said politely and extended his hand and Julie shook it.

They proceeded to walk into the stadium: Zachery first, then Eugene, Cassandra, and Julie trailing behind. They stopped at the concession stand to get food. Eugene got Zachery a hot dog and a beer for himself, Cassandra didn't get anything because she had brought her drink with her, and Julie ordered a Sprite. Then, they walked down the concrete stairs and found their seats in the club section. They were only four rows from the actual field. Eugene went in first, then Zachery, Cassandra, and Julie. That was the order they sat in.

"Hey Zachery, Cassandra and I have a surprise for you."

"Really?" Zachery said excitedly.

"Yes," Julie said as she pulled out all the candy they had purchased earlier and laid them on the ledge. Zachery's eyes gleamed with delight and Eugene's immediate responses was, "Oh no!"

'Do you like these candies?" Julie asked Zachery.

"Yes, all of them, thank you."

"You can only choose one candy; you can't have it all," Eugene told Zachery with a firm voice.

"Dad, please, I will eat just one of each candy, I promise." "Okay, just one candy."

Cassandra admired the conversation between Zachery and Eugene and knew that Eugene was an amazing father, but quickly made herself put away any ideas of her and Eugene and focus on getting to know Zachery. Next to her, Julie was quietly pouring the vodka into the Sprite Eugene had bought her.

"What grade are you in, Zachery?" Cassandra asked him as she started passing the different types of candy.

"Seventh grade. I really like these candies," he said.

"Good, me too!"

Eugene watched Cassandra and Zachery interact. He had been nervous that Zachery would not like Cassandra because Eugene had never brought Zachery into this kind of a situation. He had told his son that Cassandra was a friend, which was not a lie, but he didn't mention the underlying love he held for Cassandra. No one knew.

"Don't eat too much candy, Zachery," Eugene reminded.

"Yes, Dad."

They all continued to watch the game with Cassandra and Zachery talking most of the time. Eugene was rather quiet this evening, and Cassandra was not sure why. While Julie was talking to Zachery, Cassandra approached Eugene.

"What's wrong, you seem rather quiet tonight."

"There is nothing wrong. I just had a long day," Eugene said staring out to the field.

"I see," Cassandra said not knowing what else to say. She and Eugene had always had the best conversations and there had never been awkward moments between them. Just then Eugene put his hand on top of Cassandra's hand and she knew that he was talking to her through that form of communication. She looked at Eugene and smiled and knew that the special connection that had brought them together was still there. Julie looked over and noticed Eugene's hand over Cassandra's and was upset for a second. She wished Ryan had ever held her hand the way Eugene did with Cassandra. There was something special between them; anyone could see that.

The game lasted longer than anticipated because of the extra injuries. Throughout the game, Cassandra and Julie had given a lot of candy to Zachery and he had eaten every one of them. Cassandra had enjoyed the time with Zachery and knew he was a great kid, partially due to his mother's influence. As the game came to a close, they all left their seats and went to the main area, where they started talking about the game. Zachery pleaded to go to bathroom, and Eugene took him.

"Dad, I am not starting to feel good."

"I am sure you aren't. You ate a lot of candy."

Out of nowhere, Zachery turned white, leaned forward, and started vomiting. Eugene held his son's head and told him it was okay. Once Zachery was done, Eugene held him and gave him a kiss. He wiped Zachery's mouth and kissed his forehead, "It's okay, Son." Zachery started crying. It took Eugene a few minutes to calm him down. Zachery stopped crying and smiled, "I love you, Dad."

"Oh Son, I love you too. Don't worry, it's okay!" Eugene gave him a hug and they left the bathroom.

"What happened?" Cassandra asked worried that it had taken Eugene and Zachery so long to get out of the bathroom.

"It's okay. Zachery got sick, but he is okay now. Aren't you, Zachery?"

"Yes, Dad, I feel better."

"Are you sure?" Cassandra asked concerned.

"Yes, it's okay," Eugene said, with Zachery hugging his side.

They all walked toward the parking lot. When they reached their cars, Cassandra said goodbye to Eugene and his son. Cassandra, again, felt that stab in her heart every time she said goodbye to Eugene. It hurt her and sometimes it took a second for her to catch her breath.

"Thank you for inviting us. We had a great time," Eugene said as he hugged Cassandra.

"You are welcome. I hope Zachery is okay. Maybe we can get together for drinks."

"Definitely," Eugene said as he let go of Cassandra. "I will give you a call."

"Okay," Cassandra said knowing that he may never call again.

"It was nice meeting you, Julie," Eugene said as he extended his hand to her.

"Same here," Julie said trying to get Eugene to notice her, but knew it was hopeless. He was in love with Cassandra, and anyone could have figured that out.

Cassandra watched Eugene and Zachery walk away and somehow wished that she was walking away with them but knew it might never be her.

"Ready to head home?" Julie asked Cassandra.

"Ready to head to the bar," Cassandra said as she turned around for one last look. She would have given anything, all the money she had, to be going home with Eugene. Cassandra knew that the money she was born into was not a blessing, but more of a curse. The kind of money she had only bought happiness for one night. It was those who had less that held the key to happiness. A happiness that Cassandra longed for.

A couple of days later, Cassandra had gone into work with her thoughts on Eugene the whole time. Till now, she had not seen Ryan nor had he told her about his moving out.

"What is new today?" Elizabeth asked Cassandra realizing that this was the first time she had seen Cassandra in the office so early in the morning. It was barely 8:00 a.m. and Cassandra was seated at her desk.

"Nothing new. Everything is okay," Cassandra said not wanting to get into it with Elizabeth because she knew she asked too many questions.

"Okay," Elizabeth said rolling her eyes as she walked away. She had noticed that she and Cassandra had grown further apart over the last few weeks. Elizabeth knew she was Cassandra's assistant, but Cassandra had never treated in such a way till today.

Cassandra received a phone call on her private number at work. "Hello," Cassandra said in a professional tone.

"Hey Cassandra. It's Ryan. Sorry to call you at work, but we need to talk soon. Do you have any lunch plans?"

"No, I don't," Cassandra said, thinking to herself that Ryan sounded really serious.

"Okay, do you want to meet at the restaurant below the office building."

"Sure," Cassandra said knowing that Ryan was going to tell her about moving out because August was around the corner.

"Great, see you at noon."

"Okay, bye," Cassandra said and decided on not telling anyone about the meeting.

Later that afternoon, Cassandra and Ryan met at the restaurant underneath the building in a booth at the far end corner of the restaurant.

"What's up?" Cassandra said first as they both slid into the booth.

"Nothing much. But we should talk about the pink elephant in the room,"

Cassandra, not realizing it was a metaphor, laughed a little because she was about to look around the room for the pink elephant.

"Sure, what do you want to say?" Cassandra said staring into his eyes, Cassandra always knew that staring into your opponent's eyes would weaken them.

"Well," Ryan started as he looked away from Cassandra's eyes because he was not one to stare into her eyes for long. "I have decided to move out at the end of the month. I just think that we each need our own space," Ryan concluded, unsure of the reaction he would get from her.

Cassandra waited for a second before she decided to say anything. "Okay," Cassandra said. "That is fine. What is your last day at the apartment?"

"This weekend, since the first of the month starts on Monday."

"Cool, when are you getting your stuff out?"

"On Saturday," Ryan replied, not sure why Cassandra didn't have a more emotional response.

"Well, I hope you know you still owe me for half the rent of July, since you still haven't paid me," Cassandra said as she got her purse and started to get up from the booth.

"Okay," Ryan said, having no intention on paying Cassandra the money.

"Good, see you later," Cassandra walked away thinking, *if he knew any better, he would pay me the money and end it on a good note.*

Later that night, Cassandra walked into her apartment noticing the damage that Ryan had done all around the apartment and knew it had been a mistake letting him into her apartment. But Cassandra knew it was the kind of person she was. Cassandra was kind and always tried to help others but had to be aware that there were always those people who would take advantage of her kindness and Ryan had been one of those. Cassandra, even though she was kind, knew who was taking advantage of her. She never suspected Ryan to be one of those people, but after today's lunch, she knew he didn't intend to pay the month's rent and was going to leave just as easily as he came in. But Cassandra was not going to let him get away with it; she was sure of it.

Chapter 27

The next morning, Cassandra headed to work for another early morning. It was two days in a row and Cassandra had arrived at work before her "start" time. Cassandra was seated at her desk looking over her calendar for the week when all of a sudden she heard noises around her as if she something was shaking, and then immediately she felt her desk, chair, and everything around start to shake. Outside her office, she heard people yelling "EARTHQUAKE" and running to take cover under doorways. Cassandra, not sure what to do because she was frozen in both fear and shock, got up from her desk and could feel the building sway back and forth. Finally, after what seemed to a few minutes—in reality, it was only a minute—the shaking stopped, and Cassandra walked to join the others by the exits. She could feel herself trembling. This was her first earthquake and it had not been a good experience. As she approached her coworkers, she could hear everyone talking over the other: "Did you feel that?" "How many points do you think it was?" "Is everyone okay?" For Cassandra, it sounded more like noise at this time. She just leaned back against the wall and hoped that there would not be an aftershock. After a few minutes of standing with each other, they all decided that it was safe to go back to their desks. Cassandra, after observing everyone, was not sure why they all ran toward the exit or underneath a threshold. They were seated on the fifty-third floor of one of the tallest buildings in downtown LA. If the building came crashing down, they would be killed for sure. Cassandra was the last one to walk back to her desk.

"Are you alright?" Elizabeth asked Cassandra.

"Yes, I guess. This was my first earthquake. The ground doesn't voluntarily shake where I come from," Cassandra said still shaking.

"They don't have earthquakes in New York?"

Cassandra just looked at Elizabeth with an "are you serious?" look, then decided not to be rude and said, "No, there are no earthquakes in New York."

"Oh, okay, let me know if you need anything," Elizabeth said getting the hint and leaving Cassandra's office.

Cassandra stared after Elizabeth and then looked at her cell phone. She decided to call her mom back in New York to tell her about what had just happened. She dialed her mom's number, but the call would not go through. She tried repeatedly to call her again, but nothing. The lines seemed to be dead. Cassandra decided to use the office phone, but she had no luck either. She wasn't sure what to do. She tried calling Julie to see if she was okay but could not get through to her either. Cassandra, not wanting to stay that high up in the building, decided to call it a day and left work before the day had even begun. *There is no way I am going to die that high up in the air.* She walked to the elevator banks, pushed for the elevators, and prayed that an aftershock did not occur as she was in the elevator. *I am sure there is a time limit on using the elevators after an earthquake, but I never had an earthquake preparation class so who knows,* Cassandra thought has she got into the elevator and closed her eyes hoping she made it safely to the ground. Once Cassandra heard the elevator ding, she knew that she was okay. She opened her eyes and at the same time, the elevator doors opened. She was about to walk into the bank to see what Julie's thoughts were about the earthquake, but the doors were closed. *Standard procedure,* Cassandra thought, since the bank must have lost power. She continued to walk around and surveyed the area. Everyone seemed to be acting normal. *They must have not felt the earthquake on the streets,* Cassandra thought to herself. Instead of getting a drink, Cassandra just wanted to go home. She walked to her loft, which was the next block over, and again she tried calling her mom, but the lines were still down. She thought about Eugene for a second and wondered if he too had felt the shakes from the earthquake.

Cassandra reached her penthouse loft and was thankful that her building was only twelve floors and even though she was on the topmost floor, it was still manageable to run down the stairs. Random thoughts filled Cassandra's head from her experience earlier this morning. She chose to lie on the couch and tried calling her mother again. It had been a while since she had spoken to either her father or mother. Cassandra really never had a relationship with them both. She started remembering her childhood and how though she had been given everything, she felt as if she had nothing. Her parents always had their busy lives with each day fully calculated as to what dinner or event they had to attend for that day. Cassandra never saw her parents much. After school, she would come home and then by bedtime her parents raced in and out for the scheduled event. Cassandra's younger sister had always had her own agenda too and liked spending time by herself. It hadn't been a shock to Cassandra that Cassandra took off right after school, not opting to attend the family's legacy college in New York City. Cassandra and her parents would receive postcards from all around the world from Cassandra, and if they didn't, they would look at the monthly bank statements and know exactly where she had been. To Cassandra, her mother seemed to be proud of Cassandra—a blonde-haired beauty with light brown eyes, light complexion, and same height and build as Cassandra—for traveling the world with whatever man had filled her head with false promises. Cassandra, the complete opposite, had gone straight to college and then immediately completed her master's degree by the time she was twenty-four. Her parents' reaction had been nothing more than a mere "Congratulations, we are proud of you." Cassandra never understood and until a few years ago chose not to understand anymore. It wasn't her problem if they didn't accept her for who she was and within the last three years, Cassandra had gone from *polished student* to *bad girl* and calling her own shots. It was only then that her parents started noticing Cassandra and confronted her behavior. Cassandra, surprised by their immediate reaction, waged a war with them that had Cassandra leave New York and never look back. Even though there was a sour note between her and her parents, she missed them and today had told her that maybe she needed to keep closer communication with them. Finally, Cassandra tried one more time to contact her mother and after several rings, Cassandra heard, "Hello, hello"

"Mother is that you? It's Cassandra."

A couple of days after the earthquake, it was a Saturday morning. Cassandra woke up with a big headache and started remembering the night before, but the details were somewhat scattered. She remembered coming home after work instead of hitting happy hour, because she knew it was Ryan's last day. When she had entered the apartment, she had found Ryan packing up his things.

"Hey, how is it going?" Cassandra had asked with a bit of an attitude, because it had been the first time she'd seen him since their lunch meeting when he had informed her he was moving out that week.

"Okay, how about yourself?" Ryan had asked folding his clothes into a garbage bag.

"Good," Cassandra had said putting her stuff down and checking the refrigerator for anything to drink. Beer was her only option and she took it.

"Are you going out tonight?" Ryan had asked Cassandra.

"No, I am staying in tonight. I have a long weekend ahead of me," Cassandra had lied because she was not in a position to trust Ryan anymore.

"Cool, maybe you can help me pack then," Ryan had joked.

"Uh, no," Cassandra said. No matter how big her loft was, there were no dividers and she was able to see Ryan no matter where she positioned herself. Her only place to hide was either the bathroom or closet. Cassandra hated feeling unwelcome in her own apartment, but instead of hiding, Cassandra knew she would have to fight back. Instead of being hostile, Cassandra decided on being friendly. Using honey always caught more bees! She had changed into comfortable clothes and walked over to the couch where Ryan was sitting and packing.

"Are you excited about your new place?" Cassandra had asked sipping her beer.

"Absolutely, it's located only two blocks from the beach."

"Amazing," Cassandra had said. "Do you want a beer?" Cassandra had asked knowing that maybe she would have to get him drunk in order from him to talk. She had an amazing talent for making people feel comfortable around her, and they usually would tell her anything. This time, Cassandra was going to use her talent to the best of her capacity.

"Sure," Ryan had replied noticing how Cassandra's mood was changing and really enjoying it.

"Do you have a roommate?" Cassandra had asked Ryan handing him the beer.

"Yes, two. You remember Alice and her friend Madison? They are going to be my roommates."

"Nice, I have to come and see the house once you settle in," Cassandra had said with no intention of ever dealing with Ryan once she was done with him.

"Yes, you must."

"What about Hermosa? She must be excited that you will be closer."

"Well," Ryan had begun not wanting to say much but feeling as if he could talk to Cassandra about it. "We actually stopped talking a week ago. I am not sure why, but she said something about me dating other people and that she had proof. She went crazy and she stopped talking to me."

"Oh, no. Are you okay?" Cassandra had said pretending to be really concerned.

"Yeah, I am okay. The bad part was that she was the one with the tickets to the football game I want to go."

"That is right. What are you going to do now?"

"Well, I was thinking that if I became really good friends with Julie that she would give me one of the tickets. I know that she has them reserved for Eugene and his friend, but maybe she can give me one and Eugene can still go."

Cassandra knew she needed an immediate reaction. "Sounds like a great idea," Cassandra had said lying through her teeth. "I will help with Julie and the ticket, and I will tell Eugene that his friend no longer has a ticket," Cassandra had continued with her fake smile.

"Really?" Ryan had asked, surprised that Cassandra would help.

"Yes, don't worry, I know exactly how to get Julie on board," Cassandra had said thinking this was going to be a perfect way to bury both Ryan and Julie, Ryan before the game and Julie after.

"Cool," Ryan had said and continued telling Cassandra other things that had been happening. Cassandra had decided that she needed to play nice to get more information from him and she had to continue drinking as many beers as Ryan.

Cassandra tried moving but felt hopeless with the pain in her head. She heard Ryan stirring as he had spent the night on the couch.

"What time is it?" he said feeling the same way Cassandra was.

"I am not sure, I really can't move," Cassandra said from the other side of the loft.

Ryan forced himself to get up because he knew the movers were coming soon. He walked over to the kitchen and noticed it was 9:00 a.m.

"It's 9:00 a.m.; the movers will be here in an hour. Do you want breakfast?" Ryan asked Cassandra as he got water.

"No, thank you. I am just going to lay here hoping the pain will go away. How many beers did we drink?"

"A lot. We polished off almost two cases."

"Wow, Cassandra said feeling her belly and hoping she didn't gain any weight from the beer-drinking marathon.

"We did some damage last night. I am heading downstairs for some coffee. Be back in a few."

"Okay," Cassandra said barely whispering as she heard the front door close.

She lay in bed and knew she had to get up because the movers would be there soon. As she got up from the bed, she held her head because she didn't want it to fall off—although it was impossible, it still felt like it would happen. *Water, water would be good right now*, she told herself. She walked over to the water cooler, poured herself some water, and leaned back looking out of the living room windows at the view. She couldn't focus on any of her thoughts and went to the bathroom to look for some aspirin. After taking the aspirin, Cassandra walked in her closet to change her clothes.

Julie woke up that morning with thoughts of Ryan. Now that he was moving out of Cassandra's apartment, she was hoping that he would still continue to develop their friendship. She decided to call Cassandra to get the 411 on what was going on.

"Hello," Cassandra said.

"Hey, what is going? Are the movers there yet?" Julie asked anticipating Cassandra's response.

"No, they will be here in an hour."

"Where is Ryan?"

"He went to get coffee," Cassandra was really not interested in dealing with Julie's questions.

"Do you think I should come over? Maybe he needs my help; I did help pack the other time when he moved into your place."

"I think he is okay," Cassandra said wishing she had never picked up the phone.

"Oh, okay, but when he comes back just ask him. You never know."

"Yes, I will. I have to go, call you later." Before Julie could respond, Cassandra had hung up. *Wonder what is wrong with Cassandra?* Julie thought to herself. Julie decided not to worry and would continue with her day, in the hopes that Ryan would call her.

Ryan walked back into the apartment and found Cassandra slumped on the couch.

"How are you feeling?"

"Like death," Cassandra said. "On top of it I think I have a little bit of beer belly," Cassandra concluded as she lifted her shirt to show him her perfectly flat stomach. Ryan admired her body but changed his thoughts immediately.

"You will be okay. You are just bloated, drink lots of water and it will be okay."

"Sure," Cassandra said. "By the way, Julie called and asked if you needed her help for moving today."

Ryan looked at Cassandra with a smirk and said, "I don't know how long I have to be nice to her in order to get that ticket. Should I invite her over?"

"Well, it is going to take some time, but I am not in the mood to start entertaining today. Okay?" Cassandra said because she didn't have the energy to pretend to play both of them today.

"Okay, your call," Ryan said looking over the apartment to make sure he had everything.

Of course, it's my call!

Ryan's phone rang. "Hello, yes, I will be right downstairs."

"The movers are here. I am going to bring them up."

"Okay," Cassandra said not sure what she should do now. If she still wasn't drunk, she would head to the bar, but she was having trouble holding down her aspirin.

Ryan got into the elevator and headed downstairs to get the movers. When he reached the lobby, he got an overwhelming feeling of remorse and he started missing Cassandra even though he had been mean to her the last couple of weeks after their trip to TJ. Being like this was the only way to let go. Ryan walked to the front door and let the movers in. They were two older men in their early forties both wearing torn jeans and white T-shirts. It was a nice hot day in Los Angeles that morning and Ryan felt the sun shining as he opened the door.

Ryan and the two men walked to the loft. The men were hoping they didn't have much to move and would rather be drinking beer and playing cards.

"Everything on this side must be moved," Ryan said indicating to pile of bags he had separated in the corner.

"Okay," the older man said.

"Sure," the next one said and they both got to work quickly.

Ryan went to the kitchen and started looking around in case he had left any items.

Cassandra watched Ryan see what he grabbed and knew this was goodbye. Cassandra felt her phone vibrate and noticed that Julie was calling again. She hit the ignore button and continued watching Ryan.

At home, Julie got Cassandra's voicemail almost immediately before the first ring even completed. *Wonder what is going on at the apartment. Maybe I should go over or call Ryan?* she thought to herself. She desperately wanted to call Ryan and hang out with him but didn't want to pressure him. She thought about it and called Ryan regardless. The phone started ringing on his side. After four rings, when he didn't answer, his voicemail came on. Julie hung up.

"She just called me," Ryan told Cassandra.

"Who?" Cassandra asked knowing that it was Julie.

"Julie, but I didn't answer. Do you think it's a good idea even though I should be acting like her friend?"

"Yes, it will make her want you more. Trust me," Cassandra said watching TV. Ryan looked at Cassandra but chose to ignore her attitude and continued packing whatever he could find.

Half an hour later, the movers were still moving bags and items onto the hallway and into the elevator. Cassandra wished that the move would go quicker as she wanted to get Ryan out of the apartment and her life. He leaned against the counter and watched the movers work. He was thinking how the last two months his life had been: a whirlwind from Julie to Cassandra to Julie back to Cassandra and everything that had happened in between. Now, he only had Cassandra to help him in getting the ticket and, if he knew Cassandra, she would come through for him.

After three hours of moving everything out, the movers were finally done and were loading the last of the items onto the truck.

"They are finally done," Ryan said to Cassandra who was still on the couch.

"Really? Okay," Cassandra said getting up.

"Well," Ryan said.

"Well," Cassandra said back.

"Do you want to walk me out?"

"Sure, I will walk with you downstairs," Cassandra said looking for her flipflops.

"Are you feeling better?" Ryan asked.

"A little," Cassandra said still looking around for her shoes. Once she found them, they headed out of the apartment and to the elevator. Cassandra enjoyed the perk of having her own elevator that came to her floor. They both waited for the elevator in silence. When it arrived, they both got in and didn't say a word until they reached the main lobby.

"Don't be a stranger and remember you have to help me with the baseball game tickets."

Cassandra looked at him and with a slight delay remembering about the baseball game tickets said, "Of course, I have not forgotten." She smiled.

Standing in the main lobby, Ryan looked at Cassandra, smiled, and gave her a hug. He was truly going to miss her but knew this was the best for both of them. While Ryan was hugging her, Cassandra thought that was it. How so much had changed in two months! She didn't cry because she didn't have any-thing to cry about.

"I will call you during the week," Ryan said holding Cassandra's hand.

"Okay," Cassandra said. Ryan gave her one last smile, turned around, and started walking toward the main entrance. Cassandra quickly remembering, called out "Ryan."

"Yes," he said turning around surprised she had called his name.

"I need the key to my apartment."

"Oh, I almost forgot," Ryan said putting his hands into his pockets.

Right, Cassandra thought and just smiled at him.

"Here they are," Ryan said, pulling them out and handing them over.

"Thanks," Cassandra said holding the keys tightly in her hands.

Ryan smiled and began walking to the door again. Again, Cassandra had no feelings left. She started remembering the day when he had moved in, and they had been standing in the very same lobby. He had walked into the lobby and given Cassandra a big hug. She had been blown away and feelings had started developing then. She watched Ryan get into his car that was parked in front of the moving van, and he pulled into the street and just like that he was gone. Cassandra turned away and walked to her elevator. Without even shedding a tear, she hit PH for her apartment. Once the elevator doors opened, she walked out and opened the door to her apartment. She could see the sun shining into the living room, with the promise of a new day. Cassandra looked around the apartment and felt how lonely it was now and made her think about what she was going to do now. It wasn't Ryan that she missed, but the feeling of having someone there. She walked around and remembered where all his stuff had been, which were now empty spaces. She walked to the living room windows and stared out, hoping her answer was somewhere in the sky.

Chapter 28

*I*t was the end of the week for Eugene Conrad and he had enjoyed every minute of it—may be more than he should have. He was now in his living room trying to recover before his crazy week schedule started. He enjoyed his career, but he was not sure if he would have chosen the same career had he been given a choice. That was something he could not dwell on because growing up he knew it was something already decided. Eugene had the doors open to the balcony in order to hear the waves crashing. He had enjoyed that sound ever since he was little. The sun was starting to set, and Eugene could see the view from his couch. His phone had been vibrating uncontrollably with numerous text messages from all the different women he met the last two nights. Unfortunately, none of them had made the cut for more than just a drink at the bar. None of them were girlfriend material, but they did fit the partying bill and unfortunately, that was the only thing that Eugene was enjoying these days. He was starting to care less and less about his surroundings and his only goal was to forget and not feel anymore. The drinking brought him peace from his running thoughts; he let loose with no thoughts and concerns for what tomorrow held. At this point, it didn't matter who he met or who cared about him; he just didn't want to feel anymore and most of all he didn't want to think either.

"Your apartment looks different," Julie commented on walking into Cassandra's apartment.

"Yeah, I have noticed," Cassandra said thinking how it had been a few days since had Ryan had left and it still had that empty feeling—a feeling that

Cassandra hated and didn't know any other way to get rid of unless she drank. These days the only way she went to sleep was with a bottle or two of wine.

"Have you spoken to Ryan?" Julie asked knowing that Ryan and she had been casually texting.

"No, not really, he called me once, but I have not returned his call," Cassandra said not really having the intention of ever calling him.

"Weird how things change. He has been texting me, but nothing major, just a few hi and how are you." "Nice," Cassandra said not really caring.

"Yeah, have you spoken to Eric?"

"No," Cassandra said remembering that it had been a few weeks since their last encounter.

"I wonder what he is up to. Maybe you should give him a call," Julie said looking at Cassandra for an immediate response.

"I think I will," Cassandra said

"What are the plans for tonight?" Julie asked.

"Drink a lot and meet many men," Cassandra said with a smile.

Cassandra and Julie walked into the Rooftop Bar, Cassandra's favorite place and headed to the bar. Immediately, thoughts of Eugene and their first encounter raced through Cassandra's head. She immediately wiped them from her head; she doesn't want to ruin her night.

"What's your poison tonight, pretty lady?" Cassandra's favorite bartender asked.

"How about a shot of your strongest liquor."

"Two shots coming right up," he smiled at her wondering if she would come home with him after the bar closed.

Cassandra started making her rounds around the dance floor with Julie trailing behind her. As Cassandra was walking, someone grabbed her shoulder.

"Cassandra," the sexy man with the stunning green eyes said.

"Hi Julian," Cassandra purred.

"I have not seen you around for a while," he said.

"You know, I've been busy. By the way, this is Julie. Julie, Julian."

"Hi, I'm Julie," Julie gave him her biggest smile. Julian gave her one look, shook her hand, and turned back to Cassandra.

"Come on and dance with me," Julian said pulling Cassandra by the hand. Cassandra gave Julie a "whatever" look and followed him to the dance floor.

"You look as beautiful as the day I met you," he said holding Cassandra's face.

"Thank you," Cassandra said knowing his words had no meaning, but for tonight she could just pretend that he was in love with her. Then, he kissed her with a kiss that lasted till the next morning.

"What happened to your friend?" Julian said to Cassandra the next morning as he rolled over on his back. Cassandra with her head in the pillow said, "I don't know, I can't even think straight."

"Oh, baby, you will be okay," he said patting her back.

Cassandra was trying to keep her head from hurting any further. For a second, she had to remember who was next to her. Once she did, she turned over to face him.

"Hey," Julian said to Cassandra grabbing her face.

Cassandra was happy that her apartment was filled again with someone's presence even though she knew at any moment he would be leaving.

"Hi," Cassandra said gazing into his eyes.

He kissed her sweetly and softly, arousing himself again. "Ready to relive last night?"

he asked.

"Yes," Cassandra said as she let him take over her body. Cassandra didn't care anymore; she just wanted someone next to her.

Cassandra's phone started ringing continuously. It finally woke her from her deep sleep with a jolt; she looked to her side and it was empty. She lay back down. *Julian must have left while I was sleep,* Cassandra thought. She didn't blame him. She knew from the beginning that it wouldn't longer than a day. She grabbed her phone and looked at it, she had five missed calls from Julie. Her phone rang again, and she picked it up. "Hello," Cassandra said.

"Where have you been?" Julie yelled into the phone.

"Must you yell?" Cassandra said holding the phone away from her ear.

"Yes, I have been calling all morning. I was worried about you. Last time I saw, you and Julian were dancing really close. After that, I decided to leave."

"Yeah, he is an old friend," Cassandra said smiling and looking to her side wishing he had never left.

"I noticed. Are you planning on coming into work today?"

"No, why?"

"I saw Elizabeth down here earlier today and she was not happy."

"Oh, well," Cassandra said.

"I will call you later. Some of us have to get back to work."

"Bye," Cassandra said not listening to Julie's comment. It would be a long time before Cassandra had to actually work for a living.

Cassandra stretched and she started feeling depressed and lonely. She hated the way the next day of alcohol made her feel. She wondered whom to call and remembered that she had not seen or spoken to Eric in a while. She looked up his number on her cell phone and dialed it.

"Hello," he said casually.

"Hi sexy," Cassandra said with her favorite opening.

"Hi, how are you?" Eric said excitedly.

"Nothing much. Same old. Just lying here thinking of you."

"Really, what are you wearing?" Eric asked picturing Cassandra.

"Actually, just a sheet."

"Wow, need some company?"

"More than you know. Coming over?"

"Absolutely. What happened with your roommate? I heard he moved out."

"Yeah, things weren't working out and he was jealous of us," Cassandra said.

"I am sure. Alex told me he was out at the beginning of the month."

"Yeah, he left without much notice."

"Sorry to hear that."

"Don't worry, it was not a big loss."

"Okay, on my way."

"See you soon," Cassandra said and hung up.

Cassandra lay in her bed for a while knowing that Eric was going to take an hour or so before he arrived. She thought about Eugene and wondered what he was doing. On days like this when Cassandra was depressed, she always wondered about how life would be if she and Eugene were together. She had a gut feeling that their life would be amazing together and they would be answers to each other's prayers. Instead of thinking about him, Cassandra decided to text him.

"Hey, how are you?" she said in her first text and silently waited for his response.

"Good and yourself?" Eugene texted back.

"I was just thinking about you," Cassandra replied.

"What were you thinking about?"

"Oh, just you and I, and what could have been."

"What could have been? I never thought there wasn't a *you and I*," Eugene replied.

"Yeah, but you never said that we could be together," Cassandra typed with tears in her eyes.

"You know I am not ready to be with anyone right now. I have to focus on me."

"I know. I just want you to know you are in my thoughts."

"You are in mine as well," Eugene's text message read.

Cassandra let the tears fall from her cheeks onto the pillow. She missed him a lot, but there was nothing she could do. It was a matter of time for them. Cassandra wiped the tears away and got up to get in the shower before Eric got there. She let the hot water hit her entire body. She wished it could get rid of all the thoughts she carried in her head. Cassandra had sudden flashbacks of her days in New York. She saw herself walking the streets of New York City; she was happy on her way to work. She then saw herself in her office and working on a project. Cassandra started thinking of how much she enjoyed working in New York City and before she had left, she held a prominent position with a high profile company in New York. Before hitting twenty-six, she was making what people twice her age were making. Cassandra thought, *maybe I should head back to New York and pick up where I left off. I can get an apartment and call some of my old contacts.* She would go back to where she felt she was more in control. Cassandra knew that her life was not turning out the way she wanted in LA and maybe it was time to walk away. Sometimes you have to cut your losses before the end of unrecovered losses. Cassandra was starting to consider New York and everything it held for her.

After her shower, Cassandra dressed into something comfortable and waited for Eric. Cassandra thought about Eric and where they stood. They had not discussed whether or not they were in a relationship. They had expressed that they liked each other and even cared about each, but that line was not drawn yet. Cassandra knew Eric had a problem of trusting women after his divorce. Cassandra was starting to see a trend with the guys in her life. They had either been married and divorced or unwilling to commit. *Is this what the world has come to?* She never thought that her current life would be the way it was. Sometimes you never know what life holds. Cassandra heard her doorbell ring and got up to get it.

"Have you thought about where we stand?" Cassandra asked Eric while he held her in his arms.

"Sometimes I do, but it's kind of hard given my situation with the kids," Eric said while playing with Cassandra's hair.

"Yeah, I understand. I was just thinking that things are good between us and maybe we can take it to the next level?" Cassandra said rubbing Eric's chest.

"I don't know. I want to, I really like you, but let's take it slow," Eric said turning toward Cassandra and kissing her on the lips.

"Okay, let's. I like you too," Cassandra said smiling and returning Eric's kiss. They continued kissing all afternoon and into the night.

It was mid-August. Cassandra had been experiencing a lot of emotions and had been putting a lot of thought into where she wanted herself to be. It had been a couple of weeks since Ryan had left and not only did her apartment feel lonely, but she did as well. Her drinking at night didn't help either. If anything, she was spiraling downward fast and anyone she held onto was letting go of her hand. Although, Eric and she were talking every day and seemed to be getting closer. Cassandra at least had the comfort of Eric. Eugene has been distant and had not called or texted Cassandra in weeks. She wondered about him but knew right now there was nothing she could do. It seemed like at this moment Eugene had pulled away. Cassandra had sent him a text a few days after their last communication, but she had received no response. Ryan was still calling and texting Cassandra about the game next month; she chose to ignore him. He was trying to build a friendship with Julie and of course, Julie was letting him. Cassandra knew when the time was right, she would crush them both. During the last couple of days, Cassandra had just stayed home, staring outside her floor-to-ceiling windows wondering about life and her. *What do I really want? Where do I really want to live?* These were the questions Cassandra would ask herself. The only problem was there was no response from her or anyone around her. She knew she would need to answer these questions quickly in order to move on to the next stage in her life. Deciding to take a break from her thinking, she called Eric. Cassandra and Eric had been in constant communication barely letting a day pass without a phone call or text message. Cassandra dialed Eric's phone, waiting for him to pick up and was surprised to get his voicemail on the first ring. Cassandra thought that maybe something had happened with the line and redialed his number. Again, the same thing happened—right to voicemail. Instead of trying again, she sent him a text message, "Call me when you get this." She put the phone down and continued staring out the window while sipping her glass of wine.

Eric had just arrived at Miami International Airport and was walking toward the baggage claim. He decided to turn on his phone and immediately got voicemails and text messages. The first message he read was from Cassandra and chose not to respond to it. He put his phone back in his pocket. Eric had decided to take a week's vacation starting in Miami and then heading to the Bahamas. He had chosen not to tell anyone he was going on vacation; he just needed to get away. He also decided not to tell Cassandra; she would have wanted to come with him, but he needed his alone time. In reality, Eric enjoyed being alone. It's what he was used to. He picked up his bags from the baggage carousel and proceeded to exit the airport and look for a taxi.

Eugene was on his second glass of wine while getting ready at his house for a black-tie event he was to attend later that evening. He was walking around the bedroom looking for his socks and shoes. He had on black tailored pants, black pressed dress shirt, with a gray tie hanging around his neck. Eugene loved to get dressed up and when he did, he was definitely more than handsome. He was putting on his socks while watching the news on TV. As he watched a story about the environment, he finished putting on his shoes and walked to the mirror to look at his reflection. Eugene started tying his tie, happy he was going out with his friends. But he wished that there was someone getting ready with him. Someone he could compliment and who could compliment him back. He finished his tie, grabbed his tailored black jacket, took one last look in the mirror, and knew he was set to enjoy the night. He grabbed his wine glass and finished what was left of it, heading downstairs for another drink. The limo with his friends was about to arrive any minute. They were to pre-party at his place and he was ready to start without them.

After checking into his hotel, Eric decided to take advantage of what the sun had left to offer and headed to the hotel's beach to lay in the sun and listen to some music. He lay on the towel he had carried and took off his shirt to reveal his toned body. Eric worked out twice a week and it showed. He took his shirt and turned it into a ball to lay his head on. He put in his earphones to listen to music and fell asleep with dreams lurking nearby.

"Hey Eugene, you look good," Brad's girlfriend, who was the first to walk into Eugene's house, had commented.

"Thanks," Eugene said feeling a little uncomfortable with her remark and the look she had given him.

"My man, Eugene, you look ready to pick up lots of girls tonight!" Brad yelled as he walked inside Eugene's house and hugged him.

"Whatever is game tonight," Eugene said taking a sip from his fourth glass of wine.

Everyone else started entering the house and heading to the island in the kitchen and the counter to make their drinks.

"Please, everyone, make yourself at home and drink up. It's going to be a long night," Eugene said as he shut the door.

Chapter 29

*E*ric woke up from his nap to find the sun had set. Even though there was no sun left, the air in Miami was thick with humidity. Eric stretched and took out his cell phone from the pocket of his shorts. He had some missed calls from friends and his parents. He looked at his text messages again and went through them and found the one from Cassandra. He felt bad he had not told her he was leaving. He responded to her message. "On vacation, will call you when I get back. Miss you," he wrote and hit send. He shut his phone and continued looking at the sky that was now completely turning dark. He got up from the towel, dusted himself off, and headed back to the hotel for dinner to see what Miami nightlife had to offer.

Cassandra, sitting at home, was not sure if she wanted to go out with Julie or would rather stay home and drink enough to pass out. She heard her phone beep, got up from her couch, and headed to the kitchen counter. She saw the new message and read it. As she finished reading it, her face had a look of disgust. *So much for us getting close,* Cassandra thought. Eric had gone on vacation and didn't even tell her. *Who does something like this?* Cassandra asked herself. She threw her phone down and proceed to the fridge to make herself a drink, a strong one. She needed something to help her forget. She decided that going with Julie was her best option for now; otherwise, she would sit at home and be depressed.

After an hour of drinking at Eugene's house, everyone gathered in the limo outside his house. Eugene didn't have a set date, but there were two single girls in the group who had caught his attention, at least for tonight. Brad told the driver, "Let's go."

The entire party was headed to a gala fundraiser for breast cancer at the Country Club. The biggest gala of the year, it was sponsored by Eugene's company and no-show was not possible.

"Did anyone bring any alcohol to drink for the ride?" Brad said as he looked at the empty cups along the shelf of the limo.

"No," Eugene said.

"I think so," Brad's girlfriend said in her sweet voice.

"How about we stop at a bar before the gala? We still have thirty minutes to kill. Everyone down?"

"Sure," everyone responded simultaneously.

"Driver, please stop at the next bar you see!" Brad yelled with excitement. The driver nodded by tipping his hat.

Julie had picked up Cassandra and they were now headed toward the bars in Santa Monica.

"I can't believe Eric went on vacation and didn't tell you," Julie said repeating what Cassandra was thinking in her head.

"I know," Cassandra said, staring straight ahead. "The thing is he didn't have to tell me at all. It's not like we are dating, but if he had any respect for me, he would have mentioned something to me."

"Yes, that is true," Julie said concentrating on the road.

"A simple text or call just saying I am going on vacation that is all."

'Well, what can you do now?" Julie asked.

"There is nothing I can do. Eric already chose it for us," Cassandra said misty-eyed.

Julie looked over and understood what she was going through. It was not like she and Ryan had the best relationship, but she was trying to work on it. She continued driving to Santa Monica in the hopes that the bars would cheer Cassandra up.

Eric had just finished eating his diner at a happening Cuban restaurant. Everything and everyone around him were busy. The music was pumping loud and everyone was talking over themselves. After Eric paid the bill, he decided to head to the bar. The restaurant turned into a nightclub after a certain hour. He sat at the only stool available, ordered a beer, and started surveying the crowd. Two women bumped into Eric as they tried reaching the bar.

"Sorry," said one girl with a Latin accent.

Eric turned to look and at her, said, "No problem," and smiled.

The woman who had spoken to Eric giggled into her girlfriend's ear and they both laughed and looked at Eric. The bartender came to them and took their drinks order. Eric decided to look the other way to see the band that was playing. In the meantime, the girls were whispering to each other about who was going to make the first move to get Eric's attention. They decided that they would both approach him, and simultaneously they put one hand on each of Eric's shoulders.

Eugene and his group had entered a bar on the way to the gala. Thirty minutes must had already passed and they were all still taking shots of liquor. By now, Eugene was on his fifth shot not to mention the few glasses of wine he had drunk at home.

"Hey Eugene, we should get going. If not we are going to be late for cocktail hour," said Brad.

"Let's do it," Eugene said, slurring a little.

Everyone walked outside to the waiting limo. As they piled in, Eugene and Brad were the last ones waiting to get in.

"Hey, tell the driver we are ready to go," Brad said to Eugene.

Eugene walked over the driver's side and there was no driver, but he did notice the keys on the passenger seat.

"Hey, he is not in here!" Eugene yelled to Brad.

"What? What do you mean he is not there?" Brad asked.

"He is not in here. Look," Eugene said.

Brad walked over to the driver's side of the limo and looked inside.

"Where the hell did he go?"

"I don't know," Eugene said, his eyes glassy.

"Oh man, we are going to be late," Brad said as he stomped his foot. "Do you have his number?" Brad asked Eugene. Eugene just shrugged.

"Okay, why don't we just drive the limo? The driver can take a taxi to the gala. I am not waiting here."

"I'll drive," Eugene said.

"You sure?" Brad asked.

"Yes, I am okay," Eugene said as he opened the door to the driver seat, took the keys from the passenger seat, and inserted it into the ignition. Brad ran to the packed limo, got in, and rolled down the divider between the front and back of the car.

"Please welcome our new driver, 'Mr. Conrad!'" Brad said.

Everyone looked to the front of the car and gasped.

"Eugene what are you doing?" asked Brad's girlfriend.

"I am taking us to the gala. Unfortunately, our driver has disappeared, but don't worry folks, I will get us there safely." Eugene tried to get a grasp of the steering wheel and pedals. He finally got the limo to reverse and since Eugene had never driven a limo, he started reversing. Only he couldn't estimate how long a limo is and immediately bumped into the parked car behind him. Everyone gasped in the back. Eugene put the limo in park and hit the pedal. He got the front part of the limo out but had to reverse again. He put the gear in reverse, hit the pedal, and the limo went flying into the parked car again.

"Eugene!" yelled Brad's girlfriend, "You are going to get us killed."

"Eugene, man, are you okay?" Brad asked.

"Yes, almost got it out."

Again, Eugene put the car in drive and pulled some more of the limo out of the parking space.

In the parked car that got hit twice, the security officer who was sitting inside was stunned. Instead of getting out of the car because he was sure that his life was in danger, he immediately called 911 after the first hit.

"911, what is your emergency?"

"I am a security officer sitting in a parked car, and a limo just hit me. Oh my, it's about to hit me again," he said as the second hit happened.

"I have your location and police are on their way," the 911 operator said. "Are you or anyone else hurt?"

"No, I am okay and there doesn't appear anyone else hurt. I am not sure how many people are in the limo."

"Okay, I will stay on the phone with you until the officers arrive."

"Eugene, are you sure you can drive?" Brad asked now coming to the front where the divider was located.

"Yes, I can, I just have to get it out of this tight parking space," Eugene slurred.

"What is your name?" Eric asked the first woman who had long dark hair, caramel skin, and a dress that was tighter than his abs.

"Lucy," she said with an accent.

"I am Eric," he said with a smile and extending his hand. He turned to look at the girl next to Lucy who was a little shorter than Lucy. She had red hair, lighter complexion, and a short and tighter dress than Lucy's. "What is your name?" Eric asked now looking at the wide-eyed red-haired girl. "Nina," she said in a much softer tone than Lucy.

"Nice to meet you, Nina," Eric said taking a liking more to her because she looked more vulnerable. They both stood there smiling at him, and he offered them something to drink. "Please order whatever you like, it's on me," Eric said making room for them at the bar. They both hurried to the bar and waved to the bartender.

Cassandra and Julie walked into a bar that was semi-packed and chose to sit at a booth instead of at the bar. The waitress noticed the girls and walked over.

"Hello, what can I get you?" The waitress asked cheerfully.

"Vodka tonic for me," Cassandra said with half a smile.

"Jack and Coke," Julie said.

"Okay, one vodka tonic and Jack and Coke coming right up," the waitress said and walked away. Cassandra was left with Julie making small talk. She realized she would rather have stayed home.

Eugene put the limo in reverse for the third time. Right before he was going to step on the gas pedal, Brad said, "Wait, let me go outside and tell you how much room you have."

"Okay," Eugene said not really comprehending what Brad was saying. Brad hurriedly got out of the limo and walked to the back of the limo when he noticed that someone was in the parked car holding a cell phone to his ear. That is when Brad started hearing the sirens getting closer. He ran over to the driver's side of the window and knocked on it.

"Eugene, there is someone in the car you hit, and I think they called the cops!"

"What? Are you sure?" Eugene said now starting to get nervous.

"You need to get out of the limo now!" Brad yelled trying to open the door.

Eugene was looking for lock and his hands were moving very fast to unlock it.

Just then two police cars arrived from both directions meeting each other halfway. They put the spotlight on Brad and Eugene who was now exiting the car.

The first policeman yelled, "Stop right there, put your hand up, now!"

Eugene continued getting out the car, when the first policeman yelled again, "Stop now."

Eugene and Brad looked at each other and just stood there. The police officers seeing that it was safe to approach them, ran and threw them against the limo.

"What are you boys trying to do?" the second police officer asked them.

"Nothing, we couldn't find our limo driver and had to get to our party. So my friend decided to drive the limo. It's all really innocent," Brad said in a calm voice.

"Does your friend here have a limo license?" the first police officer asked as he patted down Brad.

"No, sir, he does have a driver's license; isn't that enough?"

The second policeman was patting down Eugene and found his wallet. The other two policemen from the other police vehicle had now approached the security man in the parked car and started taking his statement. Another officer opened the door to the back of the limo to look at the passengers, "Everyone, out!' he yelled.

"Officers, we weren't doing anything bad," Brad insisted. "Where is your ID?" the first policeman asked Brad. Brad reached into his pocket to produce his wallet and took his ID out.

The second officer was already calling in Eugene's driver's license on his radio. The first policeman noticed that Eugene was swaying a bit while standing.

"Have you been drinking tonight?" the first officer asked Eugene.

"I had a drink or two," Eugene responded with a bit of a slur.

"How many drinks again?" the officer asked noticing Eugene's intoxication.

"One or two," Eugene said trying to keep his composure.

The first officer walked over to the second officer who would have received the information over the radio: Eugene Conrad's license had been suspended due to a DUI a few months ago. The officers started whispering to each other and kept looking back at Eugene.

"What are they saying?" Brad asked Eugene quietly.

"I don't know," Eugene said. Everything was blurry.

"Brad, what is going on?" his girlfriend asked.

"I don't know, hon, let's wait to see what they say." In the meantime, the group was talking amongst themselves while the other two police officers were still taking the statement from the security guard.

"He has a prior DIU and a suspended license," the second officer said to the first.

"You can clearly see he is intoxicated right now. We are going to take a breathalyzer test and book him for driving with a suspended license and DUI. He is going to blow over the limit, I am sure." The first officer went inside the police vehicle and pulled out the breathalyzer test and walked toward Eugene.

After several drinks, both the women and Eric were now on the dance floor dancing together. He enjoyed the attention and loved the way both women were swaying their hips to the music. He could not take his eyes off of their bodies. They both grinded against each side of him: one in the front the other in the back. He wondered to himself. *Who could not love Miami?* They continued dancing to the Cuban music for several more hours.

"Well, this is some night," Julie remarked ordering her third drink. By now, she and Cassandra had moved to the bar because it required less conversation between her and Julie. "Well, there seems to be no one here," Cassandra said looking around.

"Yeah, I know."

Cassandra didn't want to talk and wished Julie would stay quiet. There were so many thoughts running through Cassandra's head that she couldn't catch one. *What do I do? Where do I go? Now what? Will anyone ever love me?* Cassandra wanted the erase the thoughts from her head but didn't know how. She just kept ordering drink after drink. She wanted them all gone now.

"Breathe into the tube," the first officer told Eugene. "We pulled up your record, you have a suspended license with a prior. Once you are done with the test, we are taking you to the police station. Now breathe into the tube." Eugene blew into the tube. The results showed he had a .20 blood alcohol, which was above the limit. The officer told Eugene to turn around and put his hand behind his head, and started reading him his rights. Once Eugene was cuffed, the officer pulled him toward the police car.

"Don't worry, Eugene, I will get you out," Brad said as the officer lowered Eugene's head into the car.

As the officers all headed into their vehicle, the limo driver came running down the street and reached Brad, "What happened?" he shouted confused. Brad turned around, took one look at him, and punched him straight in the face.

"Where are you staying?" Lucy purred with her Latin accent in Eric's ear.

"Down the block at the Concord," Eric said smiling.

"Very nice," Lucy said, "Do you mind company?"

"Not at all," Eric replied.

"Good, let's go," Lucy said pulling Eric's hand with Nina trailing behind.

"Are you ready?" Julie asked Cassandra, who hadn't said much tonight. "Yes, I am ready to go," Cassandra said finishing the last of her drink.

"Okay, let's go home."

Cassandra followed Julie out of the bar and to her car that was parked on the street. Cassandra was glad some of the thoughts had vanished from her mind because the numbness of the alcohol was starting to set in.

"Come guys, let's find some taxis. I am heading to the police station and will call Eugene's sister. Some of you should still head to the gala," Brad said, noticing his hand was swollen.

"I will come with you," Brad's girlfriend said.

They all walked to the main street and saw some taxis waiting outside another bar. Brad and his girlfriend got into one taxi, "Newport Beach police station," Brad said.

The others got into two different taxis and headed toward the Country Club.

In the taxi, Brad started calling Eugene's sister, "Hey, it's Brad. Eugene got into trouble again. Meet me at the Newport Beach police station. I am on my way there. I will explain when you get there." Meanwhile, the limo driver, now getting to his feet, had a bloody nose and his limo was still sticking out halfway onto the street. He still had no clue what had happened or what he was to do.

Eric and the two women entered his hotel room.

"Very nice," Lucy said. Nina always chose to stay quiet.

Lucy walked to the bed and sat down. Eric walked over the minibar and opened a beer. Lucy had taken her shoes off and had made herself comfortable on the bed. "Aren't you going to join me?" Lucy said with her sexy eyes. Eric, not shy at all, sat on the bed. He noticed that Nina was still standing and walked over to her, "Come to the bed; I don't bite." Nina smiled at Eric and Lucy watched. Eric sat on the bed with Nina, while Lucy came up from behind Eric, started massaging his shoulder, and took his shirt off. Lucy eyed Nina while taking Eric's shirt off. Nina then put her hand on Eric's chest and started touching it without saying a word, while Lucy kissed Eric's neck. Eric put the beer down on the nightstand and started enjoying what was about to happen. Just then Nina started caressing Eric's package and he let out a slight moan.

Julie dropped Cassandra in front of her apartment. Cassandra, confused and hurt after what had happened today, walked into her apartment dazed. The alcohol had taken its effect and Cassandra was loving the numbness. She no longer had to worry or think. Nothing mattered anymore.

At the police station, Eugene was fingerprinted and had his picture taken. Because he wasn't fully coherent, he was not sure what had just happened. He simply followed whatever the officers told him. After the process was complete, they put Eugene in a cell where he sat on the bench for a second and, in the next moment, completely passed out on his side. The amount of alcohol he had consumed had wiped him out.

The next morning, Eric woke up with an intense headache. He found himself lying in the center of his bed with just a sheet covering him. He lifted his head and looked around; there was no one in the room. He lay still for a second trying to recap last night's events, but everything was blurry and unrecognizable after leaving the Cuban restaurant. He pulled the sheet off of him and sat up for a second. He noticed his clothes were all over the floor as well as the rest of the bed coverings. He got up and found a pair of pants to put on. He went to minibar to get a bottle of water. He sat on the couch and started thinking of last night, remembering the two women who had approached him and apparently seduced him back to his own hotel room. He was surprised that they were gone in the morning. His headache intensified and a wave of nausea came over him. *Why I am feeling so nauseous? I didn't have that much to drink,* he thought to himself. Eric started taking deep breaths in order to keep himself from vomiting, but it didn't help. Within seconds, he ran to the bathroom where he started vomiting and continued to do so for the next couple of hours.

Eugene started stirring as the noise of people talking and walking around reached him. With a jolt, he opened his eyes and looked around him without lifting his head from the bed. He closed his eyes as though he would be somewhere else when he opened them. But when he opened them again, he was still in the same place. He looked around and noticed the white walls and gray metal bars. He was in a jail cell. He lay back down not sure what was going on. He thought maybe, just for a second, he was in a bad dream. He finally sat up, walked to the gray metal bars, and peered out as much as the bars would let him. He saw the officers working at a desk and walking around. He banged his head against the cold metal bars; he already knew that his drinking problem had escalated to another level.

Cassandra had a restless night of sleep and kept waking up every half hour to look at the time. All the drinks she had had did not help her during the night. After not being able to sleep any further, she finally gave in at 7:00 a.m. and just sat on her bed thinking of what to do. She definitely didn't want to drink anymore; it was pointless. She just wanted to figure out her next step. She grabbed her phone and looked through her missed calls and texts. Ryan was not giving up on going to the game and had sent her a text message saying he hoped she was still on board with the plan. Cassandra threw her phone on the bed and got up. There was much soul searching to be done, but she didn't know where to start.

"Are you sure he is okay?" Nina asked Lucy, her eyes big.

"Yes, he is okay. We only put one pill in his beer. He was still breathing when we left the room. The only problem he's going to have is a big headache and no money," Lucy said as she counted how much cash Eric's wallet had. "I love tourists, they are so naive," she said giggling.

"Vamos," Lucy said to Nina as she stashed the cash in her pocketbook and threw the rest of Eric's wallet in the trashcan of the public restroom where they'd stopped to get something to drink and figure out their next plan. "I need sleep," Lucy said as Nina followed her out.

Eric was finally able to peel his face from the bathroom floor, needing a second to stand up as he was feeling dizzy. *If I can make it to the bed, I will be okay,* he thought to himself. He slowly walked out of the bathroom holding onto the wall and whatever was on the way to the bed. Inches from the bed, he threw himself on the queen-size bed. Eric knew there was something wrong because he had never felt this way from drinking. He tried to remember what had happened after leaving the restaurant, but nothing came to him as though the memories were erased. After these thoughts, Eric fell asleep into a dark sleep.

"Eugene Conrad, your bail has been paid. You are free to go," the officer said as she started to unlock the metal gate. Eugene looked at the officer as the door opened, got up and grabbed his tailored suit jacket, and walked out.

"You have to go to the front desk to get your things," the officer said in a stern voice. Eugene looked around and saw the reception area and walked toward the area. As he went nearer, he saw his sister and Brad sitting on plastic chairs waiting for him.

"Eugene," his sister exclaimed as she ran to him and gave him a hug.

"Hi Sis," Eugene managed to say.

"Are you okay? You must feel like shit because you sure do look like it."

"I am okay. I want to get out of here and go home."

"Man are you okay?" Brad asked approaching Eugene and giving a half hug.

"I'm okay for now," Eugene said walking to the reception area where he knew he had to collect his stuff. He knew this process all too well.

Chapter 30

*C*assandra, sitting on her couch, had started planning out her two options: *stay in Los Angles and make it work, or go back to New York and pick up where she left off.* She knew going back to New York would the best option. She could continue her career that she didn't enjoy, but the status and money were the best parts of the deal. If she stayed in Los Angeles, she would have to start from scratch again, and as to the last two years she had spent here, there was nothing to show for it except a drinking tolerance she had built. She continued typing the positive and negatives for each city and hoped the answer would come to her.

"Housekeeping, housekeeping!" The maid at Eric's hotel knocked on his room door. Not hearing a response, she decided to enter the room. She slid her master room keycard into the card slot and waited for the light to turn green. She turned down the handle and opened the door. As she entered, she noticed the room was a wreck; the sheets were on the floor. She went straight into the bathroom before stepping into the area where the bed was. Disgusted with how the bathroom smelled of vomit, she threw towels on the floor and flushed the toilet. She went back outside to get the mop from the housekeeping cart and came back inside. Not wanting to start with the bathroom, she kept the mop against the wall and walked further into the room toward the bed. At first, she jumped and said, "Excuse me, sir, I knocked on the door twice, but no one answered. I can leave if you want," she said to Eric. She noticed he was lying diagonally on his stomach, his feet sticking out from the bed.

"Sir, are you okay?" she asked from afar, unsure what to do. "Sir, I can leave and come back," she said again. The maid was not sure if she should wake him up. She came closer to Eric. Since he had only pants on, she wondered if he was still sleeping off the night before; the bathroom was clear evidence he had had too much to drink. The maid decided to take peek at him and walked around to the other side of the bed to see his face. Eric's eyes were open, and blood was spilling from his mouth. The maid screamed with horror and ran out of the room yelling, "Help, please, help," through the hallways. She didn't wait for the elevator and took the steps instead. Every step she took she looked behind her to make sure the body she just saw was not following her. She made it into the lobby, running to the front desk. The receptionist immediately noticed the maid panicking and running toward her. "Help, help me." The maid was able to get words out in between each breath. The receptionist ran halfway to meet her. "What is wrong? You are starting to scare the customers!"

"Man, dead, in room" she managed to get out with every other gasp.

"What?" the receptionist said.

"Man, please help, room 3881, please," she said holding her chest and trying to calm down her heart.

"Lean against the wall, I will call security," she said and quickly went back behind her desk and called security. "Security, security, do you hear me?"

"Yes, what is the problem?" the security guard said through the phone.

"One of the maids claims there is something wrong with a man in room 3881. Can you send someone up there right now?"

"Room 3881, someone is on their way," the security guard said.

"Thank you," the receptionist said; she grabbed a bottle of water she kept underneath the check-in counter and walked over to the maid.

"Here, please drink some. Try to relax and tell me what happened."

Eugene was at home, looking over the paperwork that was given to him before he left the police station: *blood alcohol content of .20, driving on a suspended license, operating a commercial vehicle, prior DUI conviction.* The words ran through Eugene's head and he threw the glass of water he was drinking against the nearest wall and yelled, "How could I have been so stupid?!" Wanting to punch the refrigerator next to him, he stopped as tears started flowing down his face. He slid to the ground onto the kitchen floor and started crying uncontrollably. "What have I done?" he shouted at himself. Eugene knew that his second conviction would land him in jail and his entire career he had built from the bottom up was about to get wiped out. He cried for himself, his family, his son, and for the person who was meant to be his soul mate. He had ruined everything and knew the fear of losing everything hung upon him.

Two security guards entered room 3881, approaching Eric's lifeless body on the bed. The first security guard walked around the bed and saw Eric's half-opened eyes with blood streaming from his mouth that had now made its way to the floor.

"Oh my," said the second security guard as he witnessed what the first security guard saw.

"I am calling it in," the first security guard said. He picked up the phone and dialed 9 then 911. "We are at the Concord Hotel. Please send the police over, there is someone dead in our room—room 3881," he said and hung up.

"What happened to this poor guy?" the second security guard said as he stared at Eric.

A week had gone by and Cassandra had made her decision. She had told no one of her plans and with September around the corner she knew that in a few weeks, her life would be changing and that gave Cassandra hope—something she hadn't had in a few months. Cassandra still remembered when a few days ago, Ryan had appeared at her apartment ringing the doorbell until she opened. As soon as she had opened the door, she was going to yell at the visitor, but when she took one look at Ryan's swollen red face, she knew something was wrong. "What's wrong, Ryan? Come in," Cassandra had said holding the door open.

"How are you?" Ryan had begun because he didn't know else to start.

"Good. What is wrong with you?" Cassandra had asked, fearing what he had to say.

"I don't know how to say this Cassandra, but," Ryan had started and stalled.

"What? Tell me!" Cassandra had urged, now wanting to know what was wrong.

"Um. I don't know how to say this. Eric is dead," he had said and looked up at Cassandra.

Cassandra, unable to think or breathe, hadn't understood what Ryan had just said. Tears had started coming down his face and he had looked at Cassandra's unemotional face.

"How did it happen?" was all Cassandra could say.

Ryan started to tell her as he wiped his tears away, "They found Eric dead in his hotel room. The police are saying it's foul play, but no one is certain until the do the autopsy."

"Where is his body now?" Cassandra had asked. She hadn't moved from her standing position and was so numb that she couldn't shed one tear.

"On the way back from Miami. The funeral is planned in two days. I don't have all the details. I will tell you once I know. Anyway, that is all the information I have. I have to go. Will you be okay?" He had walked up to Cassandra. She had looked at him and nodded. Ryan walked past Cassandra, touching her shoulder as he left her apartment. She had been in the same standing position she was in when Ryan had first arrived. She stood frozen not knowing what to do. She was scared if she moved an inch, she would collapse in an ocean full of tears that would not stop. *Eric is dead,* was all her mind kept saying. She had moved an inch and then it had hit her hard. She had started crying uncontrollably, not stopping once to breathe, and had laid on her bed with thoughts of her and Eric running through her head.

That was two days ago and now the funeral was scheduled for this morning. Cassandra lay in her bed thinking of what to wear or what to say. She had gone through an emotional roller coaster the past two days and had even called Eric's cell phone to see if she had a chance to hear his voice. Only more news reports of a man dying in his Miami hotel room had reached everyone in California. Cassandra knew that she was making the right decision and with Eric's death it only confirmed her decision. She looked at her watch and realized she needed to get ready. Julie would be picking her up soon and she needed to be strong for herself.

Eugene sat on a bench with his right leg shaking up and down—a bad habit he had acquired—outside the courtroom waiting for his lawyer. He looked at his watch and realized his lawyer was five minutes late. Eugene couldn't call her because there were no cell phones allowed in the courthouse. He looked at his watch again; only seconds had gone by, but Eugene was anxious to get today over with. Today was Eugene's court day for his second DUI and today determined his fate, whether he would serve jail time or be given another slap on the wrist, pay a fine, and attend an alcohol program. If he was faced with jail time, he would have to explain to the partners of the company he worked for what had transpired in his life and that would be hard because his colleagues held him in high standards. Out of the corner of his eye, he saw his lawyer and her assistant walking down the corridor. Eugene jumped up and walked toward them.

"Sorry, I am late," the middle-aged attorney said to Eugene.

"It's okay, what do you think the outcome will be?" Eugene asked his lawyer again even though she had gone through all the possibilities with him in person two days ago.

"Like I said in the office, we may have a good chance that you have to pay a big fine with some volunteer services and alcohol program, and you may be lucky, but keep in mind," she said sternly to Eugene, "if this happens again, you will go to jail for a long time." She turned around and started walking to their assigned courtroom. As Eugene walked, he prayed that the judge would go easy on him.

Cassandra dressed herself in the closet. She picked out a very plain black dress with quarter sleeves that fell slightly above her knees. As she put the dress on, she had flashbacks of her and Eric rolling around her bed in each other's arms. Another one of them laughing and tears starting streaming down her face. Cassandra knew that she no longer could stay in the apartment after the funeral and packed two bags with clothes. She had no clue where she was going, but she knew she had to leave. Cassandra ordered a car service to pick her up and take her to the cemetery, and afterward, she was not sure where to go.

The next day after hearing the news about Eric, Cassandra had gone to talk to the two partners she worked for. "I am quitting; today is my last day," Cassandra had told them both.

"Why?" the older partner had asked her.

"It's time for me to move on," Cassandra had replied coldly.

"Where will you be going? To another firm?" the younger partner had asked.

"No, I have other plans that I choose to keep private."

"Very well," the older partner had said staring out of the window, with his back toward Cassandra. "Then our arrangement is off?"

"Yes," Cassandra had answered sternly. "You do not have to worry about what I know. I will never tell anyone."

"Are you sure?"

"I signed the papers, didn't I?" Cassandra had asked annoyed.

"Very well," the older partner had said with his back still to Cassandra.

"How would you like us to pay you for your final days?" the younger partner had asked worriedly. With Cassandra gone, he hoped that the secrets she knew would leave with her.

"Cash would be acceptable."

"Okay," the younger partner had replied, walked over to the safe that he kept, and taken out hundred-dollar bills. He had started counting them and when he was done, he recounted to make sure.

"Here are two thousand dollars," the younger partner said. Cassandra had taken the money and counted again to make sure.

"Thank you," she had turned around to walk away.

"Good luck," the younger partner had said. Cassandra had turned around and smiled. The older partner was looking out the window and wondering if Cassandra was indeed going to keep his secret. "What do you think? Will she say anything?" the older partner had asked the younger partner. "I don't believe so. She's given us her word and she had signed the papers in the beginning."

"Yes, but that has not kept people from talking before. Have her followed and find out where she is going. I need not have my reputation ruined or my firm brought down," he had said as he left the room.

Cassandra entered the elevators for the final time on the fifty-third floor and with her, she took the secrets of the partners of the firm—more secrets of one partner in particular.

It had always been of interest to many of how Cassandra had landed her job at one of the most prestigious law firms in LA. Without a law degree or law background, she had landed a job with the title "Business Development." On Cassandra's arrival in LA, she had met an attorney who worked for the firm, and she had started having drinks with him. One night, the partners had joined the young attorney for a night out on town. Cassandra had been introduced to the partners and they both took a liking to her quickly. They had chatted over drinks at different bars, both sharing with Cassandra their stories of opening their own firm and about their married lives. Cassandra had sat there and listened carefully to each one, looking interested. After having drank at every bar, the older partner had disappeared and the attorney and the younger partner had invited her back to the firm. They had taken Cassandra through the firm and shown her everything. After some talking, the younger partner had announced he needed to head home and had left Cassandra with the attorney, who excused himself to make a phone call and left her in the lobby of the firm. Cassandra, bored, had decided to walk around the firm again. She had walked toward the back of the firm, which was not part of the tour she had been given before. She had noticed the lights were on in the office in the back and heard some noises. Cassandra had quietly walked to the door and put her head against the door, hearing people laughing. She wasn't sure how many people were inside. Curious, she had grabbed the handle and pulled down on it. The door had opened slightly and Cassandra had peeked in. When her eyes had focused on what was happening, she had gasped with surprise and both the older partner and younger man in the room looked right at her. Cassandra not knowing what to do had opened the door completely to make sure what she saw was right. The older partner who had claimed to her earlier in the evening on how he was happily married with his wife and five children was naked in his office with his partner who was naked as well. A few days later, the partners had announced that they had decided on expanding the firm's business by creating the business development department and they had named Cassandra head of the department with a hefty salary to go with.

Cassandra could not believe it had been two years since she had started working for them. She finished packing her bags and went to the restroom to put some makeup on. She didn't want to look too pale for the funeral. After she was done, she left her apartment with her bags and decided to wait outside for her car. She no longer could bear the apartment and its memories.

"Prior DUI conviction and driving a limo while intoxicated. What do you have to say to yourself, Eugene Conrad?" the judge asked Eugene while Eugene stood with his attorney next to him. "I am sorry, Judge, I know it sounds horrible, but I made a mistake which I regret and have suffered a lot of resentment about it," Eugene said trying to keep his voice from shaking.

"What have you suffered? If anything, I notice you have not learned your lesson from the first time. It seems like you need a harsher punishment and not a slap on the wrist."

"Your honor," his attorney said, "Eugene Conrad besides his prior DUI conviction is an upright citizen without ever having a ticket, either parking or moving violation. He has made other mistakes, but he is aware of them and vows not to make the same mistake again. Maybe we can look into a restricted license and alcohol program?"

"Are you serious?" the judge said to the attorney. "Eugene Conrad, I hereby sentence you to two weeks in county jail, a fine of $1,5000, three months of volunteering service, one year of license restriction, with a year of alcohol program," and slammed his gavel down.

"Your honor," the attorney yelled.

"Next case," the judge yelled back.

Just then the officers took Eugene and handcuffed him. Luckily for Eugene, he had not told his family about the court hearing because he didn't know what the outcome would be.

"I can do an appeal," his attorney said, "to get you out of jail sooner."

Eugene just looked at her hopelessly and said, "Please call my sister and tell her the news," as they pulled him away. Eugene was lost for words.

Chapter 31

Cassandra and Julie arrived at the Catholic Church where the mass was going to be held for Eric. She was shaking a bit but didn't want anyone to notice. Outside the church, she found Ryan and Alex talking amongst themselves. Ryan noticed Cassandra and walked up to her first and gave her a hug. "How are you?" Ryan asked. He had not spoken to her since the day he had told her the news. "I am okay," Cassandra said with a slight smile. She then hugged Alex, "Hi, how are you?" she said to him. "Okay, holding on," Alex said. Cassandra knew that Alex and Eric were best of friends and Alex was probably taking this harder than anyone. Julie greeted both men. Alex grabbed Cassandra's hand and they walked inside the church. Upon entering the church, Cassandra noticed all the people who were in attendance. She wasn't sure who was who, but there were a lot of people. Alex sat down with Cassandra and Julie sat down next to her. "We have to go outside, Ryan and I are both pallbearers," Alex said. Cassandra just nodded. She looked at all the people that were there for Eric and tears started streaming down her eyes again. Right then, she heard the choir starting to sing a sweet melody and everyone stood up as they turned toward the entrance. Everyone headed to the front of their own aisles for the first sight of the casket, as it appeared at the front of the long walkway. Cassandra was standing behind Julie and turned to look at the casket that was being rolled down the aisle. Shocked and unable to hold back tears, Cassandra started crying harder than before because this was the first time Eric's death was confirmed to her. She looked at the casket being rolled down by the pallbearers with his mother and father and his son and daughter close behind, and the rest of Eric's immediate family behind his parents. His mother, dressed in all black, was crying relentlessly and almost collapsed mid-way. When the casket reached the front of the altar, everyone took their seats and the priest began, "Heavenly Father."

Cassandra did not remember much of what happened in the church. Her mind was blank and she stared at the priest's mouth moving with no words coming out. The only thing she could hear were the sounds of crying people around her. When the mass ended, she walked out with Julie whose eyes were red as well.

"What a sad service," she said wiping her eyes.

"Yeah, it was," Cassandra did not want to talk.

As they stood outside, the pallbearers were loading Eric's casket to head to the cemetery. Cassandra stood watching as if it were a movie and this wasn't really happening to her. Once they shut the door to the hearse, everyone walked to their respective cars. Eric's immediate family had piled into their limo and now the limo was waiting to follow the hearse.

"I will meet you at the cemetery," Cassandra said to Julie as they walked down the church steps.

"Okay," Julie said walking to her car that was parked in the church parking lot. Cassandra walked into her waiting sedan, got in, and closed the door. She was glad to be alone. She didn't have to indicate to the driver where the cemetery was located. He knew he had to follow the cars. Cassandra just looked out the window, trying not to bring any thoughts into her head.

Eugene had a lot of time to think as he lay on the bottom bed of the bunk beds. He was now dressed in an orange jumpsuit that had a number imprinted on the left pocket, which was now his identification. Eugene stared at the bunk bed above him. Underneath there had been words, quotes, and obscenities written by other imamates who had stayed in that particular jail cell. *How did I end up here?* Eugene asked himself. He was waiting for his sister's visit in order to give her specific instructions on how to handle his affairs and most importantly how to handle work. He knew it was two weeks, with the hope of getting out sooner, but one missed day at his office without being prepared could be disastrous. Eugene tried remembering the events of the night that had landed him in jail for the second time. He remembered starting out with the wine and escalating to shots that obviously did not sit well with him. He could only remember bits and pieces of the night. Him at the bar, him in the limo, him in the police car, and him waking up the next day. *What drives me to drink this way*, Eugene asked himself. It was going to take a lot of time to get to the bottom of his problem, but that was all Eugene had now: time.

Cassandra sat in the car on reaching the cemetery and watched everyone get out of their cars and walk toward the grave site. *How morbid,* Cassandra thought. Interrupting her thoughts, Julie knocked on Cassandra's tinted window. Cassandra annoyed that Julie was always bothering her almost didn't roll down the window but knew she couldn't avoid her. Cassandra pushed the button to bring the window down. "Are you ready to go?" Julie asked Cassandra.

"Yes," Cassandra said quietly and got out of the car. Even though it was a sunny day in LA at the end of August, the air had a certain chill to it. Cassandra and Julie walked toward the grave site and there were seats up front that seated Eric's mom and dad, huddled close together. On his mom's right side, Eric's son and daughter sat with blank looks on their face. Everyone stood behind the chairs facing the casket. As Cassandra walked by the casket, she had a flashback to the first memory of when she had met Eric at the bar in Santa Monica. She remembered how he had grabbed her and pulled her next to him and kissed her without a second thought. It made Cassandra a little sad. Julie and Cassandra stood to the side as everyone arranged themselves and the priest took his place in front of the casket and opened his bible.

"Let us pray. Heavenly Father we are here to commend Eric Dumas to the mercy of God." Cassandra had tears streaming down her face as she remembered her next memory of Eric: when Cassandra had gone over to Eric's apartment and he had just stared at Cassandra all night admiring her beauty.

"Let us recite the Our Father and Hail Mary," the priest said. Everyone began with Our Father.

"Birthday shot?" Eric had asked Cassandra at her birthday party. "Yes," Cassandra had said with a smile. She remembered them walking to the bar, both of them taking a shot, and then heading to the dance floor.

"Give us this day our daily bread . . ." everyone was reciting at the cemetery.

"Why don't you come home with me," Eric had said to Cassandra as she had taken her dress off in her apartment after coming home from her birthday party. Cassandra had never answered because she had passed out from all the alcohol.

"Amen," Cassandra heard herself saying with everyone else.

"Now the Hail Mary," the priest said.

"Hail Mary, full of grace . . ."

"I love your body," Eric had said to Cassandra as she had stood over him while he sat on her bed. Eric had taken Cassandra onto the bed and kissed her slowly and passionately. Cassandra remembered his kisses and touch.

Tears were now rolling down Cassandra's eyes like a river. "Pray for us sinners . . ."

"I think we should take things slow," Eric had said the last time he was to hold Cassandra. *"I do like you and care about you a lot; we just need to take things slow."* He had kissed Cassandra.

"Amen," Cassandra said who was now sobbing without any care, as was everyone else.

"We, therefore, commit Eric Dumas body to the ground, earth to earth, ashes to ashes, dust to dust in the sure and certain hope of the Resurrection to eternal life. Amen," the priest concluded. Everyone started walking toward the casket and began dropping a white rose as the workers started lowering the casket. Eric's mom was the first to go with the help of his dad holding her and she dropped the first rose to his eternal life. Cassandra and Julie and more people went to drop a rose. As it was her turn, Cassandra started thinking about how she never had the chance to say goodbye to Eric and never thought he would be taken in this manner so quickly. She walked toward the casket, kissed the white rose, and let it fall on Eric's casket. This would be the only goodbye she would have.

Instead of staying and talking to everyone, Cassandra continued walking to her waiting car and got in. At first, she had no clue where to go. The driver asked her, "Where to, madam?" All of a sudden, Cassandra answered, "Newport Beach," and the driver nodded. As the driver waited for the other cars to pass in order to merge onto the road, Cassandra looked out her window and saw Ryan, Alex, and Julie standing and talking amongst themselves and looking back at Cassandra's car. She didn't bother saying goodbye to them. She did not care if she never saw them again. It was a door she was ready to close. If anything, she had learned from this experience that if Cassandra had the chance to say goodbye, she had to take it. She knew that she needed to say goodbye to Eugene before she left Los Angeles to head back to New York City. If she didn't say goodbye, she would never forgive herself.

Nina was sitting on the beach admiring the waves that were crashing when a gust of air blew by and with it brought the front section of today's newspaper. It landed a couple of yards from Nina's pedicured feet. She looked down and decided to read what was going on in Miami Beach. She grabbed the paper, and even though her English was a bit rough she was able to make out the headline, "No lead in death of a Los Angeles man vacationing in Miami Beach." Nina looked down further and gasped as she saw the picture of Eric. Terrified, she ran with the newspaper to Lucy. Nina and Lucy were staying at a cheap motel toward the end of the strip in Miami Beach bordering the next city. Nina ran into the hotel, took the elevator, and barged into their room. Nina startled Lucy who was watching her favorite soap on TV.

"What is your problem, Nina?"

"Look!" Nina said with tears forming in her big eyes.

"What?" Lucy said snatching the newspaper.

Lucy read the title and looked at Nina, "So what? What does this matter to me?"

Nina then pointed at Eric's picture. Lucy followed Nina's finger to the picture and moved her hand. Lucy studied the picture carefully and finally noticed who it was. *Could it be?* she asked herself. *There is no way.* But the picture did look like Eric with his sweet smile. Lucy crumbled the newspaper and told Nina, "We are leaving now; pack your things." She grabbed whatever clothes she had lying around and threw them in a bag. Lucy did the same thing. Millions of thoughts were running through Lucy's head. *Our fingerprints are all over the hotel room. The wallet, maybe someone found it? People must have seen us at the restaurant with Eric.* They were packed in three minutes flat. They left the hotel without checking out and grabbed the nearest taxi. Lucy had no clue where they were going but they had to get out of the area fast.

"What about work?" Eugene's sister asked her brother as they sat at a table across from each other. Since it was a county jail, there were no windows or phones between them.

"I am not sure. I don't want to tell them. The truth is worse than a lie. I was thinking maybe you can talk to my assistant, tell her the situation, and she could cover for me. I am beside myself on what to do," Eugene said as he buried his head into his hands.

"I will do whatever it takes," his sister said. "Don't worry, I will call your assistant and tell her the situation. You probably won't be here for the whole two weeks anyway. You need to focus on getting better. The main point I am trying to make is what are you going to do about your drinking when you get out of here?"

"I am not sure. I am going to have to stop drinking. Get control of my life," Eugene said lying because he had no clue as to the first step in taking control of his life.

"That is a start, but there is so much more to get control of," said his sister.

"I know, but the first thing is first. Have you told Mom?"

"No, I don't think she needs to know right now; she will only be beside herself."

"I agree," Eugene said.

"Take care of yourself. I am going to call your assistant right now. I will be back tomorrow to update you on things."

"Great. Thank you so much, Sis. I love you."

"Love you too," she said with the smile that Eugene also had.

Cassandra's car drove down the coast and she peered out of the window looking at the ocean. She had not made any attempts to get in touch with Eugene. She wanted to settle in somewhere first, get her thoughts together, and then contact him. The driver and Cassandra reached a hotel in Newport Beach. Cassandra got out of the car and walked into the lobby toward the check-in desk.

"Hi," Cassandra said in a low tone, "Do you have any rooms available?"

"Hi," the receptionist said back. "Let me check. We're all sold out but let me see if anything is available." The receptionist typed away in her computer for a minute and came back with nothing. "Unfortunately, all our rooms are booked for tonight. You have some available tomorrow."

"It's okay, thank you," Cassandra said as she walked away before the receptionist could say anything else.

Cassandra got into the car and slammed the door. She did not want to be driving around all night.

"Where to miss?" the driver said.

"Down to Laguna Beach, to the Ritz Hotel," Cassandra said certain they would have rooms available.

Lucy and Nina, now on the run, took comfort for one night at Lucy's cousin's house on the outskirts of Miami. *No one will find us here,* she thought to herself. Lucy's cousin lived in a small two-bedroom, one-bath apartment in a rundown neighborhood. Lucy and Nina slept on the full-size bed in Lucy's cousin's spare room. Nina fell asleep, but Lucy stayed out all night fearing every moment and noise she heard outside the bedroom window. Lucy started recapping the events of that night. She and Nina hadn't had too much to drink because they knew the plan was to spike a tourist's drink, seduce him to bring them back to his hotel, have the guy fall asleep, and then take his wallet and any jewelry he had, but that particular night, Lucy had noticed a connection between Nina and Eric. Although, she knew that it would not work out because once he found out about her ways, he would dump her. Lucy remembered only putting one pill in his beer bottle and that had dissolved, but why would it kill him? Maybe he had a bad reaction to it? She wasn't sure what to think. Then she remembered the wallet and hoped it was somewhere in the room. Lucy tried closing her eyes, but every time she did, all she saw was Eric's face.

Cassandra opened the balcony door from her hotel bedroom to look at the ocean. She set out on the balcony and took a deep breath in from the night's ocean air. She looked around and stared out to the dark ocean with thoughts about how she was going to approach Eugene and what her words to him were going to be. But for tonight, she was too emotionally exhausted to think about anything and decided to head to bed. Cassandra lay in the bed, closed her eyes, and soon fell asleep to a night of dreams and nightmares.

Eugene woke up from his third night in jail which was like the first two: restless. He still had not heard anything from his attorney as to whether he was to serve the entire two weeks; he didn't know how he was going to survive. Eugene had spoiled himself for most of his adult life and did not how to respond to a life that was set by rules. This morning, he lay in his stiff bed, like every other morning, and thought about his life and what was next. He always started remembering his childhood. For the most part, his childhood had been ordinary with his father, mother, and sister. He had lived in a mediocre town, not having more than enough to get by. His mom and dad had been teenage parents, having tried very hard to raise Eugene with the little they had. His parents had waited a few years until his sister had been born. Given their financial situation may have been slightly better, it still had Eugene working after-school jobs from a very young age. When Eugene reached his teenage years, his parents divorced leaving Eugene and his sister with their mother, and his father moving to another state to be with his mistress. From that point on, Eugene knew that he would never cheat on any of his girlfriends, but instead of trying to find out who he was, he trapped himself in an endless relationship because he never wanted to feel the hurt he saw his mother go through. For days, months, and years. Eugene saw his mother go through emotions that only love could put you through. As much as he wanted to fix it for her, there was nothing he could do, but stand by and watch his mother break to eventually rebuild herself years later. Years is what it took for his mother to be human again. Since then, she had remarried a man that she may not be in love with, but would never make her experience the pain she once felt. Eugene knew that was one of the many problems he faced; he never let himself truly be happy because at a young age he was taught that love only brought pain. He studied his sister, who on another hand, had fallen in love young and married young. Somehow, she was not affected by what their mother had been through. His sister was still as much in love with her husband as they had been when they'd first met in middle school. Then, he thought about his failed marriage and his son, whom he wished he could have given a happy childhood, but instead had only given him his own tormented past. Tears slowly started escaping Eugene's eyes and falling off the side of his face. For all the money he had now, he would have never guessed that this would be his life: lying in a jail cell with no one to love him.

Cassandra awoke the next morning feeling the emotional roller coaster coming to an end. She lay in bed, her head resting on the pillow, just thinking and not wanting to think at the same time. Even though she had attended the funeral yesterday, she felt as if it had been a dream and that everything was okay. It was only later that she realized that everything was true, and there was no going back now. Everything had changed with Eric's death and even though she hated herself for not being able to say goodbye, she needed to make good from this tragic death. At this moment, she didn't know how, but somehow she hoped it would come to her.

Cassandra decided she could not spend all day in bed. She peered out from her bed to the balcony, which she had left open the previous night. She thought she had shut the balcony doors, but she was so emotionally drained that she could be mistaken. The sun was peering through her curtains that were blowing in the wind. Even though she felt like crying, she held back the tears and gulped them only leaving the pain in her chest. Cassandra walked into the bathroom and started running the shower. She needed to feel refreshed and alive again. Hopefully, the shower was a start.

Lucy woke up with the first sight of sunrise and nudged Nina, who was sleeping like an angel. For a second, right before she tried waking Nina, she looked at Nina and hated herself for making her a part of this. Nina was so young and vulnerable but knew this was the only way Nina was going to learn how hard life was. Nina thought life was like it was in all the love movies she watched, and thought one day her prince would come to rescue her. Lucy had to instill in her that there were no princes for women like her. The only thing that lay ahead was a hard life.

"Nina, wake up!" Lucy yelled into Nina's ear. Nina stirred a little bit.

"Nina!" Lucy yelled again, this time shaking her entire body. Nina slowly started opening her eyes to see find Lucy staring directly at her face.

"*Mi hija*, we have to get going," Lucy called Nina by her nickname: *my beloved daughter*. "Now. Before someone finds us."

"Where are we going?" Nina asked barely having opened her eyes.

"I am not sure. We have to get out of the Miami area. And we have little money, where it may take us is where we will end up."

Nina just looked at her mother, Lucy, wondering how she let herself get into this mess. Nina had spent all night dreaming about Eric and what their life would have been like if he was still alive. Nina saw the way Eric had looked at her—like no other man had looked at her before—with loving eyes taking her all in. Nina was having mixed emotions, hating her mother for taking away the only chance at happiness she had and at the same time having to trust her because she didn't want to get caught. Nina was devising her own plan; once they were safe, Nina was going to leave her mother without a word. Nina wanted to live a normal life even if it brought little. Having met Eric and witnessed what happened to her showed her what life really was about and to her it was about love.

After a small breakfast, Cassandra took off to walk on the beach. It was a gorgeous day with the sun shining down. Walking down the beach with a destination in mind, she wished she could just keep walking until she disappeared, but knew that was not an option. After walking a mile, Cassandra just plonked herself on the sand. They were people all around her enjoying their day at the beach. She observed the kids running to the water, couples holding hands as they strolled, and mothers preparing their children's lunches on their blankets. Cassandra, no longer being able to sit up, decided to lay down on the sand and look up at the sun. Cassandra closed her eyes and started envisioning the times she had spent with Eric. She started remembering the way he looked at her, the way he touched her, and the way he felt against her. It all felt so real that it scared Cassandra, and she sat up opening her eyes to the reality around her. She decided to start walking back to the hotel. She knew she was not ready to deal with Eugene; in truth, she had never been ready to deal with Eugene, but this was her only chance.

Back at the hotel, Cassandra started carefully setting her plan in place. Once she arrived in New York, she would have to visit her parents. It had been two years since she had seen her parents and her sister for that matter. At this current time, Cassandra had no idea where her sister was or with whom. Every time Cassandra thought about her return to New York, she always experienced the worst stomach pains. She should have known that it was a sign that returning to New York was not the best choice. Not feeling well, Cassandra lay on her freshly made bed, thinking about her last days in New York before departing for Los Angeles.

Cassandra had sat on the floor of her parents' New York City apartment, heartbroken and most of all dazed in the confusion of what had transpired from the past few days. Cassandra, the daughter of one of the most prominent men in New York City and his debutante mother, was set to marry a blue collar's son—who in the eyes of Cassandra's mother's family was a mere servant. Cassandra, in love with the idea of love, had never seen any of the warning signs that the short relationship was displaying. Every one of Manhattan's society knew of Cassandra and her mother's family. Everyone whispered that Cassandra, young and naive, would be making the same mistake her mother had made by marrying Cassandra's father. Cassandra knew in her heart that the man she had met, who was set to marry her, would make her happy, but she knew it was all a lie.

Chapter 32

Cassandra had met her soon-to-be husband at a party one of her "board-ing school mates"? was hosting at her penthouse apartment. She had entered the party with no desire of attending, but knew that she had promised her childhood friend. Once at the party, Cassandra had been enjoying herself drinking and dancing the night away. After a few hours, she had headed to the balcony for some fresh air. It was on that balcony that she met the boy who would become her in a short three months. Cassandra had been leaning against the balcony sipping her glass of champagne admiring the cold January air hit-ting her face when a voice next to her had asked her if she had a cigarette.

"Do you happen to have a cigarette? I have run out of them," the man had said to her.

Cassandra was ready to give a harsh response about smoking when she turned over and looked at him and stopped herself in her own words. Cassandra must have been staring at him for a few minutes because the man responded, "Do you have a cigarette or not?"

"I am sorry, how rude of me. No, I don't have a cigarette. I do not smoke," Cassandra had said politely.

"Oh, you could have said something before you decided to stare at me," he had replied double-checking his pockets.

"Again, I apologize for my behavior," Cassandra had said still staring at him.

"No problem. I could have sworn I had one left somewhere in my pocket, but I guess I was wrong," he had said as he searched his leather jacket. Cassandra should have taken that as a first warning sign. No one in Manhattan society ever wore a leather jacket to a party.

"Well, you know smoking is bad for you," Cassandra had said, wishing she had not said anything.

The man had looked at her as though she was insane, but had decided on responding politely because she was beautiful. "Yes, I know, but the champagne you have been drinking all night is just as deadly."

Cassandra had wondered for a second on how he knew she was drinking champagne and then looked down at her glass and realized how he knew.

"I guess we all have our poisons," Cassandra had said taking the last few sips of her champagne.

"Yes, we do. My name is Julian DeSmith."

"I am Cassandra Zea," Cassandra had shaken his hand.

After a few minutes of talking, Cassandra and Julian had locked lips all night never coming up for air. They had spent every minute of every day together, proclaiming their love for one another. Cassandra knew the minute she had met him he was bad news, but she hadn't cared. What had excited her was that he didn't pay attention to anyone's rules but his. Slowly as the relationship grew, Cassandra began to notice Julian was using more and more of Cassandra's money and name. After a month of heavy dating, Cassandra had introduced him to her mother and father; both her parents, before they'd known his name, had already eliminated him as a suitable match for Cassandra. After the dinner had ended and Julian had left, her parents had a screaming match with Cassandra about how Julian didn't fit the criteria as to whom she should be dating. Cassandra, determined to set her parents straight, had continued dating Julian but the only thing alarming were the lies he bestowed upon her, which Cassandra knew all along. She wanted to believe in him and most of all she wanted to believe he loved her. When during their third month of dating, Julian proposed to her with a five-carat ring, Cassandra had been beside herself, knowing that this would prove her parents wrong. She'd immediately rushed to her parents to show them the ring, but they'd objected to the marriage as soon as they saw it. Their objection had only pushed Cassandra further into the arms of Julian. They had started planning the wedding with Julian claiming to pay for everything. He had himself claimed to belong to New York society with his father's flipping commercial real estate in the early 80s and having a Central Park West address, which Cassandra had never visited because Julian had insisted on only taking her home once they were married. She never objected because she thought it was romantic and gentlemanly. As the wedding date had drawn closer, her parents gave in to attending the wedding but not paying for any of it. As the time arrived to make payments, Julian would always come to Cassandra with an excuse that his money was tied up or he would wire the money to the vendors, but that never happened and when Cassandra would approach him, Julian would get angry and start a fight. Two months before the wedding date, all the vendors had been in a frenzy because they had produced all the materials based on the fact that it was Cassandra getting married and they knew she had money. At the last minute, when Cassandra had approached Julian about paying the vendors he had gotten angry and told Cassandra that all she cared about was the money and never him, pushing Cassandra before he left—the last time she ever saw him. Not knowing what to do, she had decided on selling the ring she got from Julian to pay the vendors without it having to come out of her bank accounts. She had approached a jeweler that her family had known for years about selling the ring. At the jewelry store, she had given the manager her ring. He had taken the ring and held under his magnifying glass; after just a second of looking at it, he had shaken his head.

"Darling, I am sorry, but his ring is nothing more than a cubic zodiac. I am sorry." He had put the ring back on the glass counter and walked away.

Cassandra had just stood there as if someone had punched her heart and she could no longer breathe. She had grabbed the ring and run outside, continuing walking to Fifth Avenue. She had spent the rest of the afternoon sitting and looking at the turtle pond in Central Park never wanting to leave. While sitting there, she had started putting the pieces together and one by one they fell into place with all the lies Julian had ever told her. How naive and stupid she had been. Someone of her status to have fallen for someone like Julian—deep down inside she had somehow always known, but never wanted to admit to it. Defeated, she had left the pond knowing she had to tell her parents. They of course would be happy, but Cassandra would be left with another mark on her already broken heart.

Cassandra always cringed at those memories and the fact that she had had to admit defeat to her parents. Even though heartbreak had happened to her, she had never given up on love. She knew if she tried hard, maybe one day it would come to her. Dealing with her parents would be another issue; they never seemed to understand her or who she was.

Nina and Lucy were now on a train that would take them to Washington D.C. Lucy knew the easiest way out of the country was through Canada and not Miami; it would be too hard leaving the country through Miami as it held border portal and every given police activity. Right before they left Miami for New York, Lucy had seen the papers with big headlines: "TOURIST MAN'S WALLET FOUND IN DINER GARBAGE, DETAILS STILL DEVELOPING." Lucy knew it was their only way to freedom. She had enough money to get them to Canada and once there she would have to study a town and determine if she could play a couple of her games to win her and her daughter some money. Lucy looked over at Nina who had fallen asleep with her head against the window. She still had the same angelic face she was born with. Lucy remembered how happy she was when she found out she was pregnant and then when the doctors had told her she would be having a daughter it had brought her even more joy. Lucy and Nina's father had met a long time ago in Cuba. Being from the same neighborhood and having the same aspirations for a better life had brought them together. They never spent a day apart from dreaming what their life would be like in the United States. They would be able to get jobs and have a small home. It didn't matter if they didn't have much because they had each other. Little by little, they saved money from odd end jobs and when they knew they each had enough, they had approached a man who would guarantee their safe journey to Florida. A week before their departure, Lucy had learned of her pregnancy. Not wanting to tell her true love, she had kept it hidden until they'd arrived on safe land in the United States. All they needed to do was to touch U.S. soil and all their memories from their past life would be erased. The journey—a tough one that was prepared for—would bring upon hours and hours on a small boat with little to eat and drink and not being able to go to the restroom, but they were both ready for the chance at freedom and they knew their love would keep them strong. As the journey started, Lucy had always felt sick in the mornings and vomited during the first half-hour on the small boat. With her love by her side, she knew she would be okay. Several hours later, the small boat had entered U.S. territory waters and this was where the hardest part was about to come. All the occupants of the boat had to now lower themselves so they would not be seen. As the boat started to drift toward sea, they prayed to make sure they were not spotted by U.S. border patrol. Slowly the boat started drifting with the waves and they started hearing the sirens; they knew at any moment they would have to swim toward shore and touch the U.S. sand. It was about to become every man and woman for themselves. Lucy's love told her, "Don't worry, mi corazon, we will make it, keep faith." Lucy had smiled at him and knew everything was going to be alright. As the sirens drew closer, they could feel their small boat starting to rock more frequently. They had been instructed that when this happened, they needed to swim for life. Before they knew it, the boat had overturned and everyone was thrown into the water with the boat on top of them. In the water, they could feel the surges of waves from the speedboats that were closing in on them. "We have to swim," said Lucy's love to her. "Swim and don't stop!" he told her and gave her a kiss. They both went under water and came out from under the boat. As soon as their heads reached water, they started swimming relentlessly as they had been taught. The others started following, but were trailing behind. Lucy kept swimming never bothering to look back because she knew he would be right behind her. Within a couple of minutes, the U.S. border patrol was behind them with lights flashing on them and sirens that she would never forget. Lucy never gave up and kept swimming faster and faster. She could now see the sand on the beach in front of her and it brought her hope. She knew if she took one second to look back it would distract her and it might jeopardize her life. With her head down, she swam with more force, picturing her life with her baby and her soon-to-be husband. Lucy was the only one able to reach the U.S. land. When she made it to U.S. soil, she somehow ended up in a more deserted area where it was harder to find her. It took her a second to catch her breath but she somehow remembered her love and turned around to help him. Only there was no one behind her. She looked around, standing wet and alone. She could hear people screaming and the sirens around her were getting close. She waited another minute, waited for him to appear from the water, but knew he wasn't coming. She saw the lights and sirens get closer and knew if she had any chance she had to run right now. Lucy started running, but took one more look back just in case he was there, but he never came. That was the first day of Lucy's new life. She cried herself to sleep for many nights on any corner she could find and finally the tragedy she had faced turned her into a rock. She felt nothing and got through life day by day. When Nina was born, it was the most joy her heart had felt, but it was only for a split second. She did want to feel any joy. If anything, Nina brought her memories of her only love, a love that she would never see again until it was her time for peace.

Chapter 33

"Have you spoken to Cassandra?" Ryan asked Julie, looking at her as if he was looking at her for the first time. He started noticing that Julie had an ordinary look and there was nothing unique about her.

"No, I haven't. I have tried calling her but her phone goes to voicemail and the voicemail happens to be full,"

"What about going over to her apartment?"

"I thought about it but decided not to. You know she no longer works upstairs. Not like she ever really did," Julie said a bit annoyed.

"I kind of noticed that. I wasn't sure how she paid her rent or her bills. She never did go to work," Ryan said.

"Who knows. I am a little upset that she would leave and not say anything to me. I thought we were friends, but I guess I was wrong."

"I am sure she will come around."

"How are you holding up?" Julie asked Ryan.

"I am okay. Alex is still a mess, but getting better,"

"Yeah, it's still a shock. Has any new information developed about his killer?"

"No, I did read the papers in Miami about his death and they are still looking for leads, but nothing new has developed."

"I hope they find the person who did this," Julie said looking at Ryan, hoping he felt different about her now that this tragedy had occurred. "Did you want to maybe get some drinks after work?"

"I am not sure. I may have to visit another branch in another area and then I may head home. I will text to let you know."

"Okay," Julie said disappointed. Ryan smiled and walked away. Julie looked after him and wondered why Ryan still didn't feel the same way she did for him. Her heart ached every time she saw him; she wanted to be with him no matter what and needed to work her way to him.

Ryan started walking to his car. He had been confused and upset about Eric's death. He never did really like Eric, but for him to die the way he did was not right. Then there was Cassandra; he never did cherish their relationship when they lived together and now he was calling to apologize to her and hopefully work things out, but she was not returning his calls and he had gone by her apartment numerous times only for her not to answer. He didn't know where she was or whether she needed him. He didn't want to deal with Julie. Now that this had happened, he was over trying to be friends with her. Ryan needed to get a hold of Cassandra; he just didn't know how.

After only spending a week in jail, Eugene was free and able to go home. His sister waited for him outside the county jail. When she saw her brother, she ran to him with tears in her eyes.

"Are you okay?" She hugged him.

"Yeah, I am okay," he said enjoying his sister's hug.

"Let's go, you must be starved."

"Yes, I am," Eugene said.

"Do you want to go to your favorite Mexican restaurant?" "That is a great idea. What happened with work? Did you talk to my assistant?"

"Yes, she took care of everything. She told the partners you were out scouting properties with potential clients, and they didn't ask too many questions."

"Good. After eating and getting a good night sleep in my own bed, I will head into work early tomorrow."

"Good plan. Mom has been asking about you, I also told her you were on a business trip. You should go by her house this weekend, so she won't worried."

"I will," Eugene said looking out the window enjoying the fresh air that was not offered in jail.

Eugene and his sister drove in silence to the restaurant, while he thought about the things he had thought about in jail. He now had to put his plan into action although he didn't know how to start.

The next morning Cassandra was lying in her big hotel bed with huge pillows around her. Drained with emotional exhaustion, she had trouble sleeping and didn't know what to do in order to fall asleep. Drinking was not one of her options. She decided to get up and face the day. With a bit of an appetite, she ordered some breakfast and decided to watch TV and see what was going on in the world. She needed a distraction from her thoughts. Cassandra curled up on the couch in the living room, turned on the TV, and waited for breakfast.

Eugene opened his eyes happy to find himself in his own room and not some dirty jail cell. Even though what he experienced had been just a week, it had been the worst ever. Being restrained to a small cell and not being able to anything but sit with your never-ending thoughts was brutal. He had lost of a couple of pounds and had aged a bit from the stress he went through. He knew had to go to work this morning and get his affairs in order. He also needed to meet his attorney to find out what other consequences he now faced. *How has my life come to this?* he thought to himself. He once had it all with his marriage, but left it because he wasn't happy. *Maybe life is not always about being happy? Maybe settling is what life is all about.* He threw off the covers and got out of bed to start his day.

Cassandra, bored with watching TV, decided that it was time to give Eugene a call. It was only a matter of time before she had to leave the hotel, pack her stuff up in Los Angeles, and head to NYC. Cassandra got dressed and walked out to her balcony, took a deep breath, and dialed Eugene's number. She always got butterflies in her tummy when she would call him. The phone started ringing and she held her breath.

Eugene was sitting at his desk staring at the paperwork he needed to go through when he heard his phone ring. Cassandra was calling him. He contemplated picking it but decided to answer the call.

"Hello," he said as he leaned back in his chair.

"Hi," Cassandra said finally exhaling as her stomach turned. "How are you?"

"I am okay. How about yourself?" Eugene said, actually happy to hear her voice.

"I am okay. I am actually in Laguna Beach; well I'm staying in Laguna Beach for a few days and wondering if you wanted to get together for dinner?" Cassandra said waiting to hear his response.

Eugene surprised by what Cassandra just told him responded, "You are here in Orange County? That is good. Yes, dinner sounds great. Is tonight okay?"

"Tonight is perfect," Cassandra said relieved that he had agreed.

"What hotel are you staying in?"

"The Ritz in Laguna Beach," Cassandra said actually feeling happy in days.

"Okay, I will pick up at 8:30 p.m.?"

"Yes, I will meet you in the lobby."

"Perfect, see you then," Eugene said and hung up. Eugene had mixed emotions about seeing Cassandra because of everything he had gone through. He wanted to meet her to tell her everything that had happened to him because he knew he could trust her. At the same time, he didn't want to get close to her because he wasn't ready to be with her or anyone. Eugene turned his chair around to face the window and think about Cassandra. She was never in the plans he set when he was in jail, but that was life. You never plan for what is truly going to happen and as much as you prepare, life will throw your way whatever it wants.

Cassandra was still holding tightly onto the phone and looking out at the ocean. She was extremely excited she was going to meet Eugene for dinner. She had not seen him since the baseball game where she met his son. How funny life had been with her and Eugene; even after all this time had passed, they had managed to be friends. Cassandra was already getting butterflies in her stomach thinking about their dinner and what she was going to say to him. Cassandra knew that tonight was her only chance in telling Eugene how she felt and hopefully he would react the same to her feelings.

Eugene arrived early at the hotel, nervous, because this was the first time he and Cassandra were going to sit down and talk in a long time. The other times when they had hung out it, it had been with people around them and since Eugene was not currently drinking, he had nothing to mask his nerves. He walked around the large lobby admiring the paintings and fixtures wondering if he should have brought Cassandra flowers, but he did not want to overdo it. He walked to the end of the lobby and decided to walk outside, admiring admire the sky filled with twinkling stars promising people wishes but delivering nothing. Eugene paced around the terrace back and forth. He looked at his watch. It was 8:30 p.m. and decided to walk back into the lobby. He looked at himself in the reflection of one painting to make sure he looked okay.

Cassandra had just left her hotel room and walked toward the elevator. She was immensely nervous and wished she had had a drink before this night started, but didn't want anything to interfere with what she had to tell Eugene. She waited at the elevator and pushed the down button. She hoped she looked okay and wanted to show Eugene how beautiful she was. The elevator opened and Cassandra walked inside.

Every time Eugene heard an elevator arrive on the lobby floor, he would look up to see if Cassandra was getting off. So far she hadn't. He kept pacing in the lobby around the center table. He finally decided to lean against the table and just wait. Two elevators reached the lobby at the same time and Eugene looked at the first car and looked at the people getting off. Cassandra walked out of the second elevator car and saw Eugene leaning against the table. He looked handsome wearing black pants and a blue open-collared shirt with a belt that matched his shoes. She started walking toward him when he turned around and saw her. He was stunned by Cassandra. He'd always known she was beautiful, but this was the first time he saw in her a different light. Cassandra was wearing a strapless midnight blue dress with black high heels. Her black long hair was shining in the light as it fell over her face.

"Hi," Cassandra said to Eugene because she didn't know any other words.

"Hi," Eugene said looking at her.

They both just stared at each other for a minute before Cassandra said something.

"It's good to see you," Cassandra said.

"Same here," Eugene said not knowing if he should kiss her but decided not to.

"Hungry?" Cassandra said because Eugene kept staring at her.

"Yes, of course. I thought we could try a new restaurant that opened up this month overlooking the ocean. It's such a nice night out," Eugene said as he and Cassandra started walking toward the entrance of the hotel.

"Yes, it is," Cassandra said extremely nervous.

Outside, Eugene's car was waiting on the side and they walked toward it. Eugene opened the door for Cassandra, and she got in. He walked around, got in, started the car, and they drove off. The conversation in the car was very limited with one-line questions here and there. They both were nervous that the beginning was a little intense. They reached the restaurant in Newport Beach and pulled up to the valet.

Chapter 34

They were seated on the outside balcony overlooking the peninsula of yachts. The night's sweet air offered warmth and comfort. Cassandra and Eugene would look at each other and turn away. Neither was sure how to start the conversation and instead concentrated on the drinks menu. The waiter came to the table. "Have you decided on a drink?"

"Would you like wine?" Eugene asked Cassandra.

"Yes, sounds good," Cassandra said closing her menu.

"We will have the best bottle of your vintage red wine," Eugene said.

"Excellent, I will be back shortly," the waiter said taking the menus.

They both looked at each and smiled and both turned away. Cassandra's thoughts were running through her head as to what to say. She usually didn't have a problem talking to people, but tonight she was lost for words. She was staring at the row of yachts, when finally Eugene spoke. "I have been thinking about getting a boat, something small," Eugene said not sure if that was the correct thing to say for starting the conversation.

"Really, that would be nice," Cassandra said turning to Eugene. "I always loved boats. Every summer my family and I would sail. It was great times," Cassandra said smiling remembering one the few family trips she had.

"How is your family?" Eugene asked rearranging his silverware.

"Good, I think. I really haven't talked to them in a while," Cassandra said.

"How about your mom and sister?"

"They are both good so are my nephews," Eugene said.

Again, they both went silent and looked at each other. The waiter approached the table with the bottle of wine and showed them the bottle. Once Eugene nodded, the waiter opened the bottle and poured a small amount into Eugene's glass. Eugene tasted the wine and approved it. The waiter poured the same amount of wine into the two glasses and walked away. Eugene and Cassandra both raised their glasses to each other and said, "Cheers." As they clinked their glasses, it seemed like the ice between them just melted. They started talking and enjoying each other's company. After ordering and finishing the hors-d'oeuvres, Eugene ordered another bottle of wine and realized how comfortable he felt around Cassandra. They were laughing and looking into each other's eyes without so much of a blink. As the main course arrived, Eugene started talking about his court date and what had transpired thereafter. Cassandra listened intently without ever interrupting. She was not able to believe what Eugene was saying. She had so many questions, *why did this happen, why hadn't he called her,* but she kept silent. When he was finally done, Eugene looked at Cassandra for a reaction and she had tears in her eyes. "I am so sorry this happened to you. Why didn't you call me?" Cassandra said worriedly.

"Please don't cry," Eugene began. "I was going through so much that it never occurred to call you. I didn't want you to think badly about me."

"I would never think that," Cassandra said putting her hand over Eugene's hand. Eugene took Cassandra's hand, "Are you okay now?"

"Yes, I am doing better, but some experiences change you forever," he said looking away from Cassandra. "They make you realize things you never knew were there before."

Cassandra stared at Eugene thinking what things was he referring to. But she didn't want to ask. Eugene returned to look at Cassandra who tried to shake the tears in her eyes. She admired him for telling her what had happened. Knowing that the mood needed to be changed, she picked up her glass and said, "To new beginnings!" Eugene grabbed his glass and repeated what she had just said. "Ready for dessert?" Eugene asked.

"Absolutely, but I had a different type of idea for dessert," Cassandra said with her sexy smile. Eugene knew exactly what Cassandra was referring to.

Cassandra lay in Eugene's arm in her hotel bed. She remembered how comfortable it felt in his arms, as if they were made for her. She turned around to admire the lines and creases on Eugene's face, which revealed the few years of hard times. She kissed him on the cheek and Eugene closed his eyes and took in her warmth. He hugged Cassandra tightly, not wanting to let her go, "So what would you like to order for dessert?" Cassandra said.

"I thought I just had dessert!" Eugene said looking at Cassandra.

"Well, this will be your second severing," Cassandra said as Eugene grabbed her and rolled her over with him on top of her. He looked at how beautiful she was. She was different than any other girl he had met. Cassandra had a natural beauty that would never compare with anyone he had encountered. After staring at her, he kissed her not wanting to stop just like their first kiss had been.

"How about ordering some champagne?" Eugene said looking at Cassandra and kissing her again.

"Yes, that would be great."

Eugene got on the phone and ordered a few bottles of champagne and every dessert they offered. Cassandra got up, wrapped herself in a sheet, and walked out to the balcony to take the night air in. Shortly, Eugene walked outside to join her.

"Incredible out here, right?" Eugene said standing next to Cassandra.

"Yes, it's amazing being able to wake up to this every morning," Cassandra said staring out to the dark sky.

"I know, I would never be able to give this up," Eugene said.

"I don't blame you," Cassandra said wondering if this was the right time to tell him that she was moving to New York.

"I never asked what made you come to Laguna Beach," Eugene said.

Right when Cassandra was about to answer, the doorbell rang to the suite.

"I'll get it," Eugene said looking at Cassandra with the sheet around her.

Cassandra smiled and look back at the ocean. She was not sure how to begin to answer Eugene's question as thoughts of Eric started to grow in her head.

"Come in and have a drink," Eugene said. Cassandra took one last look at the ocean and walked inside. They sat on the bed and Eugene handed her a glass of champagne; he had laid out all the desserts on top of the bed. Cassandra thought about the time they had spent—those amazing few days in a hotel drinking, eating, and laughing. She smiled at the memory as she took the spoon Eugene had handed her.

"You never answered my question," Eugene said.

"Well," Cassandra began and started telling him the story of Eric minus the intimate encounters and how she needed a break from LA. Cassandra was going to save the part about New York and that she loved him until she felt it was time. They stayed up all night talking about everything as they laid across each other until they both fell asleep with the light of the sunrise upon them.

Nina and Lucy were now in a small motel in upstate New York, sitting on their own twin bed watching the black and white TV that kept losing the signal. Nina just stared at the TV blankly not saying much since their trip had started. Lucy had multiple thoughts running through her head as to how they were going to get across the Canadian border. Before leaving Miami, Lucy had purchased two fake passports, but was not sure how believable they were. Nina also just stared at the TV, her mind running a hundred miles per hour. She was hoping her plan would pull through. Once they were in Canada, they would have to work hard to build up some cash and get a small apartment. Her ultimate worry was Nina and what she was going to do with her. Nina was so fragile and sweet; she deserved better, but this was the life that was given to them. Lucy was also scared to read any of the newspapers in the fear that the police might have found more clues in the case. *How did everything get so messed up,* she thought. She fell asleep in the dreams she wished were true. It was only then she was at peace, being with her true love in her dreams.

Nina, even though she didn't say much, had already formulated a plan. She was not sure how many days they were going to stay in the hotel, and she knew whatever money they had left was starting to diminish. She had carefully orchestrated a plan in her head that one of the nights she would take whatever little money was left and run. She didn't know where, but Canada was not an option for her. She wanted to stay in the United States and make something of herself, but mostly she wanted to find someone who offered the same kindness Eric did with his soft eyes. Someone who looked at her for who she was not what she did. Nina falling in and out of sleep always ended falling asleep to the tune of Eric and what their life would have become.

Cassandra woke to find the afternoon sunlight hitting her face. She opened her eyes and stared at the balcony, the blue sky outside, and just did not think of anything. She just loved staring into the sky. She turned around to find Eugene asleep and studied his face. To her, she already knew every line and crease on his face. She enjoyed watching him sleep; it was as though only for a couple of hours at night, Eugene was most at peace. Suddenly Eugene as if he sensed someone was looking at him, opened his eyes to find Cassandra staring at him. He smiled and she smiled back. "Good afternoon," Cassandra said.

"What time is it?" Eugene asked stretching.

"Around 3:00 p.m.?"

"Really? We must have slept for a while."

"Well, we didn't fall asleep until 7:00 a.m.," Cassandra said.

"Yeah," Eugene said grabbing Cassandra and cuddling her. "Did you sleep okay?"

"Yes," she said. "I am starved. What about you?"

"Me as well," Eugene said. "We should eat outside by the beach," Eugene recommended.

"Good idea," Cassandra responded.

"But not until we do something first," Eugene said turning Cassandra over and kissing her. They didn't stop kissing for an hour.

Cassandra and Eugene sat down at the café by the beach. It was a perfect day and a perfect place to have lunch. Cassandra was running her toes in the sand while Eugene read the menu. Cassandra thought to herself, *I can live like this: being in love with Eugene every day*, she smiled to herself and looked at Eugene who had a sexy look when he concentrated.

"Have you decided?" Eugene looked up at Cassandra.

"How about some chardonnay?" Cassandra suggested.

"Of course, but what about food? You have to eat something as well." Eugene said looking back at the menu. "A sandwich with fries?"

"Yes," Cassandra said admiring him. She wanted to remember these moments forever.

Cassandra and Eugene drank wine and ate lunch while talking and laughing— with the occasional kiss in between. When they were done, they walked down the stairs to the beach hand in hand and then along the shore. Cassandra didn't want this to ever end, but she knew once she told Eugene that she was in love with him, she was scared he would back away, but she knew she had to tell him. After Eric's death, she knew that sometimes the brief moments you had with someone were all you could ever have. She decided that she would wait until later to tell him. They continued walking on the beach, then headed back to the hotel to make passionate love while the sun set. Exhausted, they fell asleep joined together as if that was the way life was meant to be.

Eugene woke up and looked at the clock on the nightstand that read 2 :00 a.m. Cassandra was still in his arms and he didn't want to move for the fear of waking her up. He lay in bed holding her, taking in her sweet scent. He was conflicted about what to do. The feelings he knew he always had for Cassandra was now starting to surface stronger, and he was, with all his might, trying to hold them down, but he feared the longer he stayed with her the more his feelings would grow. While thinking of what to do, he didn't realize that there were tears escaping from his eyes. He gently wiped them away because his heart had already decided for him. Slowly he pushed Cassandra away from him and placed her head on the pillow. He looked at her beautiful face, her dark hair, and clear complexion. Even when she slept, she still had a small smile on her lips. He kissed her lips ever so gently. Walking over to the desk, he found the hotel stationery and began his "Dear John" letter.

Cassandra, in writing this letter I hope you know how much I care for you. My likeness for you turned to love a long time ago, maybe even on our first encounter, whenever it may have been, it is a strong love, a love so strong that I am not able to handle it at this moment. I don't want to hurt you and I feel if I stay within this situation the probability of me hurting you is highly likely. I know after reading this you may hate me and never speak to me again, but I am willing to accept that if it prevents me from breaking your heart. You are truly a beautiful person and your heart will never be matched by anyone. I hope one day you will be able to understand and forgive me. If we are truly meant to be, then as the old cliché goes, "our paths will meet again." If not, then I will have to accept this as the biggest mistake I made and never ever finding the possibility of true love with anyone.

    With much love,
    Eugene Conrad.

Eugene reread the letter several times as if it were going to change, but it didn't. He folded it and placed it on the pillow where his head was resting a couple of minutes ago. He looked at Cassandra one last time, not knowing if or when he was going to see her. He slowly walked out of the room collecting his wallet and watch. He walked through the living room and out of the main door, shutting behind not only the door but his chance of happily ever after.

Chapter 35

*C*assandra awoke to the early morning sunshine beaming through the windows of the balcony. When she opened her eyes, it took her a second to focus and she realized Eugene was not next to her. She immediately sat up not seeing the folded white note on the pillow next to her. She rubbed her eyes, got up from the bed, and walked to the bathroom. She opened the door and there was no one. Then, she walked to the living room—nobody there either. She thought maybe he went to get some breakfast and decided to walk back to the bedroom and out to the balcony to admire the morning sun. As she on the balcony, the room phone rang. She went inside and walked around the bed to answer the phone. As she was about to answer the phone, she noticed the folded paper that had fallen off the pillow and onto the bed. She unfolded the note. She started reading the letter with a blank expression on her face, as the phone kept ringing. Once she was done, she couldn't even shed a tear. She was in complete disbelief. She sat on the bed making sure she read the letter right, but nothing changed the second time she read it. Not knowing what to do, she took a second to breathe and realized what had just happened. She had so many questions, but in the end she knew she wouldn't get any answers, Eugene had decided their outcome and there was no going back. The only thing that lingered in Cassandra's head was the fact that she never told him how she felt. *Maybe she waited too long? Maybe if she had told him sooner, he would have never left*. But she knew whatever she may have said would have never changed the outcome. She carefully placed the letter on the nightstand and went to the closet to start packing. She threw her suitcase on the bed and then threw all her things into it with any folding her clothes. She grabbed her outfit for the day and went to the bathroom to shower and change. If anything, she was now ready to get on a plane to New York without a second doubt. After she was done changing, she called her driver to immediately pick her up from the hotel. She grabbed her suitcase, the letter, and walked out of the hotel without looking back. For once she didn't want to take the memories with her.

Cassandra checked out of the hotel and got into the waiting car.

"Where to, madam?" the driver asked.

"Back to Los Angeles and then the airport," Cassandra said without looking at the driver. He nodded and they exited the hotel's entrance onto the Pacific Coast Highway. As they drove along the beach, Cassandra opened her window and the fresh breeze hit her face. She slowly started tearing up the letter Eugene had left without reading it again, and piece by piece she let the wind carry it to its final resting place until the letter was completely gone—just as her heart had vanished when Eugene left her.

Lucy awoke startled, just like she had been every morning since she had found out about Eric's death. It was when she saw Eric's face smiling at her that she woke up gasping for air. This morning she woke up and got out of bed without looking over at Nina's bed, walked into the small bathroom, and started running the cold shower. She looked at herself in the mirror; the once dolled-up woman she was instead showed her age lines and the hard life she had been handed. She took off her worn clothes and stepped into the cold shower. She shuddered at how cold the water was but knew it was not going to get any warmer. She let it sting her skin as it turned it red; she hoped the water could wash away everything that had happened. After a few minutes, she got out, wrapped the towel around her, and walked out of the room. It was then she noticed that Nina's unmade bed did not have her in it. She frantically walked to the bed and pulled the covers as if Nina was to appear underneath the flattened sheet. She walked toward the window and peered outside. There was no sign of her. Then she opened the door and looked outside. Quickly she put on her clothes, ran outside the room, down the stairs to the small coffee shop the hotel had. She walked in so fiercely that the few people in the coffee shop turned to look her way. She walked to the waitress behind the counter, "Have you seen my daughter. The girl I am always with?" Nina asked. The waitress looked at her confused and said, "No," and went back to serving coffee to the awaiting customers. Lucy looked around hoping somehow she missed Nina sitting at one of the tables, but there was nobody. She walked out of the coffee shop and looked around the parking lot. *Maybe someone took her?* But she knew she could not call the cops. She decided to go back to the hotel room and wait for Nina to return. She closed the door behind her, sat on the bed and started biting her nails. She didn't know how long she would have to wait.

Nina was able to get on the first bus to New York City. She had only three hundred dollars minus the fifty dollars she had to pay for the ticket. Wide-eyed, she sat on a window seat observing everything that went by. She didn't have a plan at all; she was just letting life take her ahead. Nina thought about her mother and how nervous she must have been not finding her in her bed that morning, but she knew that her mother had done too much harm to her already and for that, she could never forgive her. Nina decided to erase that part of her life and only look forward. At this point, there was no turning back.

Cassandra arrived at her downtown LA loft apartment just in time to meet the movers. She had not packed any of the belongings from the apartment, but she just needed a few things. She walked into the apartment and it felt as if it was still living on its own. She turned on the lights and the movers walked in behind her.

"Where do you want us to start?" the mover in charge asked.

"Pack everything up in the kitchen first, then the living room, dining room, the closet last," Cassandra ordered.

"Yes," the man said and they went to work. Cassandra, not wanting to spend too much time in the apartment for the fear of the memories rushing back, quickly walked to her closet to select with items she would take with her. She grabbed the two remaining suitcases, opened them in her closet, and started pulling clothing from their hangers and half-folding them into the suit-case. After selecting everything she wanted from the closet, she worked on her shoes and then her dresser. The movers were moving quickly and had finished the kitchen. They started disassembling the living room table and her bed. She went to the dresser, took what she wanted, and walked into her closet to make sure she had taken everything she needed. Cassandra realized that she would be leaving her furniture and everything else in storage in LA. She grabbed a few frames from her living room and put them in between her clothes in the suitcase. She quietly watched the movers move like mice around her loft. Soon they were in her closet putting the rest of her clothes in cardboard boxes. She decided to walk back to the kitchen and just watch, not really wanting to be there. Her suitcases were already taken to the car by the movers. Cassandra felt weird how she thought she had so much stuff, but within an hour they had packed up her life. Now, the last items were being wrapped up to make their new home at a storage facility. Cassandra walked to her favorite spot in the loft, which was her view. The view, which for many nights, was her only answer to many of the questions she had. She looked at the view that brought her comfort and knew she would miss it. She smiled to herself a little and then started remembering some of the good times she and Ryan had spent at the apartment.

"Miss?" the mover said.

"Yes," Cassandra turned around noticing that she was now the only item left in the apartment.

"It looks like we are done. Did you want to do a walk-through to make sure?"

"Yes," Cassandra said and went to the furthest part of the loft that started with her closet, which now had nothing but empty shelves. From there she walked to the bedroom area through the living room and dining room and ended up in the kitchen. She didn't bother checking the cabinets; whatever was left was meant to stay there. "We are good," Cassandra said.

"Okay, please sign here and initial here," the mover said. He ripped Cassandra's copy and handed it to her. "This is the address of the storage and the unit number. Will you be following us to the storage facility?"

"Oh, no. I am headed to the airport."

"Very well. Good luck," he said and walked out.

Cassandra stood in her kitchen one last time and looked around. She walked to the door and she remembered the happy times she and Eric had shared. As she was closing the door, it was as though she heard their laughter together and it brought a smile to her face. She knew that once she closed the door that she and Eric would always live in that moment in that apartment.

As Cassandra walked out of the building, it seemed like something giant was lifted from her shoulders—whether it was saying goodbye to her apartment or the fact that she was heading home, she felt a little bit better. Walking to her car, she remembered Julie and Ryan and that she had not spoken to them since the funereal. She got into the car and told the driver to drive around the block to the building on the next block. "I will be back in a minute," Cassandra said as she got out of the car and walked up the stairs to the bank. She looked at her watch and knew that Julie would be at her desk, but was not sure about Ryan. She walked into the bank confidently, looked toward Julie's desk, and saw her working on her computer. To Cassandra's luck, Ryan was seated at the desk near Julie. Ryan noticed Cassandra first and got up from his chair and walked toward her. Cassandra reached Julie's desk and waited for Julie to look up.

"Hi," Julie said shocked to see Cassandra.

"Hi," Cassandra said taking a seat and making herself comfortable.

"Hey," Ryan said walking up.

Cassandra looked at him and said a cool "Hi."

"Where have you been?" Julie started. "I have been calling you."

"I am sure that is not relevant to either of you," Cassandra said looking back and forth between Ryan and Julie.

"Well, I, we were worried and wanted to make sure you were okay," Julie said.

Cassandra laughed and looked at Julie. "First, there is no *you and Ryan,* and you clearly need to figure that out. If you haven't already, then you are in for a rude awakening. Next, I am pretty sure you didn't care if I was okay or not, because you just wanted to know where I was and finally," Cassandra said. at Ryan, she ended saying, "You will never be half the lover Eric was. Julie gasped and Ryan just had a blank look.

"Cassandra, I don't think this is the right time to bring this up," Ryan finally said.

"When would you have liked me to bring it up? When we were doing it or after it?" Cassandra said with a smirk. At this point, Julie had tears building in her eyes.

"I am confused," Julie said.

"Confused? Ryan and I have been sleeping together since he moved in. Better yet, we were having a relationship—that is until he thought of moving out without saying anything to me," Cassandra said and looked at Ryan. "I think that was a bad move on your part. I opened my home to you and you betrayed my trust?"

"Listen, Cassandra, whatever happened, I didn't mean for it to happen," Ryan said defending himself.

"I can't believe you would do this to me, Cassandra," Julie said.

"Do what? If you could be really that naïve to think that Ryan and I are living together and not having a sexual relationship, then you are crazier than I thought," Cassandra said getting up. "What you have to learn in life, Julie, is that you don't always get what you want. I do." Cassandra said starting to turn. "Oh, by the way, Ryan, every time we were together I was always thinking about Eric," she said and started to walk away. She left both Julie and Ryan stunned, knowing that they both had been pawns in Cassandra's game. Cassandra walked outside needing the fresh air. She was surprised that she told them the truth. Not that she cared, but she had to leave LA knowing that it was she who had won at the end, not them. Cassandra got back into her car. "LAX, please," Cassandra said and the driver nodded and started driving through downtown to reach the highways. She looked at the tall buildings that she had called home once. She had grown a lot with these buildings and the streets surrounding them. She took one look back as the car approached the freeway and knowing she didn't have any regrets about her time there, all she took this time were the memories that stayed with her.

Eugene was waiting in the main conference room at his office. The partners of the firm had scheduled an important meeting that morning. It was time for the meeting to take place and Eugene was a complete mess. He had no idea what the meeting was about nor did the partners give any indication about the content of the meeting. Eugene sat at the ends of the humongous conference table tapping his pen on the pad. The click of the pen was the only sound through the room. After what seemed to be an hour to Eugene, both partners walked in talking to each other. He looked up at them and sweat started building on his forehead. He wiped it off before they could notice. The partners looked at him. "Eugene, how are you son?" the main partner said.

"Great, thank you and yourself?" Eugene responded without trying to sound nervous.

"Good, please sit," the main partner said. The second partner usually didn't say much.

"Our New York office is in need of someone who can lead their business development. Since last year, they have not been able to get to where they need. On talking to the New York partners, they mentioned your name and if you would reconsider relocating to New York and working with them. By any means, it wouldn't be a permanent situation unless you would want to make it permanent. They were thinking a few years to get the business going and if you wanted to stay longer, then that's your option. They have put an amazing package together for you," the partner said as he handed Eugene a folder. "Go over the proposal, think about, and get back to me in a couple of days. The New York office would like a response sooner than later," he said as he got up and the second partner followed him. Eugene didn't say anything. "We will talk soon," the partner said and they both left the conference room. Eugene was left stunned the whole time; he thought they had found out about his jail time, but instead, they had offered him a chance to change his life—something that he needed and was looking for. Eugene didn't open the folder to read the proposal. He would wait until later when he was more clear-headed. He grabbed the folder, left the conference room, and headed back to his office. The one thing that was on his mind was Cassandra. As soon as the partner had said New York, Cassandra had popped in his head; he was trying to get rid of her, but she had already invaded his mind.

Chapter 36

Cassandra arrived at LAX and checked in all her bags. Even though she was moving back to New York, to her it felt like she was only visiting. With her ticket in hand, Cassandra walked toward security and stood in line waiting for her turn. She started thinking about the last two years of her life. Now she was faced with talking to her parents, a task she was not ready for. Then, of course, there was Eugene. Her heart was broken and somehow she knew it would never heal. She didn't want to dwell on it because the memories only brought her tears. As she passed through security, heads turned to look at Cassandra. Her beauty was always an attention grabber. Without looking, Cassandra walked toward the Emerald Room where she planned to have a few cocktails in order to make the flight to New York bearable. She walked in and handed her membership card to the attendant standing at the kiosk.

"Welcome to the Emerald Room, may I see your membership ID?" the gentleman said.

"Yes," Cassandra said handing him her card. Cassandra had been a member since her first flight at the age of two.

"Thank you, Ms. Zea. Please make yourself comfortable. You can get refreshments at the bar."

"Thank you," Cassandra said.

Not opting for the bar, she took a seat in one of the oversized lounge chairs and waited for a waitress to come around.

Cassandra was looking out on the runway watching the workers throw the luggage on the plane.

"What can I get you?" the waitress asked Cassandra.

"Vodka tonic, please," Cassandra said, without as much as looking at the waitress because she didn't like her tone.

"Okay, be right back," the waitress said.

Cassandra continued looking out the large window as she felt someone sit on the oversized lounge chair next to her and she heard the man order a drink. Cassandra didn't turn her head because she didn't want to make conversation with anyone.

The man next to Cassandra was starting to observe Cassandra. He felt as though he had seen her somewhere before.

She felt as if he was staring at her, but didn't want to make contact. The waitress came around and went in between the two lounge chairs. "Okay, vodka tonic for you, miss, and cognac for you, sir," she said handing Cassandra her drink. As Cassandra turned to face the waitress, she saw the face of the man next to her and for some reason, she stopped to stare. Cassandra didn't know what it was, but there was something about him.

"Thank you," Cassandra said to the waitress.

The man saw Cassandra's reaction when she saw his face and knew he had to have seen her before somewhere. He started racking his brain, but couldn't come up with a place or location.

"Thank you," the man said to the waitress who walked away disappointed that her gentleman customer wasn't more interested in her. Cassandra sipped her drink and started looking out to the runway. She had not told anyone about her return trip to New York and as the time was drawing near to her flight, she was getting more antsy. *A couple more of these and I should be fine*, Cassandra thought to herself. She wasn't even sure if her parents were going to be at the family apartment in New York—in a way she hoped for both situations. Then she started thinking about her sister, Cassandra, and how close they used to be when they were little. Always trailing behind Cassandra, until one day Cassandra grew up and found her own path. How distant they had become. *Maybe Cassandra would be visiting,* she thought, but it was the beginning of September and she was probably on some yacht docked on some island. Cassandra continued drinking when the man next to her said, "Have a lot on your mind?" Cassandra heard him and contemplated being curt, but didn't want to be rude." "Sort of," she said glancing at him. He was not sure how to respond and said, "Sometimes it can be difficult, but it's always easier when you have someone to talk to."

Cassandra, not sure if she should just get up and move, decided to say, "Yes, I know." *Hopefully my short answers will turn him away.*

Hi, I am Jasper White," he said with an English accent. Cassandra turned to him and said, "Cassandra Zea."

"Nice to meet you, Cassandra. That is a pretty name," Jasper said.

Cassandra just looked at him and turned her head. What was it about him that she could not determine. Where had she seen him?

"Thank you."

"Where are you headed?"

"New York, going home," Cassandra said, her own response sounding weird because she had not said *home* in such a long time.

"I love New York. I spend a lot of time there on business. I actually live in London," he said noticing Cassandra was not interested.

"London," Cassandra said. "Must be nice."

"Cold and raining most of the time, but otherwise great pubs and food."

"What are you doing in Los Angeles?" Cassandra said finally starting to open up.

"Business. I tend to travel a lot to New York, Los Angeles, and Chicago."

Cassandra looked at him. "Let me guess what you do," she said.

"Please, be my guest," Jasper said admiring her smile.

"Banker, correct?"

"That is close."

"Hmmm. Investment banker, but more like a financier. Am I on the right track?"

"Yes, sort of. Banker yes, not investment, more stocks, and bonds."

"Sounds boring," Cassandra said turning away.

"May I guess what you do?"

"Please," Cassandra said without looking at him.

"You are a heart breaker," he said.

Cassandra looked at him and said, "How did you know? What gave me away?"

"Your looks and attitude, definitely a New Yorker."

"Born and raised, but I don't break hearts. Actually, men tend to break my heart."

"I cannot fathom the idea."

"Believe it. It is definitely true," Cassandra said finishing the last of her drink. Jasper had not yet touched his drink. Cassandra started looking for the waitress and signaled her.

"Were you visiting LA?" Jasper said making sure he kept the conversation going.

"No, I lived in LA for two years and now I am moving back to New York."

"Oh, interesting. And what were you doing in LA for two years?"

Cassandra didn't know how to answer that question, specifically because she really hadn't done anything in LA except drink, party, and drink some more.

"May I have another vodka tonic?" Cassandra said to the approaching waitress.

"I was just getting a feel for the city and what it offers," Cassandra replied to Jasper.

"Oh," he said. "And what are you planning on doing in New York?"

Cassandra was starting to get annoyed with Jasper not because he was asking questions but because she didn't have the answers to them.

"I am not yet sure, but when I find out I will let you know," Cassandra said with an attitude.

"Okay," Jasper said sensing Cassandra's tension.

"Well, if you get bored of New York, maybe you should head to London?"

"Sounds appealing, but I will pass."

"I can show you the sights and really good pubs!" he said waiting for her reaction.

"How about you give me your card and I will call you if I change my mind."

Jasper looked at Cassandra; even though she was giving him the cold shoulder, there was something about her he could not pinpoint.

"Okay," he said playing her game. "Here's my card that has my mobile number as well. If you ever decide to visit, give me a call," he said getting his things together.

"You are leaving?"

"Yes, my flight should be boarding." He grabbed his suitcase and coat. "It truly has been a pleasure, Cassandra," he said extending his hand. Cassandra shook it and said, "Yes, it has. Have a safe flight."

"You as well," he said and walked away. After he left, she looked at Jasper's business card and stared at it for a moment. Why did his name sound familiar? She decided not to think about it and stuck the card in the inside pocket of her jacket. When she turned her head to see where the waitress was, she noticed that Jasper had left his drink untouched. *Weird,* she thought, but was more interested in her drink. After consuming three more vodka tonics, Cassandra was ready for her flight. At least now, she could just fall asleep. She exited the Emerald Room, proceeded to her gate, and stood in line. Once she entered the aircraft, she took her seat in first class and immediately buckled her seat belt and rested her head against the window. Before the plane took off, Cassandra had already drifted into sleep, a sleep filled with dreams of Jasper, someone who had been brought back from her past.

Later that evening, Eugene arrived home, opened a bottle of wine, and sat on his couch with his balcony door open to hear the waves crashing. It was a beautiful night out with the stars lining the sky and the warm breeze entering the house. Eugene sat back on his couch and just stared at the folder the partner had given him earlier. As he drank his wine, he thought about opening it or never opening it and passing on the opportunity altogether. Moving to New York brought a lot of logistics that Eugene was not ready for. Or maybe he thought, it was a chance for him to escape his problems here and start anew. He had lived in New York many years ago with his ex-wife and was only there for a total of eight months before he missed the sunny days of southern California. But now things were different. Maybe he should give the city that never sleeps another chance. Finally giving in, he grabbed the folder and took in a deep breath and opened it. *Dear Eugene Conrad, it is with great pleasure,* the letter began. He spent ten minutes reviewing the package. The New York partners had given him an unbelievable offer, one that if he refused would put a dampener in his career. He had many thoughts circulating in his head, and drinking more wine would hopefully calm them down. The longer he thought about his decision, the more he would prevent himself from doing anything. He finally made a decision with himself and there was no going back. Exhausted he put himself to bed and waited for morning to come; tomorrow his life would change forever.

The next morning, Eugene walked into the partner's office without knocking. "Tell New York they have deal, but I want 10 percent more on my base salary and I will make the move by the end of the month," Eugene said dropping the folder on the partner's desk. "Have them send over the new paperwork for me to sign," he said as he walked out of the office. Eugene had made the decision to make the move; if he didn't do it now, he would never make such a big commitment. As much as he was trying to play the role of the tough guy, he was trying to prevent himself from not thinking about Cassandra. He knew that moving to New York would bring more distance between them and there would probably be no chance of them ever being together, but if he believed anything he wrote in that letter to her, then he knew fate had chosen for them not to be together, at least not now. Eugene just wanted to leave California and concentrate on his new role in New York. He sat at his desk and immediately started looking for realtors in the Big Apple. He was scared and excited at the same as he didn't know what the city held for him.

Cassandra awoke to the plane's bumpy landing in New York.

"Ladies and gentlemen, we have reached our final destination. Welcome to JFK Airport." Cassandra was still trying to wake up. Apparently, the vodka tonics had done their job of getting her to New York without her being awake. Cassandra still sat in her seat as the plane made its way to the gate. She started remembering the dreams she had and they were of Jasper. Why did she dream of him? She was now worried about him, but knew she had bigger things to think about. She got up from her seat and desperately wanted to stretch, but didn't have room. She could not believe that she was back in New York. It had been two years since she had been back. Nervous of what awaited her, she followed the people out of the airplane. She thought as she exited the plane and reached the terminal that somehow her parents were waiting for her, but knew that would be impossible because no one knew of her arrival. She walked toward the baggage claim and looked for the name of the driver she had hired. Once she found him, they headed to her baggage carousel and waited for her luggage. Once he loaded the cart, they walked outside and Cassandra got into the limo. She wouldn't be in New York if she didn't arrive home in a limo. The limo took off toward the expressway, as Cassandra just looked out of the window. Once they arrived in Manhattan, Cassandra started getting chills and pains in her stomach. She felt as it wasn't home anymore and clearly she knew that she no longer belonged, but she had to give it a chance because if she didn't belong here or Los Angeles, then where? Cassandra thought of going to a hotel first, but it would upset her parents if she didn't stay at the apartment. The limo drove down Fifth Avenue toward her apartment. When it reached the apartment, she just looked out of her window to the building and to her floor which was all the way on the top. As the driver opened the door and she stepped out, she was scared of entering the building; at the same time she didn't even know why she was back here. Not recognizing her, the doorman gave her an odd look.

"Good morning, madam?" he said as he noticed all her luggage. "Are you visiting?"

"Yes," Cassandra said. "Actually, I am coming back home," she said walking toward the main door.

"Oh, and which apartment number?" the doorman asked, interested to know who she was.

"Top floor. She waited for him to open the door.

"Oh, then you are?'

"Cassandra Ciprani," she said knowing that the name sounded completely false to her, but it was her given name. It was only in Los Angeles that she changed it to her mother's maiden name.

"Welcome," he said when he realized who she was.

"Thank you," Cassandra said trying to pick up her role as the famous criminal financier's daughter that she played before she left. Cassandra paused in the lobby for a second. It was still the same marble floor-high ceilings with chandeliers everywhere and it had that same cold feeling. Exquisite, but such a lonely room. Cassandra didn't have the key to the private elevator that brought her to the floor that she once called home. She went to the lobby area.

"Hi, I don't have the key to the elevator to take me to my apartment. Maybe you can let me up?"

"Yes, Miss Ciprani! Have not seen you in a while."

"Yes, it was been a while," she said trying to remember the man's name.

"Of course, I will let you up," he said as he walked with her to the elevator.

"Your parents have not returned from vacationing this summer yet. I believe we should be expecting them shortly."

"Thank you," Cassandra said as he helped the elevator door open for her and her luggage.

"Enjoy your stay," he said as the door closed.

Cassandra rode up in the elevator as she had many times before, only this time it felt forced and not right. As the elevator bell rang to indicate its arrival on the floor, Cassandra held her breath for a second. The doors opened and she walked into the entryway of the apartment.

"Where would you like the luggage?" the driver asked.

"There is fine, in the corner," she said because she had no clue if her room was still her room.

"Okay, miss, take care," he said as he put the last of the luggage in the corner and got back into the elevator. Cassandra didn't even notice him leaving as she was just staring at everything, taking it in as if it were the first time. She started walking into the grand living room and she still felt the same cold feeling she had ever since she was little. It seemed like no one had been there for a couple of months. She walked toward the windows where there were pictures of her and Cassandra growing up. She picked one of them up. Her sister and she—how different they were in looks, but yet they resembled each other so much. She put the picture down and grabbed what was a recent picture of her mom and dad; they looked happy smiling at a recent event. It seemed like they had not aged in the two years she had not seen them. She continued walking into the dining room observing the new grand dining table and chairs. While walking into the kitchen, she remembered the days when she and her sister would pretend to cook with whatever current cook her parents had hired at the time, but their food was never edible. Cassandra continued walking through the kitchen and out to the great room and down the hallway to her room. She walked and could hear her footsteps echo throughout the apartment. Cassandra walked up to her door and stood outside as if it were to open. Finally, she turned the handle and carefully started opening the door and peering inside. She looked around the room. It was the same as she had left it two years ago. She fully opened the door and looked at the made bed with all the pillows.

Her vanity table still had the makeup and jewelry she had left behind. Walking toward the wall full of pictures, Cassandra started remembering the happy days of her young adulthood. She sat on her bed and then lay down in between all her pillows. Exhausted from her flight and emotions, she closed her eyes to rest only falling into a deep sleep of confusion.

Chapter 37

$\mathcal{C}$assandra woke the next morning to realize that she had slept through the night. The sun was barely making its way into the sky and an overcast was in sight as it was for many mornings in New York. She lay in bed thinking of what she should do today. She didn't know where to start or if she should contact her parents to let them know she was back. Hungry, Cassandra got out of bed and headed to her shower. One thing was certain: she was hungry for a New York bagel.

After breakfast, Cassandra walked the streets of New York wondering if she should call any of her old friends, but that would be grounds for lots of questions and Cassandra didn't want to answer any of them. She walked blocks and blocks, eventually making her way to Central Park. She remembered how many afternoons she had spent in this park sitting and thinking. Being in New York didn't feel right for Cassandra anymore. It was as if she was a stranger in the same town that she was raised in. *Maybe I need to give it time,* she thought, but already knew what her gut was telling her: that she no longer belonged to New York and New York had given up on her the minute she had left. But against her gut's wishes, she opted to give it a try. Maybe something would happen to prove her wrong. With that in mind, she headed back to her family's apartment. Hopefully someone had made their way back home.

A week had passed and Cassandra was now sitting at a restaurant with her parents, with little to say. She had encountered her parents at the apartment when she had returned from her walk. Her parents, happy but surprised to see her, had bombarded her with questions as to why she had returned to New York without an announcement. Since that day, things between her and her parents were more strained.

"Have you decided what your next step would be?" Cassandra's father asked as he drank his brandy.

"I am not sure, Father," Cassandra said for the hundredth time.

"We don't mean to be hard on you, darling, but you have always taught us to expect more from you," Cassandra's mother said as she drank her fifth glass of white wine.

Cassandra just looked at her mother. She wanted to cry, but didn't let the tears escape her eyes. She didn't understand why her parents put all this pressure on her. She barely knew who she was, never mind what they expected from her. Cassandra continued to play with her dessert and silence loomed over their table. She started thinking about her next move, but she didn't know what that would be. New York was no longer an option for her, but neither was California. Lost and beside herself, she didn't know what to do, but she knew she could no longer stay in New York or with her parents, for she would never understand who her parents wanted her to be nor would they ever understand her.

Eugene looked around his house one last time, as all his furniture had been covered up, all windows shut, and all balcony doors closed—as if he were leaving never to return. All the items he needed had already been shipped to New York and were awaiting which apartment he would choose to call his home. He looked around his living room and dining room, and eventually came to the front door. He hated leaving his home, but this change was good for him. He took one last look and then walked out the door, closed it, and locked it. His sister, Juliet, was waiting in her car to take him to the airport.

"Are you okay?" Juliet asked Eugene.

"Yeah, I am fine," he said closing the door and putting his seat belt on.

"This is a big change for you," she said.

"I know, big, but good."

"Yes," she said thinking about how much she was going to miss her brother. "I will visit as soon as you have everything set up."

"Of course, you better," Eugene said just staring out of the window. They drove in silence to the airport, which was only a fifteen-minute ride. Juliet pulled up to the departing lane of the airport and got out of the car with Eugene.

"You have everything," she said hiding her tears behind her huge sunglasses.

"Yes," he said not wanting to sound sad.

"Okay, give me a hug and a tight one!" she said as Eugene hugged his sister as if it were for the last time.

"I love you," he said, "keep an eye on Mom for me."

"I will. Love you too. Be safe. Call me as soon as you get there," she said.

"I will," he said as he started walking away with his bags. Eugene took one more look at his sister standing by her car and waved. Then, he turned around and entered through the sliding doors of the airport terminal. He had butterflies in his stomach and he didn't know whether they were from his fear of heights or flying, or his fear of moving to New York. He proceeded to the first class check-in line and decided that the only cure was a heavy drink.

Cassandra awoke, already exhausted from a day she had not started. After the dinner with her parents two nights ago, she was completely done with them and New York. She had not even found out where her sister Cassandra was or how she could get in touch with her. Reluctant to get out of bed, Cassandra lay in it wishing it would swallow her up. After an hour of realizing it wasn't going to, she got up knowing what she had to do. After a long hot shower, she grabbed her barely unpacked bags and put in what little she had taken out, and finished getting dressed. She knew her parents were out for the day on one of their many outings of socializing and drinking, and the coast was clear. She grabbed her bags and brought them to the front hallway. She went back into her room to grab her purse and took one look around and thought, *how funny it is when a place used to be so safe and comfortable and now it provides a different type of feeling.* Cassandra knew that can could go back to that time, and that time had passed. She looked at her room and decided to leave the memories that it held with it. That was a different part of her life and the one thing she had learned is that you can never go back: what is done is done. She walked down the long corridor of the apartment as visions of her childhood played in her head, but faded in the distant memory. She pushed for the elevator and once it arrived hauled her luggage into it. Cassandra got into the elevator, not even leaving a note for her parents, and with tears in her eyes, she pushed the lobby button. As the elevator door closed, she knew for certain that the door to her family had closed as well.

In the lobby, the doorman helped her with her luggage.

"Taxi?" he asked.

"Yes, please," Cassandra said.

"Where would you like me to tell the taxi driver to take you?"

Cassandra thought for a second; she didn't know where she was going nor did she have a plan.

"JFK," she said because it was the first thing that came to her.

"Please take the lady to JFK," the doorman said to the taxi driver as he helped load the luggage into the taxi. Cassandra got into the taxi, thanking the doorman. The taxi drove off to the highway. Cassandra sat back and thought about how she had no idea where she was headed or how she was going to get there. She wished the drive to the airport would last forever.

"Mr. Conrad, did you enjoy your flight?" the flight attendant asked him as she tried to flirt with him.

"Yes. Yes, I did," he responded with a dry mouth because he had completely held his breath during the landing.

"Great. Are you here for business or pleasure?" she purred to Eugene.

"Business," he managed to say and wished she would stop talking to him.

"Oh, nice," she said trying to keep the conversation going.

"Do you mind getting me some water?" he said.

"Not at all," she said flirtatiously.

The flight attendant walked away sashaying her hips hoping Eugene would notice.

Eugene sat in his seat looking toward the window as the plane taxied to the gate. *What a long flight,* he thought to himself and the four cocktails he had at the lounge before departing to New York did not help. If only, they intensified his fear of flying. He was glad to have made it to New York in one piece. He just wanted that cup of water that was now taking forever.

"Here you go," the flight attendant said as she leaned forward and gave the water to Eugene.

"Thank you," Eugene said hoping she would now go away.

"If you ever need a tour guide, I am as they say king of the city."

"Thanks," Eugene said looking away.

He sat back in his seat and waited for the plane to come to a complete stop. When it did, he was happy to get up and walk off of the plane.

"Which terminal?" the taxi driver said.

Cassandra not knowing how to answer the question said, "The main terminal." At least she knew that she would have options of flights of not knowing where to go. Cassandra hoped and wished that something would come to her to tell her what to do. She just sat and hoped they never reached the terminal, but when they did, she had to face reality. She had no clue where she was going or what she was going to do with herself.

"Any airline in particular?" the taxi driver asked.

"No, here is fine," Cassandra said as the taxi had arrived at the first airline. Once in the airport, she would look at the departing flights and make a choice from there. Cassandra got out of the cab and hailed a porter to load her luggage onto a trolley. She paid the driver, entered the airport, and searched for the first TV displaying the current departing flights. Cassandra reached the screens and stood in front of them with the porter behind her, staring at the screens as they flickered with constant updates on flights. She looked at the domestic list, but quickly turned her gaze to the international flights. She was going down the list when Heathrow caught her eyes. *Heathrow,* she thought as she remembered Jasper and thought about how she met him before. She thought no longer than two seconds and made her way to the ticket counter.

"Good afternoon," Cassandra said to the ticket agent.

"Hello," the ticket agent said. "Where are you going today?"

"London. Heathrow. One way. I have not purchased a ticket yet."

"Oh, let me look at the next flight. Well, we have one leaving in about two hours, but the price is 1,000 USD for one way."

"Okay," Cassandra said taking out her platinum visa and handing it to the ticket agent. "Oh, please make it first class."

"In that case, it will be 2,500 USD. Is that okay?" "Yes, please charge my card," Cassandra said as she knew it was the only way her parents would ever know where she was if they bothered to look at their statements.

After being processed and her luggage tagged, Cassandra walked through security and, instead of the airlines Emerald Lounge, opted for the regular bar located in the middle of the terminal. Cassandra sat down at one of the open stools and put her stuff on the stool next to her.

"What can I get you?" the middle-aged bartender asked.

"Something strong. How about straight vodka?" Cassandra asked. "Make it Grey Goose," she added.

"Okay," the bartender said as he walked away.

Cassandra sat at the bar looking around, observing people around her moving. Everyone was hurrying somewhere. She wished she was like them hurrying somewhere with a place to go. Instead, she had a one-way ticket to London based on the fact that she had met Jasper White a couple of weeks ago. Even now, she racked her brain trying to remember how or when she might have encountered him before, but she couldn't place him in her memory. Maybe she had never met him and it was only a figment of her imagination. She went back to looking at the bartender pour her drink; it was rather simple: some ice and lots of vodka.

Eugene escaped from the plane untouched by the flight attendant who would not stop speaking to him. He walked up the ramp to the main terminal with a million thoughts in his head. The first thing he saw was the U-shaped bar sitting in the middle of the terminal. He needed not a drink, but a quick fix and opted for a shot of whiskey to calm him down from the flight and what he was going to encounter. Walking to the far end of the bar, he didn't bother sitting down. Instead, he waved at the bartender for a drink.

"Yes, sir," the bartender asked.

"Your strongest whiskey, straight," Eugene said reaching for his wallet.

"Of course," the bartender said, wondering why businessmen always needed to drink.

"Here you are," the bartender said to Cassandra at the same bar Eugene was now at, but on opposite ends.

"Thank you," Cassandra said taking the drink and putting it to her lips. She could already smell the intensity of the drink. *Here goes nothing,* she said to herself and took the first gulp, which went down like rubbing alcohol but it would get the job done. Cassandra started looking around the bar to see who was seated around her.

Eugene took the glass of whiskey that was set before him and gulped it down in one sip. *This should work,* he thought to himself as he laid out cash for his drink. He thought about having another one but knew it would be better to get to his hotel before he didn't know how to get there. He thanked the bartender by throwing cash by the empty glass and walked away. Little did he realize that if he had turned his head, he would have a clear shot of Cassandra sitting at the bar enjoying her drink. But Eugene kept walking toward the baggage claim where his future awaited him.

Cassandra was looking down at her drink and not across the bar as she had done moments before. If she had, she would have seen Eugene walk by. Like Eugene had said in his letter, if it were meant to be, then it would be.

Epilogue

Cassandra sat in her hotel room in London. A tiny, but adequate space for her and her luggage. It had been a couple of weeks since her arrival and she still had not contacted Jasper White. For once, she felt at home; even though she was spending her time in a hotel, it seemed like home to her. She walked around London easily as if she had always lived there. She waited for the right time to contact Jasper as if she knew he held some type of secret she was not ready to learn. Until then, her days and nights were spent roaming the streets of London encountering new pubs with new and old friends.

Day in and day out, Eugene still had not become accustomed to New York life. He was now seated at a restaurant bar analyzing what he had done with his life and nothing seemed to play out the way he wanted it to. Especially, now being in New York, he had no clue where he was headed. If anything, the only thing he had managed to change was the location, but the same problems existed in New York as they did in California. Silently, he sipped his cold whiskey and thought about calling Cassandra. *Cassandra,* he thought how he missed her and talking to her. Without a second thought, he pulled out his phone and dialed her number. He needed someone to speak to and knew she was the one person who would understand. He waited for the line to ring, but to his surprise, he received a message indicating that the number was no longer in service. Confused, he dialed again and he reached the same message. *Could she have changed her number?* But she would have told him. Confused and lonely, Eugene sat at the bar not knowing what the next step in his life would be.

www.ingramcontent.com/pod-product-compliance
Lightning Source LLC
Chambersburg PA
CBHW070634180626
46817CB00006B/2119